# THREE WEEKS IN WINTER

# THREE WEEKS IN WINTER

JOSEPH LEVALLEY

Any requests or questions for the author should be submitted to him directly at Joe@JosephLeValley.com.



Published in Des Moines, Iowa, by:

Bookpress Publishing
P.O. Box 71532
Des Moines, IA 50325
www.BookpressPublishing.com

**Publisher's Cataloging-in-Publication Data**

Names: LeValley, Joseph, author.
Title: Three Weeks in Winter / Joseph LeValley.
Description: Des Moines, IA: BookPress Publishing, 2023.
Identifiers: LCCN 2023913668 | ISBN 978-1-947305-71-7 (hardcover) | 978-1-947305-84-7 (Paperback)
Subjects: LCSH White supremacy movements--Fiction. | Terrorists--Fiction. | Journalists--Fiction. | Murder--Investigation--Fiction. | Chicago (Ill.)--Fiction. | Mystery fiction. | BISAC FICTION / Mystery | FICTION / Thrillers / Terrorism
Classification: LCC PS3612.E92311 T47 2022 | DDC 813.6--dc23

First Edition

*Printed in the United States of America*

10 9 8 7 6 5 4 3 2 1

Praise for Joseph LeValley's

# AWARD-WINNING NOVELS

"Joseph LeValley's *Three Weeks in Winter* is a tour-de-force of international thrillers, a brutal and twisty tale of arms dealers and terrorists both here and abroad. So many times, my jaw literally dropped at the surprising revelations and throat-clutching moments of suspense. More people need to be reading LeValley. Like right now."

***— James Rollins, #1 New York Times bestselling author of TIDES OF FIRE***

"LeValley draws on his own experience as a newspaper reporter to give the mystery an authentic feel. Fans of reporter sleuths...will be pleased."

***— Publishers Weekly***

"LeValley skillfully weaves an intricate and involving tale even as he keeps his foot planted firmly on the accelerator. This is fiction based unfortunately on a very real problem. As such, it's both entertaining and important."

***— U.S. Review of Books***

"...a chilling tale as smoothly told as the crimes it recounts are brutal, with a reporter hero doggedly in pursuit of a story...and justice."

***— Max Allan Collins, author of ROAD TO PERDITION***

"A chilling mystery-thriller...which will have the reader captivated. A tale full of suspense and twists that builds towards the nerve-racking climax and comes to an ending with every loose thread tied up. Heartily recommend it to readers who enjoy thrillers/crime dramas."

***— Online Book Club***

"This latest installment of Tony Harrington's adventures is a gripping page turner full of excitement. It is impossible to put down!"

***— Danielle Feinberg, Director of Photography, PIXAR Studios***

*For Luke, who suggested this book.*

"Treason and murder
ever kept together,
As two yoke-devils
sworn to either's purpose."

— *William Shakespeare*

# Chapter 1

Saturday, December 27 - Chicago, Illinois
Fourteen Days to Wheels-Up, Flight 244

Even before the body completed its plummet to the pavement far below, Tenisha Wedder decided the police would never know what she knew.

The man was dead, or soon would be. Tenisha was a nurse, so she knew this without question. Her apartment was on the sixth floor. The man had fallen from above—just a flash of white skin and green parka, glimpsed as it fell past the window. A fall of seven stories or more, unimpeded, to a cold expanse of concrete was a death sentence.

The lucky ones died instantly. The less fortunate survived for a short time, in various states of consciousness and degrees of agony. In the end, they all died. Wedder had worked too many twelve-hour shifts in hospital emergency rooms to believe the man had any chance of survival.

Knowing this eased her guilt a little as she continued to rock

Fobe. She couldn't save the stranger, so it wouldn't matter if she waited until someone else found the body. When the police and EMTs arrived, if Fobe was sound asleep by then, she would venture down to the street to feign curiosity about the gathering emergency vehicles and to offer her assistance.

Her ability to turn her back on the victim now, and her reluctance to tell the police what she had seen earlier, were not a result of callousness. Her years of caring for the victims of tragedy and malice had not made her callous. It also was not the result of cowardice. Growing up on the south side of Chicago and living as a single mother in the heart of the city had made her anything but a coward.

The source of her resolve to stay away was curled up in her lap. Fobe changed everything. Having a one-year-old son to raise, to nurture, to protect, forced her to set aside any crusader impulses and think first of what was best for him.

Fobe's first smile, just hours after his birth, had awakened in her a depth of love and devotion she didn't know she could feel for anyone. It also aroused powerful maternal anxieties. Her profession had taught her firsthand how dangerous and cruel the world could be. She could not bear the thought of this precious child being placed in the path of any of those horrors. Avoiding trouble for the sake of her son did not make her a coward; it made her a strong and loving mother.

So she would not allow herself to be listed on the police report as a key witness. She would not be describing the two men who had forced the skinny white man into the building's service elevator. She would not be revealing the color of the pickup truck they drove, nor the origin of the out-of-state license plate on the front of the vehicle. She would not be risking the assailants' retributions. She would not be leaving her son to grow up without a mother.

She leaned down and brushed her lips across the forehead of her beautiful child, snuggling her nose into the dark curls at the top of his head.

In Tenisha's mind, Fobe had begun life with two strikes against him. He was Black, and he was being raised by a single mother. She knew the assumptions that would be made about him and the challenges he would face because of these two basic circumstances over which he had no control.

To compensate, she had made many sacrifices, some of them much bigger than simply hiding a few facts from the police.

Upon returning from maternity leave, she had given up the adrenaline rush and professional satisfaction of the Emergency Department at Northwestern Memorial and had taken a new job working days in the hospital's endoscopy unit so she could be home with her baby at night. She had stretched her budget to the limit and had moved from her studio apartment to this high-rise building located closer to work and featuring an outdoor playground with protective fencing. Equally important, the rental agent had assured her the owners soon would install a much-needed high-tech security system.

She looked around Fobe's room—*my son has his own room*—and smiled. He had furniture that matched, a thermostat on the wall, toys on top of the dresser and stacked in the closet, and a large bookcase filled with books, or more to the point, filled with dreams. A real home enhanced by the things so many people took for granted—things that had eluded Tenisha for the first three-quarters of her life.

She was proud of what she had accomplished on her own, and she was determined her son would have the opportunity to grow up in a safe and loving home. More importantly, she would make sure he had the opportunity to share that magnificent smile with a family of his own someday.

So, no, she would not be telling the police what she knew. And whether or not the authorities interpreted the man's death as a murder, she would not be sharing her knowledge that it almost certainly was.

# Chapter 2

Saturday, December 27 – Chicago, Illinois
Four Hours Earlier

*A quiet bar where I can sulk, or a loud bar where I can scream?* The question forced its way to the forefront of Tim Jebron's mind as he pushed forward against the icy wind. He risked pulling a bare hand out of his parka pocket only long enough to tighten the draw-strings on the coat's hood, leaning down as he did so in an attempt to protect his face from frostbite.

*Quiet or loud?* The question was answered for him by the lousy weather and the fortunate proximity of a ground-floor hotel lounge. He walked past the entrance before spotting the booths and tables through the plate glass windows. He quickly spun around and allowed an attendant to open the door for him. He almost felt guilty for not tipping the man. *They must pay him pretty well to stand out-side in December, right?*

He didn't pause to look at the lobby. He turned right, crossed the expanse of polished floor, and walked through the hardwood arch that formed the entrance to the lounge. He didn't care that it was a hotel bar as long as it was in a different hotel than the one he had stormed out of a few minutes before. The place was small, dark, and nearly empty, which suited him just fine. He chose a high-backed booth in the rear, sliding across the vinyl seat with his back to the bartender, disappearing from view.

He was angry and disappointed and confused. If a few tears found their way onto his cheeks, he didn't want some stranger seeing them.

"What's your pleasure?"

Jebron looked up to see the stocky, bald bartender approaching with a drink coaster and white linen napkin.

"Whatever's on tap. You choose."

"That's fine, sir, but do you prefer something dark or one of the local brews, or a more commercial beer?"

"Are you listening?" Jebron hissed. "I said *you* choose."

"Okay, okay. Sorry."

A minute later, a tall glass of golden ale appeared on the table. Neither man spoke.

Jebron grabbed the glass, took two big gulps, and returned it to the table with a louder-than-intended thud.

*What the hell is wrong with women anyway?* For Tim Jebron, this was a serious question. He wanted to be a good husband. He wanted to be a *great* husband. He tried hard, but he just didn't know how to…to do anything right. He rarely guessed correctly about what would make her happy, and he never foresaw what would make her mad. He didn't understand how she thought or why she did the things she did. He sure as hell didn't know how to have a simple conversation with her.

*All I did was ask her why she bought more shoes. Jesus, it was just a simple question. I mean, she's got like a dozen pairs of shoes already. I just wondered, why more shoes? She shopped all day. This is Chicago, for God's sake! She could have found lots of things.*

The mental tirade continued as he remembered their exchange. She kept asking why he didn't like them. He kept saying that wasn't the question. Then she started in on him, calling him a tightwad. Then he responded, probably a little too loudly, that he hadn't even mentioned money.

Then he pointed out that he'd brought her to Chicago for a three-day get-away. It was one of three Christmas presents he'd bought her. Three! That made the "tightwad" reference really sting. This trip wasn't cheap. Good God, the cost of parking alone would have kept food on the table for a month back when he was a bachelor.

Her response was louder than his, saying he wouldn't get a medal for it since now the trip was ruined for her.

*Ruined. Because I asked why she bought a pair of shoes?*

The sparring ended only when he grabbed his coat and left the hotel room, slamming the door behind him.

He knew walking out was a mistake, but he wasn't sure just how big of one. Obviously, it would cost him everything for tonight. There would be no bone-in ribeye at Mastro's and no skin diving back on that fantastic king-sized bed. He'd be lucky if she let him into the room at all.

Would he be able to make amends tomorrow? Maybe he could salvage a couple of days of fun before heading back to Iowa to work his New Year's Eve shift on patrol for the Quincy County Sheriff's Department. And maybe not. He held back a groan, took another swig of beer, and turned to look out of the floor-to-ceiling window beside him.

What he saw instead was his own reflection in the dark glass. It wasn't a pretty sight. His narrow face, high forehead, and recessed chin made him look like the hapless victim in a documentary about bullying. It seemed unfair to be saddled with this face and a ridiculous body too. He worked out to stay in shape, but the result was a physique so thin he looked malnourished. Muscle mass eluded him.

How he had ever worked up the courage to ask Melissa on a date was still a mystery. Why she had said yes, and then again when he had asked her to marry him, were even greater mysteries.

Tim truly loved Melissa. He knew he had won the jackpot in marrying her. She was smart and funny. She read more books than he did, she was better with computers than he was, and she was better with people. She worked hard, both at home and at her job in the Auditor's Office in the Quincy County Courthouse. And she had legs to die for.

*So why can't she answer a simple question about shoes without getting all bent out of shape? What's wrong with women anyway?*

Jebron pushed the beer glass away and shrunk further into the corner of the booth, unsure what he should do next. Flowers? Candy? A bottle of wine? Maybe grab his service revolver out of the car and put a bullet in his ear?

His agitation was interrupted for only a moment as he felt the booth jostle. Someone was sliding into the seat behind him. It didn't matter. The person or persons wouldn't bother him. They probably didn't even know he was there.

Jebron leaned his head against the window and closed his eyes.

He opened them again when he realized his position in the corner, up against the glass, allowed him to hear perfectly what was being said behind him. He had no interest in eavesdropping and was about to reposition himself when he froze.

What had he just heard? A man's voice, subdued, confidential. Had he heard him right?

A second man's voice spoke more sharply. "For fuck's sake,

Grady, don't say things like that."

The man, obviously called Grady, said, "I'm serious. I'm going to make sure the son of a bitch is dead before this is over. I've waited long enough."

"Shhh. Jesus, keep your voice down. Why are you here anyway? We agreed no personal contacts once we got this close."

"Look around. Nobody's gonna hear us. And to answer your question, I called you because there's a loose end back home. I need the okay to terminate a neighbor."

Jebron's eyes were wide, and he was barely breathing. Was this a joke? Some kind of prank someone was playing on him? It couldn't be. No one knew he was here.

*If this is real, I gotta do something.*

He reached into his pocket and slid out his phone. Making sure it was set on silent, he held it under the folds of his coat and lit the screen. He wanted to record the men, but was afraid that if he held the phone near the window, where it could pick up what they were saying, they would notice it. He settled for taking notes as they talked.

His heart beat harder and faster as the men discussed what they were planning. More than once they mentioned a word he had never heard. Eventually, he exited out of the memo app and pulled up Google. There it was. *Holy Mother of God. This can't be happening.*

His hands were shaking as he exited the browser.

Then, suddenly, the world spun out of control.

The first man, Grady, had said a name, the name of the "SOB" he was going to make sure was killed.

Again, Jebron couldn't believe he had heard him right. It was a name he knew well. Could it be?

*This has to be some kind of nightmare. I'm sitting in a bar in Chicago. Are these animals really talking about someone back in Orney?*

He was pretty sure they were, and he had heard enough. His anger and self-righteousness pushed aside his good sense. Without pausing to think what would come next, Jebron slid out of the booth, stood, and turned to confront the two men.

What came next wasn't good.

# Chapter 3

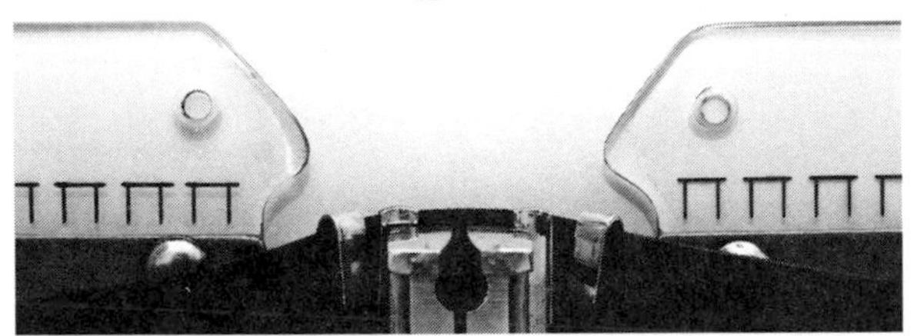

Wednesday, December 31, Orney, Iowa
Ten Days to Wheels-Up, Flight 244

Tony Harrington bit back a curse word as the bag of convenience store ice resisted his attempts to tear it open with his fingers. His parents had come for the party, and he didn't want his mother to hear what he was thinking as he grimaced and pawed at the plastic.

Suddenly the side of the bag ripped wide open, and cubes of ice slid across the counter and onto the kitchen floor. "Shit!"

"Hey, careful," Darcy Gillson said as she walked up behind him and put her arms around his waist. "If your mother hears you, it won't matter that it's your birthday."

Tony smiled. "You're right, as always. Why is it that the little things are the ones that drive me the most nuts?"

"You and everyone," Darcy said, releasing him and bending down to help retreive the stray cubes. "Why are you doing this anyway? You're the guest of honor as well as the host. You should be out there with your family and friends."

"I'll be there soon. I just needed a break, and the empty ice buckets gave me an excuse to get away."

"Who needs a break from his own birthday–slash–New Year's Eve party? Are you feeling okay?"

"I'm fine, honestly. I'm just really terrible at hosting a party. My previous house was too small, so I've had very little practice. When you combine that with the fact I don't drink much…" His voice drifted off as he lifted the remains of the bag and began pouring ice into two large buckets.

"You're doing fine. Everyone's having a wonderful time."

"It's still early. They don't know how boring I can be."

Darcy smiled. "They *do* know how boring you can be, and they all love you anyway. So try to relax and enjoy yourself."

"With encouraging words like that, how can I not?"

Darcy's grin remained but she shifted her tone. "I do have one piece of advice."

"Change the music to something more recent than 1978?"

"No, I've learned the hard way that will never happen."

He shot her a look, but she continued. "I was going to suggest that if you plan to say anything, you do it now, before people have had more to drink. It's going to be hard to get their attention later. Plus, I doubt your parents will stay until midnight."

"Do I need to say something?"

"There's no law, and it's your birthday, so do what you want, but I think it would be nice to thank people at least."

Tony couldn't think of an argument against it, so he just nodded.

They each picked up a bucket of ice and walked through the swinging door into the large family room.

Tony soon found himself standing on the second step of the staircase leading to the second floor. Someone muted the music, and the partygoers turned and shuffled in his direction. He reached down and took Darcy's hand, urging her up to join him on the step.

To the gathering, he said, "Don't panic. I'm not going to make a speech."

"Fantastic!" his best friend Doug Tenney called out from the back of the room. "Turn the music back on and let's have some fun."

Some people chuckled and some groaned. Most knew Doug well and weren't surprised by his meager attempt at humor.

"However," Tony said, "I do want to thank you all sincerely for spending your New Year's Eve with me and Darcy."

"You mean Darcy," another male voice quipped.

Everyone laughed, including Tony. He said, "Yes, you're right, of course. Even my parents are here primarily to see her. Despite that, it's my birthday, so I get to do the thank-yous and pretend you care about me too. I especially want to thank my sister, Rita, and her boyfriend, Ryan, for coming all the way from Chicago."

Rita's dark eyes smiled over the top of a cocktail glass. She raised her left hand in a small wave of acknowledgement. Next to her stood a tall young man whom Tony had met just hours before. The new love in Rita's life had been a surprise to Tony when Rita had phoned on Monday to ask if she could bring him to the party.

Ryan had curly blond hair, a neatly trimmed moustache, and an easy smile. He was far too attractive for Tony's liking.

Tony continued. "I also want to thank my parents, Charles and Carlotta, for driving up from Iowa City. Mom spent the afternoon baking, so if you gain five pounds tonight, you can blame her."

A few people applauded and Tony's petite Italian mother said, "Now, Tony, I hardly did a thing." As she spoke, her face glowed crimson. She snuggled closer to her much taller husband to hide her embarrassment. She and Charles smiled and urged Tony to get on with it. He did.

"As you can guess, I have mixed emotions about turning thirty. On one hand, it sounds more mature, even kind of cool, to no longer be a kid in his twenties. On the other hand, it means I'm a year closer to being an old guy. You know, like Ben."

"Hey!" Ben Smalley called out, feigning displeasure at the remark. Smalley was the owner, publisher, and editor of the *Orney Town Crier* and the local radio station, KKAR. Tony was a reporter, supporting the news functions at both.

Tony grinned. "Most of you probably don't know that you got cheated out of a second party, thanks to my dad. New Year's Eve and my birthday fall on the same day because of him. As the story goes, back when mom was pregnant with me, she wasn't due to deliver until January tenth. Apparently, dad insisted she be induced on December 31, so he could take advantage of the extra year of tax benefits. If he wasn't such a miser, we could be having my birthday party a couple of weeks from now."

Charles turned to the gathering and said, "Lies, all lies."

As the laughter subsided, Tony said, "On a more serious note, I also want to acknowledge the people who couldn't be here tonight. Those who've passed away or are prevented from attending by illness or circumstance."

The room grew very still. Tony said, "I especially want to acknowledge Evelyn Crowder, my longtime co-worker and friend, who left me this beautiful home in her will. It's hard to feel I deserve a gift of this magnitude, especially in light of the circumstances of Evelyn's death, but Darcy and I are working hard to make it a home. Your presence here tonight is a big help with that.

"Lastly, I want to say a word about Tim Jebron. We all were shocked to hear of Tim's death in Chicago over the weekend."

A mournful, collective sigh filled the room.

"I'm sorry to mention something so sad in the midst of a party, but I know we're all talking about it anyway. So let me just say what we all know: he was a good deputy sheriff, a good husband, and a good person. He will be missed."

Nods and mutters of agreement.

"Which brings me to this." Tony held up a glass.

Another shout from Doug. "When did they start putting Diet Dr. Pepper in champagne flutes?"

"Shut up, Doug," Tony retorted. "I drink alcohol when I have to, as you know better than anyone."

"You're right. Hey, let me tell everyone about that night in New York…"

"Shut up, Doug!"

Laughter.

Tony, still grinning, said, "Here's to wonderful friends and family, to good health, and to many more years of laughter and love."

"Hear-hear!" Everyone joined in the cheer, which soon morphed into a surprisingly terrible rendition of *Happy Birthday to You.*

Tony stepped down and headed straight for the cake that was being carried into the room by Alison Frank, a fellow reporter at the *Town Crier*.

"Nice job," Darcy whispered into his ear.

When they reached the cake, Alison smiled but shook her head, pointing the other direction. They turned and saw two friends carrying Tony's electric keyboard, a Yamaha Clavinova, into the room. His sister's boyfriend, Ryan, followed close behind, carrying two stools. Following him, carrying her cello, was Rita Harrington.

Ryan sat at the piano as Rita waved her free arm and said, "Attention everyone!" The room quieted. "We all know Tony well enough to know that when he saw the piano, he immediately assumed we were going to ask him to play for us. Sorry, brother, but tonight you only get to listen."

Tony smiled, knowing she was right, but also with a sense of relief. It would be awkward to perform at his own party, especially when several people in the room were better musicians than he was, most notably his sister, who was a graduate student in music at the University of Chicago.

Rita continued, "Tony, I wanted to get you something special for your thirtieth birthday. However, as you know, I'm a starving musician with tuition due in two weeks, so you'll have to do without the cool plaid pants I spotted in that shop in Old Town."

"It'll be tough, but I'll try to live without them," Tony said, grinning.

"Of course, I couldn't give you nothing, so I wrote you a concerto."

"A concerto? Really? Wow. I don't know what to…"

"Just be quiet and don't panic; it's not as long as a typical concerto."

A few in the room chuckled.

As Tony and Darcy worked their way through the group to stand nearer to the performers, Rita's voice became more serious. "Friends, accompanying me tonight on the piano is Ryan Stenford, my dear friend and fellow graduate student." As she gestured in his direction, the group responded with polite applause.

She said, "And now, with your permission, I would like to perform an original composition entitled, 'My Guardian Angel,' and dedicated to my *much* older brother, Tony Harrington."

Tony smiled, but his heart was pounding. It didn't stop for fourteen minutes, as Rita lovingly played a composition that began lightly, the bow tripping over the strings, then grew dark and heavy, and ended with a movement that could only be described as triumphant.

Tony had no trouble connecting each passage to some aspect of his life growing up with Rita. The music was engrossing, entertaining, and, in Tony's opinion, beautiful beyond words. When it ended, the room exploded into applause.

Tony took three strides to his sister's side, as she rose and took a bow, and then invited Ryan to do the same. The instant she was standing erect, Tony threw his arms around her.

As he squeezed, he whispered, "That was…You are…I'm speechless. My God, it was wonderful! Thank you."

She pulled back and wiped a tear from her eye as she said, "Thanks. I'm so glad you liked it."

***

An hour later, as Tony was chatting with another longtime friend, Rich Davis, an agent with the Iowa Division of Criminal Investigation, a waving hand caught his attention. Ben Smalley was gesturing for Tony to join him.

Tony excused himself and headed toward the foyer at the front of the house, where Ben was standing.

"What's up, Boss? Has something happened? You're not gonna give me an assignment on my birthday…"

Ben didn't smile. "Sheriff Mackey is here. He wants to talk to you."

Tony turned toward the front door and saw George Mackey. He was wearing street clothes and a heavy winter coat. With shoulders slumped and two days of stubble on his face, he looked exhausted and defeated. It was shocking. In more than seven years of living and working in Orney, Tony had never seen the sheriff out of uniform or unshaven.

"Sheriff, welcome." Tony hurried to greet him. "Come in, come in. Let me take your coat. Can I get you something?" Tony was babbling. "It's my birthday. I would have invited you, but in light of what happened to Tim, I didn't think…"

The sheriff looked up and stopped Tony with his stare. His eyes were red and his white hair a matted tangle. He said, "I can't stay, Tony, but I do need to talk to you. To both of you, actually. Is there some place we can sit down?"

"Sure, of course." Tony was baffled, but nodded toward the office on the other side of the foyer. As the three men entered, Tony clicked on the overhead lights and pulled the door shut behind them.

The sheriff huffed a little as he pulled off the coat and threw it across the back of the nearest chair. Ben took the other armchair, and Tony rolled the office chair from behind the desk to join the other two men in the center of the room.

Ben said, "Sheriff, I'm sure you know how terribly sorry we were to hear about Deputy Jebron. If this is about something in the *Crier*…"

"It's not," Mackey said, interrupting. "I need a favor. A giant one. I can't believe I'm here, but I don't know what else to do."

Tony recoiled as he saw tears forming in the sheriff's eyes. He had seen Mackey performing his duties in many gruesome and heart-breaking circumstances and had never witnessed so much as a flinch. He had always thought of the longtime lawman as tougher than a Siberian prison guard.

"Whatever we can do…" Tony began.

"Be careful what you say," Mackey said, his lips forming a tight grimace. "You haven't heard yet what I'm asking."

Tony held his tongue, anxious to learn what was coming.

The sheriff said, "First of all, just so we're clear, this request is off the record. Completely, absolutely secret. Do you agree?"

Tony and Ben simply nodded.

"Okay." Mackey sighed, placed his elbows on his knees, and stared at the floor for a long moment.

"Soon, maybe even on Friday, the Chicago PD and Coroner's Office are going to release their official findings in Tim's death." He looked up, first at Tony, then at Ben. "They're going to say he committed suicide."

"Oh, Sheriff, I'm sorry," Ben said.

"By the way, I know you have to print that. It will be an official report and I can't expect you to ignore it when every other media outlet will be screaming it from the rooftops."

"So?" Ben prompted.

"So it's total bullshit!" the sheriff barked. "You both knew Tim. Do you think he had it in him to take his own life?"

Tony joined his boss in shaking his head, more out of compassion than conviction. The fact was, he didn't know Tim Jebron well enough to guess at his mental state or the particulars of his life beyond the fact he had a lovely wife who worked in the courthouse. Tony also felt a pang of guilt as he thought about the number of times he had thought of Deputy Jebron as a "do-bot," a mindless minion serving at the behest of the sheriff and playing by the rules to the point of absurdity.

Ben spoke first. "I didn't know Tim very well, but I tend to agree with you, Sheriff. However, I assume the authorities in Chicago are basing this on something."

"Yes. Well, there's the rub. They've told me a couple of things confidentially, prior to the report's release."

Tony wasn't surprised. He would have expected the Chicago PD to keep Mackey in the loop out of courtesy to a fellow peace officer as well as out of respect for Tim's employer.

Mackey continued. "First, Tim and his wife had an argument in their hotel room on Saturday evening. She told the detectives about it, and the guests in the room next door confirmed they had heard shouting. According to Melissa, Tim's wife, he left the room in a huff. That's the last she ever saw him."

The sheriff paused, breathing deeply and looking at the floor once again.

"Are you sure I can't get you something, Sheriff?" Tony asked. "A beer? Or a Coke? A bottle of water?"

"Thanks, but no. Let's just get through this. The second thing is, they claim Tim sent a farewell note—a goddamn suicide note—to Melissa's cell phone."

Tony's eyes widened and he felt his torso straighten. That seemed like an extremely callous thing for anyone to do and an especially unlikely move by a man with a reputation for being courteous and devoted to his wife.

"What did it say?" Ben asked. "I don't mean to be nosy, but…"

"I don't know," Mackey sneered. "The bastards in Chicago won't tell me, and I can't bring myself to ask Melissa about it. Not yet. Not after what she's been through."

Tony could picture it. Chicago police detectives, in an attempt to be thorough or to look like they were being thorough, putting the wife of the deceased through endless questioning. It would be a terrible ordeal for someone trying to cope with the shock of losing her husband.

"In a sense, that's why I'm here. Those bastards won't tell me much of anything. They give me these two facts and expect me to simply swallow the suicide conclusion. Well, I'm not going to. I knew Tim and they didn't. Even if Tim had been chronically depressed and hopelessly impulsive, of which he was neither, he wouldn't have climbed to the top of a twelve-story building and leaped to the concrete below."

Tony winced. He had known Jebron had died in a fall—it was in the *Crier's* initial story in Tuesday's paper—but he hadn't known the details.

The sheriff was growing more red-faced and animated as he said, "Why would he do that when he had a handgun in his truck? It would have been so much easier that way. And I happen to know that Tim was afraid of heights. Not a full-blown phobia, but rooftops were places he avoided. Wouldn't he have worried that he wouldn't be able to go through with it? Besides, how did Tim find his way to the top of a private apartment building in a city he barely knew? The Chicago detectives don't know or won't say. And was there anything else on his phone that would tell us what happened? They don't know or won't say. And what in the hell was he doing in the South Loop neighborhood to begin with? They don't know or won't say. I'm telling you, this is bullshit!"

Tony interjected, as much for his own benefit as for the others. "The South Loop? That's south of downtown, near McCormick Place. It's a pretty nice area. A mix of commercial and residential, including condos and apartments. Last I heard, it was getting to be popular with young professionals. But not a place a tourist would normally wander late at night, especially in the cold."

Ben and Mackey turned to him. Mackey said, "I forgot you grew up in Chicago. That makes the favor I'm going to ask a touch easier."

"Okay, you've convinced us," Ben said. "At the very least there are some unanswered questions. What can we do?"

"Not you," Mackey said to Ben. He pointed to Tony. "Him. Put simply, I want Tony to go to Chicago and find out what in the hell really happened to my deputy sheriff."

"You want *me* to go?" Tony was gobsmacked. He had spent most of the past seven years arm wrestling with Quincy County's top law enforcement official. With a few notable exceptions, Sheriff Mackey's primary role in Tony's life had been to make himself an obstacle in searches for good stories.

"I know it's asking a lot," Mackey said. "You know I wouldn't be here if I could find another way to sort this out."

Ben said, "Sheriff, can you be more specific? As Tony's employer as well as his friend, I'd like to know exactly what you're asking of him."

"I wish I knew." The sheriff sat back and ran one hand's fingers through his wisps of gray hair. "I just want to know what really happened. The authorities won't share anything beyond the basic facts that led them to their ridiculous conclusion. I don't know how Tony does what he does, but I know he's damn good at finding answers. Sadly, I haven't got a single fragment of an idea to get him started."

The sheriff stared hard at Tony. "I do know this: if he agrees to go, if he agrees with me that the official version is BS, he won't stop until he finds the truth."

"Even assuming you're right," Ben said, "about the official version being BS, there's no guarantee Tony will succeed. He's good, but presumably so are the Chicago police detectives. Some crimes just go unsolved."

"I understand that," Mackey said. "But isn't it worth a try? For Tim, for Melissa, for all of us? Not to mention, if he succeeds, there will be a hell of a story in this for you."

Ben nodded. "Believe me, I've already thought of that, but we're a small organization operating on a shoestring budget—less than a shoestring, if I'm being honest. I can't afford to send Tony out of town for weeks on the hope he finds something worth reporting."

"I might be able to help a little with that," the sheriff said. "I talked to the County Board of Supervisors this morning. They don't want to put Tony on the county's payroll, but they said they would reimburse all of his travel expenses for up to two weeks in Chicago, if that will help. They figure if they bury it in the travel budget, no one's likely to notice."

"I'll have to think about that," Ben said. "That could open a whole other can of worms in terms of journalistic ethics and conflicts of interest." He turned to Tony. "Sorry, it seems we're getting ahead of ourselves. You haven't even said whether or not you want to do this."

Tony started to respond, but Ben held up his hand. "Before you answer, I want to point out the obvious risks. Knowing you, it's a waste of time to mention it, but please consider how dangerous this could be. If the sheriff is right, and Deputy Jebron didn't commit suicide, then it stands to reason that someone killed him. It's ludicrous to believe Tim wandered to the top of an unfamiliar building in an unfamiliar neighborhood and fell to his death by accident. We're talking about a murder that could involve anything from a mugging gone wrong to a mafia hit. Whoever did this is not going to react well to a reporter looking past the official ruling and potentially spoiling his or her escape from justice. If you'd rather pass, no one will think any less of you."

Mackey said, "I second that, times ten. I hate like hell asking you to go knock on doors without knowing what's lurking inside. You find plenty of trouble on your own without me bringing it to you on a platter."

Tony shook his head and responded in exactly the way the other two men expected. "I appreciate your concern, guys, but we all know we have to do this. As the sheriff said, Mrs. Jebron deserves to know the truth, and the *Town Crier* can always use a good story. And I think we agree I'm the best person for the assignment. I know Chicago reasonably well, and I have a boss who's willing to cover for me here, for a few days at least."

"And you'll go right away?" Mackey asked. He and Ben both looked to Tony.

"Of course," Tony said. "Not tonight, obviously. I have to talk to Darcy. Sorry, Sheriff, but I will have to tell her where I'm going."

Mackey nodded.

"I also wouldn't mind talking to Mrs. Jebron before I go. I assume she's back here in Orney by now?"

The sheriff nodded again. "She came home on Tuesday morning. There was nothing more she could do there."

"Maybe you should call her and ask her to talk with me."

"I'll do that," Mackey said, "but I'm not telling her anything more. I think the fewer people who know you're headed to Chicago, the better."

Ben said, "That means your friends and co-workers as well."

"Including Doug?" Tony asked.

Ben thought for a moment, then said, "Well, he can't go with you because I'm going to need him here, so you might as well keep him in the dark too. As the sheriff said, the fewer people who know what you're doing, the safer it is for you."

Tony nodded and stood. "Okay. Thanks, both of you. I appreciate your confidence in me. I'm not sure I can do much, but I promise to try."

Mackey stood and held out his hand, which Tony took. The sheriff said, "It's all I ask. That, and that you be damn careful. Just gather the information, then we'll let the authorities do the job they should have done in the first place."

"Got it," Tony said, dropping the handshake and heading out the door to rejoin the party.

Ben turned to the sheriff. "You know damn well he won't be satisfied to just gather intel."

"Yeah, I know. Just make sure he's telling you every day what he's learning and doing. Hopefully we can intervene before he gets himself killed."

"Is it worth it, George? Is the truth worth taking this risk?"

The sheriff sighed. "When I came through the front door, I

thought so. Now I'm not so sure. I pray to God I've done the right thing."

***

As Tony entered the great room, Doug was waiting. He grabbed Tony's arm and hissed, "What was that all about? Is there a story breaking?"

Tony shook his head, prepared for the question. "Nah. Mackey just wanted to talk to Ben about how the *Crier* will handle the release of the official findings on Jebron's death. I'm sure he only let me sit in because he's in my house."

Tony moved on quickly so he wouldn't have to look his friend in the eye.

As the countdown to midnight began, Tony pulled Darcy to the center of the room, where a handful of couples were dancing. When the guests erupted into a cry of "Happy New Year!" Tony didn't join in. He leaned down, pulled Darcy to him, and kissed her long and hard.

When they finally separated, the guests were halfway through the refrain of Auld Lang Syne.

She looked up into his eyes, "Well, Mr. Harrington, that was nice. Maybe we should tell everyone it's time to go home."

He smiled. "Soon."

"And then you'll tell me what the sheriff wanted with you and your boss."

He leaned closer, speaking quietly into her ear. "Yes, but not until after you've finished your ride on the Tony Express."

She smiled, but her eyes narrowed. "Meaning, I suppose, I'm not going to like what I hear."

"I can't be sure, but I'm guessing you're right."

For once, Tony guessed correctly. Two hours later, as they held each other, entangled in the warm, damp sheets, he found out Darcy didn't like it at all.

# Chapter 4

Tuesday, October 27, Sochi, Krasnodar Krai, Russia
Two Years Earlier

The Black Sea seemed close enough to touch, as Andros Turgenev peered out the window of the Falcon 2000EX. The plane slowed and banked, its movement less perceptible than the lack of color in Turgenev's fingers as he tightened his grip on the armrest of his seat. "Sobaka," he muttered. "Why is there no land? We soon will be swimming."

The luxurious private jet was configured to seat eight passengers, but carried only one. Turgenev had been tempted to bring with him his latest conquest, the irresistible hostess at his private club in London. She would have been impressed by the plane, and would have loved the seaside resort at Sochi, but he couldn't risk it. The fewer people who knew about this particular sojourn into Russia, the better.

Still, sitting alone in a soft chair, separated from the cockpit by a closed door, he couldn't help but think about the things he and

Prudence could have been doing for the past four hours. *Prudence. That's a laugh. There's nothing prudent about what we did in the limo parked outside the club last Friday.*

His thoughts were interrupted as a rocky coastline, concrete highway, rooftops, and lights suddenly flashed past the window. Before he had time to gasp, the Falcon's wheels screeched their welcome to Sochi, and Turgenev felt himself pulled against the seatbelt as the plane rapidly decelerated.

Turgenev glanced to the left, his eye attracted to the bright lights of a surprisingly modern airport terminal. The Falcon, however, turned right at the first exit from the runway, taxied to the far corner of the airport grounds, and rolled to a stop in front of an enormous private hangar.

As the engines wound down, the copilot emerged from the cockpit, nodded a greeting, and proceeded to the exit door. He lifted the lever, allowing the door to extend outward and down, forming a stairway to the ground.

"Any changes in plans?" the young man asked as Turgenev retrieved a coat and briefcase from the closet nearest the door.

"Such as?" Turgenev replied, genuinely curious about the question.

"Nothing implied, sir," the man said. "We've just learned from experience that distinguished men such as yourself sometimes choose to remain in Sochi overnight, once they get a taste of the… uh, atmosphere."

"Humph. I see. Okay, give me your cell number. Plan to depart as scheduled." Turgenev glanced at his watch. "Eleven p.m. local time, or about two hours. I'll call if that changes."

"Very good, sir. We'll be ready. Please do call if we're staying over. We'll need to file a new flight plan, and we'll need to get some rest ourselves."

"Yes, of course. Wouldn't want you to wait up all night." His comment was based purely on thoughts of his personal safety on the return trip, without even a fleeting concern for the comfort or convenience of the plane's crew.

Even though the young man undoubtedly understood this, his smile never wavered.

It occurred to Turgenev to ask, "Customs?"

The copilot said, "Your diplomatic passport, the fact you were alone on the plane, and the fact that this," he motioned toward the briefcase, "was your only luggage, has convinced the authorities it was not worth their time to greet you tonight. That and some… uh, grease, applied to the right wheels."

"Excellent," Turgenev said, reminding himself to use his diplomatic alias while in country.

"Enjoy your visit."

Turgenev nodded and descended the stairs. "From your mouth to the ears of fate," he said in Russian. "I sure as hell hope so."

He walked toward the giant metal hangar with significant trepidation. The building was dark and the doors closed. He looked around the tarmac and suddenly felt very alone and vulnerable. He squeezed his left arm tight to his side, just to reassure himself that his Springfield 9mm pistol was still in its holster.

*As if it matters,* he thought glumly. *Standing in the middle of acres of pavement, I'm the easiest target in history for a sniper with any ability at all. Hell, for a sniper with no ability at all.*

Turgenev was born and raised in Moscow, and was proud to consider himself a true and loyal Russian. That did not prevent him from facing the fact that today, his country was an utter disaster. The Motherland was experiencing overwhelming difficulties as it attempted to sort out who and what it was. Ever since Gorbachev and Yeltsin had destroyed the Soviet Union and dragged the empire into a nightmare of disarray, crime had become commonplace everywhere, and safety could be assured nowhere. Not even in the seaside resort of Sochi.

He hurriedly removed his phone and sent a single-word text: *Here.*

The pedestrian door at the far-left edge of the building swung inward, and a single-bulb fixture above the door popped on, casting a soft glow across a twenty-foot radius of blacktop. A woman stepped out into the light.

"Andros?"

"Yes, but only when we're alone."

"Ah, of course. Welcome home. This way."

She turned and re-entered the building. Turgenev took a deep breath and followed.

***

"My God, they're really here. You really have them."

"Of course," the woman said. "I would not summon an arms dealer, a man reputed to be ruthless and dangerous, all the way from London if I had nothing to sell him."

They were standing inside a makeshift room built out of two-by-fours and plywood in one corner of the hangar. It was obvious the room had been constructed as a temporary storeroom, hiding its contents from passers-by for the short time the merchandise would be there.

Turgenev reached out and stroked the cold metal. He said, "Yes, of course. I knew, but I didn't really think…I mean…Well, shit. They're here."

"Yes," she said again, smiling confidently. "We have them and no one knows we have them. Even better, no one will miss them."

Turgenev looked closely at the woman for the first time. She was attractive, but not in a conventional way. She was perhaps in her thirties, and clearly had lived a hard life. Her dark hair was pulled back into a ponytail, and a light scar of just over an inch in length could be seen midway between her left eye and ear. Her nose was a touch too wide for her narrow face. She wore neither jewelry nor makeup.

She was tall, but still shorter than his six feet, two inches. Her frame appeared slender in proportion to her face, but her precise shape was hidden by the long topcoat she wore with no belt.

*Roomy enough to have an Uzi hanging under it,* he thought with a tinge of anxiety.

The woman's appeal, he realized, was primarily in the way she carried herself. Turgenev was feared by many, but this woman showed no fear. It wasn't just confidence; it was her air of superiority, an energy that seemed to emanate from her soul. She was in charge, and she bore the role as happily as a child carried a lollipop. She was, he thought, royalty hidden in a day laborer's body.

"Do you have a name?" Turgenev asked.

"Everyone has a name," she said, her smile widening. "You may call me Max."

"Max. Okay. Well, Max, how is it that no one will miss these?" Turgenev stared again in wonder at two rows of trolleys, six in each row.

"It is the simple result of excess, plus chaos, plus government inefficiency, plus military incptness. All things we have learned to rely upon in Russia, no?"

"Sadly, yes."

"As you may know, nearly forty thousand of these were manufactured during the 1950s and 60s."

"I heard it was closer to thirty, but no matter."

"Yes, whatever the number, it was huge. Of course almost none of them were ever used. Deployed, yes, but fired, no. Eventually they were replaced by much smaller, lighter, and faster models. These were too heavy and too slow to be effective against modern jet fighters like American F-15s."

"So if they're too slow..."

She interrupted. "Too slow to catch a fighter at Mach 2, but plenty fast enough to catch and destroy a commercial cargo plane, or..." her smile wavered for just an instant, "...a passenger airliner. Andros, may I introduce you to my friends, the Russian Systema 25s, often still called the S-25 Berkuts, or 'Golden Eagles,' in English, even though the tag was officially dropped years ago. These are highly effective, remarkably affordable, and completely deadly surface-to-air missiles."

Turgenev could feel his pulse quicken. He pressed on. "If these are sixty years old, how can I know they work?"

"That's the next chapter of the story," she said, walking around the nearest missile and lightly tracing its form with her fingertips. "The military actually built and deployed S-25s until 1982, so these are closer to forty years old. Of more significance, once they were taken out of service as weapons, they weren't destroyed. In a rare display of rational thinking, the Ministry of Defense stored and repurposed them. The S-25s were flown for years as targets for our newer weapons systems. This helped the engineers and technicians continue to refine the radar and guidance systems for the modern weapons and created the opportunity to train our troops on the use of those systems. The Berkuts proved to be the perfect choice to mimic attacking planes."

She continued, "Some of the missiles in this room have been refurbished within the past four years. Others can be used for spare parts to finish the job for a few more. In the end, your buyers could have as many as ten in working order. I guarantee six."

"And warheads?"

"The warheads were built more recently and have been adapted to these missiles. They use just over a hundred kilograms of plastic explosives each, making them lighter, but even more lethal, than the original ordnance."

The woman's comment before, about training, began to weigh on Turgenev. He asked, "Are they complicated to operate? Who will train my buyers on how to use them?"

She nearly laughed and said, "Put your mind at ease. No expertise is required. These are nothing like modern missiles, needing complex guidance systems and programmed targets. She opened a panel on the side of the nearest missile. You set the warhead to 'Armed,' here, then you set the timer to 'Launch,' and you get out of the way. Once the missile reaches ten thousand feet, it will lock onto the nearest object in the sky, and will detonate when it strikes it. I assume you're not planning to use this in a war zone, with the need to distinguish friends from foes. The worst that can happen is that you bring down the wrong…cargo plane."

Turgenev ignored her insinuation and asked, "How did they get here, to Sochi?"

"Why should that matter?"

"Everything matters," he said, his voice inching up. "Even if it doesn't, satisfy my curiosity."

"They came from Kapustin Yar, about eleven hundred kilometers to the east, on the other side of the mountains. That was home base to the S-25s for decades. The stockpile has been there so long that no one knows how many are left. Our people took them one at a time, over months. Even if some sharp officer suspects the loss, he would be a fool to make an issue of it. His career would be over if he was proved to be right. If the missiles couldn't be recovered, he might lose more than his job."

She completed her stroll around the missile and turned to close the access panel. She said, "From our hiding place in K-Yar, we brought them here by truck, a few at a time, over the past two weeks. The trucks had common shipping company logos and made other stops while here, so no suspicion was aroused."

Turgenev was more impressed than he wanted to admit. Instead, he simply asked, "And from here?"

"We have arranged a ship."

"I didn't think cargo ships docked here. Is the pier large enough for a container ship?"

"Not of the type you mean. Only smaller supply vessels come directly to Sochi. It doesn't matter because we're using the Sophie Auguste."

"The cruise ship?"

"What better place to hide weapons? She has a hold with room for a limited number of shipping containers. We've reserved spots for three standards at forty feet each—four missiles and warheads per container. There's a little room left over if you'd like to buy a nice hat for your wife while you're here."

Turgenev realized she was making a joke. He found it difficult to smile, standing amid so much potential destruction. So much destruction and so much money. He already had a buyer arranged, at nearly twenty times the amount he was paying.

She said, "Sorry. The best part about the ship is her captain. He is a friend. He has assured us the containers will not show up on any bill of lading."

"Excellent."

"To finish the itinerary, the containers will be unloaded at the Port of Tripoli in the Mediterranean. There, they will join hundreds of other similar containers on board an ocean-going cargo ship. Their final destination, at least as far as we're involved, is a place called the Port of Charlemagne in America."

"I think you mean the Port of Charleston," Turgenev said, finding a grin on his face for the first time.

If his host was irritated or disappointed by her mistake, she didn't show it. She said, "You have the money?"

"Of course." He patted the briefcase.

"It requires a briefcase to give me the number of a bank account in Switzerland?"

"I've learned that people become suspicious of a man who travels with no luggage." He knelt and opened the locks on the case. He reached into a pouch inside the case's lid, and handed her a simple white index card with a number typed on it.

He said, "Half the money is already deposited there. The other half will show up in the same account when we have retrieved the merchandise in South Carolina."

She looked puzzled.

"Sorry, in the Port of Charleston."

"Agreed," she said, and turned.

"Before you go…"

She spun back quickly, reaching under her coat.

"Whoa, hang on." Turgenev held up his hands. "I just want to give you one more thing."

Her hands relaxed, and he pulled a manila envelope from the briefcase.

"What's this?" she said as the tension returned to her muscles.

"It's cash. Ten thousand Euros. For you."

"For me? Why? That was not our deal."

"I know. I give it to you as a gift, a show of good faith. I may want to do business with you again someday."

She reached out and took the envelope. "When that someday comes, I hope I'm no longer in this business. But I'll happily spend your money."

She turned again and strode toward the door. Over her shoulder she said, "I have much to do to meet your deadlines, but one more thing."

"Yes?"

She stopped at the door and faced him. "No matter what happens, do not contact me again. For any reason. Ever." She let the coat fall open, revealing a very nasty looking assault rifle. It appeared to Turgenev to be a Heckler and Koch G38, a model he had used himself in the past. The threat was not lost on him. He would have told her so, but she was gone.

# Chapter 5

Thursday, January 1, Orney, Iowa
Nine Days to Wheels-Up, Flight 244

Tony had no trouble finding the modest acreage that was home to the Jebrons. As he pulled onto the gravel lane and drove past a small apple orchard, he wondered if Melissa Jebron would continue living there now that she was a widow. He assumed not. The house was probably a rental, with the owners living in a newer home in town or in a senior living development in a southern state. It was common to find young couples renting area farmhouses, while the fields and orchards around them were tended by larger farm operations.

He parked on a wide expanse of gravel to the left of a double garage. A narrow enclosed walkway connected the garage to a white, single-story home. It looked to Tony like a 1960s ranch, probably with a couple of bedrooms and basement rec room, similar to most mid-century one-stories in the county.

As he walked across the paved portion of the driveway and along the sidewalk to the front door, he was happy to note the most recent snow had been cleared away. Icy walkways were one of the downsides of living in the land of four seasons.

He took his hand from his jacket pocket, but the door opened before he could ring the bell.

A woman barely recognizable as Melissa Jebron gestured for him to enter. She said, "Come in out of the cold, Tony. It was good of you come all the way out here."

Tony nodded as he stepped across the threshold. He froze his expression to ensure he didn't reveal the shock he felt at her appearance. Her bloodshot eyes and lifeless expression were the antithesis of the helpful, smiling clerk he was used to seeing in the courthouse. She wore an old Pioneer Seed Corn sweatshirt and faded blue jeans. Her feet were tucked into furry bedroom slippers, and her hair was tied in a swirl on top her head. A few strands had escaped and were caught in the left hinge of her eyeglasses.

Tony wiped his shoes on the entryway rug and said, "It was no trouble. It's only a couple of miles." He looked at her and attempted a smile. "I guess you know that. Sorry."

"It's okay. Nobody knows what to say when they get here. I've had more awkward conversations in the past three days than in the rest of my life combined. My friends and neighbors have been wonderful, but I must admit I was happy to tell them I needed the holiday to myself."

"Oh," Tony's face fell. "I'm really sorry to bother you. If you'd like me to go…"

"No, no, I didn't mean that. The sheriff said you were coming, and I'm happy to tell you what I know. Tim liked you, and I know you'll treat him as well as you can when you write your story."

Tony felt another pang of guilt as his mind flashed back to the "do-bot" sentiment he had felt toward Tim Jebron when he was alive.

"Can I get you something?" she asked, leading him into the dining nook next to the kitchen. "Coffee? Water? A dozen or so of the church ladies' casseroles?" Her lips quivered in a half-smile.

Tony admired her effort to lighten the mood. He pulled out a chair for her and took one for himself. They sat facing each other, a small maple dining table filling the space between them. "No, thanks. I have a soda in the car. But please, help yourself."

"Maybe later," she said. "How can I help you?"

Tony pulled a notepad and pen from his coat pocket and said, "Well, if it won't be too painful, could you tell me about Saturday evening?"

She nodded and began relating how she and Tim had gone to the city for a long weekend away, just for fun. She said they had no specific plans except to shop, dine, sightsee, and enjoy some time together.

"We stayed at the Grand Whitmer downtown. It's what Tim had promised. I thought he was going to faint when he found out what it cost. But to his credit, he sucked it up and stood by his word. He may have been a miser, but he was an honorable miser. He was so…so…"

Her voice broke, and Tony gave her a moment before continuing. "Nothing else on the agenda? No little errands or tasks included in the trip? Anything at all that might somehow be related to what happened?

"None," she said. "The trip was one of my Christmas presents and we…we…"

Tony could tell she still was resisting the urge to cry. He reached across the table, gave her hand a light squeeze, and waited.

"I'm sorry. The trip, the fact it was a Christmas present, it came up in our argument."

"So you had a bit of a row?" Tony asked.

She nodded and explained how they had fought in their hotel room.

"Anything in particular? I don't want to be nosy about your personal lives, but was it anything that would help me—us—understand what happened later?"

"No." Her voice took on an edge. "Tony, that's the worst of it. It was so silly. I was so stupid. If I had been more… If I hadn't…"

The brave façade slipped away, and she dropped her head and began sobbing.

"I'm sorry Melissa, really. I shouldn't have pried."

"Shoes!" She raised her head and nearly shouted, "We fought about a fucking pair of shoes I bought at Macy's. How stupid is that? A pair of shoes. If I hadn't been such a thin-skinned little brat, we wouldn't have argued, and Tim wouldn't have left. If I hadn't… Tim…Tim…would still be alive. How can I live with that?"

She crossed her arms on the table, laid her head on them and wailed in anguish.

Tony had no answer to her question and no words to soothe her pain.

After what seemed like hours, she stood and walked to the kitchen counter, where she found a box of tissues. After blowing her nose and rinsing her face with cold water, she returned to the table, this time with the box of tissues in hand.

She sniffled. "I'm sorry, Tony. I'll try harder."

"Don't worry about it," he said. "I'm not in any hurry, and I certainly understand this is difficult."

After a few more minutes of dabbing at tears, Melissa assured Tony she wanted to continue.

"Any idea where he went?"

"None at all. I mean, I know where they found him, but I don't know how he got there, or where he went when he left the room. You know how it is. You get mad, you storm out, you walk to the nearest ice cream parlor or… dress shop. Jesus, I almost said shoe store."

She bit her lower lip, obviously determined to not break down again.

"Any hint at all about why he was in South Loop?" Tony asked. Melissa looked puzzled, and he explained. "That's what the locals call the neighborhood where he was found. Did he know anyone there?"

"Not that I know of. You know Tim…sorry, *knew* Tim. He was about as worldly as one of the moles in our backyard. To him, our trip to Chicago was an exotic vacation. I think he said he'd only been there twice before when he was a kid to go to baseball games with his dad. The idea of him getting on the L by himself to ride into a strange neighborhood is just ridiculous. And before you ask, no, he wouldn't have taken a taxi, and he didn't have the Uber app on his phone. Besides, our car was right there in the hotel garage. He was far too cheap to pay for a ride."

Tony wasn't sure she was right. He could envision some circumstances that might cause a man to get in a cab. Even the bitter cold might have convinced him to forget his frugal nature and seek the shelter of a warm backseat. He kept these thoughts to himself.

"So your car had not been moved?" he asked.

"I can't be sure. When we first arrived, Tim let me off at the lobby entrance before parking. I never knew exactly where it was. The police had to search for it. After they found it and checked it out, they said it appeared to have been left overnight without being disturbed. They said they were going to check the parking garage's video footage on that. Since they never mentioned it again, I assume they didn't find anything, but who knows?"

Tony made some notes, then took a deep breath and forced himself to ask the hardest question of all. "So tell me about the text you got from him."

Melissa's eyes flashed anger. "It didn't come from Tim. It couldn't have. Someone else wrote that message."

"It came from Tim's…"

She cut him off. "Yes, it came from Tim's phone, but I swear to you, Tony, Tim did not write that message. It's preposterous to believe that for even a moment."

"May I see it?"

"No," she said, her voice rising in pitch and volume. "You can't see it because the assholes who call themselves the Chicago PD have not returned my phone to me."

"I'm sorry," Tony said. "I should have assumed they'd kept it. It's a key part of the evidence they've collected."

Melissa began weeping again. "Tony, they're going to say he killed himself, aren't they? Those bastards are going to write this off as a suicide."

"I don't know," Tony said, knowing it was a lie, "but I wouldn't be surprised. You have to prepare yourself for that."

"Please, please tell your readers it's not true. It can't be true. You knew Tim. He wasn't strong enough; he wasn't brave enough. He loved me. He did. He loved me too much to take a dive off a building like that. And even if he did decide to do something that stupid and cruel, why there? Why wouldn't he have just gone to the roof of our hotel?" She reached for another tissue.

Tony said, "Those are just a few of the million questions I have, the same as you. May I?"

He reached across the table and grabbed a tissue for himself, wiping tears from the corners of his eyes. "Melissa, I hate to ask, but can you remember what the note said? Would you mind sharing it, as closely to verbatim as you can manage?"

Her voice was hoarse and nearly at a whisper. "I remember every word. I will never forget it. I read it over and over, between my attempts to text him back and call him. It said, *'Honey, I am sorry. I can not go on like this. Forgive me. I luv you.'* The word love was spelled 'l-u-v' by the way. Does any of that sound like Tim to you?"

"You knew him best, so walk me through exactly what you mean when you say that."

Her voice grew stronger. "First of all, he never called me honey. Never. Not once. And it spelled out 'I am' instead of 'I'm' and 'can not,' two words, by the way, instead of 'can't.' And the word luv, spelled like some teenager or the print on a valentine candy. Give me a break. Someone else wrote that damn text. I know it."

Tony nodded his understanding.

She said, as much to herself as to him, "I told those detectives. I told them and told them, someone else wrote the note."

Tony spent the next hour or so asking Melissa to share happier memories of her husband. He wanted plenty of material for the *Crier's* follow-up coverage about Jebron's death. If they were forced to report the official finding of suicide, the least they could do was help everyone understand he was a good person in a loving relationship.

Finally, Tony closed his notebook and rose from the chair. "I should go," he said. "Are you going to be okay? Should we call in the church ladies?"

She brushed away her tears and choked out a small laugh. "Not the church ladies. Anything but the church ladies."

Tony smiled and pulled on his coat.

As she walked him to the door, she said, "Tony, there's one more thing."

He turned to face her, eyebrows arched.

She hesitated, then said, "I'm pregnant."

Tony felt the air leave his lungs. "Oh, Melissa, I…"

She reached up and touched his lips with her finger. "You don't need to say anything. I just…I wanted you to know."

Tony was struggling against the desire to ask, but she came to the rescue, saying, "And no, Tim didn't know. I was going to tell him Saturday night. We were going to have a nice dinner, and then I was going to give him the romp of his life in that big bed, and then I was going to tell him. If only I had…If only I wasn't so stupid and selfish…Oh, Tony, what am I going to do?"

She reached for him and he stepped forward, wrapping his arms around her, letting her bawl into the folds of his coat, as his own tears dripped into the bun of hair on top of her head.

# Chapter 6

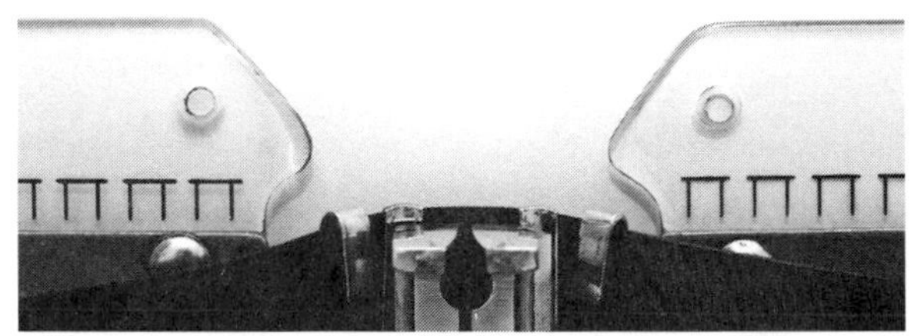

Thursday, January 1, Orney, Iowa

Darcy had finished packing and was passing the time making a list of things she and Tony needed for the house. The list included short-term items, like replenishing some of the food and beverages consumed by partygoers the night before, and longer-term needs, such as a coat rack for the foyer, a new couch for the family room, a bookcase for the bedroom, and so on.

She and Tony had lived in the house for only a month. It had come to him as a bequest from Evelyn Crowder, a fellow journalist and former columnist at the *Town Crier*. Crowder had died the previous September, but it had taken until December for all the paperwork and legal details to be finalized.

It was a fine big house, two stories tall, with three bedrooms, including a master suite with an ensuite bath. Darcy assumed this had come later as part of a renovation, since amenities like these were rare in houses built nearly a century before.

It was more house than they needed, and they had discussed whether they should keep it or sell it and buy something smaller. They had decided to stay, primarily because of the location and the grounds. The house faced west on a tree-lined boulevard that ran between downtown Orney and the new Southern Quincy Community High School at the north edge of town. Most importantly, it sat on a large property, which afforded her and Tony some privacy.

As an actress with a successful career in movies and television, Darcy was frequently the recipient of unwanted attention from fans as well as the paparazzi. Tony's previous residence, a rented bungalow on a tiny lot, had proved untenable, as people legally standing on the sidewalks or in the alley were less than a stone's throw away.

Their new abode, an old brick house with a circle driveway and landscaped grounds, couldn't guarantee privacy, but at least an intruder would need to trespass onto the property to look in the windows.

While the house did not yet feel like a home, Darcy was confident it would, as she and Tony filled it with their own furniture, decor, and memories.

Darcy was as surprised as the rest of the world that she had found happiness living in a small Iowa city with a news reporter who earned less in a year than she did in a day. However, she had no regrets. It was a good place, and Tony was a good man. Living in Iowa was inconvenient for her work, but it was a small price to pay for what she received in return. She hoped and prayed it would last.

She glanced at her watch, an old Bulova that had belonged to her grandmother, and made a face. The fact she was hopelessly in love with Tony did not prevent her from getting irritated with him from time to time, like today, for example.

The irritation was only partially due to his tardiness. It had begun the night before, when Tony had told her about the trip to Chicago. She had not welcomed the idea. More to the point, she had specific reasons why he should not go, which she had spelled out for him in considerable detail. First on the list was the fact the trip was a waste of time. Based on what Tony had told her, he had no clues to pursue, no place to start, and as a result, little hope of discovering anything the police hadn't already found. Secondly, if he did have some success, he almost certainly would be putting himself in the crosshairs of another killer or killers. She couldn't bear losing him or suffering through another near-death episode like the one Tony had endured the previous summer.

In addition, the timing of this foray into the unknown was terrible. Darcy had to go to London in two weeks to film some final soundstage scenes for her latest movie, a drama about a woman trapped in a romance with an older man she didn't love and deeply feared. She would probably be gone for a month. That meant that if Tony spent two weeks or more in Chicago, they might not see each other for six weeks. Six weeks away from him was a hard thing to contemplate. It became unbearable when she faced up to the fact that he could have said no to the sheriff's request and spent the next two weeks with her.

*Stop it.* She kept telling herself. *You say you admire him because he's dedicated to his work. Well, this is his work. You need to support him. Stop thinking of yourself all the time.*

Intellectually, she knew this was the correct attitude, but emotionally, she couldn't help feeling she was less important to Tony than the puzzle he'd been asked to solve.

In the end, Darcy had let it go and had simply suggested she accompany him to the city for a few days. She would rather have stayed at home with Tony at her side, reading a good book in front of the fireplace, but being together in the Windy City was better than not being together at all. *Besides,* she had thought, *maybe I can be helpful in some way.* She couldn't tell if Tony had welcomed the idea or simply hadn't thought it wise to tell her no. Regardless of the reason, he had agreed, and she had packed for the trip.

She looked at her watch again, her irritation growing. They had a six or seven-hour drive ahead of them, and Tony was taking much longer interviewing Mrs. Jebron than expected.

***

When Tony finally came into the kitchen from the garage, he was carrying a to-go bag from a local deli.

He gave her a weak smile, then looked away and said, "I hope you're hungry. I grabbed some lunch."

Darcy fought hard to keep her voice upbeat. "It's almost two. You're lucky I haven't eaten. You might have wasted those six bucks."

"I figured you had plenty to do, and I know you don't think about food when you're busy." He stood with his back to her, staring out the window over the kitchen sink.

"Sometimes I worry that you know me too well," she said. Her irritation was quickly morphing into concern. Clearly something about Tony's demeanor was a bubble left of center.

"Are you okay?" she asked.

"Not really," he admitted, turning and throwing his coat over the back of a kitchen chair. He pulled sandwiches and chips from the bag, but turned back to the sink as he took a bite of what appeared to be an Italian sub.

"Want to talk about it?"

His head shook and he sighed, "It's nothing. It was just a really difficult interview. Melissa, uh, Mrs. Jebron, is beside herself with grief and anger. She's guessed that the cops are going to say Tim killed himself, and she's having trouble coping with that."

"And?"

"And what?" Tony turned to her, his eyes narrowing.

"I'm sorry. I didn't mean to pry. It's just that you've done difficult interviews before. I've never seen it affect you like this. For starters, sit down and relax while you eat your lunch."

Tony pulled out the chair and plopped into it. He swallowed a bite of sandwich and looked up. "She's pregnant."

Darcy took a moment to process what he had just said.

"Their first child?"

"Yes. They've only been married for a couple of years."

Darcy took her place at the table but didn't reach for her food. "Dear God. The poor woman. Basically a newlywed, losing her husband, and then having to think about going through pregnancy and motherhood alone. Is there anything I can do…we can do, to help?"

"No," Tony said quickly, but caught himself. "Sorry. Obviously, I mean to say I don't have a clue, and there's no way to know until some time passes. In the meantime, we have to find out what happened to Tim in Chicago. Eat up while I use the facilities and grab my stuff."

Darcy could tell that Tony was purposely changing the subject, so she let it go. As she watched him stride out of the kitchen and heard him taking the stairs two at a time to the second floor, it occurred to her that Melissa Jebron was not the only person who could use some support right now. The man she loved had not even left town yet, and she could tell he was already mired in this assignment much too deeply.

She made up her mind to help him dig his way back out.

# Chapter 7

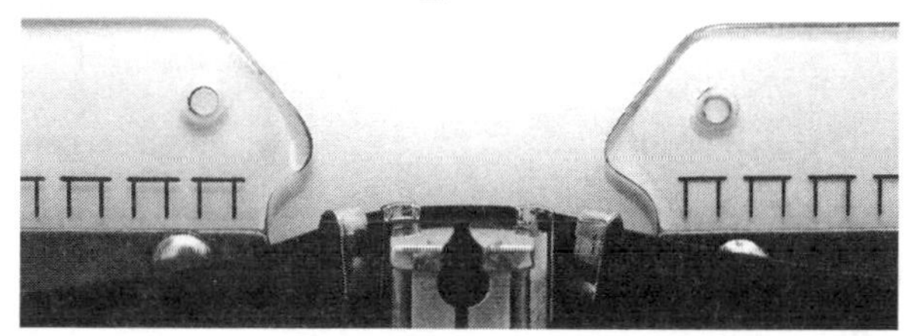

Thursday, January 1, Chicago, Illinois

Darcy gripped Tony's arm with both hands as they stood in the cold and looked up.

"Dear Jesus," was all Tony could say. He felt Darcy shiver as she pulled him closer. He glanced at her, unsure if she was just cold, or reacting to the thought of Tim Jebron falling from the top of the building in front of them to the frozen pavement beneath their feet. *Probably both*, he thought, frowning.

At the end of their long drive, Tony had insisted on going to the site of Tim's death first, even before they checked into their hotel. "I want to feel like I've begun," he had said in an effort to rationalize his urge to drive to an unfamiliar neighborhood in Chicago as the clock approached 11 p.m.

The area looked safe enough, and the parking lot of the concrete and glass apartment building was well lit. He chose to leave his automatic pistol locked in the back of his Jeep Grand Cherokee.

“The lighting bothers me,” he said.

“What? Why? I’m glad for the lights. Believe me, without them, I’d be locked inside your car while you stood out here alone. Which, by the way, is sounding like a better idea with each new gust of wind.”

Tony ignored the hint and said, “What I mean is, doesn’t this make a jump even less likely? Standing up there, on the edge of the roof, you’d see very clearly how far down it was. I could be wrong. I mean, I don’t know what goes through a person’s head when they’re contemplating suicide, but it seems to me that a plunge into the darkness would be easier.”

“If I agree with you, will you get me out of the wind?”

Tony glanced down and saw how truly cold she looked, despite her winter coat, gloves, and wool stocking cap.

“Yes, of course. Sorry.”

He opened the passenger door of the Jeep for her, then handed her the keys before closing it again. “Start the car and warm up,” he said through the window. “I’ll just be another minute.”

He heard the car start and the door locks clunk as he walked to the front entrance of the building. It was locked, with an electronic keypad for residents’ access. If the building amenities included a door attendant, it wasn’t a 24-7 service. He was surprised to note there were no security cameras in sight.

He stepped away from the entrance and turned left, walking along the sidewalk that appeared to run the circumference of the octagonal building. After making the second turn, he looked back and no longer could see his car, which made him nervous. He didn’t like leaving Darcy alone.

*Just one more minute*, he thought as he picked up his pace and made the next turn. He now had a view of the back side of the building and saw it was different from the other seven facets. It hosted two wide driveways. As he made the third turn, he had to detour around a chain link fence that ran parallel to the first drive. The fence protected pedestrians from falling onto the drive, which formed a downward ramp to a garage door at basement level. Tony assumed this was for VIP parking and storage of building equipment and supplies.

The second driveway went to a small loading dock. Tony doubted the building offered a food or linen service, so he deduced the primary purpose of the loading area was for residents to use when moving furniture or other large items in or out. Easy access such as this, combined with an oversized elevator, would be an attractive feature to prospective renters.

Once again, he could find no cameras, a curious omission in this age of ubiquitous electronic surveillance.

He climbed up on the front lip of the loading dock and tried lifting the overhead door. It was locked, as expected. He hopped down and continued his journey, spotting a pedestrian door to the left of the dock, with a keypad similar to the one in front. He tried peering through the glass in the top half of the door, but could see nothing in the darkness beyond.

He knew he was being foolish. He couldn't possibly expect to see anything helpful or even interesting. He suddenly was glad for the lack of electronic eyes. *If someone saw me, how would I explain this?*

As he turned away from the door, he heard the Jeep's horn sound three sharp beeps. *Darcy.*

Tony took off at a run, rounding the remaining two corners of the building and heading straight for the parking lot in front. As he ran past a huge mound of snow and two big trees, his sight line to the Jeep cleared. He could see a small crowd gathered at the passenger side.

It appeared to be about a half-dozen people, separated from Darcy by the thin pane of glass in the vehicle's door. *Shit, shit, shit.*

*Why didn't I get my gun?* The six-against-one situation didn't deter him. He gulped air as he pushed his legs to move even faster.

"Hey!" he shouted as loudly and with as deep a voice as he could muster. Six bodies in heavy winter attire turned to face him. Simultaneously, he heard Darcy shout, "It's okay! It's okay! They're fans."

A moment later, Tony reached the crowd and immediately saw they were young people in their teens or early twenties. He noted four females and two males, a mix of light and dark faces.

"You okay, mister?" one of the boys asked.

Tony was bent over, hands on his knees. "Sure," he gasped, "but…check…with…her." He nodded his head toward Darcy.

"What? Why?"

"Cause I'm going to kill her as soon as I catch my breath."

The teens looked alarmed, but Darcy just laughed. She said, "I'm sorry, really. I honked when I saw them coming my way. I was frightened until they reached the car. Turns out they were just checking to see if I was okay. Then they recognized me."

One of the boys said to Tony, "It's her, right? It's Darcy Gillson?"

"In all her glory," Tony said with a nod, as he stood erect. All but one of the visitors was shorter than his five-foot, ten-inch frame. As he surveyed their faces, he reassessed their ages. They were even younger than he had assumed initially. He said, "What are you kids doing out here this late, anyway?"

A girl flashed a big smile and said, "No school tomorrow! We were over at Benny's." She gestured toward the lighted façade of a diner in the distance, across the street. "And we live here."

"Yeah," the shortest boy said, "the real question is what are you doing here? Wait! Do you live here? Are you gonna live here? Oh man, that's so dope. Darcy Gillson. In our building. That's…"

Tony cut him off. "Chill out. No. We don't live here and we're not going to live here. We're just visiting."

"I know why they're here."

Everyone turned toward the girl who had spoken. She was short and wearing a winter parka with a fur-encircled hood. She had spoken with her head down, but looked up and added, "I read in *People Magazine* that Darcy Gillson moved to some town in Iowa. Okie or Ogie or some lame-ass thing. I forget. But I bet it's the same town that guy was from. You know, the guy who took a spill onto the parking lot on Saturday. He was from a small town in Iowa. Was he your friend or something?" She looked at Darcy.

Darcy, wide-eyed, looked at Tony for help. He just shrugged.

Darcy said, "I'm impressed. Smart girl. Yes, Tim was our friend. We came to town on vacation and couldn't help ourselves. We just wanted to see where it happened."

"What a dickhead move," one of the boys said. "I heard he was a cop or somethin'. What kinda troubles could a cop from Iowa have, to go an' kill hisself?"

"Any of you around when it happened? Did you see anything?"

"Now wait a min…"

"Sorry," Tony said. "I'm not a cop. I'm just curious. I knew Tim a long time."

"Sorry, man. 'Bout your friend. Still a dickhead move."

Darcy looked at the girl in the parka. "How about you? Did you see anything? Hear anything?"

The girl looked uncertain, her eyes flashing a pleading look, but just shook her head.

"Hey," the tall, lanky boy said. "It's colder'n shit out here. Can we get a selfie and get inside?"

Darcy smiled. "Sure." She zipped up her coat and stepped out of the Jeep, stepping toward the building and turning her back to it so the photo would show the teens' apartments in the background. Five minutes later, the teens were headed inside and Tony and Darcy were back in the Jeep warming themselves. She stared down at the floor.

Tony asked, "What are you thinking?"

She turned to face him. "I'm thinking I hope my coming along hasn't put you in danger."

"Relax. They're just kids."

"Yeah, kids who know you're here looking into Tim's death. Kids who could tell someone. Kids who are on social media and could tell the whole world…" Her voice trailed off.

Tony forced a smile. "Hey, kids don't even talk to their parents. Don't worry about it."

Shifting topics, Darcy said, "I'm also thinking that's a huge building. You could stay here for weeks and not get to everyone who lives here, to see if they happen to know something."

"You're right about that. But hopefully, the cops have already done that."

"So…?"

"So I have an idea how to find out what they learned." Tony started the Jeep.

"Of course you do," Darcy said, the tone in her voice implying both admiration and exasperation.

Tony reached out and gripped her hand. "It'll be okay. I promise."

"I don't want promises," Darcy said, feigning a pout. "I want something that will take my mind off my worries."

Her fingers found the inside of his thigh and lightly traced a pattern on his slacks as they moved up.

Tony tensed, put the SUV in gear, and drove across the lot toward the street.

"No comment?" Darcy asked, trying to tease out a response.

Tony turned to her, but he wasn't smiling. "I'm sorry. I'm tired and distracted. I just… Let's just get to the hotel."

Darcy pulled her hand away and sat up straight.

Tony knew he should say something more, but he couldn't. He didn't have the words to explain the emotional melee underway in his brain. He hoped a good night's sleep would help, but he was pretty sure it wouldn't.

***

Behind them, on the twelfth floor of the apartment building, a tall, broad-shouldered man with light, wavy hair lowered a pair of military-grade binoculars and muttered a string of obscenities.

He had been drawn to the window by the honking of a car horn in the parking lot; not something he normally would even notice when staying in Chicago. However, after what had happened on Saturday, his senses were on high alert. His curiosity had been further aroused when he'd seen the group of people gathered at an SUV out in the middle of the parking lot.

The implications of what he had seen were troubling, to say the least. Strangers in a Jeep talking to kids who probably lived right here in the building. Because it was dark inside the Jeep, he couldn't see the occupants, but he guessed there were two people. The teens were showing no interest in the rear seats. The vehicle was parked with the passenger side facing the building, so even the binoculars couldn't help him see the license plate. The longer the people in the Jeep kept talking to the kids, the stronger his concern and frustration grew.

As he watched from his window, he saw one of the girls pull a phone from her coat pocket. He was pretty sure it was that young Hispanic girl from the third floor. He'd seen her around. He'd never liked the idea of that family being in the building and had known it would lead to trouble eventually.

As the girl held up the phone, the group gathered with their backs to the building. A woman stepped out of the Jeep, but her features were obscured by her winter garments as well as by the group. She quickly turned away, posed for a photo, and returned to the vehicle. *Who are these people?*

"Dammit to hell," he said aloud, and pulled his latest burner phone from his back pocket.

"Six," said the voice answering the call.

"You told me the Iowa guy's case was closed," the man growled.

"It is, or soon will be. All done but a couple of signatures. What's up?"

"Somebody's here tonight, asking around. Vehicle looked private. Maybe a friend, or another off-duty deputy."

"Ah…Well, I suppose that's to be expected. They won't find anything. We've made sure of that."

"You better have," the man said, emphasizing each word.

"Jesus, relax. It's fine. I've done everything I needed to do."

"Not everything," the man said. "I need you to retrieve a cell phone for me…"

# Chapter 8

Friday, January 2, Clark County, Missouri
Eight Days to Wheels-Up, Flight 244

Jon Slapp hated the cold. He hated how it made his breath fog his glasses as he walked from his cabin to the lodge. He hated the amount of time he spent every day putting on and taking off the items of clothing required to survive outdoors. He hated how, after only a few minutes of drills, his face muscles felt frozen, making it hard to enunciate.

None of this was new to him. He had grown up in the cold. His hometown often experienced temperatures far below those thrust upon northern Missouri. Nine degrees was far warmer than twenty below. Still, human beings should not have to venture outside when it is too cold for flowers. *Flowers, hell. It's too cold for a polar bear*, he thought.

Despite his whining, Slapp was not soft. He hated the cold, but he didn't cower before it. He dealt with it, indeed mastered it, proving to himself and everyone else that he would do whatever was necessary to support the cause. If he had to stand in the winter wind until his fingers froze to the stock of his assault rifle to protect what he had built, he would. If he had to shout commands through frozen lips to a bunch of undisciplined alcoholics until they knew how to effectively breach a building, he would.

As he reached the lodge, he paused to knock the snow off his boots, then pulled open the left side of the double doors and entered. The door swung shut behind him. He removed his hat, scarf, gloves, and coat, placing them on the peg reserved for "Base Commander."

It took a moment for his eyes to adjust. The lodge was large and well-lit, with a fire burning in a huge stone fireplace at one end. However, the windows were kept covered whenever the group was meeting, and even the best lights couldn't compete with the brilliance created outside, as the morning sun reflected off acres of white snow.

The lodge was one of the thirty or so structures that had once comprised a church camp for teenagers. Located in northern Missouri on more than two hundred acres of timberland, it was bordered on the northeast by the Des Moines River, and on the southeast by a large, kidney-shaped lake.

It was the ideal setting for a camp, and church leaders had invested large amounts of money and thousands of hours of volunteer labor to build it in the 1980s. However, over the next few decades, the church's support for the camp had waned. It had proven difficult to manage large numbers of teenagers, many away from the watchful eyes of parents for the first time. Equally challenging was finding qualified staff, who were sometimes the source of trouble rather than the cure.

By the time the third pregnancy arose from teens reportedly "exploring their faith," camp enrollments were already declining. Church members' financial support was shrinking at an even faster pace. Financial woes mounted and thoughts of closing the camp began to get serious attention. Then, in 2020, the global pandemic sealed its fate.

The elders found it the perfect opportunity to close the camp for good. The property was put on the market with little expectation of a satisfactory or rapid sale as the global economy sputtered.

Needless to say, Jon Slapp's appearance at church headquarters in St. Louis was unexpected. His offer to buy the camp at the asking price, and with a check in hand, was welcomed with astonishment and joy in equal amounts. No one questioned Slapp's story that he wanted to convert the camp into a commercial hunting and fishing operation. The existing lodge and cabins surrounded by woods and with easy access to both river and lake fishing made it ideal for Slapp's purposes, the elders agreed.

Residents near the camp, whether on farms or in nearby towns, also welcomed the news. Some were outdoor recreation enthusiasts, but most were simply happy to learn the camp would be put to good use, rather than being allowed to fall into disrepair. Slapp was welcomed to the area not quite as a hero, but at least as a new favorite son.

The reception would have been quite different if they had known who had ordered Slapp to buy the property, or the origin of the funds for his certified check.

As Slapp gazed into the lodge on this cold January morning, he noted there were no empty chairs. More than forty hand-picked supporters of the cause had been summoned, and all had come. They were dressed, armed, on time, and in place.

Slapp stood a little straighter and allowed a smile to cross his features as he thought about how far they had come. He took ten brisk steps into the room.

"Ten-hut!" he heard Fitz call out. Fitz, his first lieutenant, was Joel Fitzgerald, a 29-year-old former wrestler with the huge muscles and cauliflower ears to prove it.

The lieutenant's build was the opposite of his commander's. Slapp's slight build, boyish features, and rimless eye glasses gave him the appearance of a college professor or accountant, causing many to underestimate him. A few who had made that mistake in the past had found it to be their last.

The response to Fitz's command was instantaneous. The sliding of chairs, and the clap of boots on the wooden floor, came as a well-orchestrated harmonious sound. Forty-two men and women dressed in white-and-gray winter military fatigues stood suddenly. In an instant, all were quiet, motionless and ramrod straight.

"As you were, my friends," Slapp said loudly, while thinking to himself, *It's showtime.*

# Chapter 9

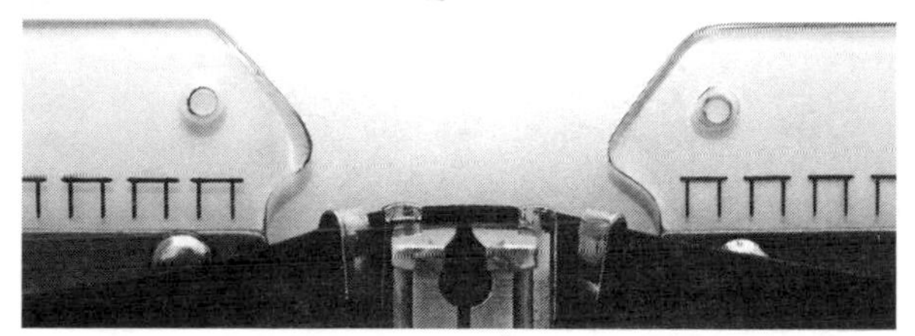

Friday, January 2, Chicago, Illinois

"'Til There Was You" began playing in Tony's pocket as he paid for his sweet roll and orange juice in the hotel lobby. He hurried to one of the small cocktail tables, set down the bottle of OJ, and pulled his phone from his pocket. Pushing the green "Answer" button, he said, "Hey. You're supposed to be sleeping."

"So are you," Darcy responded. "It's just after seven. Where are you?"

"Down in the lower lobby, at the coffee bar. I woke up and couldn't get back to sleep, so I decided to grab a roll and get started. Are you getting up? Can I get you anything?"

"Yes and no," she said. "I'll clean up and come down. I need to see what they're offering before I decide. Will you be there?"

"Yeah, I'll grab a paper while I wait. It's too early for me to accomplish much anyway."

"Okay," she said. "Thirty minutes, tops."

Less than ten minutes later, Tony finished his faux-breakfast and stood. Despite what he had told Darcy, he couldn't just sit. There had to be something he could do until she arrived. He gathered up his trash, dropped it in a nearby receptacle, and headed for the elevators.

As he stepped out onto the twenty-first floor, he was overwhelmed by a deep sense of melancholy. An Iowa couple, on holiday in the big city, had been happy just a few days ago. Walking down this same hallway, pausing to open this door…

Tony was standing in front of room 2116—Tim and Melissa's room. He stared at the door. The door Tim had slammed before he'd rushed off to…to what?

Tony turned his back to the door. He was sure the police had cleared the room by now, and that it had been placed back into service, so he had no thoughts about seeing the inside. He was here in an attempt to retrace Tim's footsteps. He knew it was futile, but it was better than sitting alone in the lobby, staring at an unopened *Chicago Tribune*.

*He came out this door. He almost certainly turned left, toward the elevators. Then what?* Tony walked back to the elevator and pushed the "Down" button. *He was mad. He wanted to get away to vent, or sulk, or whatever. Where would he go?*

The possibilities were endless and nearly overwhelming. Tony forced himself to think logically, and consider what he knew.

*It was dark and it was cold, so no ice cream shop,* Tony thought, remembering Melissa's comment. *And certainly not a dress shop.* No, like most guys Tony knew, Tim Jebron would have gone for a drink.

The elevator doors opened, and Tony strode out into the lobby. The doors to the street were on his left, on the other side of the check-in desk. The hotel's bar was another level down.

Knowing he was now straying into total speculation, Tony looked at the lounge at the bottom of the escalator and decided it was not where Tim had gone. It would have been convenient, but it had downsides that would have been important to Tim.

First, it looked upscale. Tim would not have been comfortable plopping down amid a bunch of business people in suits and dresses. Secondly, it looked expensive. Tony knew from experience that it *was* expensive. If Tim was as tight as Melissa said, he would have avoided it. Lastly, Tony thought, *if it was me, I would have gone somewhere outside the building. I would not have wanted to be where my wife could find me easily*. As Tony formed this thought, it sounded petty, even childish. It didn't change his opinion. *Men can be petty and childish. So what else is new?*

Tony walked briskly across the lobby and pushed through a revolving door. Out on the sidewalk, his challenge grew exponentially. *Which direction would Tim have headed? East toward the lake? North toward Navy Pier? South, toward Soldier Field? Did he even know where these things were? Is that how he ended up in South Loop?*

The latter seemed unlikely to Tony. Obviously, Tim's journey had ended in South Loop, but he wouldn't have walked there. He had a smart phone. In only seconds, it would have told him it was too far to walk on a bitterly cold December night. *And why would he choose that, anyway, if he didn't know the city and didn't have any connections there?*

It seemed obvious to Tony that a typical guy, fleeing a fight with his wife, would seek the closest refuge that served alcohol. Gazing across Wacker Drive and the Chicago River, Tony realized even the nearest bar would be more than a couple of minutes away. He turned and pushed through the hotel's doors, returning to the lobby to meet Darcy.

He found her sitting in the lobby café, her hands wrapped around a warm coffee mug. Her face was stoic as she spotted Tony approaching.

"I wondered if you'd run out on me again."

"Again? When have I ever run out on you?"

"You know what I mean. You weren't where you said you'd be."

"Sorry. I thought I had enough time to retrace Tim's steps, at least to the front door."

"Retrace…?"

"That's overstating it, of course. I've just been trying to put myself in his head and think about where he might have gone when he stormed off."

Darcy's tone softened. "Any luck?"

"Not really." He walked her through the logic that had taken him out to the street.

"Makes some sense, I guess," she said. "So what now?"

"We'll have to follow up tonight, when we have a better chance of finding people who were at their posts that night, but when you step outside and see the view across the river, you can see it's a good bet he headed that way. It was dark and the restaurant across the street would have been lit up. It seems likely he would have headed for an area that looked busy, rather than a sidewalk running along an empty street."

"Okay, we have a task for after dark. How about today?" She took a sip of her coffee.

"Today we get some powerful help and, if we're lucky, an insider's look at what the police have assembled."

Darcy's head popped up, and for a moment, Tony thought the coffee might escape back out through her lips.

He smiled as she asked, "Just how do you propose to do that?"

"You can't have forgotten," he chided her. "I have a friend in high places here."

"Oh, of course." She groaned, sitting back in her chair and folding her arms. "You're talking about your girlfriend in the FBI."

Tony tried to look serious. "Stop calling her my girlfriend. Anna

Tabors is a highly-respected and capable agent of our nation's most significant criminal justice organization. The fact she hasn't found a good enough reason to arrest me yet does not make her my girlfriend."

"Maybe not, but she's gorgeous and single. And I've seen the way she looks at you. If she puts you in handcuffs, it won't be to take you to jail."

"Very funny," Tony said, trying to sound as if Darcy's comment wasn't funny at all. "She and I are all business. And as I've told you before, she's too tall for me."

This comment was a longstanding joke between them, and Tony inserted it to provoke a reaction. It did.

"Ow!" he yelped. He reached up and rubbed his shoulder where Darcy had punched him.

Like much humor, his comment was founded in truth. Tony could not imagine Anna Tabors ever having a serious interest in him.

Tabors, a Black woman in her thirties, measured just over six feet—two full inches taller than Tony. Despite the fact Tony had inherited his father's easy smile and his mother's Italian complexion and dark wavy hair, he had always felt awkward with women. His average height and slender build were not confidence boosters, and his athletic skills rated ten points below horrible. Except for an occasional bike ride, and his efforts to learn tae kwon do, he preferred to spend his free time with books and music. His mother had called him "intellectually curious." Tony preferred that over "nerd."

He and Darcy had been together for nearly a year, and Tony still couldn't fathom why such a perfect woman found him desirable. The idea that she could be jealous of another woman—any woman—was laughable.

In short, Tony had no interest in Anna Tabors beyond having a friendly contact at the FBI, and he assumed that even if he did have an interest, she would shut it down faster than a crystal meth lab.

***

They met over lunch at The Palace Grill on Madison, an old-fashioned cafe with Formica tables, a checkerboard floor, and walls covered with sports memorabilia and photographs of champions long dead and mostly forgotten. It was crowded and noisy, but the aromas were captivating. In other words, it was the perfect spot for lunch on a cold January day in Chicago.

Darcy ordered a cobb salad, Tabors chose the club sandwich, and Tony asked for something called a "Sunshine Burger."

"I don't know how you can eat like that," Darcy said, with a hint of envy in her voice. "I must be in the wrong job. If I ate sandwiches and fries at every lunch, my next role would have to be as a contestant on *The Biggest Loser*."

"I run every morning," Tabors said. "I run so I can eat whatever I want. Food is my guilty pleasure."

Tony was trying to think of a clever response when he was distracted by the four young men at the next table. They were staring at Darcy.

He turned to her and said, "As long as our food's not here yet, do you want to play the accommodating celebrity for a couple of minutes? I'm not sure we'll get any privacy unless you give these guys what they want and send them on their way."

"Well, I'm not gonna give them what they want," she smiled. "But I don't mind signing an autograph or two."

Tony leaned the opposite way and spoke to the man closest to him. "If you make it quick, Darcy said she's happy to sign an autograph."

The man was stocky, dressed in denim work clothes, and sported a "Sox" ballcap. He broke into a wide smile. "Is it really her? Is that

Darcy Gillson?"

"Yep," Tony said. "But she'd like to enjoy her lunch in peace, so you and your buddies make it quick, please."

The four men were on their feet in an instant, crowding around Darcy and handing her slips of paper and, in one case, a twenty-dollar bill, to sign. Then, of course, came the inevitable request for pictures.

Darcy said, "Tell you what. Let's do one of all of us. Then you can share it with each other. Fair enough?"

"You bet!" one nearly shouted, handing his smartphone to Tony. Darcy stood and positioned herself at the center of the group, and Tony snapped one photo. After a flurry of handshakes and thank-yous, the men grabbed their coats from the backs of their chairs and headed for the door.

Tony could see others in the room were staring, probably wanting similar opportunities. However, the waitress had arrived with a full tray of food, so Tony shook his head and returned to his seat. He hoped everyone understood the message.

Tabors dipped a fry in ketchup and asked, "Is it always like this? How do you stand it?"

"Not always," Darcy said, spearing a piece of chicken in the salad. "In Orney, they're getting used to me. Most of the people who really wanted autographs or pictures already have them. If I get bothered there, it's usually by someone from out of town."

"Like the paparazzi," Tony said.

"Yeah, like the paparazzi," Darcy nodded. "But now there are days when life is almost normal there. It's one reason why I love it so much."

Tony shifted in his chair, trying to keep a frown or even a scowl from forming on his face. Something about Darcy's comment bothered him. He couldn't understand why. He pushed it to the back of his mind. There was business to do.

"If you don't mind turning to the subject at hand, may I ask if you were able to get anything helpful?"

Tabors swallowed, took a drink of iced tea, and turned to face him.

"Do you have any idea how much the Chicago PD hates it when the FBI starts nosing into one of its cases? I don't mean dislikes; I mean hates. I wouldn't have even asked if I didn't have a friend who works in homicide. And I have to tell you, Tony, I didn't enjoy calling in a favor from her for a closer look at a suicide case."

Tony set down his burger and looked her in the eye. "If you're trying to make sure I appreciate what you've done, I can assure you I do. I don't have a clue about the inner workings of the FBI or the police and certainly don't understand the politics, but I believe you when you tell me you risked a lot to make the call."

Tabors tried to look stern. She said, "But I don't care because I'm Tony Harrington and I need what I need, so spill it."

"That's a little harsh," Tony said, "but pretty much what I was thinking, yeah."

Darcy surprised them both when she interjected, "It wasn't a suicide."

"Darcy's repeating what…"

"Tony, please," Darcy said. "I can speak for myself." She looked Tabors in the eyes and said, "I didn't know Tim Jebron, but Tony did. Sheriff Mackey did. Melissa did. Rich Davis did. Not one person who knew him harbors even a tiny suspicion that Tim killed himself. That, combined with the circumstances, has convinced me this was a homicide. The Chicago PD may hate you for asking, and they'll probably hate you even more when you prove they got this wrong, but too bad. They are wrong, and we're doing the right thing by coming together to find out the truth."

Tabors leaned back and smiled. "Well said. You should be on the stage or something."

Darcy, a little red-faced, said, "Sorry…"

Tabors interrupted. "No, don't be sorry. You're exactly right. I happen to agree with you. Believe me, I wouldn't be helping you if I didn't. Tony's a nice guy, but I don't help people just because they're nice."

"So…" Tony prompted, still wanting to know whether Tabors had learned anything.

Tabors took a deep breath. "Okay, when you called me yesterday, you said you knew the basics, the handful of things the police are using to determine it was suicide. I assume Darcy is up to speed on these as well?"

Darcy nodded and Tabors continued, "Here are a few more details, but they won't be very helpful. First, there were no obvious signs of a struggle or an injury before the fall, such as an attacker's skin under the fingernails, or a bullet wound, or anything like that. But of course the body was badly damaged in the fall. The skull was crushed, multiple bones were broken, all the trauma you'd expect. The problem is, those types of injuries make it hard to say if he suffered any blows prior to the fall."

Tony nodded grimly. "What about the tox screen? Any drugs or alcohol?"

"No drugs," the agent said. "Pretty high alcohol content. About three times the legal limit. You wouldn't have wanted him driving a car."

"Could he even walk at that level? I'm pretty sure I couldn't," Tony said.

"Not everyone's as much of a lightweight as you, Tony," Tabors said. "If he was a regular drinker, he could have been reasonably functional. Visibly drunk to anyone who saw him, but probably mobile."

Tony pulled out his reporter's notepad and pen, and made a note to ask Melissa about Tim's drinking habits. He said, "So this didn't raise a red flag with the cops? They think a drunk guy from out of town made his way to the top of that building?"

"Actually, the police are saying this strengthens the suicide theory. He has a fight with his wife, storms out, goes to a bar, gets drunk, ends up dead. In their minds, this fits a pattern they've seen many times."

Tony shook his head but refrained from comment. Instead, he asked, "Anything more about Tim's vehicle?"

Tabors looked through some notes she had retreived from her shoulder bag. "No. As I think Melissa told you, all the evidence says the pickup never moved from its original parking spot. However Tim got to South Loop, he didn't drive there."

"Time of death?" Tony asked.

Tabors didn't need the notes for this one. She said, "The body was found just before midnight. Some guy half in the bag literally stumbled into it as he was returning to his apartment from the parking lot. To his credit, he risked the trouble he might face, considering his condition, and called it in right away. They think the body had been there only a short time before it was found. No indication he died earlier. The coroner is certain the fall killed him."

"Any revelations in those notes about Tim's movements that night? Why or how he came to be in South Loop?"

"No," Tabors shook her head. "The reports describe a very thorough process of talking to potential witnesses, scouring the neighborhood, following up with cab companies, et cetera. Nothing was found. No hint of what happened before he took the plunge."

Undaunted, Tony said, "They must have interviewed the guy who found him, and others in the building. Anything helpful there? Any witnesses?"

"Obviously, no one witnessed a crime, or said they did, or we'd be having a very different conversation," the agent said. "In addition to the guy who found him, they interviewed a handful of people in the building—people in apartments on the correct side of the building and in which the lights were on."

"That seems a little weak…" Tony began, but Tabors cut him off.

"They didn't go door-to-door to every apartment. Maybe they should have, but in light of the hour, and the fact that they already suspected suicide, they let it go." She turned to the next page in her notes. "There was one woman they encountered. A nurse. She lives in the building and came down to see if she could help after noticing the flashing lights in her windows. When she learned the man was dead, she left. There's no indication they talked to her beyond that."

Darcy asked, "What about the suicide text that was sent to Melissa? Any helpful information on the phone?"

"The police say no. According to the reports, they reviewed Tim's text messages and emails going back three months. They didn't find anything suspicious or anything they thought was helpful. They noted Melissa's responses after the suicide text and her attempts to call and text him back, which confirmed her version of what happened. Otherwise, the phone wasn't helpful."

Darcy persisted. "What about the other apps? Did they look at his maps, or notes, or even social media?"

"Actually, that's a good question," Tabors said. "You'd have to assume they looked at social media—that's pretty standard procedure these days—but there was no mention of it in the reports. I honestly don't know how thoroughly they looked."

Tony was impressed with Darcy's train of thought and said so. He added, "I'd love to get my hands on that phone and spend a couple of hours just digging around. I suppose it will be locked up for years as evidence."

"Maybe not," Tabors said. "Once the suicide ruling is official, they'll probably release it. The ruling's expected today. Maybe I can get it if I offer to deliver the deceased's effects to his widow."

"That's excellent!" Tony's voice rose and he sat up straighter. "Can we…"

"Easy, Tony. I said maybe," Tabors reminded him. "And even if I get it, one of us will have to ask Mrs. Jebron for permission to look at it."

"That won't be a problem," Tony said. Something in his tone caused both women to turn, puzzled looks on their faces.

He quickly said, "What about fingerprints? Any unidentified prints that they're trying to ignore or explain away?"

"That's one detail they do seem reluctant to discuss," the agent said.

"They found prints?" Tony and Darcy asked in unison.

"Actually no. They didn't find any prints."

"*Any* prints?" Tony's voice grew louder still. A couple of people at nearby tables turned to look. He sat back and took a deep breath. In a low voice, he said, "Sorry, but do you mean there were no prints on the phone at all? Not even Tim's?"

"That's what was in the report."

Tony's astonishment was turning to anger. "So their theory of the case is that Tim wrote a suicide text to his wife, and then wiped the phone clean before jumping to his death?"

"Actually, yes," Tabors said, sounding a little incredulous herself. "In the recommendation for a ruling of suicide, the detectives gave two possible explanations. They said it could be a manifestation of the 'tidying up' behavior sometimes exhibited by people just prior to killing themselves."

Tony snorted. Darcy said, "And the second?"

They speculated that the phone was wiped clean when Deputy Jebron pushed it into the front pocket of his jeans.

"Complete, utter, total bullshit," Tony said. "It was a touch-screen, yes?"

Tabors nodded.

Tony pulled out his iPhone. "Look at that screen. My phone goes in and out of my pocket a hundred times a day, and the screen is always covered in fingerprints."

He paused to grab his last two fries and said, "So this is good news."

"Good news? How do you mean?" Darcy asked the question, but Tabors's wrinkled brow demonstrated she was curious as well.

"It proves that someone's going to great lengths to ignore the facts and sweep this under the rug. It proves we're on the right track."

Tabors's face clouded. "I get your point, but be careful what you say and how you say it. It's one thing to believe Tim Jebron was murdered. It's quite another to start talking like the Chicago PD is a part of it somehow. Before you make that leap, you'd better have a hell of a lot better evidence than a clean touchscreen."

"Before I'm done, I will," Tony said. "That's why I'm here."

***

Back in her SUV, Tabors took the official police reports from her briefcase and began reading them for the third time. Tony's suspicions about a police cover-up had gotten under her skin. She knew it was unlikely. She had worked with the PD many times and had several friends who worked there. She knew the department to be filled with a lot of dedicated, hard-working, honest cops.

However, she also knew it was a huge organization. It would be hopelessly naïve to assume there were no bad apples, no political pressures, no chance of a blown investigation, or even a misdirected one. Tony's comments had forced her to acknowledge more consciously what her subconscious had been struggling with all morning.

The entire section of the report describing the investigation into Tim's actions on Saturday night was simply too tidy. If viewed through a lens of skepticism, it appeared too pat; as if someone sat down and wrote everything needed, without doing the actual work. The report simply lacked the usual holes, delays, and glitches you expect when assembling multiple detectives' notes collected over multiple days.

*Tony Harrington, you jackass*, she thought. *What are you getting us into this time?*

# Chapter 10

Tuesday, October 27, Sochi, Krasnodar Krai, Russia
Two Years Previously

"Speak."

"Turgenev is here."

"What! Where?"

"Sochi. The Black Sea, in Russia."

"I know where Sochi is. Aren't you supposed to be on vacation?"

"I *am* on vacation. Believe me, I'm not happy I saw him. But there he is, having a drink by the pool of my resort. I thought I should call. I assume you want me to follow him?"

"Christ, probably. Maybe. I don't know. Maybe he's on vacation too."

Donnette Berg had been a CIA officer for too long. She was shaking her head even before her runner in Virginia had finished the thought. She said, "He appears to be alone. He's wearing a black turtleneck and a topcoat. I'm pretty sure he's armed. He looks about as relaxed as Rambo."

"Well, shit. You better learn what you can. At least see if he meets with someone. And be careful. We don't want to ruin your vacation."

He was gone before Berg could say, "No shit."

She was in her room, where she had retreated to make the call. She quickly slipped out of her shorts and halter top, and pulled on black slacks, a maroon long-sleeved blouse, and comfortable flats. She grabbed her go-bag, exited the room, and hurried back to the pool, located outside the lowest level of the hotel, facing the sea. She was just in time to see Turgenev leaving by the exterior stairs leading up to street level. She pivoted, strode back inside the building, and took the elevator up to the lobby. She stepped out as Turgenev walked casually into view outside the front doors. Through the glass, she could see him getting into the backseat of a car. *No markings. Probably a private hire*, she thought.

She pushed through the revolving door and climbed into the nearest taxi, ignoring the bellman and pulling the cab door closed herself. Before the driver could ask, Berg said in Russian, "Do you want to make a lot of money?"

"Yes, of course," the young man said. "Do I have to kill anyone?" He smiled at her.

She said, "Go. Follow that gray car that just left, but don't be obvious. Maybe you will actually save someone from getting killed."

"Like the movies, yes?" The man grinned in the rearview mirror, but the car was already moving.

She nodded. "Like the movies except the bad guys are real, and so are their bullets."

The driver's smile faded, and his eyes returned to the road. After a few minutes, he said, "He appears to be going to the airport."

"Shit," Berg said. If Turgenev was leaving, she had probably missed any chance to learn why he was here.

"So?"

"So follow him anyway. In the traffic around the terminal, we're unlikely to be spotted."

"Ah, except he's not going to the terminal."

Berg looked up through the windshield and saw the young man was right. The gray car went past the terminal and turned onto an access road.

"Where does that go?" she asked, unable to read the small sign near the turnoff.

"The private operators. There's a drop-off area and parking lot for those getting on or off private planes. Your bad guy is rich, I think." The driver slowed as they neared the turn.

"You have no idea," Berg said. She quickly added, "Don't stop here. Go around the curve and let me out there."

"Miss, it's late and not well lighted here. It could be dangerous."

*You have no idea*, she almost repeated, but refrained. Instead, she said, "I'll be fine. Thank you for your concern. Here is perfect."

The car pulled to a stop at the curb. Berg handed the driver twenty thousand rubles, or more than two hundred dollars, for what was probably a ten-dollar ride. His eyes widened.

"The extra is to keep your mouth shut. Not a word. Understand?"

"Yes. Thank you. Thank you."

She barely heard him as she jogged across the grass, down a small slope, and into the weeds along the chain-link fence. Looking around to ensure no one was watching, she pulled a cap from her bag. She wound her long, red curls into a bun on top her head, secured it with a bobby pin, and pulled the cap on tightly. From the bag, she retrieved a pair of wire cutters, used them to snip a few links of the fence, and wriggled through. In seconds, she was running along the narrow gap between two metal hangars. When she neared the end, where the tarmac began, she stopped and listened.

A car was driving away, and a jet engine was beginning to wind to life. She used a mirror from the bag to peek around the corner. She only saw one person, undoubtedly Turgenev, walking away from the hangars toward a Falcon jet parked on the tarmac. As he climbed the stairs, she pulled out her phone, snapped a picture of him, then one of the plane's tail, and sent them to Langley. It was dangerous to communicate directly to them, but this phone was headed for the Black Sea anyway. Keeping it was not an option after using it to call her runner earlier.

Suddenly someone spoke. Berg nearly cried out, the voice was so close. A second voice replied. A man and a woman. They were right around the corner from her. They hadn't been there a moment ago, so they must have come out of the hangar through a small door. *A small, incredibly fucking quiet door*, Berg thought, then added, *Sorry, Lord. I need you now. No more swearing.*

She was sweating, trying not to breathe, and fighting the urge to run as she backed away as silently as possible into the shadows between the hangars. The couple were speaking in Russian.

"Yes, I confirmed it. The money is there," the woman said.

The door slammed shut and Berg could hear a key turning in the lock. *Sure, now the door makes noise.*

The man: "We'll start tonight."

"Start and finish," the woman said, the tone of authority unmistakable. "Our accommodating friends leave tomorrow evening."

A sigh. The man: "Understood. It will be done."

"Precision, stealth, teamwork," the woman said. "No fuckups."

"Precision, stealth, teamwork. Understood."

The woman walked past the gap and could have seen Berg, despite the agent's pleas to her guardian angel to make her invisible. Luckily the woman never glanced in her direction. A few moments later, Berg heard a car engine start and fade away as the vehicle exited the operator's parking lot.

The man spoke, apparently into a phone. "Tell everyone to get ready. We start at midnight. That's less than an hour, so get your ass in gear." A pause. "Me? I'm going for coffee. It's going to be a long night."

The man, too, shuffled past the opening, Berg holding her breath until he was gone. *Two for two. Let's hope my luck holds.*

Another car started and disappeared into the night.

Berg took a deep breath, reached into her bag for her lock picks, and took another peek around the corner. Deserted. She stepped out, knelt, and was through the door in less than twenty seconds.

Glancing around, she saw no evidence of an alarm system, no wires, no window sensors, and no keypad for arming and disarming one. It would have been unusual to encounter a sophisticated system in a Russian hangar, but in this case it seemed a possibility. Something was here—something important enough to bring Andros Turgenev all the way from London to see it.

A lone fluorescent bulb illuminated the far end of the hangar. On the right was a plywood structure with a makeshift door secured with a large padlock. To Berg, this amounted to a billboard announcing: *Look here first!*

Opening the padlock took even less time than the lock on the front door. She pulled open the plywood panel, slipped inside, and pulled it shut again. She glanced up and realized there was no ceiling on the temporary structure, making it unwise to use a flashlight. The good news was that enough light leaked over the top that she could see a little.

What she saw took her breath away. Missiles. Big, green, nasty looking missiles. But for what? *These are too big to be SAMs, or under-wing weapons, but clearly too small to be ICBMs.*

She paced it off. Thirty-four feet. She ran her hand around the edge at the top. Flat, waiting for a warhead. When fully assembled, maybe thirty-nine or forty feet long. *Or tall. What the hell?*

Her questions didn't slow her actions. She snapped a quick picture of the nearest missile, attached it to a text and wrote: *Looks like maybe a dozen of these. Private hangar. Sochi International.*

As soon as she pressed Send, she heard the plywood panel slide open behind her. A woman's voice said in Russian, "If you move, you die."

*Shit*. Berg froze.

The voice repeated, this time in English, "Assume you American or British. Say again. If move, you die."

Berg nodded, responding to the English in the hopes the woman wouldn't know she spoke Russian.

The woman said, "Give. Phone. Gun. Papers."

Berg turned a quarter turn to the left so the woman couldn't see her right hand. As she did so, she tapped the phone's Down Volume button in a pre-designated pattern. She continued her turn and faced her assailant.

When the woman saw Berg already held a phone in her hand, the woman's face contorted into concern, then into anger. "What have you done? Show me!" She held out her hand.

Berg handed her the phone while silently ticking off the seconds. When her internal clock reached four seconds, she spun away and dropped. She landed hard on the floor just as the phone's self-destruct mechanism reached five. A burst of light and sound was instantly replaced by the woman's scream.

Just as quickly, Berg rolled back onto her feet and ran out of the storeroom into the hangar. She could smell the woman's burning flesh and hair. The phone's self-destruct charge made an effective weapon at close range. Berg didn't pause to inspect the damage. She darted left and pulled her gun from the go-bag on her shoulder. Two men burst into the hangar through the front door, spotted Berg at a dead run, and saw the other woman writhing on the ground.

The first man lifted an automatic rifle and pointed it at Berg. "Stop!" he screamed. "What have you done? What have you…"

Berg shot him twice in the heart and never slowed. She was three steps from the door when the second man, without speaking a word, pulled the trigger on his assault rifle and dropped her in her tracks. She fell to her knees, then forward into the back of the door, and came to rest on her right side, looking back into the hangar. She could see blood pooling in front of her face. She was pretty sure her pistol was still in her hand, but she couldn't feel it. She tried to lift her hand to shoot back, but her arms wouldn't move.

*Dear God in Heaven. He's severed my spine*, she thought.

The man walked up and stood facing her, staring into her eyes. Quietly, in Russian, he said, "Did Max ask who you are? Your name? Your country? Your business here? I care for none of those things. You hurt Max. You die."

The man aimed the rifle again. It was the last thing Donnette Berg ever saw.

***

### Tuesday, October 27, CIA Headquarters, Langley, VA

At Langley, a communications tech recognized the significance of the photo and message that had just arrived. He significantly improved his chances for a future promotion when he jumped on it immediately.

He typed an alert code into his keyboard, then forwarded the text to his boss. Then he looked up the agent assigned to the phone code, and sent the message to her boss.

His comm set buzzed immediately. Donnette Berg's runner took no time with niceties.

"You just got this?"

"Yes, sir. At 4:48 p.m."

"Nearly midnight in Sochi."

"Yes sir."

"This real? We haven't been hacked or something?"

"No sign of that, sir. I think it's more likely than not to be authentic."

"Shit. Anything else from Berg?"

"No sir. And uh… sir?"

"Spit it out."

"Her phone went offline immediately after sending it."

"Aw, hell. Any way to tell how or why?"

"Well sir, we got the code."

"What code? For God's sake, man, spill it!"

"The code the phone sends when it self-destructs. All indications are that she sent this one text, and then destroyed her phone."

"Well, fuck."

"My thoughts exactly, sir."

"You religious, son?"

"Sir?"

"If you believe in a higher power, get out of your goddam chair and get on your knees. I fear our operative is going to need all the help she can get."

"Yes, sir."

"But before you abandon your seat, send out a situation alert and tell everyone to gather in whatever conference room is biggest, and available. We'll get started with those who are still here at five in the afternoon."

"Yes, sir."

"If those missiles are real, and on the loose, we have to find them and secure them. If our agent is in trouble, we have to find her and save her. And it all has to be done in a hostile country five thousand miles away."

"And sir."

"Something else?"

"The message says they're at the airport. I would only add you have to find and secure them in hours, maybe in minutes. They could be in the wind faster than…"

"Faster than a Nimbus 2000 crosses a Quidditch field. I get it. So stop talking and hop to it."

The tech didn't pause to wonder at the runner's knowledge of *Harry Potter* lore. He focused and began typing fast.

Sadly, it didn't matter. Two years later, after thousands of hours of effort and millions of dollars of resources, the missiles and Donette Berg still were missing.

# Chapter 11

Friday, January 2, Chicago, Illinois

Tony and Darcy spent the remainder of the afternoon in their hotel room working. Darcy read a script her agent had forwarded to her a few days previously, and Tony wrote an email summary of their findings so far, miniscule as they were, and sent it to Ben and Sheriff Mackey.

At seven, they changed out of blue jeans and into clothes more appropriate for dinner at a nice restaurant on a Friday night in Chicago. Tony remained in his sweater but put on khaki pants and dress shoes. When Darcy emerged from the bathroom, she was wearing a red dress, wool scarf, and teardrop gold earrings.

"You look lovely," Tony said, stepping forward and kissing her on the cheek. She didn't respond except to pick up her purse from the long bureau that doubled as a TV stand and walk the three paces to the closet to grab her coat.

It wasn't the first signal Darcy had sent that something was amiss. Fearing what it was, Tony was determined not to ask. He was not ready to talk about it. Instead, he opened and held the door as she passed into the hallway.

Down in the lobby, they joined a line of couples waiting for cabs. Tony took the opportunity to signal the elderly Black man at the bell stand. The uniformed gentleman immediately approached.

"May I help you, sir?"

"Yes, thank you. I'm wondering if you were on duty last Saturday night."

"I'm certain I was." The man's deep voice resounded with pride. "Every weekend, right here, for seventeen years. I'm Jonathan Hightower."

"It's nice to meet you, Jonathan," Darcy said, smiling. "That's an impressive record of service. You don't find many people who stick with their jobs like that anymore."

"Well, I'm lucky," Hightower said. "I love what I do, and these here folks seem to like me." He paused. "Wait a minute. I know you, don't I? You're in the movies or somethin'."

Darcy held out her hand. "Busted," she said. "I'm Darcy Gillson. I've been fortunate to be in a few movies and TV shows. I love my job too."

"Sure, Darcy Gillson. Well, I'll be. See, that's why I love doing this. I get to meet all kinds of interesting people. Now how can I help you two?"

"We're friends with this guy," Tony pulled a photograph of Tim Jebron from his jacket pocket. "We're wondering if you happened to see or talk to him Saturday night."

"Ah, of course. The deputy."

Tony's eyes widened. "You know who he is?"

"Sure. When a guest in our hotel dies, the word gets around pretty quickly. Especially in a weird case like that, the body found on a sidewalk in another part of town and all. I heard today that he committed suicide. Damn shame. I'm sorry you lost your friend."

"Thanks," Tony said, realizing he shouldn't have been surprised that hotel staffers were talking about Tim's death. The police, both uniformed officers and detectives, would have been in the hotel after the body was found to interview Melissa and others and to search the room.

Tony asked, "So did you know him? I mean, had you seen him around?"

"Matter of fact, I had," Hightower said as Tony and Darcy glanced at each other. "And I talked to him very briefly that night; you know, before he… Um, anyway, he was walking toward the doors in his coat, so I asked him if he needed a cab. He said no, he wanted to walk. I was gonna warn him about the cold, but he didn't seem to be in the mood to chat. The only other thing he said was that he wanted a beer. Asked if I knew anyplace nearby. I told him there were plenty and offered to get him a map from the desk, but he said 'never mind' and left."

"Any idea where he went, or even which direction he headed?"

"No idea where he ended up, but he turned left at the end of the drive. That won't help you much. From there he coulda stayed on Wacker, or gone right at the crossing that leads to the bridge over the river, or left and walked along Columbus. If he was smart, he woulda pulled out his phone and found the nearest pub."

"I doubt he used his phone, but let's say he got lucky and found the nearest place. Where would that be?"

"Well, I gotta think. The nearest stand-alone club would probably be farther west, or maybe north across the river. But the actual nearest place to get a beer, besides the bars here in the Whitmer, would be in the hotel in the next block. They've got a small corner bar at street level. If he went that way, he probably woulda seen it."

"By the way, do you happen to know what time this was?"

"Not for sure, but around seven," Hightower said. "There was a line like this waiting for cabs, and that usually peaks around that time."

"Thank you, Jonathan," Darcy said. "You've been very helpful and generous with your time."

"Sorry, but I gotta ask," the bell captain said. "What's this about, anyway?"

Tony was prepared for the question. "Sadly, it's just two friends trying to understand how Tim could do this. It's so terrible, so permanent. We're just trying to follow his footsteps from that night, to see if we get any sense of what he was thinking."

"Well, good luck to you," Hightower said. "But I gotta tell ya, it won't help. Take it from someone with experience, only time and a little grace from above can ease the pain of losing someone."

"I'm sure you're right," Tony nodded, "but thanks for understanding and helping us."

"No problem. God bless." Hightower tipped his hat and returned to the desk. Tony and Darcy headed out the doors and turned left.

***

In less than a minute, the cold penetrated every layer of clothing and every pore of skin.

Tony put his arm around Darcy and pulled her close. "Are you okay with this?"

"Long enough to get to the nearest pub. After that, I'm going to insist on a cab ride and a nice dinner."

"Deal," Tony said, spotting the older, smaller hotel up ahead. "I think we might be there already."

The bar was busy, with a mix of what appeared to be business people who had stayed too long after happy hour and couples having drinks to begin their nights on the town. Light jazz played softly through overhead speakers.

A waitress with pink-and-green braids and a string of piercings in each ear nodded them toward the only empty table, a booth in the far corner. After a few minutes, the waitress approached with coasters and a wine list. Waving away the list, Darcy asked for a glass of Moscato and Tony ordered orange juice. They stared out the plate glass window at the cars passing by. There were almost no pedestrians braving the cold.

When the waitress returned with their drinks, Tony asked her if she'd been working the previous Saturday night.

"Saturday? Well, yes and no," she said. "I got here late. My babysitter didn't show and I had to take my kid to my mom's. That's always a treat, especially on a Saturday night. Like she's got anything better to do. Anyway, I didn't get here until after nine. Why do you ask?"

Tony explained that they were looking for a friend, and showed her Tim's picture.

"Sorry, I can't help. I doubt I was here but even if I saw him, I probably wouldn't remember. He doesn't look like somebody I'd give a second look. Know what I mean?"

Tony did, and bit back his response.

The waitress said. "You should talk to Dale, the guy behind the bar. He was working alone Saturday until I got here. He was plenty pissed, but it was quiet, so he didn't have any real reason to bitch. Saturdays are always slower than Fridays 'cause you don't get the office workers pouring out of all these high-rises."

Tony nodded his understanding and asked her to pass on a request to speak to Dale when he had a lull in his duties.

A few minutes later, a stocky bald man in an apron appeared next to their booth.

"You rang?" he asked in a raspy voice.

"Sorry to bother you when you're busy," Tony said, holding up Jebron's photo. "We're wondering if you saw our friend in here last Saturday night."

The bartender took the picture, gave it a quick scan, and handed it back to Tony.

"The asshole?" he said. "This guy's your friend?"

"Yes," Tony said, sitting up straighter. "He's usually a really nice guy, but we've heard he was in a foul mood on Saturday."

"Yeah, I'd have to agree. He had one tall glass of pale ale, and barely said two words to me. Then he left without paying."

"Left without paying? That's a little hard to believe. Are you sure this is the guy?"

"Oh yeah. That's him. Ironically, he was sitting right where you are now. After he left with those other two guys, and I realized he hadn't left any money for his beer, I wanted to chase him down and punch his lights out. Unfortunately," Dale paused and turned to look at the waitress, "I was working alone and couldn't leave."

"Wait, wait," Tony said. "What other two guys? Can you start at the beginning and tell us exactly what happened.?"

"Maybe," the bartender said. "You a cop? And if you are, why are you hanging out with Darcy Gillson?"

Darcy forced a smile through tightly pressed lips.

"Not a cop," Tony said. "I'm a friend of Tim's and just trying to find out what happened to him on Saturday."

"He missing or somethin'?"

"No. Sadly, he's dead. He left behind a young wife. We told her we'd try to find out what happened."

"Hey, I don't wanna get in the middle of something. I mean… dead…That's some serious shit."

"Please just tell us what you saw, and we'll be on our way. It would mean the world to us and to his wife."

As Tony spoke, he removed a crisp, new $100 bill from his wallet and slid it across the table. It disappeared into the bartender's beefy hand faster than Tony could blink.

"As I was saying," Dale said, "he came in around seven. The place was nearly empty but he walked straight back here, to this last booth. We had a very brief, unpleasant exchange, in which he ordered his beer. Then he basically disappeared into the corner of the booth. I almost forgot he was here.

"A few minutes later, two other guys came in. They sat in the booth next to this. It wasn't long before your friend stood up and joined the other two guys. I assumed they had agreed to meet here, and the two guys who came in later just hadn't realized the first guy was already here. The three of them chatted quietly, finished their one round of drinks, and left. That's when I saw the money on the second table for two of the drinks, but nothing on the first table. I'm sorry your friend is dead, but if he treated anyone else like he treated me, he might not have lived long anyway."

Tony thought the remark was completely out-of-bounds, but didn't risk alienating the bartender by responding to it. Instead, he asked, "Did you hear any of the conversation? Get any sense of what they were discussing, or where they might be going when they left?"

"No, no, and no. Sorry."

"Can you describe the other two men?" Darcy asked.

"Boy, I see a lot of people in here, and they were just kinda ordinary. White guys in winter coats. Now that I think about it, one might've been dressed better than the other. I think he had a long dress coat and business attire, and the other man was in blue jeans and a sweater."

"Bald, bearded, gray, dark, anything?" Darcy pushed.

Dale took a deep breath and said, "Let me think. One guy, the casual guy, had a dark beard and short, dark hair, kinda unruly. He looked like a working man, you know, a lumberjack type. The other guy was more clean-cut. No beard, lighter hair, fit. He looked like ten thousand other white guys who work in offices around here. That's all I know, really."

"Sounds like they paid in cash, so no credit card charge to indicate who they were."

Dale nodded but said only, "I gotta get back to it. Any chance I can get a picture before you go?"

"Sure," Darcy said, sliding out of the booth and standing next to him.

Dale handed Tony a phone. After a quick pose, snap, and handshake, Dale was gone.

As Tony stood and helped Darcy into her coat, he said, "I'd bet my life savings that Tim Jebron never cheated anyone out of a bar bill in his life. I just can't imagine it."

"So what does it mean?"

Multiple possibilities occurred to Tony. "He could have been really excited, or maybe the opposite, to see the guys who sat in the next booth. Maybe he knew them, like bumping into old friends from school, or maybe someone he had arrested in the past. You know, someone who got him so worked up that he forgot to pay. Or he could have left under duress, and never had the opportunity. Or he could have done it on purpose to send a message to someone that he was in trouble."

Tony pulled on his own coat. "Actually, I'd scratch that last idea. I don't think Tim was that clever." He paused to look at Darcy and said, "That sounds like I'm being harsh. What I mean is, I don't think that's the way Tim's mind worked."

"What did you mean by duress?" Darcy asked.

"I'm not sure. Maybe these guys confronted Tim for some

reason, or vice-versa. If they were having some kind of argument, or the conversation devolved to the point where Tim was perceived as an enemy, maybe they forced him to leave with them."

"Seems unlikely," Darcy said, "but with the bar nearly empty and a bartender not really paying any attention, I suppose it's possible."

She looked at the two booths with the high-top padded backs separating them. She said, "I'm betting the bartender was right, that the guys who came in later didn't know Tim was in the next booth. Unless they specifically looked, how would they? I wonder if Tim overheard something he shouldn't have."

"Makes sense," Tony said. "If you're right, I'm dying to know what it was."

Tony had no idea how close he had just come to speaking the truth.

# Chapter 12

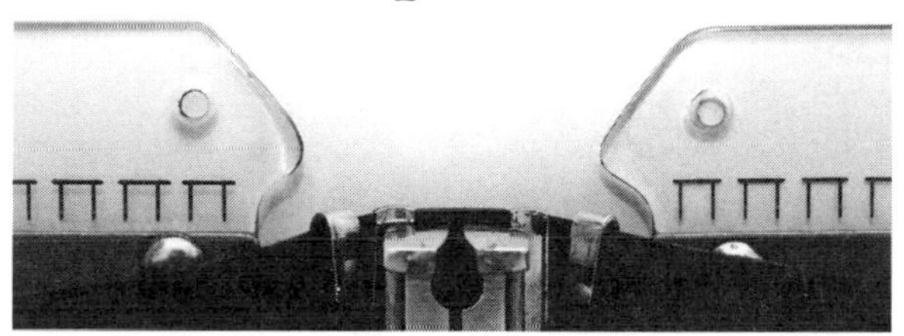

Friday, January 2, Chicago, Illinois

Tony and Darcy debated as they ate their generous portions of sea bass and salmon. The tone of the discussion had an edge to it, but both appeared determined to ignore it.

Darcy's point of view was as simple as it was compelling. The fact that Tim had left the bar with two other men clearly called into question the police's conclusion that his death had been a suicide. At the very least, it showed something significant had happened after Tim had left his hotel room—something the detectives had not uncovered, or at least not reported, in their investigation.

"We need to take this to the police," she argued. "They need to interview the bartender and follow up on this. They have the resources to do it properly."

It was a difficult position to dispute, but that didn't stop Tony from doing so. "They may have the resources, but do they have the desire? We already know they've been ignoring evidence. What if that's because there's something more going on here? What if someone in the department really is in on it? Telling them what we found might only put a target on our backs. We uncovered this much in one day. We should keep digging, at least until we stop making progress."

Darcy shook her head, exasperated and fearful, as she came to understand better every day why Tony kept finding himself in situations of genuine peril.

She was about to push back when Tony's cell phone buzzed on the linen-covered table top. He had set it to vibrate, to be courteous to the other diners, but had left it out so he wouldn't miss a call.

Glancing at the screen, Tony said, "It's Ben. I'd better answer it."

He grabbed the phone off the table and walked into the hallway leading to the men's room. "Hey boss, what's up?"

"Hi. Sorry to bother you on a Friday night, but I got a strange call. I think you'll want to hear about it. Do you have a minute?"

"We're at a restaurant, but I'm nearly finished. Go ahead."

"A kid called the office, asking for you. The desk didn't want to give out your cell phone, so they forwarded the call to me."

"A kid?"

"Yeah. He said his name was Jalen. Said to tell you he was one of the kids you met in the parking lot last night. Does that make sense?"

"Sure. I mean, Darcy and I chatted with a half-dozen teenagers. We were at the place where Tim died. We just wanted to see it, get a sense of the place. It was a very brief exchange. It was too damn cold to stand around outside for any longer than that. So what did he want?"

Ben's voice conveyed as much question as answer. "He said his friend, a young girl named Elena, is in the hospital. She was attacked as she was getting out of her car."

"That's horrible," Tony said, wondering if Elena was another one of the teens they had met, and then wondering what all this had to do with him. Ben soon answered both questions.

"Jalen said this girl, Elena, was with the group last night. Now, from her hospital bed, she's asking for Darcy. She won't tell anyone what happened. She won't talk to her mother, or the doctors, or even the police. Jalen sounded almost angry that she wouldn't talk to him. She just kept saying she wanted to talk to Darcy."

Tony was more than a little surprised, but said, "Ben, hang on. If this concerns Darcy, I want to get her in on it. Give me one minute."

Tony walked to the edge of the restaurant's dining room and waved at Darcy, motioning for her to join him. She got up from the table and did so, asking what was going on.

Tony urged her to hold her questions for just a moment, and led her to the maître d' stand. To the hostess, he said, "Do you have an empty dining room, or lounge, or even an office, where we can take this call? It's very urgent and we don't want to bother your other guests."

The young woman looked uncertain, but said, "The group that was in the board room—that's what we call our smaller private dining room—has finished. The room hasn't been cleaned yet, but it should be fine for you to use for a few minutes."

Tony nodded his appreciation, and the woman led them down another hallway. Into the phone, he said, "One more minute."

They sat at the table and pushed a few dirty dishes out of the way. Tony set the phone down and punched the "speaker" button.

He said, "Okay, Ben. Darcy's with me now and we're alone. If you have time, please start at the beginning and tell her what you told me."

Ben did, and at the sound of her name, Darcy let out an audible gasp. "Why me?" was all she managed to say.

"Jalen didn't have a clue," Ben answered. "He said the only thing the two of you talked about was the 'dead guy,' and only for a few seconds."

"Oh, no," Darcy looked stricken. "Is this the girl who figured out why we were there?" She looked at Tony but spoke to Ben. "I think I know who he means. There was a girl there who guessed we were friends of Tim's. She's really the only one I talked to about him. She was pretty shy but seemed nice."

"Does Jalen think this had something to do with what happened there last Saturday?" Tony asked.

"I'm sorry, guys, but I just don't have any answers to your questions," Ben said, his voice thick with concern. "You have to understand that I spoke very briefly to a distraught teenager who didn't seem to know anything either."

"A very smart and resourceful teenager, too," Tony said. "He must've Googled Darcy and found my name, then did a search on me and found the *Town Crier's* number. Pretty impressive."

Ben remained focused on the situation.

"How about the two of you? Any guesses what this is about?"

Tony looked at Darcy, who simply shook her head.

"Nope," Tony said.

Darcy took a deep breath and said, "We all know there's only one way to find out. Assuming you got them from Jalen, give us the name of the hospital and Elena's last name and room number."

***

Cook County Hospital's official name was longer. Tony thought it probably was named for a significant donor, or perhaps a local political leader. It made little difference because everyone still called it Cook County Hospital, or CCH. The large medical center and its services were housed in a relatively modern facility. Tony was pretty sure it was younger than he was. He could remember seeing it under construction when he was a kid growing up in Chicago. As expected, the hospital was a madhouse at 10 p.m. on a Friday night. The only open entrance was for emergencies, and the waiting room was filled with a wide variety of human suffering. As a Level I Trauma Center located in the heart of a city of nearly three million people, it was always busy and rarely pleasant.

They decided to don COVID masks as much for anonymity as for protection against any airborne threats. After passing through security, Tony and Darcy waited in line to speak to a woman behind glass at a reception desk. Darcy gripped Tony's arm as they both tried not to get caught up in the tragic situations all around them.

When they reached the front of the line, Tony explained that they were there to see Elena Church and gave the room number. The clerk expressed her regrets that visiting hours were over. This led to a pleasant back-and-forth exchange, which quickly became less pleasant as Tony tried to convince the clerk it was urgent, and they were there at the patient's request.

The clerk looked as if she had heard every conceivable argument and excuse. In any case, rules were rules.

Finally, Darcy interjected, "Perhaps, if you could spare one more moment of your time, you could call the nursing station up on the floor. If we're as needed as we think, maybe someone there can help."

The woman looked hard at Darcy for a moment, then said, "One call."

"Thank you," Darcy said as the woman dialed.

Less than two minutes later, Tony and Darcy were in an elevator, escorted by a young man.

Darcy was about to ask the man's role when he said, "I'm an aide in the Trauma Center. Sometimes I get asked to escort visitors after hours. You know, we can't have strangers just wandering the halls."

"Of course," Darcy said, nodding.

"A big hospital like this has, you know, like a billion dollars' worth of drugs around." The corners of the man's eyes crinkled, and Darcy could imagine the smile behind the mask. "And then with all that crap about patient privacy, not to mention some of the nut jobs we get here. You wouldn't believe… I mean, not that you look like nut jobs or anything."

Darcy laughed.

The man shook his head and said, "I guess I'll be quiet now. We're almost there anyway."

The elevator doors opened and they walked a short distance through a lobby and a doorway, up to the nurses' station.

"They're all yours," the escort said to the woman behind the desk.

"Thank you," Darcy and Tony said.

"No problem," the man said. "Stay safe out there. If you think it's no fun comin' in here as a visitor, just try it as a patient."

Darcy and Tony waved a quick goodbye and turned to the woman at the desk. Before they spoke, another woman emerged from a patient room a short distance down the hall and approached them.

"Are you Darcy? Darcy Gillson? Do you know what happened to my girl? Why's my girl hurt? Who would want to do this to Elena?"

The desk clerk stood and turned to the second woman. "Mrs. Church, I know you have questions, but our guests have just arrived. Let's get them out of their coats and introduced, and then we'll see if they can help you."

"I'm sorry. Of course. I just…This is so…I'm sorry." She brushed a tear from the corner of her eye and said, "I'm Marta Church, Elena's mother."

The desk clerk returned to her seat to answer a ringing phone, and Darcy and Tony turned to face the petite Hispanic woman.

"I'm Darcy Gillson. This is my boyfriend, Tony Harrington. And, sadly, I must answer all your questions with a simple 'no.' I don't have any idea what happened or why. I have to confess, I'm baffled as to why Elena is asking for me."

Church tried to hide her skepticism and said simply, "Then I suppose it was kind of you to come. I hope Elena will explain this to you, 'cause I can't get the girl to say a thing to me."

Darcy asked if it was okay to bother Elena now, considering the hour. The girl's mother said yes. Elena had refused to take a sleeping pill until after she had talked to Darcy.

"And the police?" Tony asked.

"They took off a long time ago," Church said. "With no evidence and a victim who refuses to answer their questions, who can blame them?"

Darcy and Tony removed their coats, and Tony folded them over one arm. As they entered the hospital room, they were saddened by what they saw. Elena was lying back on the bed, inclined about halfway to a sitting position. An IV line was attached to one wrist, a splint was attached to the little finger of her left hand, and a host of wires leading to an EEG monitor were attached to her head. Most disturbing was the sight of her left eye swollen shut, and a cut along her left cheek below it.

Marta Church said quietly, "They're most concerned about the concussion. They would have sent her home, but they want to be sure her brain function is normal and there's no swelling. They said everything else will heal." As she spoke, her voice cracked and she wiped away more tears.

At the sound of her mother's voice, Elena opened her eyes. When she saw Darcy, she immediately began to cry.

"Elena," her mother said, rushing to her side. "Are you okay? Is this okay? You wanted to see her, right?"

"Yes, yes." Elena nodded and fought to stop crying. She looked straight at Darcy and said, "I'm sorry. I'm *so* sorry."

Darcy approached the bed. “Is it okay if I remove this?” Both mother and daughter nodded, so Darcy pulled off her mask and handed it to Tony. He retreated to a small chair next to the wall.

Darcy smiled and took Elena’s good hand. “Please don’t cry. You have nothing to be sorry about. You didn’t do this.”

“You don’t understand. It’s my fault. I took your picture. Now he knows.”

Darcy tried to keep a smile on her face as she felt her body stiffen. She said, “I don’t know what you mean, Elena. Why don’t you just tell me about it? Tell me everything from the beginning.”

Elena recounted that she had spent the middle part of the day swimming. Still on semester break from high school, a group of friends was invited to join one of their classmates who lived in an apartment building with an indoor pool.

“I headed home about 3:30. My mom gets off work at 4:30, and she likes it if I’m home when she gets there. It’s just a short drive, so it was maybe fifteen minutes later when I pulled into the parking lot.”

“You had a car?” Darcy asked, then added, “By the way, Tony’s going to take a few notes while you talk, if you don’t mind.”

“I guess it’s okay,” Elena said, looking doubtful.

Darcy glanced in Tony’s direction, seeing him nod his appreciation and pull his notebook from his coat pocket.

Elena said, “Yes, I had my mom’s car. She rides the L to work and doesn’t mind if I use the car, as long as I pay for gas with my babysitting money, and don’t go too far. Anyway, when I stepped out of the car, this man was there. I mean right there. When I stood up, I was blocked by the car door and this man in front of me.”

“Can you describe him?”

“I’ll never forget him. He was big.”

“Big like tall, or big like fat?”

“Big like tall. Not fat, but not skinny either. When I tried to push past him, he felt like stone, even through his winter coat. He had a wide nose that twitched when he got mad, which was right away, and a mean face."

"A beard?"

"No, nothing like that. He just looked like a bully. The kind you avoid in school. He had on a blue stocking cap, so I don't know about his hair. His eyebrows were dark."

"You're doing great, Elena. A grown man or young, like a teenager?"

"No, he was old. Maybe even forty or so."

Darcy forced back a smile. She asked, "What did he say?"

"I'm not sure at first. I was so scared. I…honestly, it's like I went numb. I didn't hear anything. Then he grabbed my arm like, you know, like he wanted to wake me up. I started to scream but he slapped me." She began to cry again.

"Are you sure you're okay?" Darcy asked. "You don't have to tell us anything you don't want to."

"No!" the girl said. "I *do* have to tell you. He wanted…he's…" She stopped and took a deep breath. "Sorry. You wanted me to tell you everything. I have to think. So, after he slapped me, he pulled on my arm until I was right up against him. He spoke quietly but it was horrible. He hissed as he spoke. It was like a snake. He said if I screamed or if I didn't cooperate, he would kill me."

"He said 'cooperate?' That was the word he used?"

"Yes, I remember because it surprised me. I thought he was going to…you know…" She looked at her mother, then looked away. "Anyway, now I wasn't sure. I was still scared, but I asked him what he wanted. That's when he asked about you."

"Me?" Darcy suddenly felt cold. She looked at Tony and saw he was staring back.

Elena continued, "Well, it was you but not you. I mean, I told you this is my fault. I'm sorry."

Darcy fought to keep her voice calm and friendly. "It's okay, really. Just tell me what he wanted."

The girl said, "He asked me who the woman was that I was talking to last night. I said 'When?' You know, like I talk to a lot of people. He slapped me again and told me not to play dumb. He meant last night, there in the parking lot. I said I didn't know. I mean, I did know, of course, but I didn't want to tell *him*. That's when he hit me."

She reached up and touched her face. "This time it wasn't a slap. He hit me with his fist, hard. It made me hit my head on the car behind me, and I could feel blood on my face. I started to cry. He told me to stop it and answer his question. I might have told him… I was so scared, but before I said anything, he asked what we talked about. I said me and some friends just asked the couple in the Jeep if they were moving to our building. He didn't believe me. He held my arm tighter and twisted it. It hurt, a lot. So I told him. I'm sorry. I told him how I noticed your Jeep had Iowa plates, and how I guessed maybe you knew the dead guy."

She paused again to breathe deeply. "I'm so stupid. It was the wrong thing to say. Suddenly, he *really* wanted to know who you were. I kept saying I didn't know, and he started hissing again, calling me all kinds of terrible things. I couldn't stop crying, so he said, 'Give me your phone.' I shook my head. That's when…that's when…"

Darcy glanced over her shoulder and saw Marta Church, seated in an armchair in the corner of the room, weeping.

Darcy said, "Elena, please don't keep going if this is too hard."

"I want to, please," the girl said. "When I didn't give him my phone, he grabbed my hand and broke my little finger. Just snapped it like it was piece of a KitKat Bar or something." She paused to blow her nose into a tissue, then said, "When I felt my finger snap, I screamed, really screamed. That's when he hit me again. It must have been a lot harder this time, 'cause I woke up here, at the hospital. Jalen told me… Sorry. Jalen is my friend. He told me my phone was gone when they found me on the ground next to my car."

Darcy gave Elena's good hand a light squeeze and said, "You were very brave. You suffered all this to protect me. I won't forget it."

"But don't you see," Elena was crying again. "I didn't protect you at all. He has my phone. To open it, all he had to do was put it in front of my face before he walked away. Now he knows exactly who you are."

# Chapter 13

Friday, January 2, Chicago, Illinois

"I'm sorry I got you into this," Tony said. "It's all my fault. I should have come alone."

He and Darcy were lying back-to-back under the covers of the king-sized bed in their darkened hotel room.

Darcy's tone surprised him when she said, "Really, Tony? That's your answer? I shouldn't be here?"

"I just meant…"

"I know what you meant. You want to protect me. You want to be the hero. You feel guilty because you brought your woman along and now she's at risk. You did it all for you, and now your guilt is keeping you awake. Do you sense a pattern here?"

Tony was desperate to avoid this conversation. He didn't want to hear about his faults. Not tonight. He didn't want to deal with his feelings, or Darcy's. He just wanted to be left alone. Fortunately or unfortunately, he knew better. He knew if they didn't talk, he was going to lose her.

He said, “Is that how you think I feel? You think I just brought you along to meet my needs?”

“Jesus, Tony. You’re not listening. Stop thinking about yourself for one minute and ask how I feel. Maybe I don’t need a hero right now. Maybe I don’t want to be treated like an add-on, like someone who’s good company when everything’s fine, but needs to be sent packing when things get dicey. Maybe I want to be your partner. A real partner, in every sense.”

“You are, I swear. I’m just so scared when I think about…”

She cut him off. “Bullshit.”

“Wha…?”

“Calling me a partner is total BS, and you know it. You don’t keep secrets from a partner. You don’t refuse to talk to a partner about what’s eating you. You don’t change overnight from a happy, caring, attentive lover to a stranger who’s lost interest in sex and kisses me on the cheek, and call yourself my partner. And tonight, when I most needed you to love and support and comfort me, you don’t turn your back and try to go to sleep. I don’t know anymore what we are, but we’re not partners.”

Tony reached out to pull her close. She looked back over her shoulder. Even though he could barely see her face, Tony had no doubt about the expression on it.

She said, “Please don’t touch me. No matter how badly I want you to—need you to—just keep to yourself until you’re ready to tell me what in the hell is going on.”

# Chapter 14

Saturday, January 3, Chicago, Illinois
Seven Days to Wheels-Up, Flight 244

"I have a question for you," Anna Tabors said as she strode into the small conference room at the Chicago field office of the FBI.

"Good morning to you too, Agent Tabors," Tony said, surprised at the agent's abruptness.

Tony and Darcy were seated on one side of a modest gray table. They had come at Tabors's request. A woman, probably an administrative assistant, had called Tony's cell at 8 a.m. and had issued the invitation and instructions to get there.

"Sorry," Tabors said. "It's been a crazy morning and I'm wondering what you may have stumbled into." She pulled out a chair opposite the couple and sat.

Tony and Darcy looked at each other, then returned their gazes to the agent. "We're wondering too," Tony said. "You have our attention, now what's your question?"

"Was Deputy Jebron into guns?"

"I'm not sure what you mean."

"You know, was he what someone might unkindly call a gun nut? A guy with a big collection, survivalist talk, anti-government attitudes, any of that?"

"Not that I know of, but isn't that a better question for Sheriff Mackey or Tim's wife?"

"I've already asked them both. Now I'm asking you."

"I never saw a hint of any of that from Tim. My impression, he was a milquetoast type. If I had to guess, he had two guns, his service pistol and a rifle or shotgun for hunting. Maybe one of each."

"That's pretty close to what both Mackey and Mrs. Jebron said," the agent said, sitting back in her chair and sighing.

Tony waited a moment, then said, "Not to change the subject, but when talking to the sheriff or Mrs. Jebron, did you tell either of them what we've found so far, that Tim was seen leaving the bar with those two men?"

"I mentioned it to the sheriff. He said he had heard from you already. I didn't report anything to Mrs. Jebron. I don't work for her and didn't think it was my business to tell her anything."

"Thanks," Tony said. "Just trying to keep up with who knows what." The room grew quiet again.

Tabors seemed to make up her mind about something. She leaned forward and asked, "What do you know about POVO?"

"The city in Utah?"

Tabors didn't smile. Tony hadn't meant for her to. His mistake had been an honest one. He said, "Oh, sorry, that's Provo."

Darcy said, "POVO is that fringe group claiming to be preparing for the 'next society,' right?"

Tony turned and looked at her, his mouth agape. Tabors smiled.

Darcy said, "I looked at a script once that involved them. I don't think the movie ever got legs. Quite frankly, I think the studios were afraid to make it. These guys are nuts and no one wanted to take them on."

Tabors nodded. "POVO is an acronym for 'Patriots of Victory One.' They began as a ragtag group in northern Missouri. Maybe twenty or so men and women who liked to stockpile guns, drink beer, and drive around in modified pickup trucks while shooting things out-of-season. In fact, it was the game wardens who first brought them to our attention. Sadly, they're not so fringe anymore. As politics and society changed, and anti-establishment sentiments came to the forefront without much retribution, the leaders of POVO jumped onto social media and began to actively evangelize." She paused. "And recruit. Today we estimate they have more than a thousand members, mostly located in a dozen or so states in the Midwest and South. And they're not just bigger; they're better organized and more coherent in their messaging."

"This is all very interesting, and more than a little disturbing, but what does this have to do with…?"

Tabors held up a hand to cut him off. She pulled a manila envelope from her briefcase, removed a cell phone, and pushed it across the table.

"Tim's phone?" Darcy asked as Tony picked it up.

"Yes," Tabors said. "The magic phone that doesn't collect fingerprints, except mine, and now yours."

"Sorry," Tony said, putting it down.

Tabors couldn't restrain a chortle. "No, it's okay. I want you to look at it."

Tony eagerly picked it up again.

Tabors said, "Mrs. Jebron gave us the password. You probably assumed that." She shared it, and Tony opened the phone.

"I'll give you a minute. See if you reach any of the same

conclusions I did, or at least uncover the same questions."

Tony held the phone so Darcy could see the screen as well. He began opening various functions. The suicide note, Melissa's responses to it, and all of Jebron's other texts were there. Tony scanned through them quickly. When he got back twenty days before Jebron's death, he stopped.

"Nothing worth noting in the texts," he said.

As Tabors nodded, Tony added, "Except a bogus suicide note." He repeated the process with the emails. He said, "Emails are even more boring. He must have ordered something from High Trails Sporting Goods once, 'cause he gets about three promos from them every day."

Tony opened the call history and found nothing worth noting. He opened the memos app. Empty. He tried the voice memos. Empty. He didn't comment but assumed Tabors could guess what he was doing.

He saw the Garage Band app. Tony didn't think Jebron had been musical, but a lot of phones had it. He checked the recordings.

"Nothing recorded in Garage Band," he said.

Tabors raised her eyebrows. "Very clever of you to think to check it," she said. "Gold star."

"Great," Tony grimaced. "It still doesn't tell me what I'm looking for."

Darcy said, "Check his browser history."

Tabors smiled. Tony opened the browser. The icons for the most-used sites were displayed in rows. One was the government site for Quincy County. One was ESPN. A few were for specific sports teams, such as the Chicago Cubs. Tony ignored these and opened the browser's History tab.

"Well I'll be damned." At the top of the list was the website: PatriotsOfVictoryOne.com.

"I see you found it," Tabors said. "Another gold star, but this one goes to Darcy."

Tony nodded, then asked, "So what is my milquetoast deputy doing on the website for a radical group advocating for a second civil war?"

"That's what I'd like to know," Tabors said, "but I fear we have a hint."

Tony looked again and saw the date and time the website had been opened. "Oh man," he said. "This is the night Tim was killed."

Darcy leaned closer, gripping Tony's arm. She said, "So what does this mean? Was Tim mixed up with these people somehow?"

"I don't know," Tabors said, "but it seems unlikely. No one I've talked to has given any indication he was interested personally, and Mackey assures me he would have known about it if Tim had been investigating them. More to the point, I've spent time going further back through his history. As far as I can tell, he only visited that site once."

Tony said, "This is likely the very last thing he did before he died." The room grew very still. Tony said aloud what everyone was thinking.

"So Tim Jebron goes into a bar alone. Two men come in and sit in the next booth. Tim takes out his phone, searches for and finds the POVO website. Soon after, he leaves with the two men. Then he gets thrown off a roof. Did I miss anything?"

"Only the conclusion you draw from all that. I'm actually rather proud of you for stopping where you did."

Darcy said, "You two may not want to say it out loud, but I will. Tim overheard these guys talking and checked them out. Then, they caught him at it or he confronted them, and they took him out and killed him."

"Yes. Well, that's a scenario that fits what we know. Of course, there could be other…"

"Bullshit," Tony said quietly. "That's exactly what happened and we all know it. So the big question is, why? Why would two guys murder someone just because he overheard a conversation?"

"They could just be hotheads." Tabors said. "You know, a couple guys who think they're above the law, who think they're tough. They don't like Tim's eavesdropping, so maybe they take him to the roof to teach him a lesson and, well, things get out of hand."

"Maybe," Tony said, "but it feels like a stretch. More likely, Tim heard something really onerous. Something these guys couldn't afford to have a stranger overhear. Maybe they were talking about something they've done, like another murder or something, or perhaps a crime they're planning. They feel compelled to silence the problem."

"So how did they get him to leave with them?" Darcy asked.

"Who knows?" Tony said. "Maybe they came up with some story that convinced him to go. Maybe they were armed and simply forced him at gunpoint."

"Maybe they threatened someone else, like his family," Darcy said, joining his train of thought. "You're right. I can imagine a lot of ways they could have done it. Of course, once they're alone somewhere, maybe even in a vehicle these guys were driving, Tim's completely at their mercy."

"Right on all counts," Tony said, "but speculating about the how doesn't really matter. The fact is, he left with two men after looking at this website." He tapped the phone. "This is the key to finding out why they killed him."

Tabors looked from Tony to Darcy and back to Tony. "Again, I agree with you," she said.

"Which brings us to the biggest mystery of all," Tony said. "Why in the hell are you having this conversation with a newspaper reporter and an actress?"

Tabors squirmed. Tony thought it might be the first time he'd ever seen her looking uncomfortable.

She said, "It's pretty simple. I'm scared. These POVO creeps are growing bigger and more dangerous. They're no longer the wannabe tough guys we like to call 'gravy seals,' who couldn't throw a tantrum, much less an insurrection. We've learned that POVO is better funded and more intense than other similar groups. Their leaders, at least the ones we know about, have quit their day jobs and devote all their time to the cause. It just feels like something is coming. Another Oklahoma City, or worse."

"God forbid."

"I'm scared enough that I've decided it's worth it to go beyond our normal methods to track this down."

Tony didn't know what he had expected to hear from Tabors, but it wasn't this.

He said, "You're asking for our help?"

"Yes," she said, instinctively lowering her voice. "Understand, I'm not suggesting you do anything crazy. Nothing dangerous. I just need someone to connect with them on social media, gain their trust, maybe become on online member. See if you can get connected to their site on the dark web. Maybe get a hint about what they're up to."

Tony nodded his understanding, even enthusiasm, but asked, "Okay, sure. But why me?"

Tabors said, "I'm nervous about asking the Chicago PD for anything more. After looking at how they either botched or buried the investigation so far, I don't know who I can trust. Besides, if this really does involve POVO, then it goes far beyond the city limits of Chicago."

"Okay, I get that," Tony said, "but you're with the..."

"The FBI, of course," the agent finished for him. "And believe me, I'm doing what I can to light a fire under my colleagues. But bureaucracies move slowly. I've reported everything to my boss, and

I've filed my written report. He and others will talk about this and they'll decide maybe I'm on to something, but they'll also note there's no real proof of any crime committed, let alone substantial evidence that one may be coming. So they'll probably let me continue to work it but not give me much help. I'm not going to have a team and a bunch of resources at my disposal, at least not until I learn something more."

Tony understood. He had great respect for the FBI, based on what he had observed in the past and his experiences with Tabors, but he also understood that what she was saying was true. In giant organizations, especially those rooted in government, some barriers are just inevitable.

"Lastly," Tabors said, "you may not have noticed, but I'm a Black woman."

Tony and Darcy couldn't help it. Laughs escaped their lips.

Tabors smiled but quickly grew serious. "Think about it. I'm the person least likely to have any success in getting close to POVO. Some of them actually wear hats that say, 'Make America White Again.' There are Bureau resources I can use to dig into the organization from afar—electronics and so forth—but I can't meet them online or talk to them."

"Well, crap," Tony said suddenly. "I'm not sure we can either."

Tabors looked puzzled. She said, "I assumed Darcy would be out of this going forward, just because she's so recognizable, but it sounds like you mean something else."

"Yeah," Tony said. He explained to Tabors how he and Darcy had gone to the apartment building to see where Tim had died and had talked to a group of teens. Then, one of those teens had been assaulted and had been forced to tell her attacker why they had been there.

He said, "The assailant took her phone, so he knows who we are and what we look like."

"You're assuming this is connected." Tabors said it as a statement, not a question.

"Of course, yes. What else could it be? This guy wanted to know what we were asking about when we were there Thursday night, and he demanded to know what Elena and her friends had told us. He put a teenage girl in the hospital to get answers. This all ties together somehow."

"Well, shit," Tabors said. "Obviously, you're going to have to steer clear of this. I'll find another way to approach it."

"Hang on," Tony said. "Just give me a new email address and put me in a disguise. I'd probably need that anyway. The FBI must have people who do disguises."

"Of course," Tabors smiled. "But just how do I explain to them that I'm bringing a civilian, a news reporter no less, into the heart of an active investigation?"

"Ah… well."

Darcy said, "This isn't a problem."

Tabors and Tony turned to look at her.

"I mean, it *is* a problem because I don't want Tony to do this. I'm very tired of visiting him in hospitals. But I know him well enough to know he won't listen. He's excited to go after these guys, so he will."

"So…?" Tabors asked.

"So, I just happen to know people who work in makeup, wardrobe, special effects, props, you name it. I'm guessing the people I know would put the FBI's disguise experts to shame."

***

As they drove back to the hotel, Darcy said, "I'm going to arrange this for you, and then I'm going home."

"Honey, I hope…"

"Just stop," she said, turning away and gazing out at the snow-lined streets. "It's clear I can't be involved in whatever it is you do next, so I'm just in the way. Probably, my presence helped the killers identify you faster, so I've actually put you in more danger."

"That's just silly. Please…"

"Don't pretend you disagree. At least be honest enough to admit that you'll be relieved when I'm gone. Less to worry about, and no one to object when you decide to do something foolish."

Tony wanted to tell her she was wrong, but he knew he couldn't.

"Okay," he said. "I'll be honest. Yes, I worry about you. When an FBI agent tells me she's scared of these people, it makes me want to send you as far away as possible."

"Don't pretend this is about protecting me." Darcy sighed and looked out the passenger window. "This is about meeting your needs. You want to be left alone. There's something else…"

"Please don't read more into this than it is," Tony said. "I love you, and I want you to be safe. End of story."

"Call Melissa."

"What?" Tony almost sprained his neck as he whipped around in reaction to the change of subject.

Darcy said, "Melissa needs to know about the two men. She deserves to know that we've found real evidence that she was right, that Tim's death wasn't a suicide. Call her now. I can drive if you like."

"I'll call her later," Tony said.

"I think you should call her now."

Tony's face reddened, and he nearly barked, "I said I'll call her later."

"I thought so."

Tony's exasperation was morphing into anger. He held it in check because he did not want to have this conversation.

She said, "What happened when you went to Melissa's?"

"What do you mean, what happened?"

"Something happened. You haven't been the same ever since you interviewed her. You're distracted, unhappy, and you've barely touched me. I think I deserve to know."

"Darcy, I just… I can't…"

"Dear God. I knew it."

Tony pulled the Jeep to a stop at a red light.

Darcy looked up and said, "I just remembered, I need some hand lotion. Pull around the corner and stop. I'll be right back."

"Darcy…" Tony reached for her but she was out the door. The cold air was like a physical presence that invaded the car in the moments it took for the door to swing closed. Tony did as instructed and parked in the first open spot in front of a fire hydrant on the side street.

After about five minutes, his cell phone buzzed. He dug it out of his jeans pocket and glanced at the screen. "Ah, shit."

It read: *Headed home. I'll have the makeup and costume people call you. Don't forget to bring my things when you come. Be safe. D*

Tony looked back and saw the L station a block away. He could see a train pulling away. The Blue Line. To O'Hare. "Ah, shit," he said again.

# Chapter 15

Saturday, January 3, Chicago, Illinois

Rather than stew in his hotel room waiting for Tabors to send information on a new email account, and for Darcy to send contacts for her friends in the world of show business, Tony decided to spend his time pursuing more traditional approaches to investigative reporting. The most obvious avenue, and if he was being honest with himself, one of the few available to him, was talking to witnesses from the night of Tim's death.

Tabors had given him, on his promise of confidentiality, a copy of the police report. It included a ridiculously small number of names of people at the scene on Saturday night. Considering the bitter cold and the late hour, Tony could understand why few people had been present when police arrived.

Five names. That was it. Five people who had seen the body and had bothered to remain close enough, probably inside the building lobby, for police to identify once they had arrived. The man who had actually discovered Tim's remains had been interviewed, along with three others.

Tony reread their statements, confirming that none contained anything helpful.

The fifth person listed in the report was the nurse, Tenisha Wedder. She had come down to the scene from her apartment six floors above to offer her assistance. The report said officers told her the victim was deceased and that there was nothing she could do. They encouraged her to return to her apartment.

She wasn't mentioned further, indicating she had not been interviewed. Tony decided that was the place to start. Rather than rehash what the police had already learned, he would take an even longer shot and talk to the one person who had been there, albeit briefly, and hadn't been asked what she had seen.

Tony glanced at his watch. It wasn't quite noon. The report said Wedders was a nurse at Northwestern Memorial. She had told the police she had trauma experience. If that meant she worked in the ER, maybe she'd be on duty on a Saturday. *Worth a try,* Tony thought, *but just barely*. He knew there was no good reason to do this except that he had the time, and being thorough was what good reporters did.

***

As Tony drove into a parking ramp on the medical center's campus, he gazed up at one of the enormous buildings and realized how unbelievably naïve he had been. Finding a specific nurse within this vast complex was not a needle-in-a-haystack problem; it was a needle in an entire hayfield.

He knew he couldn't just walk up to the information desk and ask for Tenisha Wedders. There was no way the hospital was going to direct him to one of its employees. He thought he might go to the hospital cafeteria and ask some of the Emergency Department staff if they knew her and could help, but when he reached the main lobby, he was reminded again of the depth of his foolishness.

He picked up a Visitor's Guide at the reception desk and learned that the complex had multiple dining options in multiple locations. It also noted that thirty-six restaurants were within walking distance of the campus. If Wedders and/or her co-workers were having lunch, they could be anywhere.

Tony decided to seek out the people whose job it was to help him. Every hospital had an office of public relations or something similar, and a hospital the size of Northwestern undoubtedly had a media relations specialist at work or at least on call on the weekends.

He took out his cell phone, looked up the medical center's website, and called the main number. He told the operator he was a reporter working on a story, was in the building, and needed to talk with someone. After a wait of just a couple of minutes, the call-back came.

"Tony Harrington."

"Mr. Harrington, this is Greg Belcher from Northwestern Memorial Healthcare Media Relations. I understand you're on campus and have asked to speak to someone. How can I help you?"

Tony explained he was working on a story unrelated to the hospital but needed to reach one of the nurses employed there.

Belcher first needed reassurance the story did not involve the medical center in any way. Tony did his best to convince him it didn't.

Belcher asked what it was about. Tony reluctantly explained that he couldn't disclose the subject, but he quickly added that Ms. Wedders was in no trouble of any kind. He was simply hoping she had some information about a topic he was looking into.

Belcher didn't react well to Tony's unwillingness to share more.

He then said he couldn't really help anyway, explaining that the medical center never releases contact information or other details about any of its employees.

Tony tried to sound pleasant as he said he understood this. "However," he said, "I thought perhaps you or someone could reach out to her and make her aware of my efforts to reach her. You could give her my cell number and ask her to call me."

Belcher resisted.

Tony pushed back, saying he wouldn't have called if it wasn't important.

Belcher said he wasn't sure he could find the information, even if he was inclined to help.

Tony pleaded with him to try.

Belcher finally sighed and said, "Where did you say you're from?"

"The *Town Crier* in Orney, Iowa."

Belcher chuckled. "I have to be honest with you, I haven't heard of it."

"I'd be surprised if you had. It's the smallest daily paper in Iowa in a town of about fifteen thousand."

Whether it was Belcher's dismissal of the *Crier* as "harmless," or Tony's persuasive skills, Tony couldn't say, but in the end, Belcher promised to try and to call him back either way.

"Sit tight," he said.

Tony found a bench in the lobby and sat.

Twenty minutes later, his phone rang.

"Tony Harrington."

"Mr. Harrington, I suggest you go out and buy a lottery ticket."

"I hope that means you have good news."

"It means Ms. Wedders doesn't normally work on Saturdays. She happens to be here today because she agreed to cover an extra shift for a co-worker who went on maternity leave earlier than expected."

"And?"

"And she's not excited to talk with you, especially since I couldn't tell her what it's about."

Tony felt his shoulders sag and he scrambled to think of something more he could say.

Belcher interrupted his thoughts. "However, she said she would give you a few minutes at the end of her shift, assuming you're willing to wait or come back at three, and willing to have the conversation there in the lobby where it's safe."

"Completely reasonable requests," Tony said. "Tell her I agree. She won't have any trouble spotting me. I'm wearing black Levi's and a gray parka. I'll be on a bench near the reception desk in the main lobby at three. And tell her thank you."

"Mr. Harrington."

"Yes?"

"The next time you need a favor not related to breaking news or the medical center, do me a favor and call on a weekday."

"I promise," Tony said, smiling.

***

At 3:07 p.m., a petite Black woman in nurse's scrubs appeared at the far end of the lobby and made a beeline for Tony. He smiled, stood, and held out his hand.

Wedders returned the shake but with a noticeable lack of enthusiasm.

Tony introduced himself and said, "Thank you so much for taking the time to speak with me."

She said, "I'm not sure I should and not sure I will. Before we go any further, do you have some identification?"

"Of course." Tony took out his press pass and driver's license.

She examined them carefully and handed them back, saying, "Now what's this about?"

Tony indicated they should move away from the desk. They found seats in a corner of the lobby and sat facing each other.

"I think you've probably guessed why I'm here. The man who died in front of your building last Saturday was a deputy sheriff from Orney, Iowa. As you just saw, that's where I live and work."

"Yes, well, if you're here to ask about that man's death, there's nothing I can tell you. I only went down to the parking lot for a moment. I saw the flashing lights of emergency vehicles in my apartment window. Being a nurse, I thought I should make sure my help wasn't needed."

"I understand," Tony said. "Maybe you don't know anything helpful. But Tim Jebron was a good person, and he left behind a young widow. The Chicago PD is calling his death a suicide, but I'm sure it wasn't."

Tony saw Wedders stiffen. "What do you mean?" she asked. Her question came out a half-octave higher than her normal speaking voice.

"I'm sorry, but I can't share what we've learned, except to say we've uncovered some information the police didn't have when they closed the case. I'm convinced Tim was murdered, so anything you can share, anything you might have seen before or after the incident, could be important in finding his killers."

"Killers? Why do you say that, like more than one person was involved?"

Tony debated how much to share. He knew he was on the trail of an important story—maybe one far bigger than anyone had realized before today. He didn't want to start any chatter about it. On the other hand, he could tell the mention of a likely murder had struck a nerve with Wedders. Was she simply concerned, as anyone would be, that a murderer might be in the building, or did she know something? Tony decided he had to do whatever he could to enlist her help, on the chance she might have information he needed.

"Ms. Wedders…"

"Please, call me Tenisha."

"Tenisha, okay. Tenisha, we now know Tim was seen Saturday night with two men. Men who apparently were strangers, but either way, it doesn't matter. The fact he wasn't alone right before he died basically scuttles the PD's findings of what occurred that night."

"I'm sorry. This is all very tragic and, quite frankly, deeply troubling to someone who lives in that building. But I wasn't involved. I can't help you. I should go."

Wedders refused to look at Tony as she said these things, convincing him she was lying.

She shifted in her chair, as if about to stand.

Tony said, "Tenisha, one more minute, please."

She settled back, but still looked away.

He said, "Do you have children?"

She turned to face him. "How did you know that? Why does that matter?"

*Another nerve struck,* Tony thought. He said, "I didn't know, I swear. I asked because I want to make a point. Almost no one knows this, but Tim's widow is pregnant with their first child."

Wedders sucked in a breath as her face contorted. It was obvious she immediately grasped how this magnified the tragedy for Mrs. Jebron.

Tony continued, "I'm asking you to think, as a mother, what it means to have Deputy Jebron's death officially declared a suicide. That child growing up believing his or her father took his own life. Wondering why and, well, you get the idea. I'm just trying to emphasize…"

"I get it," Wedders said tersely. "It's horrible. My heart aches for that woman and for the child. I just…I mean…" She took a deep breath. "It's *because* I have a son that I can't help you. He, too, has no father. I'm raising him alone. I cannot get involved and risk having anything come back on me."

Tony leaned forward and lowered his voice. "Tenisha, I can promise you, whatever you tell me will be kept in strict confidence. As a reporter, I know what it means to protect a source. No one will ever know you talked to me. Not my boss, not the police, and certainly not any criminals involved. It's obvious you know something. Please, I'm begging you, tell me."

She bit her lower lip, glanced around the room, and leaned forward herself. Their foreheads almost touched. In a whisper, she said, "You swear?"

"I swear. No one. Ever."

She sighed, sat up a little, and again looked in all directions. Still speaking quietly she said, "Okay, you're right. I saw him. I mean, I assume it was him. Saturday night. I took a full bag of garbage down to the bin near the loading dock. It's not well-lit, so I'm always nervous when I'm down there. I heard a vehicle outside, so I took a quick look out the narrow window in the door. I could see men getting out of a pickup truck, so I stepped back into the shadows, out of sight. Three men, late on a Saturday night, in a remote part of the building. Well, I'm sure you can imagine as many horrible things as I can."

Tony nodded, but held his tongue. He didn't want to say anything that would interrupt her.

"I say three men because that's who came through the door. I could tell something wasn't right. Beyond the fact they were coming in the back, which residents almost never do, it was clear the second guy was the odd man out."

Tony's wrinkled brow prompted her to say, "It was a procession, where the first man was leading and the third man was prodding, and in the middle was this skinny white guy who didn't seem happy at all. They were past me in seconds, but I got the clear impression that he was questioning, or even resisting, and the other two guys were pushing him along."

Tony felt compelled to ask, "Did he seem to be drunk?"

"The middle guy? Not really. Of course it's hard to know from watching them walk from the door to the service elevator. I didn't see any obvious signs. And they spoke to each other softly enough that I couldn't hear what was said. In my experience, drunks are rarely quiet."

"So you don't know…"

"Again, it was over like that," she made a sweeping motion with her hand. "I heard no words, but from the tone of their voices, I got the impression that the middle guy—shit, let's just call him Jebron, okay?—Jebron asked something, and the lead guy told him to shut up. I didn't actually hear that. It was just the impression I got."

"I understand," Tony said. "What time was this?"

She paused. "It wasn't very late. Fobe, my son, was still in his playpen. I hate leaving him in the apartment alone for even a minute, but sometimes when I have to do something quickly, inside the building, I do it."

"Of course," Tony said, genuinely empathizing with her and any single parent who must decide between dragging a child along or leaving him alone every time some menial task needed doing outside the apartment.

Wedders said, "Anyway, it was probably eight or so. Eight-thirty at the latest."

*Three hours before Tim was killed. Three hours for the two strangers to question him, get him drunk, send a text message to Melissa, and carry him up to the roof.* Tony knew he was making a lot of assumptions, but it all made sense.

"Can you describe the other two men?"

"Please, I don't want…"

"Sorry," Tony said, holding up his hands. "I don't mean to push."

Wedders looked into his face for a long moment and said, "Ah, crap. The guy in the lead, he was tall, maybe a little taller than the deputy. He was dressed nicely. No specifics. They were in winter coats, of course. But his coat was long, like a businessman's dress coat. He could have been any one of dozens of office workers who live in my building."

Tony nodded.

She said, "The third man was much more casual. Short coat, jeans, work boots."

"I'm impressed," Tony said. "You noticed a lot considering it was dark and you only saw them for a few seconds."

"I suppose," she said, looking down at the floor, "it's because I knew it was trouble. I could just tell something was up."

Tony asked, "Did you call anyone? A security guard or the police?"

Anger flashed in her eyes, and Tony immediately regretted asking. "And say what?" she said. "Officer, I just saw three men, and one of them looked unhappy? Even if I had called, do you think the police would have come and searched the building or something, based on that?"

"You're right, of course," Tony said. "I'm sorry for how that sounded."

She swallowed and wiped a tear from the corner of one eye. "Believe me, I've asked myself a hundred times if there was something more I should have done."

"There wasn't," Tony assured her. "You couldn't have known what was about to happen." He looked at her. "What?" he asked.

"There is one other thing I did."

Tony felt goosebumps rise on his arms. "I'm all ears."

"After the elevator doors closed, I took another look out the window."

"You checked out the vehicle?"

"It was a truck. A pickup truck, but one of those big monsters, with the oversized tires and elevated suspension. I hate those things. Why would anyone want to drive one, especially in Chicago traffic?"

Tony didn't know and didn't care. Instead, he asked, "Any details?"

"It was silver, and it was a Ford. I know the make because the logo on the front grille was enormous."

"Did it have a front plate?" Tony asked, trying not to get his hopes too high.

Wedders nodded.

"I suppose it would be expecting too much to think you wrote down the plate number."

"I didn't have to."

Tony looked at her and waited.

"It was a vanity plate, from Iowa. Remembering it is easy. Just four letters: POVO."

***

"I need a favor."

"Of course you do. Why else would you call me on a Saturday evening? You do know I have a life, right?" The voice was Tony's friend, DCI Agent Rich Davis.

"Sorry, Rich, but this is important."

Davis sighed. "It always is. What is it this time?"

"I need you to run a plate number. It may belong to one of the guys who killed Tim."

"Jesus Christ!" Rich said. "Why didn't you say so? Wait, where are you? Are you in Chicago? And what do you mean 'one of the guys?' How do you…?"

"Rich, stop. I'm sorry you're out of the loop on this. Mackey swore me to secrecy. But now I have real evidence Tim was murdered, and maybe a link to the killer. I know the sheriff won't mind me asking for your help." As he said this, Tony wondered if he should have just called Mackey to run the plate. He had reached out to Davis out of habit, or perhaps just because he was more comfortable bothering his friend on a Saturday night.

Davis said, "So what have you…?"

Tony interrupted him again and gave him the basics of what he and Darcy had discovered, including Tim's encounter with the two strangers and the possible link to POVO.

"And how'd you get the plate?"

"Sorry. I can't tell you that. I got it from a source and promised him complete confidentiality."

Davis's groan could be heard clearly over the cell connection. "You know I hate it when you do that. It could be a real problem if this leads to a prosecution."

Tony tried to keep the exasperation out of his voice as he said, "Let's worry about that when we get to it. First, we need to find the owner of this truck, and try to understand what he said or did that was important enough to kill Tim over."

"That's a hell of an accusation to make, based on the little I've heard so far."

"Look," Tony said. "It doesn't matter if I'm right or wrong. I have to follow up. I've got a source telling me the driver of this pickup truck was with Tim, in the Chicago apartment building, right before he died. Now please just take the information about the plate and get me a damn name!"

"Okay, I get it," the agent said. "What's the number?"

"It's simple. It's an Iowa vanity plate that simply says POVO."

"Oh, fuck."

Tony sat up straight in the seat of his Jeep. "What?"

"I don't have to look it up. I know that plate."

Tony's head swam with questions and speculations about what that could mean. He said simply, "Tell me."

Davis was silent.

"Rich, dammit, talk to me."

"I'm thinking. I'm worried. What have you…? I mean, why in the hell did Mackey ask you to do this? Didn't he know that if he was right, he was sending you into harm's way again?"

"We talked about that. He asked me to just find out what I could and come back home. To turn it over to the authorities."

Davis laughed. "For Christ's sake, does he know you? You won't be back in Orney until all the assholes in three states are in cuffs, or dead. Or you are."

"That's a bit much."

"Okay, then come on home. You've learned enough to assure Mrs. Jebron that Tim didn't die by suicide, and you have a solid lead to give to law enforcement. Your job is done."

Thoughts of Darcy flashed through Tony's mind as he said, "You win. I get your point. I'm a jerk. But I can't just walk away now. Are you going to help me or not?"

"I am, but only because I know that if I refuse, there are other places you can go to get the information. Plate numbers aren't exactly state secrets."

Tony bit back more profanities, and felt his fist pounding on the center console of the Jeep as he waited.

Finally, Davis said, "The truck belongs to a guy named Grady

Benning. He lives over near Viscount. We've been watching him for a while. He keeps his nose clean, but his lifestyle is one of those that scares us."

"A POVO type, you mean? Likes guns, hates immigrants, talks about a revolution?"

"Exactly. There are a lot of those, of course. We couldn't pay attention to them all even if we wanted to."

"But...," Tony prompted.

"But when he bought the vanity plate, identifying himself as a member of POVO, or an admirer at least, we took a closer look at him. Turns out he's got a history that could be stoking a serious firestorm."

"How so?"

"Again, I wouldn't tell you this, but it's all in the public domain. When you Google him, you'll find it. Back twenty-some years ago, when Benning was a kid, his family was part of commune up in Montana. They called it New Eden. The feds called it a cult. The local cops got some reports of child abuse going on, and went out to investigate. It went badly. Guns came out, people got threatened, and suddenly the authorities were locked in another of those hopeless standoffs."

"It didn't end well?"

"Sadly, no. The ATF got called in. That only escalated the situation. In the end, a little girl was shot and killed."

"Oh my..."

"Yeah," Davis said. "The girl was Benning's sister. He was about fourteen at the time. She was younger. I wouldn't be surprised if he's carrying a chip on his shoulder the size of Mount Rushmore."

"I don't know what to say. I feel for the guy. He was just a kid. It must have been horrible."

Davis said, "There's more. About a year ago, Benning quit his full-time job and began leaving town for extended periods of time. I can't tell you how we know, but he's been making regular trips to Chicago and to the POVO camp in Hamilton County, Missouri."

Tony had no trouble imaging the "how." It almost certainly was as simple as asking the FBI to track the movements of Benning's cell phone.

"One more thing," Davis said. "I'm gonna share this, even though it's confidential. I'm doing it in my feeble attempt to keep you alive."

"I'm all ears."

"POVO is bad news."

"I get that."

"No. Listen carefully. A few years ago, they had a huge influx of cash from somewhere—more than their membership could have provided, unless they signed up Warren Buffett or Bill Gates. They're using it to recruit and train a core group of members, and to support their 'officers' so they can do POVO business full-time."

"So Benning's a POVO officer."

"Almost certainly. He hasn't worked in a year, but bought a new truck and added a stone patio to his home, complete with a hot tub big enough to host a swim meet. When he's in Chicago, he stays at the Omni downtown. Remember, you didn't hear any of this from me."

"So, money, organization, discipline. Pretty much what I heard from Agent Tabors. What're they up to?"

"I wish I knew. A lot of people wish they knew. But they're very careful. They're not the group of drinking buddies out for some fun like when they started. They're becoming a seriously frightening militia. Whoever invested in them has to have a purpose in doing so."

"So how do I find Benning?" Tony asked. "As I just told you, I can't go to the Chicago PD and ask them to put out an APB on the truck."

"Don't bother. He isn't there."

"Really? Where…?"

"Sorry, Tony. That's all you get from me. I've said too much already. I can't help you trail a guy you've just identified as a potential killer."

Tony understood Davis's point and said so. He added, "I appreciate what you did share. Really."

"You're welcome. So come home now, and you can buy me a beer to thank me."

"Not yet, but soon. I promise."

"Tony…"

He quickly changed the subject. "Does Mackey know about Grady living in his county?"

The agent said, "Of course. His deputies have the Grady place on their watch list, for those rare occasions when they have time to patrol. And it really pissed George off when Grady put those vanity plates on his truck."

"Why is that?"

Davis said he wasn't sure, but added, "I assume it feels to the sheriff like he's being taunted. You know, Grady's basically saying he's not afraid to have everyone know he's a part of a group that's anti-law enforcement. But I don't really know. Could be something else. In any case, I know Mackey'd love to have a good reason to throw Grady's ass in jail."

"Well, if we can prove he killed Tim, that would do it."

"That's a gigantic if," Davis replied, "but I agree. You get the goods on Grady, and you'll have more than one friend for life in law enforcement. Now, any other questions, or can I actually enjoy my night at home with my family?"

"No, I'm good. Sorry I bothered you. I won't call again until I've solved another murder for you."

"Good. Night. Tony."

Tony took advantage of the agent's tone and ended the call. He didn't want Davis to ask what he was planning to do next. He didn't think it a good idea to mention makeup and costume artists, or the fact that he had a pretty good guess regarding Benning's current location. Tony's next step was obvious. He would go there, even if it meant walking into the heart of the lion's den.

He opened the map app on his phone and looked up the best route to Hamilton County, Missouri.

# Chapter 16

Saturday, January 3, Quincy County, Iowa

"Those little bastards are at it again," Darrell Fishbone muttered. Raising his voice, he said, "I see you, ya little bastards. I see you, and I'm gonna get you."

He set his beer down on the floor and lifted himself out of the overstuffed chair he kept turned toward the south window of his observatory. *Time to get my shotgun and go hunting for Ferengi, or whatever these little bastards are.*

Fishbone wasn't sure when he had begun calling it an observatory. Originally, it was just a spare bedroom in his modest farmhouse on his modest farm, where he grew a little grain, grazed a small herd of cattle, and raised a few hogs.

He was perfectly happy with his little piece of God's Earth. He had no desire to own more or to earn more or, especially, to work harder. He was content to live alone and not bother anyone. All he asked was that others return the favor.

Being left alone, which seemed the epitome of simplicity to Fishbone, was growing more elusive every year. The livestock and the barn cats had overheard him muttering a thousand times about the "government bastards" and their rules, the "commodity bastards" and their prices, and a long list of other "bastards" who wanted him to join something. The Farm Bureau, Triple A, the AARP, and even the local Lutheran pastor, all fell into the same category of "bastards who won't mind their own business."

Then, three years ago, the aliens started stealing his cattle. The first time a steer went missing, he wasn't sure what had happened. He double-checked his count and only became more convinced the herd was short. He immediately checked the fences, assuming a breach had allowed a steer to wander off. The fences were intact. The loss puzzled him, but, as with most things in life, his curiosity and irritation faded with time.

Six months later, it happened again. Because the fences appeared undamaged and the gates remained securely locked, Fishbone dismissed the notion of rustlers. *Nobody in Iowa rustles cattle, do they?* Instead of pursuing this possibility further, Fishbone made an abrupt left turn and began wondering about UFOs.

He had read about outer-space creatures stealing cattle. It had happened in a lot of places. Aliens had stolen or mutilated cattle in Texas and Oklahoma, and even as close as Nebraska. *That's what that magazine said! The one by the checkout lane in the grocery store.* The next day, he moved the chair into the spare bedroom and began watching the pasture at night.

If two losses from the herd were it, Fishbone was willing to let it go, he told himself. *Call it my contribution to intergalactic peace. But I bet it don't stop. I bet those little bastards think they can just keep coming back.*

They came back. This time, Fishbone was watching. It was dark and they were too far away for him to see much. But he could see the lights hovering around and, no surprise, the next day his herd was short another steer.

This time he added a telescope and camera to the observatory. He also called Sheriff Mackey to report the incident and to ask the sheriff to call the Air Force, or NASA at least, to see if they could do something.

The sheriff declined, saying if Fishbone wanted to report a legitimate theft of his property, he would be happy to send a deputy out to look around and take his statement.

Fishbone told the sheriff, "Go piss up a rope."

His next call was to the editor of the *Town Crier*; that new guy, Smalley. He didn't really expect a city fella like Smalley to be interested, or even to understand what it meant to a small farmer to lose valuable cattle. *The bastard probably doesn't know an Angus steer from a lab rat.*

He was surprised when the receptionist at the paper put him right through, and when Smalley answered on the first ring. For a guy from New York or wherever, Smalley seemed nice enough, but in the end, he gave Fishbone the same brush-off he had heard from the sheriff.

The people who *were* paying attention were the folks in town. As the word spread about the aliens, Fishbone suddenly found himself the butt of a lot of bad jokes, and the recipient of even more rude stares. A few people tried to tell him he needed to get help, like with a doctor or something. *Like I'm the one who's causing the problem! The bastards should just mind their own business.*

Before long, Fishbone got his shotgun out of the closet and loaded it, adding it to the corner of the observatory.

Now, two years later, Darrell Fishbone was an angry and frustrated man. He had lost eight more head of cattle, one or two at a time over the preceding months, and he still had no decent photographs or physical evidence he could use to convince the authorities to help him.

He always had avoided going to the pasture when the aliens were there. He didn't want to get abducted himself. He had read about what happens to people on those spaceships. He didn't want some alien bastard messin' with his privates.

"But enough is enough," he said to the empty room. "At some point a man's gotta stand up for what is his."

He grabbed the shotgun, pulled on his winter coat and boots, and headed out the door.

***

"Smalley," Ben said into the handset on his desk in the newsroom. He glanced at the clock. It was after 10 p.m. He hoped this wasn't someone calling to report breaking news. It was too late to add anything to tomorrow's paper, unless it was big. And if it was big, that was worse, because it would mean working later than usual, and tearing apart an already designed front page.

A raspy voice said, "Smalley? Is this Smalley? Oh my God. They're here. They're here! You have to come. Oh my God, I never thought. I mean I thought… but, oh my God, you have to come!"

"This is Ben Smalley," Ben said evenly, letting a sigh escape his lips. "Can you settle down just a little for me? Who is calling, and how can I help you?"

Even as he asked the question, Ben feared he knew the answer. He was right.

"It's Darrell Fishbone. My God, didn't you hear me? They're here! I saw it. A rocket. It's here in my pasture."

"Mr. Fishbone, as you know, we've had this conversation. I'm sorry, but I don't believe in aliens and the *Town Crier* can't print your claims without some kind of evidence."

"You dumb bastard!" Fishbone screamed. "I'm telling you they're here. I got your evidence. It's thirty feet tall and standing in the farmyard next to my pasture!"

"Mr. Fishbone, please, you have to settle down. If you're going to call me names and yell, I'm going to hang up."

"I'm sorry," Fishbone said, still animated and not sounding sorry at all. "I know we talked before. I know everyone thinks I'm batshit crazy. But this is different. They're here. I saw the ship. I *touched* it!"

Ben took a deep breath and rubbed his eyes with his free hand. He said, "Okay, I get it. It's different."

"Are you gonna listen this time? This is the biggest story in the history of… of… of anything!"

"Mr. Fishbone, it's late. I'm tired, and I'm short-staffed."

"You dumb…"

"Let me finish," Ben interrupted. "I'll make you a deal. You said you have photographs. If that's the case, then it won't matter if we take this up on Monday. We don't publish a Monday paper anyway, so there's no point in coming out there tonight or tomorrow. If you're willing to let me and my staff enjoy our day off, I'll send someone out to see you Monday morning. We'll take a look at the photos and see what evidence may or may not be in your pasture."

"That's it?"

"That's the best I can do."

"Alright. Monday then. Tell your guy to honk his horn four times when he gets close to the house. I don't want to shoot him by mistake."

"Yes, please don't do that. His name's Doug Tenney. He's a good reporter. Show him what you've got, and we'll go from there."

"Okay, and Smalley…"

"Yes?"

"If you got a gun, put it by the bed tonight. I'm telling you, those little bastards are here."

The call ended. Ben stared at the receiver as he returned it to its cradle.

*Lord, spare me. I'm pretty sure I didn't sign up for this,* he thought. *Before I moved out here, I thought Iowans were relatively normal.* Then, thinking about Doug Tenney's likely reaction to his new assignment, he added, *Lord, protect me.*

# Chapter 17

Sunday, January 4, Chicago, Illinois
Six Days to Wheels-Up, Flight 244

The call came at 7:30 the next morning.

"Mr. Harrington? I'm Dante. I have a last name, but no one uses it, including me. Just call me Dante. Darcy Gillson asked me to call you. I'm sorry it's so early, but I'm doing some of the cast for one of the big road companies performing in town this month. If I'm going to help you, I simply have to squeeze it in between shows. Can you meet me now? I have to be back at the theater at eleven. I'm sorry. I'm being rude. I should explain. I do makeup. I guess that sounded funny, huh? Me saying I'm doing some of the cast. You, know, I'm not *doing* the cast. Oh, but there's a couple I wouldn't mind… Never mind. Where was I? Can you meet me? Like an hour ago? I wouldn't blame you if you said no. Who gets up at this hour on a Sunday? Did I wake you?"

Tony grinned and waited for Dante to take a breath, then said,

"No need to apologize. I was up, and I'm glad you called. Just tell me where and when."

"Ward-Roby Costume Shop, on the northwest side. Is that the dumbest name you ever heard for a store? Rodney Ward owns it. He thinks it's a clever name, because of his name and the fact he sells, well, you get it, wardrobes. Anyway, he agreed to meet us there, so we could take care of makeup and clothing all at once. Of course, when Darcy asks a favor, who's going to say no? I mean, really? Get serious. But still, opening the shop just for us on a Sunday is pretty great, so don't tell him how dumb the store's name is. Darcy said you have a car? It'll take you a few minutes. So hurry please. I'll see you at eight."

"I'll be…" Tony stopped when he realized the line had gone dead. "I guess I'll just look up the address on my phone," Tony said to no one, as he shook his head in wonder. Fortunately, he was showered and dressed already. He grabbed his coat, scarf, keys, and wallet, and headed out the door.

***

### Sunday, January 4, Petersburg, Missouri

The sun was setting as Tony drove into the parking lot of a roadside motel on Highway 136 near Petersburg, the county seat of Hamilton County. He was tired from the five-hour drive, and his eyes were sore from the bright afternoon sun. He was glad to have the benefit of good weather as he travelled, but he wished his destination had been east, rather than southwest.

He climbed out of his vehicle, a white, late-model Chevy pickup he had rented from Avis on his way out of Chicago. He was wearing well-worn denim jeans, hunting boots, a plaid shirt, and a down-filled vest. On the truck's passenger seat lay a pile of cold-weather hunting gear. Behind the seat was a case containing a 16-gauge Browning shotgun.

Dante and Rodney had astonished Tony with their ability to transform him from book nerd to avid outdoorsman. The shotgun had been a surprise. Rodney had explained that a big part of his business was renting costumes and props to movie and theater companies. The gun was real, he had said, but probably hadn't fired an actual load of shot for more than twenty years.

Equally surprising was the Illinois driver's license in the name of Ward Roby.

"Clever, yes?" Ward had said. "Don't get caught speeding. This won't pass muster with a state trooper, but it'll get you through a checkout line at a store, or past a motel clerk."

"Why do you have…?" Tony had begun to ask.

"Hey, the movies need everything! This ID has made appearances in two movies and at least one Netflix series. Pretty good, yes? My store name, right there on the big screen."

Tony hadn't argued.

The most impressive change of all was what they had done to Tony himself. He now had longish red hair and a full beard. A temporary, but realistic, tattoo of a wolf's head decorated his right bicep. Special inserts in his nostrils made his nose appear wider. Makeup provided the ruddy appearance of a man who spends hours in harsh conditions. A stain to dim his teeth and some dirt under his fingernails completed the look. He could have asked his own mother for directions, and she would not have known him.

A photo of this new "Ward Roby," graced the fake license in his wallet.

"The best part is, it's all free," Dante had said, enjoying the surprise on Tony's face. "Miss Gillson said she's paying."

Tony had tried to object, but Dante had stopped him. "She said you wouldn't like it, but too bad. The deal's done."

It was true that Tony didn't like feeling reliant on Darcy. On the other hand, a part of him was pleased she was being supportive. Her abrupt departure stung a little less, knowing she still had his back.

The getup was uncomfortable and would require daily attention, but Tony knew it was necessary. He hoped it would be worth it.

He also hoped he had thought of everything he might need as he had made another stop in Chicago, at a giant sporting goods store. There he bought camping gear, skis, shotgun shells, binoculars, packets of chemically activated hand warmers, a battery extender for his cell phone, a backpack, a hunting knife, a crowbar, a mess kit, and a host of other items. He didn't know what he would find or would need to undertake in northern Missouri, and he wanted to be prepared.

A sign on the front entrance of the Hamilton Motor Lodge said, "Come on In," so Tony did. The lobby was small with two wooden chairs, a coffee pot and cups on a small table, and a registration desk. Behind the desk sat an elderly man. He was stretched out in a threadbare desk chair, his feet on a padded stool, staring at a small TV mounted in the corner near the ceiling.

As Tony approached, the man reached over to a remote control and muted the sound. Instantly, the talking heads from the preview show for Sunday Night Football went silent.

The man stood. "Help you, sir?"

"Yeah," Tony said. "Need a room. Maybe a couple of nights. Maybe more. That okay?"

"Sure. Rate's $89 a night. Cash in advance, or any major credit card."

"You kiddin'? For this place?"

The man frowned. "If that's your idea of negotiatin', you suck at it. Learn some manners, son. You'll go further."

"Sorry," Tony said. "It's been a long drive. That the best ya can do?"

"Well, if ya pay three nights in advance, I'll do $79."

"Deal." Tony said. He took out his wallet and counted out the cash. "You got a book I'm 'sposed to sign or somethin'?"

"Nah, I give it up," the man said. "All these POVO types, coming here to visit the camp, they keep refusin'. I got tired of arguing with 'em. They usually stay just the one night, probably while they wait for the camp to arrange their lodgin.' You one of them? A POVO member, I mean?"

"Not yet," Tony said, "I been readin' about 'em. I'm here to hunt turkeys, but I thought I might stop out there and see how to go about it. Any advice?"

"Nah, I don't know squat about it." He squinted at Tony, then said, "Well, I do know it's no huntin' club like they told the town council. Pretty much everybody's figgered out by now that these boys are preparin' for World War III or an alien invasion or some such nonsense. I stay outta it. Long as they pay their bills, I don't give a shit if they're nudist Satan-worshipers. Here's your key. Coffee's free. If you wanna eat, there're a couple of pizza places in town, and one family restaurant that grills up a pretty good steak dinner."

Tony smiled. "Fair enough. Won't bother ya anymore. Thanks."

# Chapter 18

Monday, January 5, Hamilton County, Missouri
Five Days to Wheels-Up, Flight 244

The approach through the woods and up to the camp's entrance was not the winding rustic asphalt or gravel path Tony had expected. Despite the hilly terrain and proximity to the river, Tony found himself driving on a surprisingly straight, modern concrete road, as wide or wider than a typical state highway.

Glancing left and right, he could see that enormous amounts of earth had been moved and scores of trees sacrificed to create it. He puzzled over why someone would spend a huge amount of money just to make access to a camp less attractive. He didn't dwell on it. As he reached the entrance, he found himself blocked by a closed gate constructed of what appeared to be four-inch steel I-bars. An enormous sign greeted him with: *Camp POVO. Members Only. No Trespassing. Ring for Access.*

A call box was mounted in a station to the right of the gate. Tony had to exit his truck to use it.

The voice that responded to the call button expressed no greeting or pleasantries. "Member number and access code?"

"Uh, sorry, I'm not a member. I'm…"

"State your business," the voice commanded.

"I, uh, my name's Ward Roby. I'm not a member, but I wanna be one. I'd like to talk to someone about joining."

"Sorry, sir. POVO is not taking new members right now."

Tony was surprised. Everything he had learned about POVO indicated that it was constantly recruiting. He fumbled for a response and only found a lame one.

"Could I please speak to someone? I drove a long way to get here. I've been following POVO online, and wanna support the cause."

"Stay there."

Tony waited, glad he was wearing the winter hunting attire. It was warmer here than in Chicago, but still damn cold to be standing outside waiting.

The box squawked: "Drive forward. Look for the sign to Parking One. Turn left and park near the largest cabin. Someone will meet you there. Do not deviate from your instructions. Understand?"

"I understand. Thank you," Tony said. There was no reply, but the steel gate began sliding silently to the left. Tony climbed into the pickup, checked his disguise in the mirror, and drove into the camp.

***

"My name's Fitzgerald. Our gate officer said you're Ward Roby?"

"That's right," Tony said, having no trouble putting on an air of excitement at being welcomed into Fitzgerald's office. "Thanks for lettin' me in. I was hopin' to meet up with others like me."

"And what does being 'like you' mean, Mr. Roby?"

"Well, ya know. Like you guys say on the website. Tired of people who don't belong here stealin' our jobs. Tired of the government takin' all our money while rich politicians get whatever they want. Tired of havin' to tell every fuckin' customer service telephone robot what language I speak. This is the U.S. of A. for God's sake. Tired of the feds attackin' our way of life and killin' our women and children. We shouldn't have to take this crap from nobody."

"Well said, Mr. Roby. Unfortunately, as you heard at the gate, the camp is full right now. We simply can't accept you into the cause, at least not as a camp participant. You can still join online and support us that way."

"Ah, shit," Tony said. "I coulda done that before I ever left home. I drove down here 'cause I wanna be part of it. I wanna kick some ass. I can pay, if that helps."

Fitzgerald looked at him for a moment and said, "I'm not sure you could. Because accommodations are tight, we're only allowing our most, uh, ardent supporters to join us here. The fee is $25,000."

"Holy shit! Twenty-five grand? You guys hand out free blow and hookers, or what?"

Fitzgerald smiled. "No, Mr. Roby. We use all the resources we can muster to support our cause. To prepare for, and to create, a new white nationalist state."

Tony squirmed, trying to decide what to say next.

Fitzgerald said, "I assume you're not ready to make that membership investment today, so if you'll excuse me, I'm going to get back to work. When you leave, please exit the camp by the route you came in. Training ops are underway. It would be very dangerous to wander into the wrong area."

The threat was less than subtle, but Tony tried to ignore it. Staying in character, he allowed his shoulders to slump and his voice to lose its lilt. "That's it? Shit. Okay. I get it. I'm outta here. Maybe I'll come back when I win the lottery."

"I hope you do. In the meantime, thank you for supporting the cause. Goodbye Mr. Roby. Victory One for America."

"Yeah, sure," Tony said, and shuffled back to his truck.

Once inside the cab, he took a deep breath and started the engine. He had not been fooled. Fitzgerald's sky-high membership fee was simply a way to get rid of him without having to explain why POVO was turning away a potential recruit. Tony didn't know the reason, but he knew there had to be one. It made him uneasy.

Driving out of the parking lot, he made up his mind to take a chance. He needed to learn *something* on his visit here. Something more than the fact that one of the leaders was named Fitzgerald, and worked in a surprisingly stylish and comfortable office, inside what appeared to be a former camp dormitory. When the truck reached the turn he had taken to go toward Parking One, Tony turned the opposite direction from which he had come, toward the center of the camp.

He drove for a couple hundred yards through the forest, past signs for Parking Two, Range One, and Patriots Hall. The road widened into an expanse of concrete fifty yards square, with buildings on three sides. The one directly across from him was huge. Tony wondered if it had been built for boat storage. Through the trees on the right, he could see the glimmer of the lake.

Vehicles were parked three deep outside the large building. Clearly, it was the center of a lot of activity, at least at the moment. Tony kept moving forward, slowly, taking in all he could. As the pickup cleared the trees and entered the courtyard, he heard a shout, then several more. Seconds later, two large SUVs pulled to a stop in front of him, blocking his passage.

A passenger from each vehicle jumped out, grabbed something from the respective backseats, and approached his pickup from each side.

"Uh-oh," Tony muttered. The men, now motioning for him to step out of the truck, were carrying semi-automatic assault rifles.

"Hey, fellas. What's up?" Tony said, climbing out of the driver's door.

"Member number and access code," the man closest to him said.

"Uh, sorry. I'm not a member. I just got turned around. I was trying to leave."

"Driver's license." The man said, holding out his hand.

Tony stretched and tugged to get to his wallet from his back pocket, under his parka, and finally handed over the fake ID.

"Why are you here?" the second man asked.

"I uh, just met with Fitz. When I left his office, I musta turned the wrong way."

At the mention of Fitz, the two men looked at each other, then back at Tony. The first raised his weapon just enough to be pointing at Tony's knee.

Handing the license back, the man said, "You turn around and leave now. You don't get a second chance. Out the front gate. No stops, no turns. This time, we'll be following you."

"Okay, okay, guys. I'm on your side. I get it. Cool weapons by the way. This is so great. I'll be back."

He climbed into the truck, maneuvered a three-point turn, and left. The advantage to being followed, he realized, was that the gate opened before he reached it. He didn't even have to slow down as he departed Camp POVO.

# Chapter 19

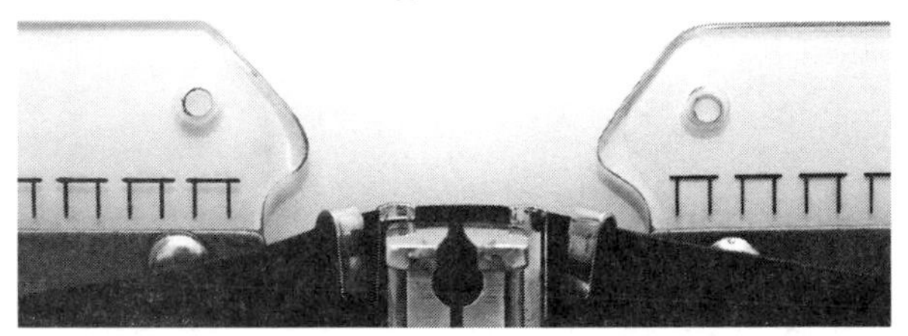

Monday, January 5, Quincy County, Iowa

It took a lot to upset Doug Tenney. It was his nature to take the world in stride, ignoring the problems he could and making jokes about the ones he couldn't.

This time, however, he'd been pushed over his limit. As Tony Harrington's best friend, he should not be in the dark, shut out from any hint of what Tony was doing. For three days, Tony hadn't answered his phone, and Ben hadn't answered his questions. It was as though his friend were on some kind of secret mission or something. Doug was pissed. *Where is that asshole, anyway?* he wondered for the hundredth time.

Then, to top it off, his assignment for this morning was an insult. Ben Smalley had asked him to go talk to Darrell Fishbone about aliens. *Aliens! For God's sake, everyone in the county knows Fishbone is off his rocker. Certifiably nuts. So why is Ben doing this to me?*

He tried to recall what he might have said or done at Tony's party to either tick off his boss or to make him seek revenge by way of a practical joke.

He recounted every exchange in his mind and concluded that he hadn't acted badly. Well, not *that* badly. A couple of minor jabs—mild compared to the usual banter. That's how he remembered it, anyway, and he had been reasonably sober. Doug liked to drink beer, especially when it was free, but he had been careful on New Year's Eve. With his boss there, as well as his best friend's family, and with his girlfriend, Alison Frank, at his side, he had gone easy, both with the alcohol and the jokes. *I don't deserve this*, he concluded confidently.

As he turned into the lane to Fishbone's farm, he found himself hoping there *were* aliens sitting in the kitchen with the old man, sharing a bowl of Froot Loops. *It'd serve 'em right,* Doug thought. *Send me on an assignment as bogus as this, then find out they handed me the scoop of the century.*

It turned out to be a case of "be careful what you wish for."

Doug zipped up his parka and pulled on a stocking cap before getting out of his Toyota RAV4. He took two steps toward the house and stopped, remembering what Ben had told him. He returned to the vehicle, pulled open the door, and honked the horn four times.

*With my luck, the crazy old coot will shoot me anyway.*

He trudged through the snow to the front of the farmhouse and climbed the two steps onto the porch. There was no bell, so he rapped on the storm door. After a few moments, he used the side of his hand to pound a little harder and called out, "Mr. Fishbone? It's Doug Tenney from the *Crier*. Ben Smalley told you I'd be coming." Doug pounded again. "Mr. Fishbone?"

No one came. Doug sighed and stepped off the porch, walking around to the side of the house. Fishbone's old truck was parked in front of the single-stall garage. It was the only vehicle Doug had ever seen the man drive. The implication was that Fishbone was home or at least somewhere on the property.

Doug hoped the old farmer wasn't already out in his pasture looking for aliens. He had no desire to wander around in the cold trying to find his interview subject. Unsure of what to do, he called his boss.

"He said he'd be there," Ben said, sounding genuinely surprised.

"So this isn't just some prank?" Doug said. "I thought maybe you'd sent me out here just to get even for that very funny remark I made about your inability to hang onto a woman."

"No, I didn't, but now that you mention it, I should have."

Doug winced, wishing he hadn't offered the reminder of one attempt at humor that had fallen flat Wednesday night.

"So what do I do? You want me to hang out a while or head back in?"

"Probably should just come back, but before you do..." Ben's voice trailed off, then returned. "Sorry, I was checking my call history. Fishbone called me on a cell phone. Let me give you the number. Maybe he'll answer. If he's out in his barn or something, that'll take care of it."

They ended their call, and Doug immediately looked at Ben's text and entered Fishbone's number. A few seconds later, Doug could hear a standard iPhone ringtone. It sounded like it was coming from behind the house.

What the hell? Doug walked around the corner to the backyard. The phone stopped ringing. Realizing it had rolled over to voicemail, Doug ended his call and redialed. The phone began ringing again, definitely louder from here, but not quite outside.

He looked up and to the left. The ringing was coming from inside the house. It was louder here because the window was open. No, not open. The glass was missing.

Doug looked at the ground below the window, and then out into the frozen snowbank that ran parallel to the house, about ten feet away.

"Ah, shit." He reluctantly walked closer to examine the debris on the snow. Glass was strewn all around, intermixed with frozen liquid and some thicker material. This, Doug realized, was what any fan of horror movies might call "blood and gore."

He resisted the urge to vomit and dialed the authorities.

"Nine-one-one, what is the nature of your emergency?"

Fighting to stay calm, Doug explained who he was and where he was, and said he feared someone inside the house was hurt, probably dead.

The dispatcher asked him to explain how he knew this, undoubtedly reluctant to send an ambulance and officers to the scene without some assurance there was a problem.

"I know," Doug said, choking to get the words out, "because I just saw his brains scattered across the snow in his backyard."

# Chapter 20

Monday, January 5, Hamilton County, Missouri

Tony was in his motel room, using Google Earth on his laptop to try to get a good sense of Camp POVO's layout, when his cell phone rang.

"Hey, boss."

"Hi. How are you? Making any progress?"

"Yes, but I'm not sure what to do next. Maybe you can give me some advice."

"Maybe," Ben said, "but I need to fill you in on what's happened here."

Tony sat up straight. "Everything okay? Everybody?"

"We're fine, but Doug's a little rattled. I sent him out to interview Darrell Fishbone this morning…hang on, I'll explain why in a moment. What matters is that Doug found the old guy dead in his house."

"Fishbone is dead? What happened?"

"Well, it looks like he went to bed with his shotgun. He actually had told me he was going to. I didn't think he'd meant it literally. Anyway, the shotgun went off while Fishbone was in bed. Half of his head ended up in the snow outside his bedroom window."

"Dear God. The crazy old fart. What a horrible...So how's Doug?"

"He's making terrible jokes about it, which tells me he's trying to cope. It wasn't a pretty sight."

"I'm sure it wasn't. Should I talk to him?"

"Not just yet. Alison is there for him, and to be honest, he's more than a little pissed that I won't tell him where you are. Where *are* you, by the way?"

The idea of lying flitted through Tony's mind but quickly dissipated. "I'm in Petersburg, Missouri."

"The POVO Camp?"

"Yeah. I've got a professional disguise, thanks to Darcy, so I paid a visit to the camp today. Told them I wanted to join." Tony knew how Ben would react to this news. He wasn't disappointed.

"Dammit, Tony...Why do you do these things? We've had this discussion. You're not an undercover agent. You're not a cop. You're a reporter! You're supposed to gather facts and write news articles. Which, by the way, I haven't seen yet."

"I know. I am. I was. I mean, I'm just gathering information. I haven't done anything risky. I just went out to talk to them. What I learned is...well..." He realized he didn't know how to explain why he was so concerned.

"Just tell me," Ben said. "I may be pissed, but that doesn't change the fact that I've learned to trust your instincts."

"Something is happening there. Something big. I could sense it. They turned me away, even though they've been recruiting for years, but it's more than that. Everyone is on edge, hyper-sensitive. I swear, it's locked down tighter than Fort Knox."

Ben was quiet for a moment. "And you think this is somehow connected to Tim Jebron's death?"

"Can't be sure, but there's pretty good evidence that at least one POVO leader was involved in killing him."

"How did…"

Tony interrupted his boss and said, "You'll also be interested to know that a POVO leader lives near us."

"What? By 'us,' you mean here in Orney?"

"Near Viscount, actually, but close enough."

"Holy shit. That's a story worth chasing. If Tim was killed by one of our own, well…Who would've thought? Are you sure?"

Tony explained about the truck with the POVO plate, seen at the building where the deputy was killed, and the owner of the truck.

"Well, shit. I don't know what to tell you. Except," his boss added, "that's one more reason I need you back here. You've done great work, but we're short-handed without you. This Fishbone story is exactly the kind of thing you normally would be covering. Now you've got background on this Grady guy to do. Not to mention, you've done everything the sheriff asked of you. You've provided him with enough to push the Chicago PD into revisiting the finding on Tim's cause of death. Leave the rest to the cops, or the DCI, or the FBI, anybody but you."

"I'll come home soon," Tony said, unsure why he was stopping short of telling his boss that Agent Tabors had asked for his help. "There's just one more thing I need to do here first."

"Dammit, don't be taking chances down there. Those POVO guys are dangerous. You do something stupid, you're gonna get yourself killed. That would be very inconvenient. Did I mention I need you back here?"

Tony smiled. "You know me, boss. I'm always very careful."

Ben groaned. "I do know you. That's what scares me."

Tony ended the call, pocketed his phone and returned to Google Earth on his laptop. Using the 3-D view and zoom function, he was able to identify just what he needed—the fastest route to get into and out of the POVO camp at night.

***

Growing up in southern Italy, Tony's mother, Carlotta, did not experience ice in nature until she was in her early twenties. Her first exposure to it was after she married the dashing young American writer, Charles Harrington, and moved with him to Chicago, Illinois. She was uneasy about the approach of winter that first year. Her sense of foreboding grew each day as she watched the trees lose their leaves and the grass turn from lush green to a grayish brown.

Then the snow fell. It transformed the earth, and Carlotta along with it. She gasped in awe the first time she looked out the apartment window and saw an unfamiliar city. *This* Chicago was bright and clean and new, as if God had swooped in during the night and left a fresh coat of paint on everything.

Every aspect of winter fascinated her. She giggled at the sight of her own breath, marveled at the giant icicles reaching almost to the ground from the eaves of some buildings, and reveled as she felt each flake of snow lightly touch her outstretched tongue.

She insisted Charles take her sledding or cross-country skiing as often as his schedule allowed. Later she learned to ice skate and, eventually, to downhill ski. So it was no surprise to anyone that once her two children, Tony and Rita, were old enough to walk, Carlotta strapped them into ice skates and ski boots.

Now, at 11 p.m. on a cold January night, as Tony Harrington knelt in the snow behind a fallen ash tree, he was thanking his mother for teaching him to embrace the outdoors in winter. After years of recreation on snow and ice in Illinois and Iowa, Tony knew all the tricks that would keep him warm and dry for as long as necessary.

Using the binoculars from his backpack, he studied the POVO camp. He held his breath each time he raised them, to prevent the lenses from fogging over. His position was southeast of the camp, on the far side of the lake. Worried about electronic sensors and alarms hidden in the woods, Tony determined his best chance to approach the camp undetected would be by crossing the lake. Northern Missouri rarely got the below-zero temperatures experienced in the upper Midwest, but this was January, and Tony believed, or at least hoped, it was cold enough. The ice would be thin, but passable, especially since Tony's weight would be distributed over the lengths of his cross-country skis. The skis had been a last-minute thought as he had filled two carts at the sporting goods store. At the time, Tony had wondered if he was crazy. The bill had been staggering.

Now, of course, he was glad for his impulsive nature, and for his choice of skis over ice skates. He was better on skates, and could move faster, but crossing rough, ungroomed lake ice would be too risky on skates, especially considering the thick clouds that obscured the moon. With luck, the skis would get him there and back fast enough.

The Camp's massive building—the one Tony had observed from the opposite side earlier that day—was at least a half mile away on the western shore of the lake. In Tony's forty minutes of surveillance, he saw just two people. Both exited the building and did not return. He hoped it was a sign the activity was winding down for the evening. He desperately wanted to see what was inside the structure, and even more desperately wanted not to get captured or worse.

He raised the binoculars again, examining the building as best he could from this distance. He could see no sign of doors or windows on the side of the building that faced the lake. *Not a boathouse.*

*So what is it?*

He returned the binoculars to his backpack, sat, and strapped on the skis. Then he stood, hoisted the pack into place, and picked up the Browning shotgun. His Walther automatic pistol was in the truck. He was here to find information, not to shoot things. The Browning was for show. Tony knew that if he was caught on camp property, he would need to convince the POVO guards that he was a hunter who had unwittingly wandered onto their land.

He checked the shotgun's barrel to ensure no snow or debris had found its way inside. He then loaded a shell, checked the safety, and slid the gun across his shoulders under the straps of his pack. He picked up two ski poles and pushed off toward the expanse of frozen lake, barely visible on a moonless night.

Tony crossed the lake slowly, encountering a mix of wind-swept ice and snow. Occasionally the skis vibrated over rough patches. Tony hoped the ice's texture was due to the wind and not to the thawing and refreezing of surface water. His concern was amplified by the fact he encountered no evidence of snowmobile tracks. People who drove snowmobiles loved riding on the open expanses of frozen lakes. If they were avoiding the lake, it was a clear sign that Tony was at risk. He tried not to dwell on it.

As he neared the shore of the POVO compound, he slowed and crouched low, uncomfortable that his only cover was darkness. He looked up at the sky and prayed the dense cloud cover would hold for at least another hour. Of course, he understood it might all be moot. If this well-financed and well-trained militia was using night-vision surveillance or other early warning technologies focused on the lake, the guards might already be waiting for him to waltz into their grasp. Once again, he tried not to dwell on it.

He inched forward until he felt the tips of the skis scrape on the beach rising up above the water line. Setting the poles down on the slope in front of him, he turned, sat, and removed the skis. He crawled up into the snow and scurried to the nearest stand of trees off to his left, dragging the skis and poles with him.

A snow drift along the tree line provided a convenient place to hide his backpack and other gear. He nestled everything but the hunting knife and his cell phone up against the base of the drift and pulled snow down to cover it.

Despite the cold, Tony realized he was sweating. Taking a deep breath, he forced himself to relax. *Slow your breathing. Ease the tension in your jaw. Remember, you're just a hunter. You're lost. You're glad to find someone who can tell you where you are. No need for concern. No need to hurry.*

Tony nearly laughed out loud. None of this was working. He was scared. He was out of his element, and he knew it. As Ben had reminded him, he was a writer, not a spy, and certainly not some kind of commando. He was in reasonable shape and knew some basic martial arts thanks to weekly sessions with Master Jun for the past couple of years. But he knew that in no way qualified him to take on a private militia. Staying out of jail, and perhaps staying alive, relied solely on not getting caught.

*So don't get caught, you dickhead,* Tony thought, and began crawling toward the back of the massive building he had come to see.

***

Finding the exterior of the building was easy—the molded steel walls rose thirty feet into the air. Tony didn't bother to guess the other dimensions, but it appeared to him to be at least as big as the high school gymnasium back in Orney. His desire to see the interior was proving to be a much bigger challenge. The only windows on the back were two narrow horizontal openings on what could be a second story, more than twenty feet above Tony's head. The only portal visible from Tony's position at the back and to the left was a small side door from which he had seen the two people exit an hour before.

Tony knew he dared not stray into the courtyard in front of the building. It was well-lit and wide open. A person would have to be crazier than Tony, and far braver, to attempt access from there. It was the pedestrian side door or nothing.

Tony mentally crossed his fingers, took a deep breath, and made a dash for the door. Locked.

*Of course it's locked. Only an idiot would expect otherwise. So what now?*

He noted the door had a sophisticated security system, with a touchpad for entering a code and a faint red glow from a bulb indicating it was armed. The crowbar would stay in his pack buried in the snowdrift. There was no sense in forcing a door if all it did was announce his presence to armed guards.

Tony leaned down to examine the keypad, thinking perhaps worn buttons would give a clue to the code. As he did so, the red bulb blinked out and was replaced instantly by a glow from a neighboring green bulb. The door clicked.

Tony jumped back, pressing his back to the building's cold steel wall. The door swung open toward him, stopping just short of the toes of his boots. He heard voices. Two people, he thought. A man and a woman.

As the door swung back toward the closed position, Tony could see the couple walking away from him, in the direction of the courtyard. He held his breath, not wanting to move, but knowing this was his chance. He took one quick step to his right, grabbing the handle just before the door settled back into place. He prayed the couple didn't hear his movements. His prayers were aided by a combination of the couple's heavy clothing and conversation, and the muffling effect of the snow around his feet.

The couple disappeared around the corner of the building without looking back, and Tony immediately refocused his attention on the door. Being careful to not allow it to latch, but also not opening it enough to draw attention from anyone inside, he sidled around until he could look through the remaining gap.

All he could see was a small foyer, a design feature to improve energy efficiency, Tony assumed. He quickly pulled open the door, stepped into the foyer, and returned the door to its not-quite-closed position. He tugged off his stocking cap, dropped it to the floor, and used the toe of his boot to push it into the gap of the open door. He let the door slide up against his makeshift wedge. He knew there was some risk the door would sound an alarm if not closed completely within a certain period of time. However, he believed the risk was greater if he allowed the door to close and it required a code to get back out.

The interior door had a narrow vertical window and no lock. Tony moved to the side, away from the window, and leaned over to take a quick look. The room was cavernous and dimly lit. He hoped this was a sign that everyone had left for the night. He pulled open the second door, stepped in, and quickly shut it again.

As he tried to comprehend what he was seeing, he removed his gloves, unzipped a pocket on his parka, and extracted his cell phone. He began taking pictures of everything in sight. First and foremost were three tractor-trailer rigs parked in tight formation and filling about a third of the total space. They faced large garage doors leading to the courtyard outside.

Tony was not an expert on trucks, but Doug Tenney's dad was an over-the-road driver, so he had an idea of what he was seeing. He fought the urge to whistle. These were late-model Kenworth diesel tractors. The logo emblazoned in chrome on the sides of the hoods gave away the brand, and the streamlined designs and flawless white paint attested to the newness. *How much money do these assholes have?*

The trailers appeared to be standard full-sized boxes. Tony couldn't remember exactly, but he thought each was about fifty feet in length. He snapped pictures of the license plates on the trailers, then stooped down to get the plates on the tractors. The cabs and trailers bore no other markings.

He looked around. A big portion of the room was clearly a work area—large steel tables, metal racks, chests of tools lined up against the wall, and ceiling-mounted chain lifts. Something heavy had been there or was expected. To Tony's left, in the front corner, was a small enclosure with glass windows—probably an office. The balance of the space held a long table surrounded by a dozen folding chairs, probably for coffee and lunch breaks, and a row of wooden shipping crates stacked two high.

Tony examined the crates, trying to nudge one quietly to gauge its weight. It wouldn't move, indicating it was full. All of the crates were sealed with metal brackets and screws. As much as he wanted to find a lever and begin prying, Tony knew he didn't have time, nor could he risk the noise.

He headed for the office. If he was going to find any information about what POVO was doing, that was his best shot. Even before he reached the door, he knew this shot was a misfire. The locked door featured another alarm pad with a glowing red light.

"Shit," he hissed.

He looked around. He had to find something beyond a few license plate numbers to make this worth the effort and risk. With only one other thing he could think of to try, he placed the phone back in its pocket, and jogged to the back of the nearest semi. With his left hand, he raised the safety catch on the nearest of the two doors, and with his right, he grabbed and lifted the handle. The mechanism moved easily enough, but not without scraping and groaning.

To Tony, who was trying to work silently, it sounded like the scream of an electric guitar at a Slipknot concert.

The door swung open. As its shadow receded, allowing the glow from the room lights to reach the interior of the truck, Tony let go of the handle. It fell with a clunk against the front panel of the door. Tony didn't notice.

"Oh my God, oh my God, oh my God." He stumbled back, unable to accept what he was seeing. *Get a grip,* he tried to tell himself. *What is…? How…? Oh, my God.*

He dug in his pocket for the phone, nearly dropping it. Digging deep for a calm that was eluding him, he spread his feet, used both hands, and managed to take a clear photograph of what was obviously the tail end of a very large missile.

Taking a deep breath, he raised himself up on the bumper step and snapped another photo. The missile was painted white. Blue and red letters down its side said simply: *Patriots of Victory One.*

He quickly pulled up the photo gallery and selected his eight most recent pictures. Pushing his text app, he attempted to send them to Tabors. Nothing. No bars. No internet. It could be the metal building and the remote location, or it could mean a jamming device was in place. Either way, he knew he needed to get moving. If he was caught now, no one would know that…that…what? That a group promoting the creation of a new white nationalist state was in possession of missiles? Tony pushed the trailer door shut as quietly as he could, sliding the handle back into place. Then he ran.

***

In the foyer, he pushed the phone into its pocket, zipped up his coat, pulled on his gloves, and bent to grab his hat from the bottom corner of the door. Through the gap, he saw a man round the corner of the building, headed his way. Clearly a security guard, the man was dressed in military white snow gear. A rifle with a scope was slung over his shoulder.

Knowing that shutting the door would trap him inside an alarmed building, and leaving it ajar would summon the guard, Tony did the only thing he could. He straightened his shoulders, exited the door, turned left, and began to walk toward the stand of trees and snowdrift where his shotgun and backpack were stashed.

"Hey!"

Tony kept walking.

"Hey! Halt!"

Tony slowed and turned. "Sorry, did you mean me?"

The guard stomped through the snow toward him, taking the rifle from his shoulder and cradling it in his hands. "Yes, you! Stop right there."

Tony smiled, held his hands out in front of him, and stepped toward the guard. "No problem. Sorry to have troubled yo…" In mid-sentence, Tony lashed out, striking the man in the throat. As the guard stumbled back, Tony kept coming, kicking the guard's left knee with the toe of his right boot. The knee buckled, and as the guard fell, Tony grabbed the rifle and swung it hard. It made an ugly sound as it connected with the side of the guard's head.

The man lay motionless in the snow. "Sorry, pal," Tony said, breathing heavily. "I learned that trick the hard way last year, when I was the one left lying on the ground."

He grabbed the man's feet and dragged him into the trees, then went back for the rifle. Knowing two guns would be more burden than benefit, Tony threw the rifle as far as he could into the woods. He found his skis easily, clipped them into place, then donned the backpack. He reached deeper into the snowdrift and retrieved the shotgun. Once again, he checked the barrel and slid the gun into place across his shoulders. He quickly headed for the shoreline, and once there, kept going out onto the ice.

Less than a minute later, a sledgehammer slammed into Tony's back, raising him off his feet and throwing him face-first onto the frozen lake. *No, not a sledgehammer,* he thought, as his ears registered the sharp crack. *Dear Jesus, I've been shot! A second guard? Of course there's a second guard, numbnuts.*

Tony struggled to breathe. He'd been hit in the back. He had no way to know how badly he'd been hurt. He could taste blood and the eye closest to the ice was filling with something. *Blood? That can't be good.* His face hurt but not as much as his ankle. It had been twisted badly when his ski tried to go a different direction than the rest of him. Slowly, he managed to suck in bits of air, indicating the wind had been knocked out of him, rather than his lungs having been torn up by a bullet. Of course the shooter was still there, probably getting closer every second. Tony knew he had to move but couldn't seem to manage it. He gritted his teeth, and cried out in pain as he kicked the skis free from his boots. Then he pushed as hard as he could with his right arm and rolled over onto his back just as a second shot ricocheted off the ice where he had been lying.

*This bastard isn't even shouting warnings,* he realized, and forced himself to roll again, this time in the opposite direction. As he did so, he rolled onto the shotgun. It obviously had dislodged from its perch on his shoulders when he had fallen.

Flailing his legs and twisting, Tony managed to get ahold of the gun. He used the stock to push himself up onto his knees. When he looked up, the world stopped. The shooter was there, ten feet away, raising his rifle to his shoulder.

Tony did not want to kill the man. He had been down that path and still had nightmares about it. He was even less interested in dying on a frozen lake in Missouri, having completely failed at whatever it was he was supposed to be doing.

All of these thoughts flashed through his mind in a millisecond. Without hesitating, he raised the stock of the shotgun, dropped the barrel until it was pointed at the man's feet, and pulled the trigger.

The blast knocked Tony onto his back, banging his head onto the ice. In a daze and with eyes pointed toward the missing sky, he couldn't see what happened next, but he knew the sound. The ice shattered and the shooter dropped, the weight of the rifle and winter gear pulling the man into the icy water.

As Tony's head cleared, he resumed pumping his feet along the ice, scrambling away from the open water created by the shotgun blast. He still couldn't stand, but he managed to get onto all fours and crawl, dragging the shotgun with his right hand. Soon he heard splashing and cries for help. *Splashing from two hands.* He smiled. The guard had dropped his rifle. The man had a chance to survive, which is more than he had been willing to offer Tony. If the guard made it back onto the ice, he would be forced to seek warmth immediately. This was one killer who wouldn't be coming after Tony tonight.

He kept moving, but as the adrenaline drained away, he began to take stock of his own situation. His right eye was now frozen or swollen shut. His back hurt like hell, his face hurt worse, and his head was throbbing. One ankle was next to useless. He had a big lake to cross and another mile to trek through the woods to his truck to have any chance of survival. He not only faced the real threat of Mother Nature's wrath, but the possibility of another guard, or another dozen guards, coming after him.

*Okay, great. Now on the plus side?* He struggled to think of something. *I have my backpack, which means I have water, food—if I can count two Milky Way bars as food—handwarmers, and a few tools.* The thought of the handwarmers brought a surprising lift to his spirits. Something about having access to heat in the face of freezing to death brought a degree of comfort. He also had matches and lighter fluid, but he knew starting a fire would be the equivalent of offering a homing beacon to his pursuers.

He stopped. *I have a phone. I can call for help. What is wrong with me? I have a phone! I have a…*

"Shit!" The scream was answered by a dog's bark off in the distance. The phone was gone from his pocket. He had failed to zip it, and obviously had dropped the phone in the scuffle. "Tony Harrington, you are a total dickhead," he said, meaning every word. The loss of the phone was catastrophic on multiple levels. Not only did it exacerbate his immediate peril, it also meant the loss of the license plate numbers and other photos he had taken. Worst of all, if the POVO people found it and managed to hack past the security code, it would lead them right to Tony and everyone he cared about.

"Dickhead is way too nice a word for you," he muttered.

Up on his knees, Tony eyed the shotgun. He now was more determined than ever to survive and get the word to everyone about what he had seen. He knew the gun was empty; he had fired the only shell he'd loaded. He lifted the gun, pointed the barrel down toward the ice, and used the stock to raise himself to his feet. The pain made his head swim. He realized he was crying. It made him wonder how an eye that's frozen shut manages tears, which made him begin to laugh.

*You're losing it, Tony. Get moving.*

The gun made a poor crutch, but he managed to hobble forward. He moved slowly, but a lot faster than a crawl. He decided that when he made it to shore he would stop for water and a Milky Way. He debated removing the wig and the beard, knowing the disguise would do nothing to save his life if POVO members found him now. However, he decided to leave them on as extra protection against the cold.

*Hang in there,* he told himself. *With a little luck, and grace from above, I may live to see Darcy again. Oh, Darcy…What am I going to do…?*

# Chapter 21

Tuesday, January 6, Chicago, Illinois
Four Days to Wheels-Up, Flight 244

Arvin Jugg was instantly awake. In one motion, he sat up, swung his legs to the side of the bed, and scooped his phone off the nightstand.

"One," he said.

"It's two."

"What happened?"

"We're not sure, but I know you like to be in the loop. Sorry about the hour."

The screen on the phone read 1:46 a.m. "It's okay. Talk to me."

"We had an intruder," said POVO Camp Commander Jon Slapp. "Two guards are down."

"What the fu…?"

"Hang on. It may be nothing."

"Nothing?" Jugg's knuckles were white on the edges of the

phone. "How can two guards be down and it be…?"

"Bottom line," Slapp said, "the building is secure. The locks are on and armed. No sign of forced entry anywhere. No alarms. Someone came into the camp. Based on where he was spotted and the tracks in the snow, it's pretty obvious he came and went by the lake."

"Shit. I knew we should have posted guys full-time on the lake side. Especially now. We're so close."

"Hindsight and all that," Slapp said, risking the further irritation of his commanding officer. "In any case, we know someone was here, but we don't know why. It could have been completely innocent. Could be some ice fisherman wandered ashore, got spooked by the guard, fought back and ran."

"Don't be a fuckin' idiot. Our guys are well-trained and well-armed. If two of them are down and the intruder…Wait a minute. What about the intruder?"

"He's gone."

"Shit. This is some kinda pro at work. It has to be. You're sure we're secure?"

"Every indication is that the guy never made it past the back of the building."

"What do the guards say?"

"Nothing so far. One got his head bashed in. He was in bad shape so I put him down."

"Ah, man."

"I know, I hate it too. Had to be done. Never know how a thing like that will affect how a man thinks. Don't worry, I did it myself, so no one here knows it. I told them I sent him home."

"The second man?"

"He's in the hospital with severe hypothermia and frostbite. He's heavily sedated. Some of the other guards spotted him coming across the ice on the lake. He'd been in the water. They had him loaded up and on the way to the ER before I could intervene."

"It's okay. By the time he's awake and talking, we'll be gone."

"That's what I'm thinking too."

Jugg paused to think, then said, "Get everyone up at dawn. Have them search the camp thoroughly."

"Probably a good idea."

"That guy was there for a reason. Maybe we chased him off before he did something, but maybe not. Look for cameras, bugs, anything he could have planted."

"Understood."

"Three more things."

"Sir?" asked Slapp.

"Make sure everything is ready for this afternoon. I'll be down there soon after lunch. But first, get a team into the woods on the other side of the river. Maybe they'll find this guy's trail. If we're lucky, maybe he's stuck in an animal trap, or bleeding out from his fight with our guard."

"Already underway. The third thing?"

"Post some fuckin' guards on the lake side of our camp."

# Chapter 22

Tuesday, January 6, Hamilton County, Missouri

Tony tried to open his eyes. Only his left responded. It saw white, too much white, and closed again.

"Ah, welcome back," a woman's voice said. "Sorry about the light, but I need to check your eye."

"Eye?" Tony said. "One?" He slowly opened his left eye, letting it adjust to the light. He saw a woman's face. It was attached to a woman's body, wearing a white lab coat.

"One?" he asked again, "Uh… doctor?"

"Very good," the woman's voice sounded soothing, with a touch of humor in it. "You didn't assume I was a nurse, so I won't have to bash in your other eye."

Tony smiled, but it instantly vanished as he felt the sharp pain that accompanied the gesture.

"Don't fret," the doctor said. "Your right eye is patched because the lid was lacerated. We didn't detect any permanent damage to your eye ball. A good plastic surgeon will have you looking like Tom Cruise in no time."

"You mean old?"

A nurse standing to the right of the doctor laughed. "We should all look so old."

"Where am I?"

"Traner Family Medical Center. That's what we started calling the county hospital after the Traner family gave us $20 million."

Tony forced himself not to smile.

"We're a small hospital in northeast Missouri, but we have a great staff of doctors. We try not to ship every scrape and bruise off to St. Louis."

"Scrape and bruise? I was shot in the back."

Tony could feel the doctor tense, but her voice never changed.

"I'm pretty sure you weren't. Shot, I mean. I've been practicing emergency medicine for more than two decades. I don't think I'd miss a bullet hole in the back."

"But he…"

She interrupted. "You do have a nasty bruise back there. As large and as deep as I've seen in anyone other than a few construction workers over the years who've fallen off roofs. Did you fall off a roof?"

"No." Tony said, beginning to guess what had happened.

"Do you have my backpack?"

"A backpack? No. Nothing like that. A local farmer brought you in. He said he found you lying next to the lake road. All you had were the clothes you were wearing, a wallet, and a strange collection of injuries. By the way, I hope you have a good story, 'cause the sheriff is out in the hall waiting to talk to you."

"The sheriff? Oh shit! Sorry, doctor. I need a phone. I need it now. Please."

He tried to sit but cried out in pain and fell back onto the bed.

The doctor said, "In good time. First we need to…"

"No!" Tony ignored the pain enough to raise himself onto one elbow. "I have to make a call now. What day is it?"

"It's Tuesday. Please, Mr. Roby. I need to complete my examination, and the sheriff needs to talk to you."

Tony fought to control himself, to sound as calm and rational as possible.

"Doctor," he looked at the name embroidered on the coat, "Erickson, please listen carefully. My name is not Roby." He held up his hand. "No, I'm not delusional. I was working undercover using that name. My real name is Tony Harrington. I'm working with the FBI. I was shot last night, or early this morning I suppose. The reason you found no slug in me is that I was wearing a backpack. In it was a metal mess kit, a crowbar, a bunch of stuff. The bullet must have been slowed by the material and supplies in the backpack, and then hit the mess kit or crowbar, which saved my life but left a nasty bruise. Are you with me?"

The doctor looked skeptical, but said, "I'm inclined to think the blow to the head made you loopy—that's the technical medical term for wacko—but the fact you were wearing a wig and a fake beard when you arrived gives a little credence to your story."

Instinctively, Tony's free hand reached up and confirmed the wig and beard were gone. He knew it didn't matter and the movement didn't slow his plea to the doctor. Simultaneously he said, "What I learned must be passed to the FBI as quickly as possible. Please. I'm begging you. A telephone."

A shadow passed behind the doctor, materializing into the figure of a man. He was elderly and slender, with white receding hair and a bushy moustache. All Tony saw was the gold star on his shirt pocket.

"Mr. Harrington, I just heard everything you said. If it's true, you're the luckiest bastard to ever walk the Earth."

"I'm happy to agree," Tony said, unsure what to think of the sheriff's appearance. *Is his involvement a blessing or a threat? Who can I trust?*

The question was quickly answered. The sheriff said, "It was those POVO bastards, wasn't it?" He said it as a statement, not a question.

Tony nodded.

"I knew it. I knew those bastards would come to no good. Give a bunch of cowboys weapons and a playground, it's bound to get out of hand."

"Sheriff, please."

The sheriff smiled. "No worries, son. If I can listen, you can use my phone to make as many calls as you want."

***

Anna Tabors didn't recognize the number as the screen in her SUV reported an incoming call. She didn't want to extend the warranty on her vehicle or change her health insurance, so she was tempted to ignore it. On the other hand, she was driving, with nothing else to do, so she pressed the "answer" button.

"Anna Tabors."

"Anna. Agent Tabors, thank God."

"Tony?"

"Yes. Can you hear me okay? Listen carefully."

"I hear you fine, but you sound terrible. Are you okay?"

"Not great. In the hospital, but…"

"The hospital? What happened?"

"Later, please. I need to tell you what I found at the POVO camp."

"What do you mean *found* at the POVO camp?" Tabors's voice rose. "What have you done? What happened? I thought we agreed…"

"Anna, shut up."

Astonishment, more than compliance, compelled Tabors into silence.

Tony said, "I'm sorry, but listen to me. They have a missile. Do you hear me? A missile! Probably more than one."

Tabors hit the brakes, swerved over to the highway's shoulder, and stopped.

Throwing the SUV into Park, she said, "Tell me everything."

Tony did.

***

Ninety minutes later, Agent Tabors was standing next to Sheriff Wallace Ballister at Tony's bedside. She had been on her way to northern Missouri when Tony had called. Even so, Tony was impressed.

"Didn't know you cared so much," he deadpanned.

Tabors shut the door to the hospital room and closed the window shades. Tony noticed the light dimmed in the room, reminding him he had no idea what time it was.

His question was forgotten when Tabors said, "You may be the most important person in the country right now. At least my bosses think so, assuming you saw what you claim and aren't hallucinating or making shit up. And by the way, if this turns out to be BS, I'm gonna come down on you so hard, you're gonna wish that bullet had killed you."

"I know what I saw," Tony said. "I mean, I don't know a moon rocket from a pop gun, so I don't really know what it was, but there's no doubt there was some kind of missile or rocket in the back of that truck. So why does that make me important?"

Tabors looked at both men, then said, "This is strictly confidential. And Tony, we're off the record here. We're so far off the record, that the record hasn't been invented yet. Understand?"

Both men nodded.

Tabors took a breath. "Okay. Based on Tony's description of a missile about two-and-a-half feet wide and roughly forty feet long, with its large fins placed a third of the way up on the fuselage, it is possible—not a given, but possible—that we're talking about a Russian V-300 Berkut missile."

"Russian?" Ballister and Tony spoke in near-unison.

Tony noticed the tightness in Tabors's jaw muscles and the grimness in her tone when she said, "About two years ago, a CIA officer planted in Russia spotted an arms dealer in a resort city on the Black Sea. She followed him to an airport hangar, where she found and photographed a dozen missiles. She didn't know what they were, but the CIA quickly identified them from the photos she sent them. They are V-300 missiles, which were part of the Soviet S-25 Berkut missile defense system. They apparently had been stolen from a Russian military installation on the other side of the mountains.

"Sadly, the agent disappeared after sending her transmission and is presumed dead. The missiles have never been seen again."

The sheriff asked, "Of course we've been looking?"

"Oh yeah," Tabors said. "The CIA sent a whole team to follow up. The missiles were gone from the airport and no trace was found regarding where they went. They searched for a year before they finally notified the FBI about the potential threat. They hate sharing anything with us, and only did so because they wanted our agents to keep an eye out for them. If that's what you saw, it's the first time in two years that anyone has provided a clue about where they went."

"What kind of threat?" Tony asked. "These aren't nukes, I hope."

"Not likely," she said. "The photos from Russia showed no warheads had been mounted on them yet. But assuming the warheads came from the same base in Russia, they probably were conventional chemical explosives. That's what was stored there. These are older model surface-to-air missiles, designed and built back in the Soviet era. They're too slow to be a big threat to our modern military aircraft, but they have a range of 25 miles and a max altitude up to 60,000 feet or so. As we learned from 9-11, terrible things can be done to non-military targets—things that can kill innocent people and wreak havoc in immeasurable ways."

No one spoke for a long moment.

Eventually, Tony said, "The missile I saw was painted white and carried the POVO name. That could indicate that it's not just arriving here; it's ready to ship out."

"Exactly what my FBI superiors said when I called them. By now, most of the brass in Washington, in both the intelligence agencies and the military, are gearing up to deal with this." She looked at the sheriff. "I'm afraid your county is about to be the focus of a lot unpleasant attention."

"POVO bastards," the sheriff said. "I knew they were trouble, but who coulda imagined a *missile*?"

"So if hellfire is about to rain down on Camp POVO, why are you telling me all this?" Tony asked.

Tabors said, "Three reasons. First, we don't want you to tell anyone or, God forbid, publish anything about what you saw. We have to keep this contained until we deal with it."

"I have to tell Ben, and Sheriff Mackey too. They're expecting reports from me, and I'm not going to lie to them."

"You understand what's at stake here? There could be a dozen enemy weapons on American soil right now. We have to find and neutralize them before something catastrophic happens."

"I do understand. I also know that you know these are men we can trust. What else?"

Tabors sighed but moved on. "The second reason I'm talking to you is that we don't want you charging back in there. It would only confirm to POVO that someone's on to them. For you, it could be even worse."

"Worse?"

"My boss said it would be best if you didn't get killed when our commandoes raid the place. I told him I wasn't so sure."

"Very funny," Tony said. "What else?"

"The final thing is the obvious one. We need to know everything you know."

"I already told you..."

"You told me in one quick telephone call what you saw. Now I need every detail. A Boeing C-17 full of people and equipment is going to land in St. Louis in about five hours. The strike force will be here in Hamilton County before dawn. They want everything you can remember, plus any other thoughts you have."

"Such as?"

"I don't know, your assumptions, speculations, best guesses. Anything that might help them overrun that camp without getting a lot of people on either side hurt or killed."

"And me?" The voice was Sheriff Ballister's.

Tabors turned to him. "I suggest you go back to the office and try to forget we had this conversation. Gather your deputies at dawn. Tell them it's for mandatory diversity training or something. Give me your card, and I'll call you and let you know the plan and how we can best use you."

The sheriff nodded, and Tabors added, "You have any veterans on your staff?"

"A couple of the guys were Army. Served in Afghanistan. Another does his monthly weekend with the National Guard."

"Good. Come to think of it, before you go home for the day, email me their bios, or give me access to your personnel files. These are the kinds of details the strike force leader will request. I'd like to be ready."

"Got it." The sheriff turned to go but stopped and turned back to Tony. "You were damn fool to go to that camp alone. By all rights, you should be dead. Wouldn't have helped anybody."

"Can't argue with that," Tony said.

"Glad you're not dead," the sheriff said.

"Me too," Tony said, as the sheriff disappeared out the door.

***

Tabors grilled Tony for nearly two hours, asking about everything he'd seen during his two visits to the camp, including people, weapons, vehicles, buildings, other landmarks, and of course, the interior of the largest structure. Using a combination of Google Earth and Tony's memory, they drew a map of as much of the camp as they could.

After Tony described the tractor-trailer rigs, Tabors said, "Can you remember any license plate numbers, or even portions of them?"

"I'm sorry, but I didn't even look at the numbers. You know how it is. I was snapping pictures, so I didn't pay any attention to what was on them. I think a couple of them were white and blue, but I couldn't even swear to that."

"No worries," Tabors said, looking like she meant the opposite.

An aide delivered hospital food to the room, a standard fare of chicken breast, mashed potatoes, and green beans, with a tiny, sealed cup of vanilla ice cream for dessert. Someone had been thoughtful enough to order an extra tray for Tabors.

As the aroma reached him, Tony realized he was famished. He finally thought to ask, "What time is it?"

"Almost three," the agent said. "You doing okay?"

"Yes, but it wouldn't matter if I wasn't. What else can I do to help?"

She said, “We’re almost done, but since we’re alone, there is one more thing I want to ask you.”

Tony waited while she opened her bag and removed an envelope. She took out a photograph and handed it to him. “Have you seen this man?”

It was obvious to Tony that it was an official FBI photograph, not from a wanted list but from a personnel record. The man in the picture was young and clean-shaven, with light-colored hair cut short, and gray eyes set in a narrow face.

He looked up from the picture and said, “I live in Iowa. I’ve seen at least ten thousand guys who look just like this.”

“This is serious, Tony. Please.”

“Sorry.” He looked at the photo again. “I don’t think so. He’s not anyone I interacted with at the camp, if that’s what you’re asking. Unless, of course, he was one of the guards bundled up in snow gear.”

“I doubt that,” she said. “I can promise he’s not the one who took a shot at you.”

“I take it he’s one of yours?”

“Yes. The FBI has an agent planted with POVO.”

“So why did…?”

“I didn’t know. I wasn’t part of the operation watching POVO. If I’d known we had someone there already, I never would have asked for your help in connecting with these bastards.”

“So…?” Tony prompted.

“So, no one’s heard from him in a month. He’s way past his deadline to report in. I was hoping you’d seen him, so at least we’d know if he’s alive.”

“You knew him?” Tony could tell from her face that she did.

“We trained together at the academy in Virginia. Ted was a good man.”

“Ted?”

"Theodore Roosevelt Janssen. Always quick to point out his surname came from his Dutch heritage, and not from the British. He was an arrogant prick, but I never met an agent who was smarter or more capable. He loved being where the action was. I wasn't surprised when I heard he'd gone undercover with POVO."

"I wish I could help," Tony said, handing the photo back to her.

Sounding almost desperate, Tabors said, "He was assigned to Cabin Six. Just him, I think. Did you see that cabin? Any activity around it?"

"Again, I'm sorry," Tony said, shaking his head. "I didn't see any of the cabins. The only bunkhouse I saw appeared to be from the original church camp. It had been converted to offices."

The agent's grim expression and slumped shoulders made him wonder if Tabors was feeling something more for Janssen than just concern for a colleague. She stood and said, "I should go. You need to rest, and I have work to do before the storm troopers arrive."

"Before you go, may I use your phone?"

Tabors hesitated. "You swear this won't get out ahead of us?"

"Hey," he said, "if you can't trust the media, who can you trust?"

She groaned but pulled out her phone, let the facial recognition software turn it on, and handed it to him. "God help us all," she said.

# Chapter 23

Tuesday, January 6, Orland Park, Illinois

The crowd jumped to its feet as the hockey puck shot across the ice in a perfect line to catch the corner of the net. At the last possible instant, the goalie's glove appeared and slapped it away. Half the room cheered while the other half groaned. All heads turned to follow the puck to the other end of rink.

Randy Lundgren was one of the cheering half. His son, Archie, was playing goalie for the Naperville Redhawks hockey team.

"Way to go, Troll!" Lundgren screamed, using the nickname the team had bestowed on his son two years earlier, when Archie was a sophomore. The name, presumably, was a reference to a fairy tale, or perhaps even the movie *Monty Python's Holy Grail*, in which a troll refuses to let anything pass.

Archie liked the nickname, which allowed Randy Lundgren to like it too. The boy, now a senior and nearly a man, didn't take his eyes from the action to acknowledge his father's cheers, yet another sign of a good athlete.

As Lundgren returned to his seat, he found himself looking around the arena for his ex-wife. He hadn't seen Laura in months and he was certain she would be here watching. The ice arena in Orland Park was only about thirty minutes from the home in Naperville they had once shared, and where she and Archie still lived.

He gave up looking. With everyone bundled in coats, hats, and scarves, it would be difficult to pick her out of the crowd. Her raven hair and perfect curves would be obscured. Not seeing her caused a small pang in his heart he couldn't explain, because he knew from experience that seeing her would only hurt more than her absence.

The marriage had been over for nearly a decade. Throughout those years, Laura had become an expert at avoiding him. Lundgren couldn't blame her. He had hurt her deeply when he had cheated, and had slammed shut any door to reconciliation when, despite his promises, he had done it again.

Like many military officers, and especially fighter jocks, Lundgren was proud to serve his country, and was dead serious about the oaths he took. His lack of faithfulness as a husband was the one mark of shame on his record that he had to accept.

Lundgren had been flying for nearly thirty-five years, a good share of those as a fighter pilot for the US Navy. He had seen more than his share of action, launching off of aircraft carriers in the Persian Gulf during two wars.

After twenty years in the military, he retired with his officer's pension and became a pilot for Wingdance Airlines, a regional commercial carrier based in Chicago.

He loved his job, but it had a major downside in addition to the temptations and opportunities it presented to him daily. Flying made it difficult to participate in many of his son's activities. It was why, every year during Archie's holiday break from school, Lundgren took two weeks of his vacation time to be in Chicago. Every year, he enjoyed a father-son Christmas with Archie, and spent several days watching him play hockey in various leagues and tournaments as he advanced through the ranks.

Because flying was as much a part of Randy Lundgren as eating, he was eager to get back to work on Saturday. But there was no question it would be hard to resume his busy schedule and fade into the background of Archie's life. Next year, his son would go off to college, maybe even the Naval Academy like his dad. There wouldn't be many more holidays like this one.

# Chapter 24

Tuesday, January 6, Hamilton County, Missouri

Arvin Jugg wore an all-white jumpsuit and carried no notes as he stepped up onto the dais. An American flag waved on a huge digital display behind him. The POVO logo was superimposed on the image. To his right stood Camp Commander Jon Slapp, and to his left, First Lieutenant Joel Fitzgerald. The three POVO leaders faced an audience of nearly fifty men and women: thirty-nine trained soldiers plus a handful of technicians and support staff. All were dressed in winter miliary fatigues. They were in formation, as perfectly aligned as China's Terra Cotta warriors, and just as quiet. They were assembled in the main lodge at Camp POVO. It was 2 pm on Tuesday.

Jugg's smile exuded confidence and excitement. When he spoke, his voice was strong and clear. No microphone was necessary.

"At ease, ladies and gentlemen," he said. The movement of feet created a single, crisp *whoosh*.

Jugg said. "Today, we reach the end of one journey and embark on the beginning of the next. Regarding the journey just ended, I offer you my sincere congratulations and my deepest admiration. You've worked hard. You've learned and prepared, and you've passed every test. You've been carefully selected, and you have proven yourselves worthy."

Every face in the audience beamed with pride.

"More importantly," Jugg said, his voice rising in pitch and volume, "you have committed yourself to a great cause. You are the men and women who are going to rescue our nation from the chaos. You are the ones who will return America to its former greatness. You are the ones who will spark the revolution and the creation of a new society!"

Slapp and Fitzgerald began applauding vigorously, so everyone in the room instantly joined it.

Jugg leaned forward, elbows on the podium, and spoke quietly. The room fell silent.

"It all begins today, when we show Americans, the true Americans, the white, God-fearing Americans, that they don't have to cower before big government. A government that cares more about giving handouts to losers, and queers, and immigrants, than it does about helping the hard-working people who built this country." His voice grew louder. "We show them we won't tolerate a government that protects the Muslims who bomb us and the Chinese who grow deadly viruses, while good, white Americans die by the tens of thousands."

Louder still, "We show them we no longer will tolerate a government that sends agents to kill our women and children."

His bark was nearly a scream, "Like in Texas! Right?"

Fifty voices screamed, "Right!"

"Like in Idaho! Right?"

"Right!"

"Like in Montana! Right?"

"Right!"

Jugg knew he had them where he wanted them. He said, in a normal tone of voice, "That's right. So please be seated, and let's talk through what we are going to do about it."

Everyone sat.

The digital display behind Jugg changed. A map outlined five Midwestern states: Missouri, Iowa, Illinois, Kansas, and Nebraska. The states were colored a simple gray, with black lines showing their borders. A small white star gleamed from one location in each state.

Jugg stepped to the left edge of the dais, pulling the podium with him and giving everyone a clearer view of the display. He said, "As many of you know, our generous supporters made it possible for us to procure a dozen surface-to-air missiles. These missiles were not new and required some work. As a result, some were sacrificed to provide parts for others. In addition, two of the missiles were damaged in engine tests and could not be repaired. What remains are five powerful weapons, armed, tested, and ready to fly."

A murmur passed through the assembly.

"Each missile will be deployed to a separate location, seen here on the map. The towns are not labeled because not everyone needs to know the destination of every weapon. If one team fails and is captured, its members cannot be forced to divulge the locations of the others." He paused and waved his finger. "By the way, do not be the team that fails."

He smiled, and the POVO members laughed.

"Those of you helping to prepare and paint the trucks in the assembly building have seen that only three trucks remain. Two teams have already been dispatched. We did this to avoid the spectacle of five big rigs departing our camp in a short period of time. Spreading out the timing reduces the risk of getting unwanted attention and awkward questions."

Two stars on the display disappeared—those in Iowa and Nebraska.

"Most of you here today will be assigned to one of the three remaining teams. Your orders are in envelopes at the back of the room, labeled by your POVO number. Do not share your orders with anyone else. This is why we asked you to forfeit your phones when you arrived at camp. Now I'm asking you not to tell even your fellow POVO members. The less each person knows, the safer for all of us and for the mission."

A hand went up.

Jugg said, "Please hold your questions until the end. I may cover it as we proceed."

The hand disappeared, and Jugg said, "Your first assignment is to deliver the missiles safely to their designated locations. You will change into civilian clothes, and except for the truck drivers, will travel in groups of two to four people in a variety of vehicles and by different routes. We want to avoid any appearance of a convoy accompanying the trucks.

"The destinations have been selected to minimize the chances of discovery of the missiles during the short time they are in place. You may find yourself in an abandoned warehouse, or an old barn, or some other, equally unpleasant working environment. I'm sorry, but the temperatures can't be helped. It's winter in the Midwest. You're equipped with the best gear money can buy, so I know you'll cope just fine. Waiting until spring or summer just isn't an option. We are at risk every day of being discovered. We learned this the hard way when Number Twenty-Two was found to be a traitor in our midst."

A groan escaped from the group, and many nodded their agreement or at least their understanding.

"To speak the obvious, once you're on site, your job is to unload, set up, and prepare the missile for launch. Everything you need to complete these steps is loaded into the trailer with the missile. When completed, some of you will depart and return home or to wherever you like. Four people will remain at each location to guard the missile and conduct the firing sequence at the designated time. As you know, our technicians are trained as soldiers as well, so they're able to respond if there are any last-minute problems.

"The bottom line, ladies and gentlemen, is that if you all do your jobs, do them well, and stay alert, in a few short days, the entire world will know that a new white nationalist state is emerging in America. The pitiful group of soft, greedy bastards who call themselves the leadership of this country will be cowering in their ivory towers, suddenly aware that the real men and women of America are ready and able to call the shots whenever we want. And best of all, we accomplish it without harming a single person."

"But how can…?" a voice in the group began.

Jugg cut him off. "As we've told you from the beginning, these missiles, once fired, are designed to lock onto the nearest flying targets. The locations we've selected ensure these targets will be commercial airliners flying on established routes across the Midwest. However, as a result of the brilliance of our tech team, new programming will direct the missiles to a pre-designated distance from each airliner, where they will explode in spectacular fashion. The crews and passengers of these planes will know they narrowly escaped death. When this happens to five airliners almost simultaneously, and we announce to the world how easy it would have been for us to destroy the planes, it will be apparent to everyone that we have the means and the will to do whatever needs to be done to set America back on the right track. No one in leadership, from the state houses to Congress to the White House, will be able to ignore our demands. Are we clear?"

"Yes, sir!" said fifty voices in unison.

"Maybe you didn't hear me," Jugg said, standing tall and raising his voice. "Are we clear?"

"Yes sir!" came the thunderous response.

"Good. So let's go to work. You have your assignments. You're dismissed to go perform your duties as Patriots of Victory One!"

The crowd applauded and began to disburse. Jugg called out, "Number Twelve!"

A middle-aged man with a square face and a crew cut turned toward the dais.

"Please join me for a minute. I have a special assignment for you that just came up this morning."

As the man strode briskly toward the front, Jugg thought how fortunate he was to have a few men and women on his team like Matt. He was one of those rare people who had washed out of the Army Rangers because he liked killing people too much. His behavior in an Afghan village had resulted in a dishonorable discharge. Matt's resentment had grown into an all-out hatred of the established military. He channeled this anger into his devotion to POVO and its mission.

Matt trained like his demons possessed him. More than one POVO recruit had limped off or had been carried off the training grounds after an encounter with him. Matt wanted to hurt his colleagues and wanted to kill his enemies.

This made him the perfect choice for what Jugg needed—a quick trip into town to visit a patient at the Traner Family Medical Center.

# Chapter 25

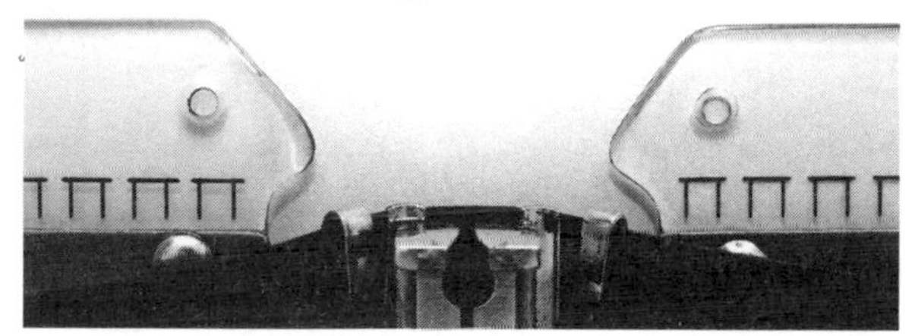

Wednesday, January 7, Petersburg, Missouri
Three Days to Wheels-Up, Flight 244

Pain, Tony knew, could be an enemy. It could push you into corners, make you afraid to move. It could slow you down at critical times when survival required action. It could interfere with all that is beautiful and push a person into the darkness of resentment, anger, and even vengeance.

But not today. Today, pain was his friend. As the physical therapist pushed him to walk with one ankle in a brace and a cane in his hand, the pain provided a distraction. Focusing on his ankle allowed him to think less about dead deputies, missing missiles, an angry boss, and his uncanny ability to screw up the relationships he most treasured.

*Darcy...How can I tell you? How can I not tell you and expect you to understand? I know I can't hold onto you forever, but I also know I'll be lost without you.*

He was nearly as distraught when he thought about Ben Smalley.

Tony loved his boss and hated doing anything to make him mad. When he had called Ben earlier that morning to report he was in the hospital, Ben had erupted in a way Tony had never heard before. Now, he had two precious relationships to mend, both with people who might never trust him again.

The only good news was that Ben's anger had subsided a little when Tony had told him the excursion onto the POVO camp had resulted in the discovery of missing Russian missiles. Although frustrated that he couldn't publish a story of that magnitude immediately, Ben had acknowledged that Tony had achieved something important.

Tony's thoughts were interrupted when the therapist said, "I think we're done. You're doing fine."

Tony looked at the young man and said, "You have an odd definition of 'fine.' My ankle hurts like hell."

The therapist smiled and said, "It's a nasty sprain. Keep it elevated and iced when you can, and take ibuprofen as needed. Use the cane to keep your weight off of it for a few days. If you don't overdo it, you'll be good as new in a couple of weeks."

Tony pushed aside his skepticism and nodded, saying, "Thanks. I do appreciate your help."

"That's why we're here," the man said, nodding toward the door. "I'll walk with you back to your room."

***

Darcy Gillson hurried through the glass foyer into the main lobby of the Traner Family Medical Center, glad the automatic sliding doors allowed her to keep her hands tucked into her coat pockets. She had been fooled by the late afternoon sunshine and had left her hat and gloves in the car. It was far colder outside than she had expected, and the short walk from the parking lot to the hospital entrance had turned her face into a rosy porcelain.

Standing in the lobby, she worked her jaw muscles to reawaken the sensation in her face and reached back to sweep her blonde locks out from beneath the collar of her coat. She approached the desk.

"May I help you?" asked an elderly woman in a blue smock with a "Volunteer" label.

"Yes, thank you," Darcy said. "I'm here to visit Tony Harrington."

"Let's have a look. Harrington. Harrington." The woman's face clouded and she said, "H-A-R…right?"

"Yes, that's right."

"Well, I'm sorry miss, but I don't see a patient by that name. Could he have been discharged already?"

Darcy didn't try to mask her surprise. "Maybe, but I was just told this morning that he was here. I drove as fast as I could."

"I'm sure you did, dear," the woman said, "but I don't see…"

Darcy had a thought. "Could you look up Ward Roby? Is he a patient?"

The woman frowned, shook her head, but went back to her computer screen. She said, "Why, yes, Mr. Roby is here. Would you like to visit him instead?"

"Yes, please."

"He's in room 127. You won't have any trouble finding it. When you walk past the cafeteria and gift shop, you'll see the hall splits in two directions. There are just the two wings of patient rooms. Take the one to the left, and the room will be about halfway down on the left side."

"Perfect. Thank you so much."

Darcy made a brief detour to use the restroom near the cafeteria, then ducked into the gift shop. She was surprised and happy to find it had a get-well card that would be perfect for Tony. It featured a black and white photograph of Gene Wilder on the front, taken from the movie *Young Frankenstein*. Wilder's hair was in disarray and his eyes wild as he stood alongside his monster lying prone on the laboratory table. Darcy didn't even care that the joke printed inside the card was lame. Tony loved vintage stuff like this.

Knowing what to write in the card proved to be much harder. She was still angry. All the issues she had raised with him in Chicago were only exacerbated by the fact he had done exactly what she'd predicted. She didn't know the details, but clearly he had ventured into dangerous territory and had come damn close to getting killed. Now, here she was, once again visiting him in a hospital.

On the other hand, when Ben had called her early this morning, Darcy had nearly collapsed. The anguish she had felt upon learning Tony was hurt had been quickly obliterated by the sheer joy she had experienced when Ben had quickly assured her that he was safe. It had been a stark reminder of how much she loved him and did not want to be without him.

As she had driven like a crazy person from central Iowa to northeast Missouri, she had resolved that she would set aside her questions and suspicions and anger and would focus on helping Tony through his ordeal.

Now, as she walked down the hallway with her coat draped over her left arm and a silly get-well card in her hand, she just wanted to see him. She wanted to know he was okay, wanted to hold him and tell him she was sorry for leaving, wanted to see him smile and hear him say they were fine.

What she saw instead was another surprise. Reaching the door, she knocked once and pulled it open. A big, square man in a winter ski mask was on the far side of the bed, facing the monitors and equipment. His head jerked left, clearly surprised by her entry.

"What…?" Darcy began, but then stopped as she saw the man withdraw a syringe from the IV bag hanging from a pole next to the bank of electronics. She didn't get a chance to finish her question. In three quick motions, the man leapt onto the bed, then back to floor, then lunged the final step to reach her.

Darcy cried out and raised her arm as the syringe flashed and plunged into her.

The man jammed the plunger to its limit, retracted the needle, and swept Darcy to the side with one brutal backhand to her face. She screamed as she crashed against the wall and fell to the floor.

Tony and his therapist were just thirty feet away, headed back to his room, when they heard the crash and scream, and saw a man in a ski mask run out. The man stopped outside the door for a brief moment and turned to face Tony. He pointed an index finger in his direction, made the pantomime motion of firing a gun, then turned and fled.

Tony let him go. He had recognized the voice that had cried out, and now his only concern was Darcy. The therapist seemed torn about what to do. As Tony hurriedly limped into the hospital room, he called out, "Let him go! Call for a doctor and call the cops, then get back here and help me!"

He knelt next to Darcy and took her arm as she struggled to sit up. Tears sprang from his eyes.

"Darcy, oh my God. Darcy! Are you hurt? What happened?"

"I…I'm not sure. My face."

"Let me see." Tony gingerly took her face in his hands and pushed her hair back. He could see a bruise forming on her left cheek. A surge of anger erupted in his soul, but he kept his face and hands stoic. Quietly, he said, "The skin's not scraped or broken. You're going to have a bruise, but nothing worse that I can see. Of course there are plenty of people here who can tell better than I…"

She interrupted him. "He stabbed me."

Tony froze. "What!?"

"He had a syringe. He stabbed me in the arm with it."

"My God," Tony said, turning his face to the open door and shouting, "Nurse! Doctor! Somebody get in…"

Three people were in the doorway before he even finished. The therapist was there with two women, a nurse and an aide. Tony quickly told them what Darcy had said, then stood and got out of their way. They did a quick assessment regarding her mobility, then lifted her up and laid her gently on his hospital bed.

Turning to the aide, the nurse said, "Call the ER and tell them we're coming, then grab a gurney and get back here." The aide left without a word.

To Darcy, the nurse said, "Show me."

Darcy indicated her left arm. Her winter coat was still wrapped around it. She said, "I held up my arm to protect myself. He was so fast. I… I didn't think. I just reacted."

The nurse began to unwind the coat. Suddenly her muscles tensed and she bent down.

"What?" Tony asked.

The nurse shook her head. She stood, reached into her pocket and pulled out a pair of latex medical gloves. Once in place, she bent down again, putting her face up close to Darcy's coat.

The aide arrived at the door, guiding a hospital gurney toward the bed. Without looking at her, the nurse said, "Call a code."

"What?" the aide appeared mystified. "She looks…"

"Call the goddamn code!" the nurse barked.

"What's happening?" Darcy asked, tears welling in the corners of her eyes.

"Don't worry," the nurse said, "I'm just being extra cautious."

Darcy reached out with her right hand and grasped the nurse's forearm. "I don't care if you're being Clara Barton, tell me right now what in the hell is going on!"

“Almonds,” the nurse said.

Tony staggered. “Oh, no…” It escaped his lips before he realized he said it.

“What!” Darcy barked, her fingernails digging into the nurse’s arm.

“Try to relax,” the nurse said. “I smell almonds on your coat. That’s an indication of cyanide.”

“Cyanide?” Darcy looked at Tony and began to cry. “Am I…? What’s going to…? Tony, help me.”

Ignoring the pain in his ankle, Tony nearly flew to the opposite side of the bed from the nurse. He took Darcy’s hand, leaned down, and kissed her forehead. He tried to smile. “You’re going to be fine,” he said. “The nurse could be wrong. And even if she isn’t, you’re in the right place to get treated quickly.”

As if summoned by his words, Dr. Erickson, the aide, the therapist, and another nurse all arrived at once. Tony was pushed to the side, and in seconds, Darcy was on the gurney and on her way to the Emergency Department.

All of the air in the room seemed to leave with them. Tony gasped and collapsed into the nearest chair. His head fell into his hands, and he began sobbing like a baby. After a few short minutes, he forced himself up onto his feet. Grabbing his cane from the floor, he hobbled down the hall toward the ER.

***

Tony glanced at his watch for the fiftieth time. It had been less than an hour. He shook his head in disbelief. It felt like he had been sitting in the ER waiting room for days.

A phone at the desk rang. Tony looked up as a clerk answered it, listened, nodded, and hung up. He said, “Mr. Harrington?”

Tony jumped up, cursing under his breath at his ankle. "Yes," he said through gritted teeth.

"This way, please."

Tony hurried as fast as he could through a set of double doors to the right of the desk. The clerk led him down a short hallway and indicated a room to the right. Not a patient room, but a room labeled "Consultation 1."

*Oh, no*, he thought. *Please, God, no.*

When he pulled open the door, relief washed over him like a tsunami. Seated at a small table were Dr. Erickson, Anna Tabors, and a smiling Darcy Gillson.

Tony reached her in two hops and threw his arms around her. He buried his face in the hair on top of her head as the tears came flooding back.

Dr. Erickson placed her hand on Tony's arm. She said, "You might want to ease your grip a little. It would be a shame to kill the patient after she cheated death once already today."

Tony released his embrace but kept his arm around her shoulders as he slid into the empty chair next to her. He noticed Sheriff Ballister standing in the corner, but only for an instant. He returned his attention to Darcy.

"You're okay? You look fine. What happened?" He turned to the doctor. "She's okay?"

"She's perfect. It turns out she's just as lucky as you are."

Tony glanced at the sheriff and then at Tabors. "Tell me."

The doctor spoke first. "As suspected, the substance the nurse smelled was cyanide, one of the most toxic of all the poisons."

Tony nearly interrupted her. He had many questions, but he bit his tongue and let the doctor continue. "Darcy's luck came in the form of a heavy winter coat. It was draped over the arm she raised to defend herself. The attacker's syringe penetrated the coat but never made it to her arm."

"Thank God," Tony said, overwhelmed by a flood of emotions ranging from relief to astonishment to anger. "That's…that's…I don't know what to say. You could have been…" His anger took center stage. "Who did this? Who would do this? Why?"

The sheriff responded. Everyone turned to look at him as he said, "Darcy saved two lives this afternoon. Her own and yours."

"Mine?" Tony was thunderstruck, but just as quickly grasped what was meant. The attacker had been in Tony's hospital room. Darcy was simply unfortunate enough to get in his way. It explained the attacker's gesture toward Tony in the hallway before the man had fled.

Tony said, "Was he waiting for me in the room?" It seemed a risky tactic, considering it was hard to know when Tony would return and who would be with him.

"No," Ballister said. "He was injecting that syringe into your IV bag. He didn't know you were being released today. He must've assumed you'd be re-connected to it when you returned to your bed. Ms. Gillson interrupted him before he finished emptying it, so he turned it on her."

Darcy said, "Note that the gallant sheriff has exaggerated my role. I didn't save your life at all. That creep was just stupid. I don't want you getting all gushy about what you owe me."

Tabors laughed and said, "Harrington, you better hang onto this one. She could've had you by the balls for months, and she just gave it all away."

Tony said, "She didn't give away a thing, because she knows she has me tied in knots anyway."

"Okay," Darcy said, "Moving right along…"

Tony said, "I don't suppose anyone caught this jerk before he got away."

"Nope, but that's why we're here," the sheriff said. "Did you notice anything that would help us identify him? Or better yet, do you have a longstanding enemy or a signed death threat from someone who matches this guy's description? Then we can just go pick him up."

The doctor stood, "I need to get back to work. You folks are welcome to stay here and use the room to play detective for as long as you need it." She looked from Tony to Darcy and said, "I'm glad you're both okay. Try to stay that way. If I see you back in my ER, I may have to take away your TV privileges for a week."

"Considering how crappy your TVs are, that wouldn't be any big loss," Tony quipped.

The doctor smiled but added in a serious tone, "Your discharge papers and care instructions will be waiting for you at the ER desk as you leave. A little attention to your injuries, and a little rest, will go a long way toward your healing."

"Aye, aye," Tony said as the doctor disappeared out the door.

The sheriff took the chair left vacant by the doctor's departure, and the conversation returned to the attacker. Unfortunately, Tony didn't have much to add. He said, "Taller than me, but not by much, stocky build, black knit ski mask. He was wearing jeans and a down-filled coat sewn in a large diamond pattern. It had a logo on the breast, but I didn't notice which brand. That's about it."

"He was fast." They turned to Darcy, and she continued. "I couldn't believe a man of that size could react so quickly or jump so high. If they put a move like that in one of my action movies, no one would believe it."

"Anything outside?" Tony asked. "Cameras or a make on a vehicle? Anything?"

The sheriff shook his head. "We're checking everything, but so far we're coming up empty. I'm afraid he's in the wind."

Tabors said, "So what's your best guess, Tony? Who was this guy?"

"Well, considering where we are, it has to be one of the POVO guys. No college buddy who thinks I stole his girlfriend..." Tony stopped as Darcy looked up. "Sorry, bad example. You know what I mean, there's no one from any other aspect of my life who might have followed me to Missouri to murder me; especially since I came here in disguise. It's pretty obvious what happened. The POVO camp leaders knew they had a breach Monday night and thought I might be injured. They had someone check the local hospital to see who had been admitted and for what types of injuries. I don't think there are more than twenty inpatients here. It would have been easy to spot me."

Ballister said, "They couldn't have known their intruder was admitted. And I doubt they would have attempted to kill you unless they were sure."

"So what are you saying?" Tony asked.

"I'm saying it's far more likely someone who works here at the hospital is a sympathizer, maybe has ties to these SOBs, like a spouse or something. Probably when the FBI and I showed up to talk to the patient in Room 127, someone called POVO and tipped them off."

Tony hated to think that was true, but the sheriff was right. It seemed the most likely answer. He found his mind wandering to other possible leaks. For example, how long would it take for someone to call one of the entertainment shows to tell them Darcy Gillson had narrowly escaped being killed? He pushed the thought aside to address something far more urgent.

He said, "Speaking of POVO, what happened at the camp today? Did the raid happen? Have the weapons been recovered? Are people in jail?"

Tabors sighed. "Sadly, none of the above. The raid was executed perfectly, but..."

"But what?" The strain was evident in Tony's voice. This was too much to handle in one day.

Tabors said, "But no one was there."

"No one?" Tony was incredulous. "You mean that literally?"

"Yes, literally. The camp was completely empty. There were no trucks in the large building you saw Monday night. There were no people or vehicles anywhere. The desks and file drawers in the offices were empty. We have a team still there, checking everything more carefully, but it's clear we're not going to find anything."

"Surely those gleaming white semis can't just disappear," Tony said. "They're huge."

"Yes, they're huge, but they're also commonplace on America's highways. Plus, they left a camp that's out in the middle of nowhere. If they went different directions, no one would think anything about a semi passing by on the way to a delivery. Within minutes, they could have joined the traffic on any of a number of state and US highways, including the Avenue of the Saints just to the east of us. In a couple of hours, they could have been on I-70 or I-80. Three other interstates aren't much farther. We're looking at videos from every camera we can find, but so far, we have zilch."

"Okay, I get it. It's harder than it seems. What about your mole... I'm sorry, your friend. Any sign of him?"

The muscles twitched in Tabors's jaw. She spoke quietly. "His cabin was empty, just like all the others. But we found some signs they had caught onto him. His cabin had been torn apart in a search. Also, in another building, it looked like someone had been handcuffed to the center support column. It's a warehouse that was used to store food and other supplies. We recovered some blood from the floor, and we're having it analyzed, but I fear the worst. These assholes discovered what Ted was doing and locked him in the warehouse. I can guess what they've done with him by now."

Darcy reached across the table and laid her hand on Tabors's wrist. "You can still hope. They must have been keeping him alive for a reason."

"I'm sorry," Tabors said, her face a stoic mask, "but today dashed what little hope I had. Think about it. They sent a man here to murder Tony in his hospital bed. They were ready to kill a complete stranger just because he *might* have seen or heard something. There's no doubt in my mind that come spring, we'll be fishing the body of Theodore Roosevelt Janssen out of that lake."

# Chapter 26

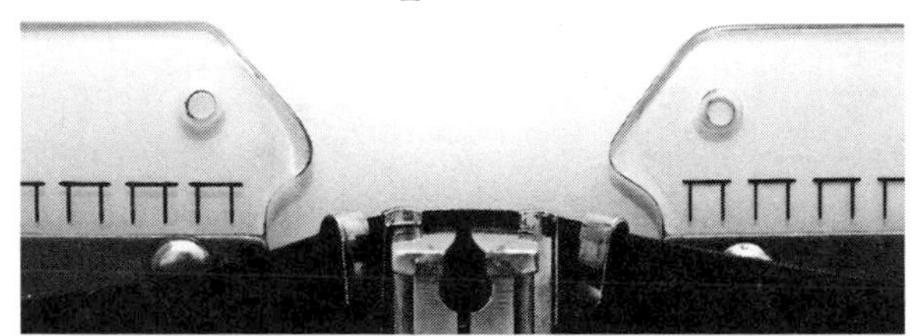

Wednesday, January 7, Langley, Virginia

The government of the United States of America has a well-earned reputation for moving slowly. It can take months to get a passport, years to get an FCC license to use a broadcast frequency, and even longer to get a needed improvement to an interstate highway. However, when a clear and present danger is identified, the cogs in the machine turn at a different rate, and in a different gear.

Today, Francis Harken, known as "Frat" to his friends and closest associates, was very clearly in high gear. Harken was the deputy director for counterterrorism at the US Central Intelligence Agency. He was on his third telephone call in eight minutes. The first was the one he had received from the FBI. His contact in the director's office had called to tell him the missing Berkut missiles may have been spotted. *Finally, after two years, but in fucking Missouri?*

He would think about it later. First, he had to act. His second call was to his boss, the director of the CIA. The third he was placing now to Colonel Terrence "Tar Pit" Jackson, the commander of one of several Air Force units housed at Offutt Air Force Base in Nebraska. He and Jackson had served together in the US Strategic Command, also headquartered at Offutt. After four years of working side-by-side, Harken had moved on, accepting a leadership role at the CIA. He believed he could better serve his country by identifying and eliminating threats *before* they required military interventions.

Jackson had stayed in the service, moving up from major to lieutenant colonel to full colonel in record time for the Air Force, a branch of the military notoriously stingy in granting promotions. Harken called Jackson's encrypted cell phone, a number known to very few people. He was confident Jackson would answer. He did.

"Frat!" the colonel's voice boomed. "It's been a while. You still a lowly major?"

"Yep. No excuses. I just couldn't cut it. You still bald?"

Jackson's laughter rolled like thunder out of the phone's speaker. "Sadly yes, but I'm still better looking than you, so I don't let it bother me too much."

"Everybody's better looking than me," Harken said. "No comfort in that."

"True, so true." Jackson paused and took a breath big enough to be heard across the miles. "I assume you didn't call to give me shit about my hair, so what's up?"

"You're very, very right," Harken said, and then told Jackson about the twelve missing Russian missiles, and how at least one of them had been spotted in Missouri.

"Missouri? My God."

Harken knew the location would get Jackson's attention. Jackson had grown up in St. Louis. It wasn't core to why Harken had called him directly, but Jackson's knowledge of the region couldn't hurt either.

He explained how a newspaper reporter had gone to the POVO camp in the middle of the night and what he had found there.

"We, and by 'we,' I mean a interagency operation of CIA, FBI, and the military, had a strike team on-site at the camp just twenty-four hours after receiving the report. Thing is, the bastards had cleared out by then."

Jackson kept silent, knowing his friend would cover the important details quickly.

Harken said, "We didn't find much, but we did find packing crates and some heavy equipment. The bottom line is, this Harrington guy didn't imagine it. We believe there's evidence that at least three of the missiles were there, maybe more. They've been serviced and repainted with the POVO logo. And now shipped out."

"All signs say that they're gonna get used, probably soon?"

"Exactly."

"Any idea about targets?"

"Lots of ideas, but no actual clues. However, if I was still stationed at the home of the Strategic Command, which is practically next door to Missouri, I might find an excuse to sleep somewhere else, like in Canada."

"Not funny."

Harken realized he was nodding, even though only he could see it. "You're right. It's not funny."

"How can I help?"

"I want it all. I want the command's radar and other missile detection capabilities focused on the Midwest, at least for a few days. I want everything you got up in the air, serving as spotters and potential responders to a missile launch. I want everyone from the cadets in Colorado Springs to the Air National Guard bases throughout the area to be flying, watching, and ready to act."

"You ask a lot, and all of it's a waste of time. But you worked here, so you know that. Our air defenses are designed to protect our borders. Our anti-missile systems need a window of twelve to sixteen minutes to identify a missile threat and to launch, to have any chance to take it out."

"You're right. I know all that. I helped you plan those response scenarios. In this case, a missile launched at Offutt, for example, from somewhere nearby, would give you three or four minutes to respond. Maybe even less."

Jackson was quiet for a long moment. He said, "You realize, of course, the Berkuts were designed as surface-to-air missiles."

Harken sighed. He knew what was coming.

"If these people are planning to take down airplanes, our window is nearly zero."

Harken didn't respond. He could hear Jackson punching a keyboard. The colonel said, "A launch at a nearby airliner flying at thirty-five thousand feet would allow you about ninety seconds to respond. That means meeting the threat in-air in ninety seconds. You'd basically have to launch simultaneously."

"We understand that and are working on alternatives. Believe me, we're talking to the president and the FAA about shutting down commercial air traffic for that portion of the country until we find these things."

"That's not gonna happen," Jackson said. "You close down the air lanes in the Midwest, you close down almost everything. It's pretty hard to get from New York to LA without flying across the middle of the country. They'll need a lot more proof than one possible sighting by a civilian and a few empty crates."

"Right again, of course," Harken said. "That's why our next request will be to your bosses at the Pentagon. We want as many commercial flights as possible to be escorted by military planes."

"Logistically difficult, to say the least. Even if it happens, there's no guarantee they could save the targets."

"Well, most of the fighters and bombers will have countermeasures and other defenses, even if they're not equipped to shoot down a missile at full speed. Worst case scenario, they sacrifice the military plane."

"You're talking about suicide missions."

"You got a better idea, I'm all ears."

Jackson was silent.

Harken said, "I'm not disagreeing with you. There just aren't any good options. Which brings me to the main point of my call."

"You're joking. Mobilizing the entire US Air Force isn't enough of an ask?"

"I want you to deploy the PADs."

"The what?"

"Terry, don't play dumb with me. I know that Offutt is hosting four banks of Prioritized Area Defense units—what you like to call PADs."

"Those are still on the drawing board."

Harken was raising the issue of a new defense capability that had been proposed a few years earlier to meet this very need—protecting targets from short-range tactical missiles, nuclear and otherwise, launched from nearby locations. The PAD system was proposed to have multiple interceptors loaded on a mobile platform that could be deployed, set up, and operated quickly and easily. In publicly available information, the system was still a dream being discussed. Harken knew better.

"Dammit!" he nearly shouted. "Stop messing around. We're not just talking about hundreds, or maybe thousands, of lives. We're talking about a strike that will paralyze our nation, shut down *all* air travel, and probably plummet us into the greatest recession since 'This Land is Your Land' was the number one song on the radio. I know you have the PADs. Four banks, built as prototypes and delivered to Offutt for testing out in the middle of bum-fuck Nebraska somewhere."

"How do you know all this? You're talking about a project so secret that some of the other commanders on base don't know about it."

"Tar Pit, c'mon. We're the CIA. We know shit. Play dumb if you must. Keep your promise to your boss, but figure out how to get those PADs in place. Put them under the major flight lanes and near major airports."

"Even if they exist," Jackson said, unwilling to concede the point, "and even if they're deployed, the chances of being in the right place at the right time, and successfully terminating a strike, are miniscule and smaller."

Harken responded very quietly. "My dear friend, we have to do *something*. We can't just sit on our hands and wait for the first plane to fall or government building to collapse. If that doesn't convince you, take a moment to consider the alternative."

Jackson was silent, so Harken pushed on. "When this catastrophe occurs, what happens later when someone finds out you had these systems available and didn't deploy them? I'm not sure the Air Force would survive the backlash. I'm not sure the entire US military command would survive it. Maybe not the government itself. We must *do* something."

"Ah, fuck me," Jackson groaned. "I'm on it."

Harken kept pushing. "Don't go chasing the command structure for approval. Just do this. Now. Today. Get forgiveness later, but get those PADs in the field."

"Enough." Jackson's voice sounded an octave less deep and carried a sharp edge. "I said I'm on it. You don't have to tell me how to do my damn job."

"You're right; I'm sorry. I trust you completely. That's why I called you."

"Wonderful," Jackson said. "Your deep and abiding respect for me has resulted in the biggest shitstorm in history being dropped into my lap."

"You're welcome," Harken said.

# Chapter 27

Wednesday, January 7, Petersburg, Missouri

Tony and Darcy lay on the lumpy mattress in his room at the Hamilton Motor Lodge. One piece of a large pizza remained in the box on the nightstand beside the bed. The lamp was on, its faded shade creating a soft, pink glow in the room.

The lump Tony was feeling under his head was not from the decades-old pillow, but from the Walther he had placed under it. In addition, Sheriff Ballister had insisted on assigning a deputy to protect them. The young man was outside, presumably drinking the motel's free coffee while sitting in his SUV. Tony knew a single deputy could not slow down, let alone stop, a POVO attack. The Walther probably wouldn't save them either, but having it close at hand made him feel better.

Darcy said, "It's weird, but having that guy outside makes me more nervous, not less. It's like having a neon sign saying, 'Here they are!' I wish he'd just go away."

Tony rolled to his side to face her. "I agree, especially since no one's coming. If I thought they were, we wouldn't be here."

"How can you…?"

Tony said, "POVO's gone. Whatever it is they're doing, it's started. Plus, they have to know that if I learned anything at the camp, I've shared it with the authorities by now. There's no point in risking an attack to shut up someone who's already spilled the beans."

"But you said that guy pointed at you; made a gesture that looked like he would be coming for you."

"Yeah, maybe later," Tony admitted. "I just think he and his pals have bigger fish to fry right now. Believe me, if I thought we were at risk, we'd be on our way home or to a hotel in Chicago or St. Louis. Or anywhere."

"Gosh, I'd hate to give up these posh accommodations for a room at the Ritz-Carlton."

Tony smiled and lightly brushed an errant strand of hair from her forehead.

She said, "By the way, why *are* we still here? Just too tired to travel?"

"The room's paid for," Tony said. "I forked over big bucks for three nights, but spent the second one in the hospital. I'm not gonna throw away the third one too."

Darcy giggled, then said, "And the serious reason is…?"

"The truth is, I want to go back to the POVO camp tomorrow. Tabors said the FBI experts will be done by then, so it's no problem."

"You can't expect to find something. As you just said, they had a whole team of experts go through the place."

"No, it's not that. I just want to see it. I want to get a sense of its size and layout. I want to understand better how they organized things, the kinds of activities that went on there. If I'm going to write about these clowns, the camp will tell me a lot about them."

"Makes sense. I wish I could go with you."

"I assumed you would."

"Have you forgotten? I don't have a coat. My cyanide-soaked parka is in an evidence locker at the Sheriff's Department."

"Way ahead of you," Tony said. "I talked to Ballister. He's loaning you a coat. They have some serious cold weather gear available in a size that should work for you. He said he would leave it at the motel desk tonight and you can just ship it back to him after we get home."

"That's perfect. Thank you for thinking of it. After years of living on the coasts, I forget how nice and trusting people can be here."

Tony resumed his position on his back and closed his eyes. He said, "So tomorrow's gonna be a long day. We should get some rest."

"No."

Tony's eyes opened. "No?"

"We're not going another night without talking about what happened with Melissa."

"Please, Darcy, I don't want…I can't…"

She sat up and turned to face him. "Tony, we must. Please, trust me. I'm not angry. I'm a big girl. I can handle it. But we have to talk about it. What happened can only destroy us if you keep it a secret. Surely you can feel what it's doing to us. You haven't touched me since that day. You've barely kissed me. It's like loving me is off limits now that you've had sex with another woman."

"I've *what?*" Tony sat up and ignored the pain as he twisted around to face her.

"It's obvious, Tony. But really, it's okay. Things happen. I wish it hadn't, but I understand. I just don't want to lose you."

"No, no, no," Tony shook his head vigorously. "I did not sleep with Melissa."

"Really, Tony. I meant what I said."

He reached out and took her face in his hands. "Listen to me

I did not…Well, I mean…Ah, crap, let me just tell you exactly what happened."

He could feel Darcy grow tense even as he realized how right she had been. He had been stupid not to tell her everything from the beginning.

"I was at the door, ready to leave. That's when she stopped me to say there was one more thing, and she told me she was pregnant. It stunned me. The pain I felt for her was palpable. I instinctively reached out and pulled her close to hug her. I started to cry and buried my face in her hair."

He paused and looked into Darcy's amazing blue eyes. She nodded for him to continue.

"She clung to me. Slowly the awareness came, probably to both of us, that this was no ordinary hug. She wasn't letting go. As it began to get awkward, I tried to pull away, but she wrapped an arm around my neck and pulled my head down to kiss me. I resisted but she was so insistent, so desperate. I wanted to be nice, I wanted to help her…"

Darcy's face was a mixture of grin and grimace. She said, "You're a guy. You wanted to…"

"Okay, fine, I didn't resist much. We kissed. But it was so much more. I was shocked. It was all wet lips and tongue and…"

"Okay, Tony. I get it. I don't need every detail."

"Sorry, but I need you to understand. I was getting aroused. She could sense it. She pressed against me and whispered, 'Please.' She said she just wanted to forget for a while. She said she needed this. She kept saying please."

"And so you…"

"I said no. I took her hands and pushed her away. I told her I was sorry. I even told her that I wanted to, although she undoubtedly could see that for herself. But I told her I couldn't. When I left, she was a sobbing heap on the floor. I felt like I had delivered another death to her door."

"You really said no?" Darcy couldn't help smiling.

"Don't you understand?" Tony felt tears welling. "I left there feeling like I'd done something horrible. I'd hurt someone deeply who was already hurting so much."

"But you should..."

"But even worse," Tony said, "At least worse for me... for us, I *wanted* to say yes. I wanted to take her, right then and there. It took every ounce of willpower I could muster to walk away. I couldn't come to grips with that. I still can't. How could I have wanted her so much, when I've committed myself to you? When I know I'm in love with you?"

He pulled Darcy close, not wanting her to see his face as he cried. "I'm so sorry."

Darcy pushed him back, looking him in the eye. Her voice danced like music as she said, "Tony, you're the most naïve thirty-year-old who's ever lived."

His brow furrowed.

She continued, "Wanting to say yes is no reason to feel ashamed. Wanting to have sex is the norm. Human beings are made that way. We all want to have sex. You think that when I'm half-naked with a handsome co-star, filming a love scene, that I don't feel those urges? That I don't fantasize about sneaking to his trailer later and having a good romp?"

Tony felt his face flush. Apparently he was less understanding than the woman he loved.

She said, "Relax, and listen to me. Loving a person doesn't mean our human nature disappears and we never again desire other people. Loving a person means we care enough to set aside our urges, our desires, and stay true to the promises we've made. That is exactly what you did. My dear Tony, thank you. I've never felt more loved in my life than I do right now."

"Really?" Tony was genuinely surprised. He was even more surprised by what Darcy said next.

"Yes, really," she said, as she pulled her nightgown off over her head and reached for his belt. "And now I'm going to prove it."

# Chapter 28

Thursday, January 8, Hamilton County, Missouri
Two Days to Wheels-Up, Flight 244

Darcy liked her borrowed coat. It was as far from stylish as a garment could get, but it was heavy and warm, and reached to her midthighs. Clearly its owner was a lot taller than Darcy. The coat was dark green and featured a lining with a thin layer of Kevlar sandwiched between two layers of down. A note left by the sheriff in the coat pocket noted that it wouldn't stop a bullet from an assault rifle, but it would provide a modest amount of protection in case of trouble.

*What kind of trouble can I find at an empty camp?* Darcy wondered. In any case, she wasn't complaining, especially because the coat was adorned with "Hamilton County Sheriff" patches on the shoulders. She thought it was cool, and insisted Tony take her picture posing in it. He was forced to use her phone since his was presumably being examined by the fish at the bottom of the lake.

The day was sunny and significantly warmer than the previous few days. The trees were dripping water from the melting snow in their boughs, and the ground was mushy in spots. Each time she stepped into a puddle or a muddy spot on a trail, Darcy tried not to think about what her Moscova boots had cost. She didn't complain. Watching Tony limp through their walk with a cane in one hand eliminated any thoughts of feeling sorry for herself.

As Tony had predicted, their walk around the camp was eye-opening. They found a huge parade training ground carved into the woods. Surrounding it was every conceivable type of outdoor obstacle, just like those seen in Army recruiting commercials. Beyond the climbing walls, concrete culverts, and mud pit, they came across a simulated village street, lined on one side by faux building fronts, but on the other with actual buildings. Signs on the fronts read "Restaurant," "Hair Salon," "Hardware Store," and "Bank." The insides featured mock-ups of fixtures and furniture built of plywood.

At one point Tony gasped, and Darcy turned to look. He was probing a series of holes in the bank's "teller counter" with his pinkie finger. He said, "Mother of God, they were training with live ammo in here!"

Once they started looking for them, Darcy and Tony found the bullet holes in many places. Each new discovery sent a chill through them.

Living accommodations were about what they expected—a series of bunk houses clustered together, each holding a dozen single beds and a communal bathroom.

They also found six cabins nearer to the front of the camp, behind the office building Tony had seen on his first trip there. Each was smaller but was designed to house just one person. A double bed, a kitchenette, a bathroom, and a living area with desk and couch identified these as officers' quarters.

"Tabors said her friend Ted had served as the camp's accountant.

He was staying in Cabin Six, at least until they took him away and shackled him to a pole," Tony said. "Let's take a look."

What they found confirmed the FBI agent's fears. Cabin Six had been nearly destroyed inside by someone's thorough search. Cabinets had been pulled off walls, floorboards had been pried up, every piece of furniture had been smashed to kindling.

"The FBI team didn't do this?"

Tony reminded her that Tabors said the FBI found it like this. "Obviously, POVO didn't want any chance that Agent Janssen left behind information that could be found by the authorities."

Darcy's face darkened, and she brushed back a tear. She said, "All that effort and risk for nothing. If he's dead…and if he died before he could share what he knew, it's…Well, it's just heartbreaking."

Tony nodded his agreement, and they moved on.

At noon, Tony said his ankle needed a break. They climbed into the rented pickup and started the engine. Once they were warm enough, they removed their coats and pulled a plastic bag from behind the driver's seat.

"Chicken salad sandwich, cold pizza, or a ham and cheese Lunchable?" Tony asked.

"It's a tough choice," Darcy grinned. "Kind of like having to choose between the twelve-ounce Duroc Chop and the Broiled Alaskan Halibut at the Cherry Circle Room in Chicago."

"Okay, wise-ass, I get it. Gas station food is not a preferred choice for either of us. But it beats starving," Tony dug into the bag for the Hostess Cupcakes he had purchased for dessert. He held up the smashed package and made an exaggerated pout with his lower lip. "Just barely beats starving," he muttered.

Darcy giggled. "I'll take the sandwich. I actually like chicken salad on a croissant. If it's been in their cooler for less than three weeks, it might be okay."

Tony took a bite of the pizza and made a face.

Seeing this, Darcy set the sandwich on a napkin in her lap, and used her fingers to break it in two. She handed half to Tony.

As he reached out to take it, he said, "Have I ever mentioned how wonderful you are?"

She took a bite of her half and smiled. She chewed, swallowed, and said, "Well, yeah, last night you said it several times, but considering what we were doing at the time, it probably doesn't count."

"Oh, it counts," Tony said. "It counts, and counts, and counts…"

The giggle returned, and she said, "We should change the subject before clothes start coming off again."

Tony reached out with his free hand, touched her hair, then moved to her face, down her neck, and stopped to linger on the mounds in her sweater. He said, "I rather like the idea of clothes coming off, but, alas, considering the bright sunshine and the clear glass in this truck's windows, you're probably right."

They leaned in for a brief kiss, then finished their lunch.

***

They entered the vast steel-and-concrete building far more easily than Tony had experienced a few nights previously. It appeared the strike team had used crowbars to force open the pedestrian door on the side. With no way to lock it again, the door had been propped shut with a piece of lumber. A sign read, *No Trespassing by Order of the Hamilton County Sheriff.* Tony swept aside the length of board and pulled open the door.

Except for the missing semis, much was the same as the night he entered the camp: the office, the work benches, the ceiling-mounted winch, and the paint booth where the missiles apparently had been painted white and adorned with the POVO logo.

Tony pointed out a few differences in the room—empty packing crates and other signs of the POVO exodus. One change he immediately noted was the open doors on a row of large metal storage cabinets on the far wall. As they approached, Tony could see they held a variety of supplies and tools.

"Speaking of organization," Tony said, "these cabinets are arranged more neatly than any closet I've ever had."

"Not a high bar," Darcy quipped, "but I see what you mean. The one on the left has cleaning supplies and tools, the one in the middle looks like stuff for mechanics, and on the right, paint and sprayers."

Tony limped closer and examined the large plastic buckets stacked two-high in one cabinet.

"Remind me to look for a dumpster when we go outside."

"A dumpster?" Darcy asked.

"These are twelve-gallon buckets of paint. That's a lot of paint."

"It's a big camp," she pointed out. "It shouldn't be a surprise that they used a lot of paint."

"I agree," Tony nodded, "but look at the labels. Most of these are automotive paint. Is it here because they didn't use much paint for vehicles, or because they did?"

"Ah, I get it. Dumpster contents will tell you what they actually used."

Tony turned and looked to the corner of the room, left of the cabinets. A garden hose with a spray handle hung from a large wall-mounted reel. Then he looked at the floor where the trucks had stood. A long horizontal drain ran for twenty feet along the middle of the floor.

"I wonder..." he said, hobbling over to look at the drain. He looked up and suddenly moved as quickly as he could to the disassembled crates across the room. He found a large piece of cardboard and carried it to the workbench. There he grabbed a pair of sheet metal shears and used them to cut a long, narrow strip from the cardboard's edge. As he moved back to the center of the room, he could see Darcy watching him, her face a mix of puzzlement and amusement.

Tony pushed one end of the cardboard strip through the grate in the floor drain and moved it back and forth, scraping it against the sides of the drainpipe.

When he pulled it out, he cried, "Son of a bitch, I was right."

Darcy could see what he had found. Blue and red paint was clearly visible on the edges of the makeshift probe. She had her phone out even before Tony asked for it. She allowed the phone to recognize her face and open, then handed it to Tony.

"Thank goodness, a cell signal," he said as he dialed Agent Tabors. "The strike team must have disabled whatever was jamming the signal when I was here before."

"Darcy?" Tabors's voice said from the phone's speaker after a single ring.

"It's both of us," Tony said. "I found something at the camp. Your folks may have found it, too, but in case they didn't, I thought I should call."

"I'm all ears," Tabors said.

Tony tried to keep the excitement from his voice. "They painted the trucks."

"What? Why do you say that?"

"There's blue and red paint in the floor drain."

"We already knew they painted the missiles. Is this just…"

Tony interrupted, "No, this isn't the drain in the paint booth. This is the floor drain under where the trucks were parked. There's paint in the drain."

"We looked at the floor," Tabors said, sounding a little defensive. "There was no sign of overspray, so we dismissed the idea."

"It's an old painters' trick," Tony said. "They used a hose to keep the floor wet. The overspray fell onto the water and ran down the drain. As long as they kept the floor wet, no paint would have stuck there."

"How do you know all this crap?"

Tony smiled. "I read a lot. You should try it sometime."

"Bite me," Tabors said.

Darcy laughed and said, "Hey! Don't give him any ideas."

Tony said, "I'm serious, Anna. I'll bet you a thousand bucks that we're not looking for white trucks. They're red or blue or some combination of those colors."

"No bet," the agent said. "You may be right, and I can't afford it. We'll get people going back over the videos with that in mind. If we find them, I'm going to owe you big time."

"Music to my ears," Tony said, "but I'll call it even if you just find these jerks before they start killing people."

"Roger that," Tabors said, and hung up.

***

The next stop was the warehouse. Tony wanted to see where Agent Janssen had been held. Darcy said she wasn't sure she wanted to, but she stayed at his side as they went in search of another large building. They found it immediately, facing the same expanse of concrete ninety degrees to the left.

The building was the epitome of simple—built of concrete blocks with narrow horizontal windows high enough to be shaded by the eaves. There was one wide door in front, and a garage door on the left side, no doubt used for unloading supplies.

When they entered the building, they saw immediately that the garage door had been chained shut and secured with a massive lock. The front door had dual deadbolt locks. Both were wired to an alarm system. However, the system was not armed, and the front door was not locked.

"Would have made the perfect jail," Tony observed. "Concrete floor and walls, impassable doors, and a roof made of metal."

"Plenty of food," Darcy said, eyeing rows of boxes and shelves filled with canned goods.

"Nice for the prisoner if he hadn't been shackled to that pole."

"Actually," Darcy said, "I was thinking about something else."

"Oh?"

"Think about what they left behind." She turned to face him. "Really think about it. They walked away from what, millions of dollars' worth of land? Millions more in buildings and equipment? And all these supplies?"

"Pretty crazy," Tony said.

"Not just crazy," Darcy said, reaching out and gripping his arm. "What does it say about what they're doing?"

"I'm not sure I…"

She continued, "It says to me that they're planning something so big, so catastrophic, that walking away from millions of dollars of investments doesn't matter. These lunatics really believe they're sparking the end of…of…I don't know, maybe everything. If there's a 'new white supremist state,' and you're in charge, who cares about a few million left in Missouri?"

Tony felt his mouth go dry and his heart rate quicken. *Could she be right? Good lord, what are we up against?*

He chose his words carefully. "Let's hope there's another answer. Maybe they were simply planning to return. But in case you're right, let's find something that helps the FBI nail these pricks."

A tear began to roll down one of Darcy's cheeks. Tony pulled her close and held her. He was silent only because he could think of no other words of comfort.

After a few moments, Darcy pushed away and wiped her face with the back of her hand. She said, "You're right. Let's keep searching."

Tony nodded and said, "We should locate their armory. I doubt we're going find any answers here among the soup cans." He turned to walk out but noticed Darcy wasn't moving. He turned back to her. "Darcy?"

She was staring at the shelves full of cans.

"What is it?" Tony asked.

Her eyes remained fixed, but she said, "Did I ever tell you about my dad's patio?"

"What?" Tony was baffled.

"My dad's house in upstate New York. Did I ever tell you about his patio?"

"Pretty sure you haven't," he said.

"Dad had the patio rebuilt several years ago. He replaced the ordinary concrete slab with bricks. There are two colors of pavers, light and dark brown. It's beautiful."

"I assume there's a point to this, and the stress hasn't pushed you over the edge."

"The bricklayer was this elderly Irishman. He did a beautiful job and was very proud of his work. He was one of those guys who's worked hard all his life to perfect his craft."

"Okay…"

"I happened to be there visiting when the work was nearly finished. I naturally wandered out to see it. When I complimented the bricklayer on his work, he took me aside and said, 'Don't tell your father, but I signed it.' Of course, I said I was sure Dad wouldn't mind, but the workman wanted me to see it. He took me over to the first row of bricks and asked me what I thought. I told him I thought it was lovely, but I didn't see a signature. I said he must have hidden it well. The man nearly cackled with glee. He wanted me to guess how he had done it. I couldn't guess, so he finally told me."

"Darcy, I really…"

"The bricks, Tony. He used the light bricks as dashes and the dark bricks as dots. The first row of bricks spelled 'Flaherty' in Morse code."

Tony turned to look more closely at the shelves that had captured Darcy's attention. He said, "You don't think…"

"Maybe. Look at how all the cans on three of the rows are facing out, perfectly aligned in one direction. Then notice the two rows in between. They're a jumble. If the labels facing out mean dashes, and the labels in mean dots, or vice-versa, it could spell something."

"But how could Janssen have done that if he was tied to the pole?"

"No way to know, of course, but if he was held in here for any period of time, they would have had to let him loose for a little while each day to eat and relieve himself. They wouldn't have wanted him to use their food storage room as a toilet. Maybe he had enough time alone to devise a message. Do you know Morse code?"

"No," Tony said. "Whatever I learned as a kid is long forgotten. It doesn't matter. Your phone knows."

"Of course," Darcy quickly extracted her phone from her pocket. "Here it is, the alphabet in code."

"This could be complicated," Tony said. "How do we know where to divide the longs and shorts to make the letters?"

"He did it for us," Darcy said, now completely committed to the idea that the cans were a message. "See, some of the cans are turned sideways. I bet those are dividing points."

Tony glanced at the phone screen, then up at the shelf, then back to the phone, then up.

"Holy shit!" he said. "You're right. "Look! Look at this."

He pulled his reporter's notebook from his coat pocket and began writing down letters. Within minutes, they had it all:

CAB SIX NINETY PACES NNW
SIXTY P N L IN FALL TRUNK

"Make sense to you?" Darcy asked, while her face betrayed her certainty that it did.

"Yep," Tony said. "We go to Cabin Six, walk ninety paces north by northwest, then sixty more paces due north. There's something for us there, in a fallen tree trunk to the left."

"Do we dare hope?"

"Hope and pray," Tony said, "but first..." He grabbed Darcy and bent her back over his left arm, giving her a long, warm kiss. When they separated, he said, "You, my dear, have once again proven you're a damn genius."

"Just lucky this time. Without a crazy bricklayer in my past, I never would have thought of it."

"We'll debate it later. Right now, we have work to do."

They hurried to the truck and drove back to the parking lot nearest the officers' cabins. From there, using the compass on Darcy's phone, they followed the directions as best they could. In addition to his cane, Tony brought along a hammer from the tools in the truck and the steel handle from the tire jack.

They needn't have worried about the directions. An enormous ash tree lay on the ground exactly where Janssen had said it would be. The lower part of the trunk was split in multiple places, likely the result of a combination of wind and the weight of the upper tree.

"Kinda sad," Darcy noted.

"It may have been dead before it fell," Tony said. "The emerald ash borer kills every tree it infects."

"This couldn't have helped," Darcy said, looking more closely at where the trunk was splintered. "The tree is hollow."

Tony nodded. "Bad news for the tree, but good news for us." He reached his gloved hand into the opening. An instant later, he whooped and pulled out a plastic bag. It was an ordinary two-gallon freezer bag with a zipper-style seal. Tony brushed it off and held it up for Darcy to see. Inside was a thick notebook with what appeared to be a leather cover.

She gasped. "A journal! My God. Have we done it? Do we finally have a way to…?"

"Do not move!" The voice was a cross between a bark and a snarl.

Darcy froze, but Tony spun to see the source of the command. It was a slender man with a boyish face and glasses. He would have looked about as threatening as a wisp of cloud on a sunny day, except for the Smith and Wesson automatic pistol he held at arm's length, pointed at Darcy's head.

"Who are you?" Tony demanded, trying to push the threat to Darcy out of his mind.

"Shut up, Roby, or Harrington, or whatever you're calling yourself today. You're in my camp, and I have the gun, so do exactly what I say."

Tony held up his hands in the universal sign of surrender, and took a step forward.

The man's thumb clicked off the gun's safety as he barked again, "Not one more inch! It won't bother me a bit to splatter the bitch's brains all over you. I've killed before, and I'll kill again, so just stop."

The gun moved to the right, focusing on Tony instead of Darcy. "In fact, I should kill you right now for what you did to my two men Monday night. I had to kill that guard myself, thanks to you. He was a good man."

Tony saw the muscles in the man's jaw tighten. Fearing his trigger finger would soon follow, Tony opted to remain silent and motionless.

To Darcy, the man said, “Okay, sweetheart. Take one step back toward me, and hand me that bag very slowly.” He repositioned the gun again, this time aiming at her torso. “If you even flinch in a way I perceive as a threat, I’ll shoot you in the leg, and then your boyfriend in the head. That’s right. Nice and easy.”

Darcy reached back, and the man plucked the bag from her hand. Seeing the journal inside, he stuffed it into an oversized pocket on his winter coat and said, “I’ve been following you two most of the day. After weeks of looking everywhere for that traitor’s journal, I didn’t think you’d find it, but I figured it couldn’t hurt to watch and see. And what do you know? You succeeded. Don’t expect me to thank you.”

Suddenly, the man threw his free arm around Darcy’s neck and dragged her back against him.

“Hey!” Tony shouted, hobbling a step closer.

“Sorry, but only she gets to live. A guy just never knows when he might need some insurance or…” he stole a glance at Darcy, “… a good fuck. You, I don’t need.”

He swung the gun to point it at Tony. As he pulled the trigger, Darcy’s right arm was already moving up and to the right. The gun exploded, deafening her right ear. The Kevlar in the coat’s sleeve didn’t stop the bullet.

An ugly sound escaped from Tony as he spun 360 degrees and landed on his back in the snow. Spots of blood fell into a small pool next to his left ear.

Darcy screamed and tried to tear away from the man’s grip. His arm squeezed tighter around her neck, and he pressed the gun’s barrel up against the bottom of her chin. The heat from the barrel burned her flesh, and she screamed again.

“Shut the fuck up!” the man demanded. “Stop now, or I swear, I will shoot you and throw you over my shoulder. You’re just as valuable to me with one good leg as two."

Darcy managed to stop screaming, but she was still sobbing. "Tony? My God, Tony! What have you done? You bastard!"

"I did what needed to be done, as always," the man said, releasing his grip and shoving her ahead of him along the path she and Tony had made through the snow just minutes before. "Stay three steps ahead of me—no more, no less—until we get back to the parking lot. I've got a snowmobile parked in the shed. We're going for a little ride together."

***

Once Darcy and the man had made the turn in the path and disappeared behind the trees, Tony sat up. His scalp hurt like his hair was on fire, and he felt dizzy. He could also feel blood running down the left side of his face. His hand instinctively rose to find the source. It found a long, narrow, horizontal wound above his left ear. It was obvious that Darcy's attempt to deflect the bullet had mostly succeeded. The slug had ripped through his skin and hair, but had failed to put a hole in his face and an even larger one in the back of his skull. Once again, she had saved his life.

Tony climbed to his feet. He was desperate to chase down the path after Darcy and the man, but knew he had to stop the bleeding first. Patting his parka, he was reminded that the hammer was in the large pocket on the lower left. In the right pocket was his winter scarf. He pulled it out and tied it tightly around his head. It made a terrible bandage, but it was better than nothing. In any case, it would have to do until he had time to use the first aid kit in the truck.

He picked up his cane, limped to the fallen tree, and recovered the tire iron from where he had left it. He turned and began walking as fast as he could toward the parking lot.

The pickup parked outside the POVO office building came into view on his left just as he heard the whine of a snowmobile engine off to the right. The sled was moving away from him to the southeast, as it crossed his field of view for a few seconds. Darcy was driving. Her abductor sat behind her with the gun pressed against the back of her skull.

"Dammit," Tony muttered, picking up the cane and breaking into a jog. Determined not to let Darcy out of his sight, he ignored the pain as he hurried to the truck.

When Tony drove onto the main road and turned toward the center of the camp, the snowmobile was already disappearing across the courtyard near the largest building.

*You're driving too fast*, Tony wanted to shout. Then it occurred to him what she was doing. She was speeding in order to take control of the situation on the snowmobile. By driving dangerously fast, the man behind her would be forced to lower the gun to hang on with both hands. He also couldn't harm her without risking a serious accident.

Tony stomped on the accelerator, and the pickup leaped forward. He was going fifty when he entered the courtyard, and the snowmobile was already past the building and nearly to the lake. To Tony's horror, he realized Darcy wasn't turning.

"You can't go on the lake!" he shouted as he began honking the truck's horn. "It's too warm! The ice is melting!" He knew Darcy couldn't hear him, but he kept shouting and honking. Then he saw it—a large pool of open water only thirty yards or so offshore. His dread exploded into terror as he drove the truck over the curb and onto the ground next to the building. His left tires were on the walkway and his right were in snow. He kept his foot on the gas and a hand on the horn.

The man must have also spotted the open water because he suddenly took a dive off the snowmobile to the right and rolled to a stop in what remained of a snowdrift. He leapt to his feet and turned to face the pickup as it came bouncing toward the lake.

Tony's intent had been to stop at the lake's edge and proceed on foot to save Darcy. However, Tony had caught the assailant's attention. The man smiled and raised his weapon, pointing it directly at Tony.

Without thinking, Tony twisted the truck's steering wheel to the right. The truck slid in the snow but turned just enough. The right corner of the truck's front bumper struck the man mid-thighs. From inside the cab, Tony could hear bones snap as the man was thrown backward into the snow.

Tony slammed on the pickup's brakes, jammed the shifter into Park, and jumped out. He ignored the man and began hop-jogging onto the ice just as the snowmobile reached the open water.

Once again, he screamed. "Darcy!"

To his amazement, the sled didn't do a nosedive into the lake. It hydroplaned for nearly a minute across the open water, regained solid ice, and drove another fifty yards in a wide arc before slowing to a stop. Tony could see Darcy turning to look back, undoubtedly wondering what had happened to her abductor and how she could get back to the scene of the shooting to try to save Tony.

He waved, wondering whether Darcy would even recognize him from that distance, without his cane and with a scarf tied around his head. His question was answered immediately, when he heard the machine's engine wind up again, and saw it turn and head straight toward him.

Breathing heavily in response to a mix of pain, exhaustion, and relief, Tony hobbled back to the snowbank where the POVO gunman lay. He was tempted to get his own weapon from the truck before approaching the man, but it was obvious the figure on the ground was no threat.

The man, whom Tony would later learn was Jon Slapp, POVO

camp commander, lay staring at the blue sky. Despite the open eyes, Slapp was not seeing anything. Tony might have been surprised to find the man dead, but the amount of blood in the snow, and the bone protruding from the man's left leg, told a clear story. In shattering the man's leg, the truck's bumper had also severed a femoral artery. The man had bled to death in less time than it had taken Tony to walk out to the shoreline and back.

Tony felt revulsion at the gruesome sight but felt no remorse about the death. This bastard had shot him and had attacked Darcy, not to mention he had been a part of whatever horrific plot had been hatched by POVO.

"You can rot in hell," Tony said to the corpse.

He turned and moved a few paces away so he could greet Darcy without her having to see the horror scene in the snow.

She was off the sled even before it came to a full stop, nearly knocking him over has she threw her arms around him.

"You're alive, you're alive, you're alive…!" she kept repeating, her face buried into the thick fabric of his coat.

Tony gripped her shoulders and pushed back so he could look into her eyes. "You saved me," he said.

"And that prick with the gun?"

"He wasn't so lucky."

"Good."

Tony didn't respond to that. He expected Darcy would experience a more profound reaction later, but he couldn't take the time to think about it now.

"Nice work on the snowmobile. I thought for sure I was going to have to pull you out of the lake. Was that luck, or did you know the sled would do that?"

"I not only knew it; I've done it before."

The shocked look on Tony's face almost brought a smile to

Darcy's lips. "As you know, I'm from upstate New York. Watercross is a big sport there."

"Watercross?"

"That's what they call it when snowmobiles ski on open water. They run races every June on Lake Placid. I never owned a snowmobile, but I dated a guy in high school who was really into it. He took me up there one weekend and convinced me to try it. I had a lot of fun."

"I'm pretty sure I don't want to know anything more about your weekend at Lake Placid with a boy. In any case, we have work to do, and we should hurry," he said. "Call 911, or better yet, call Ballister directly and tell him what's happened. I'm going to get Janssen's journal and try to find this guy's gun. If you feel up to it, you can help search for it in the snow. Just don't look in the direction of the body. It's not a sight you can unsee."

Darcy nodded, already pulling her phone from her pocket.

Tony added, "If you find the gun, pick it up by the barrel with two fingers. I killed this guy, so we'll want to be sure the evidence is clear that he held the gun in a firing position."

He turned and limped back to the body. It only took a moment to reach into the man's pocket and pull out the bag containing the journal. He turned his attention to the man's hands, which were empty, then began scanning the ground for signs of the gun. He hoped it wasn't under the body.

His eyes moved in wider and wider arcs, trying to spot any break in the snow that looked unnatural. About thirty feet southwest of the body, he saw it. Gray gunmetal and a portion of the black vinyl grip protruded from the snow at the base of a tree.

"Found it!" he called out, deciding to leave it in place for the authorities to recover.

"I found it too!" Darcy cried.

Tony spun in time to see her racing toward him, a huge smile on her face. In her hand was Tony's smartphone.

"Holy shit!" he cried. "Where…how…?"

"It was at the base of the snowbank over there," Darcy said.

Tony looked in the direction she was pointing and realized it was the snowbank in which he had hidden his gear Monday night. The phone must have fallen from his pocket into the deep snow when he was retrieving his skis, and not later, on the ice, as he had assumed. Then today, as the snow receded in the warm sunlight, the phone was exposed.

He gave her a quick squeeze and excitedly took the phone. "Now let's see if that overpriced protective case did its job." At the touch of the screen, it came to life. "Hallelujah," he said, opening the photo storage app. He selected the pictures of the three semis' license plates and sent them to Tabors.

Less than fifteen seconds later, his phone buzzed.

"Hi, Agent Tabors," Tony answered cheerfully.

"You found your phone."

"And they say the FBI has lost its analytical edge."

"Okay, smart guy, I'm sorry. I spoke the obvious. I've already sent the photos on to the task force. These will be a huge help."

"Thank Darcy," Tony said. "She's the one who found it."

"Of course she is. You couldn't find your way out of an open garage door without her help."

"Sad but true," Tony said, grinning at Darcy. "She also just saved my life again. And I probably should mention, we found Janssen's journal."

"You what?!" Tabors's shriek caused him to flinch and pull the phone from his ear. As he returned it, Tabors was spouting questions like Fourth of July fireworks. "What does it say? Is he okay? Does it give you what we need to stop these…?"

"Slow down," Tony said, "I'm sorry, but I don't know anything more about your friend. We haven't even opened the book yet. We found it hidden in a hollow tree. Before we had a chance to look at it, I got shot in the head and Darcy got kidnapped."

"What the..." Tabors's tone shifted to skeptical, even irritated. "You're telling *me* to slow down?"

"A lot's happened today, and we can talk about it later. Right now, we want to get someplace warm and get a look at what Janssen wrote."

"You're right," the agent said. "Do that. Tell me where you land so I can join you, but don't wait for me. I'm almost halfway to Chicago. Find out everything you can and get me the information."

"Ten-four," Tony said. After a moment, he added, "Why don't you go to Iowa City? It's right on I-80. We can meet there. It's on our way home, and you won't have to backtrack as far."

She agreed, and they ended the call.

Darcy climbed into the truck. The engine was still running, so the cab was warm. She turned to look at Tony. "Aren't you coming?"

"Just a sec."

Tony trod back through the snow to where Slapp's body lay facing the sky. Trying to not disturb anything on or near the body, he gingerly patted the man's pockets with the back of his hand. When he found the lump, he reached into the man's coat pocket and pulled out an iPhone. He held the phone over the man's face until it unlocked, then returned to the truck.

He could see Darcy was in the driver's seat. He didn't object. He undoubtedly looked like a cadaver that had been worked over by first-year medical students, and he felt worse than he looked.

When he climbed into the seat beside her, Darcy said, "Before we go anywhere, we should tend to whatever wound is hiding under that scarf on your head and get a look at the journal."

Tony said, "We need to go now. If the sheriff arrives while we're still here, we'll be tied up for hours. I also worry that the dead guy might not be the only POVO member who stayed behind. We can't be sure we're safe until we put some distance between us and this place."

Darcy nodded, put the truck in reverse, and backed away from the body in the snow. As she turned and guided the truck up the hill to the parking lot, she said, "I don't suppose the fact that you stole the dead man's smartphone has anything to do with your desire to get out of here before the sheriff arrives."

"I didn't steal it. I retrieved it for the FBI. I'll turn it over to Tabors when I give her the journal."

"So you're helping rather than hindering the investigation? You keep helping like that, they're going to reward you with five years in Leavenworth."

"I'm serious," he said. "This needs to get to the right people, ASAP. It can't help us find and stop POVO if it's sitting in an evidence locker in Hamilton County."

"So you're not going to look at it?"

"Well…I didn't say that."

Darcy released a quick chortle, then grew serious. "You sure you'll be okay for a while?"

"My head's pounding the beat to 'Ballroom Blitz' and my ankle's screaming obscenities at me, but I'll live." He unwrapped the scarf from his head and confirmed the bleeding had stopped. "Just get us out of here."

# Chapter 29

Thursday, January 8, Hamilton County, Missouri

Once they exited the camp, Darcy drove east toward US 61, where they would turn north to reach Iowa. She said, "I have a rental car back there in the hospital parking lot."

"Good point," Tony said. "I'll send a text and let them know someone will be back for it later, if that's okay."

"Of course." Darcy nodded, her eyes focused on the road.

Tony turned his attention to the dead man's phone and opened the camera app. He was pretty sure the phone wouldn't go to sleep and lock him out while the camera was on. He then checked the battery life, set it aside, and pulled the journal from the plastic bag. He began skimming through the pages.

"There's so much detail here," he said. "It's no wonder the POVO leaders were anxious to find this. Finances, inventories, schedules and…" Tony gasped.

"What?"

"Three years ago, POVO got an influx of cash—$30 million."

"*How* much?" Darcy exclaimed incredulously. "From where?"

"Janssen writes that the source was a mystery, at least to him. The POVO leaders told him the money was in a numbered account in an offshore bank. He was instructed to transfer it to POVO's own funds, presumably in a different offshore bank. When he did so, he had to exchange the money from Euros to US dollars, so he had the impression it came from a foreign source."

"Foreigners investing in white supremist extremists in America? What the hell is going on?"

Tony didn't try to answer. Turning a page, he said, "Wait, here it is—$17 million of the money was paid two years ago to another numbered account, this one in Zurich. Janssen says the missiles arrived at the camp a couple of months later." He paused, then gasped again. "Oh, my God. Twelve missiles!"

"*What?!*" Darcy nearly drove off the road.

"All twelve of the Russian Berkut missiles came here."

Darcy's face was white, and she spoke in a whisper. "Tony, what are they doing? What's going to happen?"

"I don't know, but they have to be stopped." He resumed reading.

A few minutes later, Darcy glanced over and wrinkled her brow. Tony had switched to the last page of the journal and was scanning the pages in reverse. In answer to her obvious question, he said, "I'm hoping at some point Janssen just tells us what this is all about. If he does, I thought maybe it will be nearer to the end of what he..." Tony's voice trailed off as the air left his lungs. "Holy mother of God," he squeaked.

"What? *What?* Tell me!"

Tony pulled out his phone and put it on speaker. Tabors answered before the first ring had finished.

"Talk," the agent said.

"They're going to shoot down airliners," Tony said, finding it incomprehensible that he had spoken the words.

Tabors was silent for a beat, then said, "Tell me more."

"They bought twelve missiles. After test firings and scavenging parts, they ended up with five fully functional weapons."

"Five?"

"Five surface-to-air missiles, armed with warheads containing C-4. They're going to shoot at commercial passenger planes flying in air lanes in the Midwest. Apparently, someone had the bright idea that terror unleashed in middle America would make everyone in the US feel unsafe."

"Probably right," Tabors said. "What else?"

The plan was to ship them out in five semis to different locations."

"Five trucks? You saw three."

"That's right. Agent Janssen's journal entries end just before Christmas. I'm guessing two of the trucks had already been deployed before I ventured into the camp."

"Shit. Did, uh, does Ted know where? Please tell me you have locations."

"Yes and no."

"What the hell does that mean?" Tabors was animated.

"Janssen lists towns and cities, but not specific addresses."

"Give me the list."

Tony took a deep breath and tried to keep the quiver out of his voice. "Lincoln, Nebraska; Sioux Falls, South Dakota; Rochester, Minnesota; Manhattan, Kansas; and, you're not going to believe this, Orney, Iowa."

"Orney? How did your town make this list?"

"Who knows? One of the POVO leaders lives nearby, so maybe it's connected to that."

"No matter," the agent said. "Anything else?"

"There's a lot of intel here about the money, camp operations, other stuff."

"That can wait. I have to get the alert out about the weapons and their locations ASAP. But before I go, I have to say thank you. This is incredibly good work. Because of what you and Darcy have done, we now know what we're looking for and where to look. You may have saved countless lives today. You may have saved more than that."

"I hope so," Tony said, "but it's not over yet. Once you have those missiles secured and a bunch of lunatics in prison, then we can talk about who gets credit for what." He turned and saw Darcy was crying. He said, "I need to go. We'll see you in Iowa City in a couple of hours. In the meantime, keep us posted on what happens."

At the next intersection, Tony encouraged Darcy to exit the highway. They found a truck stop and pulled to the far end of the lot. Tony had filled the pickup that morning, so there was no need to park closer. Once the truck was stopped and in Park, Tony pulled Darcy closer and wrapped his arms around her. He had no words to comfort her, nor she him. They simply clung tightly to each other, praying that they had discovered enough information, and in time to make a difference.

***

Once back on the road, a fresh coffee in the cup holder for Darcy and a Diet Dr. Pepper for Tony, it didn't take long for things to heat up. The first call came from Sheriff Ballister, who wanted to know why Darcy and Tony had left the scene of a violent death. Didn't they know they were key witnesses? Didn't they know leaving was a crime? Didn't they know they were needed there?

"It's dusk, and soon it'll be dark. We're stumbling around here with our heads up our asses. We haven't even found the alleged gun."

"Oh, sorry. I can help with that," Tony said, describing exactly where the gun lay.

"Don't expect me to thank you," Ballister said. "You could have saved us a lot of trouble if you'd been here to tell us that when we arrived."

Tony apologized again and explained the reasons they had left.

"Okay, I get that," the sheriff said, "but I still need to know exactly what happened here."

"No problem. Darcy's driving, so I'm happy to give you my statement now."

The sheriff grumped about trying to do his job over the phone, but then agreed on the condition that Tony provide him with a full written statement within twenty-four hours. Tony agreed, and then walked the sheriff through the day's events at the camp.

When Tony finished, the sheriff said, "Unbelievable. You're saying you got shot *again*, this time in the *head*, and you're okay?"

"To say I'm 'okay' would be overstating it, but I'm not gonna die," Tony said, irritated to acknowledge that his scalp still burned and his ankle still ached.

"You know I'm gonna need that journal," Ballister said. "It's a key piece of evidence."

*You don't know the half of it*, Tony thought, but said, "The FBI wants it first. My guess is they're gonna classify it and bury it deeper than the Mariana Trench."

"Yeah. Hell, you're probably right."

"Anything else for now?"

"Considering what happened here, I'm sure I'll think of something. You made a mess of Mr. Slapp."

Tony could envision the sheriff looking at the body as he spoke. Tony said, "That's his name, Slapp?"

"Yeah, Jon Slapp. In town, he called himself the camp director, but people who know these guys better'n I do say Slapp was the base commander."

"So he was the top dog in POVO?"

"No, it don't mean that. Slapp reported to somebody somewhere else. Rumors are the big boss is in Chicago, but who knows?"

"Chicago would make sense, since that's where Deputy Jebron first bumped into these guys."

"Not my worry," Ballister said. "I got enough to keep me busy here, trying to be sure you didn't commit first-degree murder when you killed this guy."

"I swear I didn't, sheriff. When you see the crease he left in my scalp, you'll believe me."

Darcy interjected, loud enough for the sheriff to hear, "I have a nice burn on my neck where that asshat's hot gun barrel jabbed me. Trust me, I didn't do that on purpose."

"Okay, okay," the sheriff said. "I'm convinced. You're innocent, and the bastard had to die. To be honest, I can't say I'm sorry."

"Me, neither," Tony and Darcy said in unison.

Seconds after hanging up, Tony's phone chimed again. It was Sheriff George Mackey. Tony didn't even get a chance to offer a greeting. Mackey barked, "Is it true? There's a Russian missile in my county? Tabors called me. She didn't know much. Is it true? Any idea where?"

Tony waited for the barrage to subside. He could understand the sheriff's agitation because he shared it.

He said, "Sheriff, I honestly don't know. As Anna probably told you, an undercover FBI agent wrote in his journal that Orney was one of the locations named. There's no way to know if that's what actually happened, if they ended up transporting a missile to Orney and setting it up."

"Jesus Chr…"

Tony pressed on, "Plans could have changed, and even if they didn't, we don't know exactly where they chose to do this. Was it in Orney itself, or just the vicinity? The thing's nearly forty feet long. Presumably it would have to be at least angled toward the sky, if not completely vertical. There can't be many buildings in the entire county that could accommodate that."

"You're right. Good point." He was gone.

Tony would have smiled if the threat they were facing wasn't so terrifying.

Darcy said, "We should think about that too. Maybe we'll come up with an idea of where to look that wouldn't occur to the sheriff."

"No one knows the county as well as George," Tony said, "but you're right, of course. It can't hurt to put some thought into it."

Tony's next call was to Carlotta Harrington.

"Hey, Mom."

"Tony! Is everything okay?"

Tony smiled. "We're fine. Darcy and I are on our way back from St. Louis. We thought we might stop and steal a free meal from you."

"Tonight? Well, of course, of course! I'll just have your dad run to the store."

"Please don't go to any trouble. Anything you have on hand will be fine."

"Nonsense. Don't worry. We'll do this right."

"Believe me, I'm not worried. Agent Tabors will be joining us, so set a place for her too."

"The FBI lady? What's this about? Are you sure everything's alright?"

"It's fine, really. We just agreed to meet in Iowa City because we knew you would take good care of us."

"I'm not dumb enough to believe that, but I do like hearing it. Drive carefully."

"Darcy's driving, so we're fine. See you soon."

He looked over to see Darcy grinning.

"What?"

"You didn't tell her you'd be arriving with a damaged eye socket, a bad ankle, and a bullet hole in your head."

"Yeah, that shitstorm can wait another hour or so. Can you imagine? If I'd told her, she'd have the police and the paramedics lined up in the front yard waiting for us."

"Nice to be loved," she said.

"Yeah, right," he replied, with all the sarcasm he could muster.

# Chapter 30

Thursday, January 8, Offutt Air Force Base, Bellevue, Nebraska

Colonel Tar Pit Jackson picked up his phone on the first ring. "What makes you think I'm still speaking to you?"

"You are. Trust me," said Frat Harken from his desk at Langley. He hadn't been home since Tuesday, but all the weariness had left him when he'd received the call from the FBI with the details from Agent Janssen's undercover efforts. To Jackson, he said, "I have the intel you need to save us, or at least to have a shot."

"I'm listening. What do you got?"

Harken described the POVO plans Agent Janssen had outlined in his journal.

"Five sites? Shit. Speaking hypothetically, of course, I only have four prototype launcher platforms."

"I know. We'll have to find one or more of these birds before they're set up and ready to launch."

"My hypothetical MLRS are already on the roads," Jackson said, pronouncing it "Millers," the military slang for Multiple Launch Rocket System. "They're headed for four monitoring areas, a couple of which were suggested by you, I believe. Now you're gonna tell me our five tangos are in different places."

"Cry me a river," Harken said, "but do it later. Here's where you need to be: Lincoln, Nebraska; Sioux Falls, South Dakota; Rochester, Minnesota; Manhattan, Kansas; and Orney, Iowa."

"Slow down…"

"Don't bother. I've already sent the list to you on JWICS," Harken said, referring the secure intranet service used by the military.

"Hang on." A moment later the colonel said, "I don't know where this town in Iowa is, but Rochester's almost certainly the farthest from us. That's the obvious place to cut to get the list from five to four."

"I agree," Harken said. "We'll just have to make sure those bastards are tits-up before it's too late."

"Roger that. We'll have our PADS onsite in Nebraska, Kansas, and South Dakota by morning, hypothetically speaking, of course."

Harken was growing tired of the language game, but said, "That's three."

"I can count," the colonel said, his irritation returning. "We have one platform in Iowa already. We sent it east on I-80. Unfortunately, the mobile carrier lost a bearing in the rear axle. If this prototype actually existed, it would be parked in a weigh station waiting for parts to arrive. Then it would get its ass in gear as fast as possible."

Harken knew better than to make an issue of it. In a military operation, shit happened. All you could do was respond, adapt, and move on.

The colonel added, "On a serious note, I appreciate the intel. Our odds are still as small as your dick, but there's at least that tiny chance we'll get one if they launch."

"If they launch, you better get more than one. Tell these guys…"

"We sent our best people," Jackson said. "We included an officer in each crew so there would be no hesitation in making the call. They've all been instructed to fire instantly at the detection of a launch. In other words, I've done everything possible to give us that chance. Still…"

The colonel's voice trailed off, and Harken said, "Terry, I know you have. Thank you. And rest assured, we've got a shitload of people working on this from the other end. We may find and terminate these things before the go-code even gets issued."

"Your lips to God's ears," Jackson said.

# Chapter 31

Thursday, January 8, Chicago, Illinois

Arvin Jugg took a large swallow of vodka and tonic and hit the send button. He knew it was risky to drink before talking to his superiors, but he couldn't resist. He had been a mental train wreck all day, unable to sit still or concentrate. His jaw hurt from being clenched tightly for hours, and his fingernails were chewed to the point his fingertips were bleeding.

This operation was his from start to finish. He conceived it; he convinced the Russian security service, the Federal'naya Sluzhba Bezopasnosti or FSB, in Moscow to support it; and he later had the same success with leaders in the Kremlin. Once approved, he prepared and trained, adopted an American identity as Arvin Jugg, and moved to the US. He worked hard and actually made it all happen. Now it was done—all except the actual attack.

*If this works, my name will be immortalized in the Motherland as the man who singlehandedly brought America to its knees. If it fails, I will be the one to take the blame.* If he failed, he had no doubt that no one in the Kremlin nor the FSB would admit to even knowing who he was. *I'm the one driving the bus. If it goes over a cliff, I'll be the first to die.*

It was evening in Chicago, which meant it was just 6 a.m. in Moscow. Jugg had asked for the early meeting. He wanted to have this conversation when the men on the other end were sober, and at an hour that made it difficult to create excuses to be absent.

"Your connection is complete," an automated voice said.

"Speak," came the command from the conference room in the Kremlin. The man spoke Russian, and it sounded as if he were standing next to him. Jugg marveled at the special SATCOM telephone with encryption software. Who needed codebooks and spycraft when you could speak directly and confidentially to Moscow whenever you wanted?

"Use no names or ranks," came the additional command. "You may refer to me as Number Eight."

Jugg smiled wryly, knowing it must pain the leader of the FSB not to refer to himself as Number One. Another sign of how desperately the FSB and political leaders wanted to distance themselves from this operation.

*They think I'm going to fail,* Jugg mused. *They want deniability. When I succeed, they'll be killing each other in their mistresses' beds to get the credit for creating and supporting this.*

Aloud, he said, "Thank you, Number Eight. Our business today should be short. While the operation is complex, the potential results are enormous. The decision to move forward is easy."

"We will be the judge of that. Report on your status."

"Thank you, sir. In summary, more than fifty loyal men and women have been trained, indoctrinated, and deployed. They are convinced of the facts they have been told and will execute the plan without hesitation."

"Facts such as what?" a second voice in the room in Moscow asked.

Jugg sighed. He had hoped to avoid delving into details. He resisted the urge to tell the man to stop wasting time. Instead, he said, "The members of POVO believe they are loyal Americans, fighting to restore the country to an ideal they call the 'New Society.' These are people who are angry and resentful by nature. They blame their problems on the government, immigrants, and people of other colors and religions. Somehow, they have convinced themselves that America is supposed to be a nation comprised only of people who are white and Christian, even though that has never been true. We have encouraged these beliefs. We have stoked the fires of resentment and hate and have nurtured their misguided dreams. We have used these techniques to build an operational force of carefully-selected and highly-trained men and women who are ready to act."

Jugg heard a voice for a moment, perhaps attempting to interject a follow-up question, but he ignored it and forged ahead. "Secondly, the POVO members have been told the missiles are programmed to explode near the planes, but not to destroy them. They believe this operation is a demonstration of POVO power that will frighten the leaders in Washington and force them to take POVO seriously as it makes demands. I believe this ruse is essential to our success. Even the most ardent anti-government extremist might hesitate to fire a missile if he believed it was going to kill hundreds of innocent people."

Number Eight, who obviously was the general in charge of the FSB, said, "Proceed with your report."

"Five missiles have been prepared and transported to five separate locations. The POVO members are completing final assembly and fueling. Two of the missiles are ready and operational. The other three will be ready in two days."

"How do you know you will have appropriate targets? What about weather and other delays? Are you not at risk of being caught?"

Jugg's jaw clenched again as he wondered if any of the fat dimwits around that table could remember the previous briefings about this. He tried to hide his snarl as he said, "Of course there is risk, but it is minimal. Many precautions have been taken and plans carefully devised to prevent detection. Also, remember, these are Americans working in areas familiar to them. The normal risks, such as citizens wondering about the activities of outsiders, are not factors in this operation."

"Yes, yes," another voice said. "That was a key part of this plan, and I don't mind acknowledging, a brilliant one."

"Thank you, sir," Jugg said, genuinely glad to hear at least one word of praise.

The previous voice said with a note of irritation, "I believe I asked you about targets."

"Yes, sir. That is not a problem. More than two thousand commercial airliners fly over the chosen locations every day. These are large jets which fly far above the weather. They come from every part of North America. In short, a major storm would have to impact airports in a radius of five hundred kilometers to eliminate all potential targets. No storm of that magnitude has ever existed. We will have targets."

"What about your breach?"

Jugg was stunned that a general in Moscow had learned about a lone newspaper reporter entering the camp Monday night and escaping. Jugg had only known about it for a couple of days. Believing it of no consequence, he had not reported it. Then the point of the general's question dawned on him.

He calmly said, "I assume you are referring to the FBI mole who infiltrated our training camp. As I reported, the agent was caught and eliminated before any critical information was reported to his handlers. It is a non-issue."

"I would not call an FBI agent in your midst a non-issue," a third voice said.

The first voice, the general, said, "Enough about that. It was a mistake. It was unfortunate. It was dealt with quickly and completely. We will move on."

Jugg bit back a laugh. *So much for being Number Eight.*

"I have one final question," the general said. "As you look seriously at every aspect of this operation, how do you assess your chances of success?"

Jugg knew it was unwise to say how certain he was that every missile would bring down a target, and that America would be crippled within hours, and perhaps destroyed within days. Instead, he said, "With all due respect, gentlemen, I have spent considerable time analyzing and evaluating this very question. I am convinced that if you give this final approval, we have a seventy-five percent chance of bringing down five American planes on Saturday, and a ninety percent chance of bringing down four. And best of all, there is no chance of anyone ever knowing that Russia was a part of it. America will soon be at war with itself."

He could hear rustling sounds over the phone. He couldn't be sure if the FSB and Kremlin leaders were expressing skepticism or excitement; perhaps a mix of both.

Jugg pressed on. "Do I have your permission to proceed?"

He heard the general say, "Any other comments or questions before we answer?" His tone did not invite a response, and there was none.

Still speaking to his colleagues, the general said, "When you decide the final question, consider not only what our comrade has told us about his readiness; consider what success will mean. The fall of America will be a glorious thing for the Motherland, but it undoubtedly will cause a global recession for a period of time. We may, and probably will, have to deal with other unforeseen consequences. In the end, we will stand tall as the new world leader on every front, but the process will carry a measure of pain. We agreed at the outset that the pain was worth the final success—a world free of an enemy that has stalked us for a hundred years. Now that the end is in sight, I still believe this to be true, but I encourage you to decide your position independent of mine. If we move forward, we do so as one body, fully committed to Russia's future glory and the rebuilding of the Soviet state."

Jugg knew the general's words were utter bullshit. He had just told the group his own decision, which was the equivalent of daring anyone in the room to disagree.

"I call the question," a voice in the room said.

After a short pause, the general said, "It is decided. You may proceed." He added, "Добре ходити и добр вы путь буде," an ancient Russian expression wishing him success: "Walk well, and your path will be good."

"I am honored to serve and pledge myself to Russia's glory," Jugg said, and ended the call.

# Chapter 32

Thursday, January 8, Johnson County, Iowa

As the pickup approached Iowa City on US Highway 218, Tony was furiously snapping pictures of the journal's pages. He wasn't surprised that Darcy hadn't even raised an eyebrow. She was smart enough to know that Tabors would seize the journal immediately upon meeting them, and they would never see it again.

Tony had no qualms about photographing the pages. He was causing no damage, and the document was not classified. So far, no one had told him he couldn't make copies, and perhaps most importantly, he and Darcy had been the ones to find it. Without Darcy, it would have stayed in the hollow tree trunk until it was too late.

*Not to mention my head may never stop throbbing,* Tony thought. *A bullet wound should entitle a guy to a little extra information.*

He finished his task and returned the journal to the plastic bag. He returned to typing on his phone.

"What now?" Darcy asked.

"I'm sending the pictures in batches of ten pages each to my email at the *Crier*," he said. "Tabors is smart, and she knows me. She might guess I've taken the photos, which means she might confiscate my phone."

"Considering the nature of this stuff, and the government's history of keeping terrorist activities secret, they may come and confiscate the newspaper's computers too."

"I doubt it, but it's possible. Where else can I send them?"

"How about to me?"

"Too obvious. Besides, I don't want to get you into trouble, or create a giant hassle for you if they do start locking up accounts. Give me a minute." Tony continued typing and then said, "Done. They're all sent to the *Crier*. Now, let's think…"

"Lawrence Pike," Darcy said, naming an attorney in Orney who had represented Tony in the past. "He'll have attorney-client privilege. Seems like it would be harder for them to get the images back from him."

Tony smiled. "Do you ever tire of being so damn smart?" He composed an email to Pike, then followed it with a series of emails with photos attached. When finished, he picked up Slapp's phone and opened the Recent Calls list. He used his own phone to take a picture of the numbers on the screen, then scrolled down for the next set of calls. He took another picture, then repeated the procedure twice more.

"You could take screen shots with Slapp's phone and email them to yourself," Darcy pointed out.

"I could, but that would leave evidence on Slapp's phone that I'd done it. These might be poorer images, but this way, my activities are kept secret." He paused and said, "At least I hope they are. Who knows what the feds can learn from the computers in these things?"

Tony began reviewing emails. He took a couple more pictures, but knowing he was running out of time, he moved on to the texts.

***

Ten minutes later, they turned into the driveway of Tony's parents' home. They saw Tabors's Cadillac SUV parked on the street in the dark shadow between streetlights, with the motor running. She shut off the engine and climbed out of her vehicle at the same moment they did.

"Agent Tabors, glad to see you made it. You could've waited inside."

Tabors smiled. "Your mother's been out here a half-dozen times to make the same point. When I declined, she kept me supplied with coffee and snacks, if you can call an apple torte with ice cream a snack."

Tony returned the smile and gestured toward the house.

Tabors said, "Not yet. First I want to say thank you again. I can't mention in front of your parents what you've done to help us. You've given us a chance to stop this horror show before it happens."

"Just…"

Tabors cut him off with a raised hand and continued. "Secondly, I need the journal. Right now."

"Of course." Tony reached into his coat pocket, pulled out the bag, and handed it over.

"And I have to ask, do I need to take your phone?"

"You're asking if I copied the book?"

"Not really asking," Tabors said, "since I have no doubt in my mind that you did."

"You know me well, Agent Tabors. You're right. I did. However, there's no point in taking my phone. I've already emailed the pictures to a couple of locations where they're safe."

"You did what?" the agent barked. "Don't you know what you're saying? Do you *want* me to arrest you for obstruction, for tampering with evidence, for sharing state secrets, and a dozen other crimes I can think of?"

"Bullshit," Tony said. "I haven't obstructed anything, and good luck convincing a jury that I tampered with something that I didn't damage and voluntarily turned over to you immediately. You wouldn't even know about this journal if we hadn't found it and brought it to you."

The agent's red face could be seen in the glow from the streetlight a block away. She started to speak, but this time, Tony interrupted. "Agent Tabors, you know me well enough to be certain I won't publish anything from that journal until this is over. I would never do anything to jeopardize an investigation of this magnitude, nor hinder your efforts to catch these cretins and put an end to this nightmare. So please, let's go inside and get back to work. When we're done, you're gonna win a medal or two, and I'm gonna have the story of the century."

"If we stop them," the agent hissed. She turned and started up the walk.

"One other thing."

The agent stopped but didn't turn.

"I also have the camp commander's phone."

"You *what?*" the agent spun to face him.

Tony held out the phone, and Tabors's hand shot out to snatch it.

"Careful; it's unlocked. Leave it in camera mode, and it should stay that way."

"This is unbelievable," the agent muttered as she minimized the camera function and began looking at Slapp's emails. Without looking up, she asked, "So you used a corpse to open this, and then you looked through it?"

"Of course," Tony smiled. "That's my job."

Tabors looked up. "Your job." She nearly spat out the words. "You think it's your job to tamper with a body at a crime scene, to steal evidence, to invade someone's privacy, to illegally access his information, and to use it for your own purposes?"

"When you say it like that, it sounds so harsh."

"Dammit, Harrington, I'm serious! What's wrong with you? I swear, I should put you in handcuffs right now. And don't look so amused, Ms. Gillson. You could easily be charged as an accomplice in all this."

Tony's smile disappeared, and he said, "You want to talk seriously, let me tell you what's serious. A group of people plotting to destroy our country is serious. Finding and using every possible clue is serious. Keeping the damn camp commander's phone out of an evidence locker and getting it to the FBI within hours of recovering it is serious. So get off your damn pedestal, stop making threats, and come inside. Maybe we'll actually make some progress, not to mention getting out of the cold and enjoying a home-cooked meal for the first time in days."

Tabors didn't respond except to glare at him. After a few seconds, she turned and resumed her walk to the house. Tony and Darcy followed close behind.

***

At 8 p.m., Tony, Darcy, Anna Tabors, and Rich Davis were gathered in the study at Tony's boyhood home. His father, Charles Harrington, a.k.a. C.A. Harker, used the study primarily as an office and writing room. Charles had turned out a dozen novels and screenplays in the fourteen years since moving to Iowa City from Chicago, all while teaching and directing the writing program at the University of Iowa.

Tonight, the room's usual occupant was excluded from the conversation. Rich Davis had driven over from Orney to join them at the request of Tabors.

In the ninety minutes since they had arrived, they had survived Carlotta Harrington's anguish over Tony's injuries, anger over not being told, fears that he and Darcy were in some kind of peril, and determination to ignore it all and treat her guests to a great meal. Shrimp and pasta in a wine sauce with steamed broccoli and tortellini soup, topped off with a choice of three desserts, had not disappointed.

To Carlotta's dismay, they had eaten quickly, expressed their thanks and apologies, and retreated to the study.

Tabors had not joined them in the dining room. She had taken her meal to the study, sitting at Charles's desk and stealing bites between phone calls, texts, and emails. Despite her anger, she had known Tony was right. Slapp's phone almost certainly would provide important intelligence for the anti-terrorism team. She had furiously searched its contents, looking for communications between POVO members that would aid in their efforts to find and stop them. She had found hundreds of emails and texts, mostly encrypted, and nearly as many records of phone calls.

Now they were faced with a classic case of a poverty of riches. There was so much information on the phone, it was impossible to know where to begin. It would take weeks just to decode, read, and analyze what was there.

Tabors suddenly set her jaw, closed her eyes, and pushed Slapp's phone away from her, across the desk. She placed her elbows on its polished surface and dropped her head into her hands. "I could scream. I know what we need is there, but these assholes communicated constantly. I've sent almost a hundred copies of messages to the task force, but who knows whether they include addresses for places where we can disarm missiles or orders for shaving cream for the camp?"

"And the phone numbers?" Tony asked, picking the phone up off the desk and beginning to scroll through it.

"It's a huge list from dozens of area codes. If he was coordinating a major operation in addition to operating a training camp, it makes sense that he was on his phone all day. But again, we don't know which calls are relevant, or if they're even calling registered phones. They could be using burners. I've sent a list of numbers to the task force, and I'm sure they're tracing them, but it will take time."

Almost as if speaking to himself, Tony said, "Ballister mentioned a rumor going around that Slapp reported to a big boss in Chicago. I see five calls in the past three weeks to the 872 area code."

Tabors sat up straight. "That's the relatively new code added for Chicago."

"Right," Tony said.

As he spoke, the phone in his hand vibrated.

"I'll be damned," he said, holding the phone out for Tabors to see. "Speak of the devil."

"Seriously?"

Darcy moved her chair closer to look, and Tabors and Davis got up and walked over to where he sat.

"It's a text, but it's in code."

He moved the phone in an arc so everyone could see the screen. It said: *Xpp yprxf?*

"What do I do? If this is the boss in Chicago, it could be a mistake to not respond."

"Let me think," Tabors said. Everyone looked at her.

Darcy was the last to look up. She said, "The message is asking 'All Clear?'"

Three faces all turned, open-mouthed, to stare at her.

She said, "I assume it's a simple letter-substitution code, which isn't much of a stretch considering many of their members are volunteers and part timers. They probably don't use anything too sophisticated. Even if they use a method like the daily newspaper or some other source to change the encryption each day, it still boils down to substituting one letter for another."

"And you deciphered this from eight letters how?" Tabors asked.

The first word probably is 'all.' How many three-letter words can you name that have a single letter followed by a second letter twice? There are two common ones: 'see' and 'all.' When put in the context of Slapp being left behind to ensure nothing more happened at the camp, it makes sense his boss would want a report. If they really are close to launching the missiles, then what he really wants is reassurance there are no problems. Hence a message asking if everything is okay. If the first word is all, then the second letter of the second word is an L and fourth letter is an A. That fits with the word clear. 'All clear?' makes sense and it fits. No guarantees, but I'll bet that's it."

Once again Tony found himself shaking his head in wonder at the woman he loved. He was jerked out of his reverie when Tabors said, "So how do we respond? Using the same code?"

Tony said, "Darcy's right, I'm sure, but we can't compose a message since we've only deciphered five letters of the code. We also don't know if they use a different key for messages going to and from the boss. I say we just send the emoji for 'thumbs up,' and leave it at that. It's universal, and even if it violates POVO protocol, the big boss or whoever this is, might overlook it. If he's getting the reassurance he wants, maybe he'll want it to be true."

"Do it," Tabors said, and Tony typed and sent the quick response.

Before he was done, Tabors was talking to someone on the task force, telling them their new top priority was a location for the phone that had just texted Slapp and the name associated with it. When she was finished, she turned to Darcy.

"Remarkable work. Truly fantastic. I have no doubt our code-breakers would have reached the same conclusion quickly, but once again, the fact you pulled that out of your ear allowed us to respond to the text immediately. That might have bought us the time we need."

"Let's hope it did," Darcy said, shifting in her seat and looking at the floor.

Tabors stood and walked out from behind the desk. "I'm sorry, but I need to get back to Chicago. I can't search for missiles in five different regions, so I'm going to focus on catching and removing the head of this snake. I suggest you three get back to Orney and help Sheriff Mackey find and eliminate any threat that made its way there."

The other three rose from their seats. Tony said, "Darcy, if you don't mind, hitch a ride back with Rich."

"Tony..." Darcy and Tabors spoke almost in unison.

Tony said, "Relax. My issue is that I have to return a pickup truck to a rental agency in Chicago and retrieve my Jeep. On top of that, it may take me a while to pry myself loose from my mother. You all get moving, and I'll join you as fast as I can."

Davis and Tabors nodded and pulled on their coats.

Tabors's phone buzzed. She returned to the desk and set the device on top. She answered it and put it on speaker.

"Anna Tabors."

"Agent Tabors, this is Frat Harken. I'm deputy director for counterterrorism at the CIA in Langley. Can you talk?"

"Yes. I'm in Iowa with the people who discovered the missiles at the POVO camp, found our agent's journal, and brought us Jon Slapp's cell phone. I think you can speak freely in front of them."

After a long pause, Harken said, "Very well. I'm leading the joint task force that's charged with finding and eliminating this threat. The phone number you sent us belongs to a man in Chicago named Arvin Jugg. I need you and your colleagues in the FBI's Chicago office to help us find and capture him."

"Understood. What more do you have for us?"

"I've just texted you his picture. You'll see he looks like an all-American boy. We've pulled some basic facts about him from our data sources. He appears to be as wholesome as he looks. Single, a good job selling imported medical devices to hospitals and clinics, a member of the Knights of Columbus, season tickets to the Chicago Bears. No known ties to extremist groups and no visible anti-government sentiments. Not even a registered gun."

"Doesn't sound like our man."

"You'd think that, wouldn't you." It wasn't a question.

"Sir?"

Harken said, "He has this very clean-cut, very visible life going back about five years. Before that, there's almost nothing. The proper official record's in all the right places, but nothing in any of the other usual spots."

Tony stared in awe at Tabors's phone. Harken had pulled all this information about Jugg in perhaps three minutes. The abilities of the CIA were exhilarating and terrifying at the same time.

When Tabors spoke, Tony's awe instantly changed to shock.

She said, "A spy."

"Very likely," Harken said. "It's a good cover, but not one of those planted deeply and in the US for life."

"In other words, an operative here for one specific purpose. One single horrifying mission."

"Can't be sure, but I'd bet my pension on it."

"A spy from where?" Tony sputtered.

"No way to know. We have enemies in lots of places. The simplest answer is Russia, just based on the fact the weapons came from there and Jugg doesn't look Asian or Middle-Eastern. But it's still just a guess. At this stage, it doesn't matter. I don't care if he's from Venus. You must grab this bastard. And do it in a way that's private and quick. He can't have a chance to signal an alarm or, God forbid, a go-code."

"Understood. Do you have a location on the phone?"

Harken said he did, and gave them the address.

All four people in Iowa gasped.

"What?" Harken demanded.

"The address," Tabors said. "It's the building where Deputy Tim Jebron was killed. His death was what triggered the…"

"Yes, I've been briefed," Harken said. "It makes sense, I suppose. Tell your friends in Iowa I'm sorry for their loss, but Deputy Jebron's death put us on the trail of this nightmare. Let's make sure he didn't die for nothing."

"Understood, sir," Tabors said. "I'm leaving now."

Tabors and Davis resumed buttoning their coats and headed for the door.

Tony said, "Anna, would you share Jugg's picture with us?"

"I'm not sure I can."

"Think about it," Tony said, displaying more patience than he felt. "You need to find this guy fast. You can't put his mug shot in the media, so the more insiders who have it, the better your chances."

"But you're going to be in Iowa," the agent said.

"After I get my car, yes, but you never know. It can't hurt for us to have it, and maybe it will help."

Tabors sighed, pulled out her phone, and forwarded the picture that Harken had sent her. She said, "This better not show up in the *Crier* until after this prick is chained inside a cell at Gitmo."

Tony smiled and saluted as Tabors and Davis went out the door. Before Darcy could follow, Tony reached out and pulled her up against him.

"You are extraordinary beyond words," he said.

"What can I say?" she smiled. "I do the Cryptoquote in the newspaper every day. Spotting the word 'all' is a well-ingrained trick."

"That does not diminish your intelligence, nor your resourcefulness, nor your humanity, nor the magnificent curves pressed against me right now."

She smiled and looked up at him. "You know you're a dick, right?"

"Alas, 'tis so. But a dick who loves you so much it hurts."

She kissed him. "Keep hurting, newsboy, and hurry home."

# Chapter 33

Friday, January 9, Orney, Iowa
One Day to Wheels-Up, Flight 244

Doug Tenney was eating a bagel and reading the morning paper when his phone rang. It was Ben Smalley.

"Good morning."

"Good morning. You up?" Smalley asked.

"Of course. I assume my most excellent boss has noticed I've been coming to work early every day to cover for my former friend who's disappeared."

"Yes, I have," Smalley said. "No joke, Doug, I really appreciate everything you've been doing. What's on your plate for today?"

"The usual stack of stuff, plus I went to Fishbone's funeral yesterday. I talked to people about him. Thought I'd write a short feature. He was a pretty well-known figure around town. Rather 'colorful,' if you know what I mean."

"Good idea. I should have thought of it myself."

"Bottom line is, I've got no meetings or scheduled commitments if there's something you want me to do."

"Yeah, well, it's probably a waste of time, but I was actually thinking about Fishbone this morning. The timing of his death makes me uneasy."

"Not sure I follow."

"Like I said, it's probably nothing, but he calls me one day, excited out of his mind that he's actually found something on his farm, and then a couple of days later, he's found dead."

Doug sat up in his chair. "You sayin' maybe it wasn't an accident?"

"No, well, I don't know. Hell, it probably was an accident. The old coot told me he was sleeping with his shotgun. Still, it nags at me."

"So what do you want me to do?"

"I want you to bundle up in your warmest gear and go take a look around his farm. There must be something there that set him off. It's probably just some trash that blew in from a neighbor's farm, or maybe, if you're lucky, a meteorite. I don't know. Just have a look around. At the very least, you'll learn more about him. Maybe something to help with your feature piece."

"Happy to do it," Doug said, thinking he was anything but happy to be asked to tramp around in the snow for several hours in search of a farmer's trash. "You okay if I go this afternoon, after I get my routine stuff filed?"

"Sure, that makes sense. And thanks. I appreciate it. Keep me posted."

The call ended, and Doug thought, *Yeah, you'll be the first to know if it's a cardboard box or a rusty seed corn sign.*

***

## Friday, January 9, Chicago, Illinois

Tony sat in the parking lot of a Hilton Garden Inn on the west side of Chicago, waiting for the pickup to warm up. His head still throbbed with every heartbeat, and he was in no mood to scrape frost off the windshield. He took advantage of the downtime to scroll through the photographs he had taken the day before of texts and emails on Jugg's phone. He picked a relatively long and recent text and attempted to decipher it. If Darcy was right about it being a simple letter substitution, he should be able to figure it out. After six or seven minutes, he gave up, put the truck in gear, and headed for the rental car agency.

He had arrived in Chicago after 1 a.m. He had hated taking the time to sleep, but had known he had no choice. He had taken two of the pain pills supplied by the hospital in Missouri, washed them down with a Diet Dr. Pepper, and fallen asleep in minutes.

It was now nearly 9 a.m., and he was anxious to get moving. The problem was, he was utterly dumbfounded regarding which way to go. He desperately wanted to drive over to the apartment building in the South Loop and find Arvin Jugg before he could launch Armageddon. The problem was, he also desperately wanted to get back to Iowa, find the missile hidden in or near Orney, and destroy it before it could murder several hundred innocent people.

Perhaps most frustrating of all was his knowledge that he wasn't really needed in either place. The FBI would be all over Jugg by now, and Sheriff Mackey and his deputies had a far better chance of finding a weapon hidden in Quincy County than Tony could ever hope to have. Ben's words echoed in his ears: *You're not a cop. It's not your job to find the bad guys or to administer justice. Your job is to learn the facts and report them to the public.*

"So where do I want to stand to watch other people save the

day?" Tony muttered to himself. "Chicago or Orney?"

He decided he needed more information. As he drove to the rental agency to retrieve his Jeep, he opened his phone and told Siri to make a call.

"Good morning," Agent Tabors said, sounding like it was anything but good.

"Was he home? Did you get him?"

"No, and no. And we're still off the record."

"Of course. So what happened?"

"Nothing happened." The agent's voice was strained. She was clearly exhausted, frustrated, and a little angry. "We surrounded the building, covertly, of course. Then a team went in posed as installers for the new security system. When Jugg didn't answer his door, they breached it. He was gone. Clothes, personal items, computer, all gone. He's either finished in Chicago, or our response to his text last night tipped him off. They probably had a code word to indicate everything was okay."

"Well, shit," Tony said. "Sorry, excuse the language."

"Oh, I've been screaming much worse for the past ninety minutes."

"I suppose his phone's off the grid?"

"Yes. No sign of it. We've got people covering the airports, train stations, and even the buses, but we can't cover every car leaving the city. There are ten thousand ways out of here."

Tony had a thought. He said, "You have someone monitoring Benning's phone?"

"As a matter of routine—you didn't hear that from me—but why do you ask?"

"Put yourself in Jugg's shoes. If you're right, if he's running because he knows Slapp is down, he's gonna be anxious to talk to someone who can reassure him that the plan isn't compromised, that everyone else is moving forward. You or Rich or someone told me that Benning is an officer in POVO. If he gets a call or text from a new number today, something you haven't seen before, that could be Jugg calling from a new phone."

"Good thinking. I should have thought of it. I'll get ahold of Harken and make sure someone's on it. I wouldn't be surprised if the CIA is as smart as you are."

"Very funny," Tony said flatly. "Call me if anything happens. I'm headed home."

Tony paid the bill for the pickup, transferred his gear into his Jeep, and drove across the street to a Dunkin' Donuts for "breakfast." He retrieved a bag with four chocolate-chocolate donuts from the drive-up window, just as his phone chirped. To his surprise, it was Tabors.

"Didn't expect to hear…"

She cut him off. "Where are you?"

"West side of the city, at a donut shop. Why?"

"You were driving a Chevy truck. Did you rent from Avis?"

"Yes…" Tony was baffled.

"Their shop off I-290 in Oak Park?"

"Yes. What's this about?"

"He's there. Jugg. At least it might be him. An unknown phone called both Benning and a guy named Fitzgerald, the number two at the camp, early this morning. That phone is at the Avis center."

Tony already had his Jeep in gear and was headed back toward Avis.

"God in Heaven," Tabors said. "I hate involving you in this, but you're right there. We can't let him get away before we get people over there. He could toss the new phone at any moment. So I need you to try to spot him. *Just* spot him, understand? Stay out of sight. If he's moving, follow him. Do *not* approach him or attempt to apprehend him. If he's what we suspect, he'll be well-trained and well-armed."

"I understand," Tony said, pulling the Jeep into a drug store parking lot near the Avis lot. He thought he was less likely to be spotted if he didn't drive into the rental car place directly. It was a relatively small location, which was good for spotting suspects but bad for staying out of sight.

Tony grabbed his laptop shoulder bag from the rear of the Jeep and slung it over his shoulder. He assumed he would look more like a traveler if he wasn't empty-handed. He pulled a stocking cap from the pocket of his parka and pulled it down to his eyebrows. He then reached into the storage compartment at the rear of the SUV, pulled out a vinyl case, and removed his Walther automatic. He pushed the gun into the now empty coat pocket.

After closing and locking the Jeep, he headed for the Avis building. When he was close enough to see through the glass doors, he stopped in his tracks and turned away.

*I'll be damned. That's him.*

Tony began walking slowly through the car lot, trying to appear as though he was a renter looking for the correct car. One nice thing about a January day in Chicago—no one was casually hanging around outside. It was unlikely anyone would observe him wandering around or, worse yet, offer to help.

A couple of minutes later, Arvin Jugg hurried past him, pulling a large suitcase. He didn't even turn to glance in his direction. As Jugg walked between two cars, he pushed a button on a key fob and unlocked a Chevy sedan on his right. He collapsed thc handle on the suitcase and hoisted it into the back seat. He followed it with the satchel hanging from his shoulder. Then he stood, closed the back door, and opened the front.

Moving as silently as he could, Tony quickly closed the gap between them. When he was close enough, and before Jugg could lower himself into the driver's seat, Tony nearly shouted, "Arvin!"

Jugg jumped, then spun, in a blur of motion, but Tony was ready.

Almost simultaneously, he thrust upward with his knee, driving it into Jugg's groin. The POVO leader emitted a horrible sound and doubled over. Tony instantly brought the butt of the Walther crashing down into the back of Jugg's skull.

Jugg collapsed at Tony's feet.

Tony casually looked around, then reached down and lifted Jugg into the car and pushed him over into the passenger seat. He retrieved the key fob from the ground and placed it in the cup holder, climbed into the driver's seat, started the car, and drove out of the lot.

"Did you spot him? Are you safe?" Tabors barked as soon as she answered her phone.

"I only have one question," Tony said, smiling broadly. "Where would you like him delivered?"

***

To say that FBI Special Agent Anna Tabors stormed into the interview room would have been an understatement. Tony was convinced the anger spewing from the agent could have uprooted trees if released in the wild. The agent slammed the door behind her, dropped her shoulder bag onto the floor, and collapsed into the chair on the opposite side of the small metal table from where Tony sat.

They were back in the FBI Field Office in Chicago. An hour before, Jugg had been whisked away by armed guards and paramedics, his rental car had been returned to Avis, and Tony had been locked in the back of a police cruiser and brought here. Two FBI agents who could have moonlighted for the WWE had brought Tony to this barren room with a locked door.

Now Tabors sat staring at him, red-faced. She finally hissed, "You dumb son of a bitch. What were you thinking?"

"I..."

"Shut up! It was a rhetorical question. You injured a key suspect. You ignored my specific instructions. You put yourself in deadly peril unnecessarily."

"I…"

"Not to mention, without any authority, you assaulted a man who was committing no crime."

"Anna…"

"You will address me as Special Agent Tabors."

"Okay Agent Tabors, aren't you getting tired of these conversations?"

"I sure as hell am. I'm getting tired of making lists of all the crimes you commit because you have some uncontrollable death wish."

"What I mean is, don't you get tired of throwing these accusations at me when you know they're BS? What I did was approach a man who was wanted by the FBI and initiate a citizen's arrest. When he resisted and attempted to assault me, I defended myself, subduing the suspect. I then called you and immediately turned him over to the authorities. You should…"

"Don't you *dare* say we should be thanking you. If you want our thanks, you'll start by doing what you're told. I've already lost one friend to these POVO assholes. I do not want to lose another one."

This comment caused Tony to squirm for the first time. He hadn't considered that Tabors might actually be concerned for him personally.

"I'm sorry if I caused you any anxiety," Tony said. "I know you have enough to worry about already. But I swear I was never at any risk."

Tabors shook her head, reached down to her bag on the floor, and pulled out a plastic bag. It made a loud thump when she dropped it on the table in front of him.

"Do you know what that is?" the agent asked.

Tony could see it was a chrome-plated revolver. He didn't speak.

"That's a Ruger Super Redhawk 454. It's called the Casull. It's one of the most powerful handguns sold commercially. People have used the Casull to shoot big game. This one was in Jugg's pocket. If he had used it, you'd be lying back in that parking lot with a hole in you the size of a softball."

Tony swallowed and looked away from the gun. "Okay. You've made your point. I'm sorry. But I'm not dead, and you have Jugg, so that's good, right?"

"Yes. If he ever wakes up, that's good." Tabors stood. "Now get the hell out of here and go back to Orney. If you interfere in my investigation again, I'm going to shoot you myself."

# Chapter 34

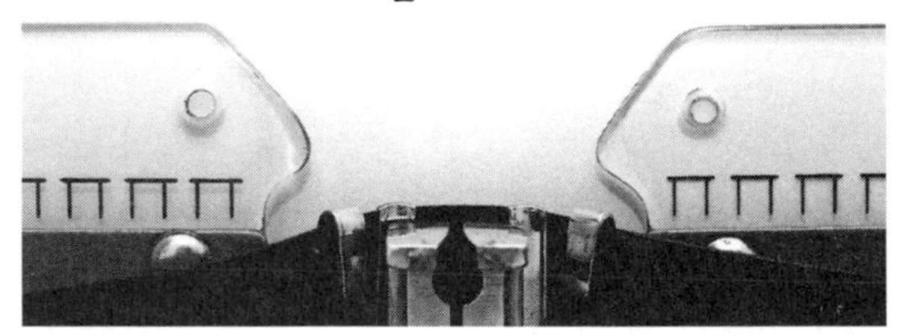

Friday, January 9, Orney, Iowa

Grady Benning looked up at the forty feet of cylindrical metal towering over him. Even though there was minimal light inside the enclosed space, the freshly painted surface seemed to sparkle.

*One more day*, he thought. *One more day*. He had waited a long time for POVO to finally make its mark in the world. He had waited even longer to exact his revenge on the shithead who had murdered his sister. Tomorrow would bring the satisfaction of achieving both—the ultimate two birds with one stone.

The world would react in shock to the power POVO would demonstrate with its missiles. Even better, George-fucking-Mackey would react in horror and shame that one of the weapons had been fired from his county, very nearly from his own backyard.

*Then, Sheriff, when you come to my place to arrest me, I can put a bullet through your brain. I may not survive, either, but I'll die knowing that you suffered while I celebrated.*

He stepped away from the Berkut to get out of the way of two technicians. The men carried portable LED lanterns. They were checking and re-checking every part of the weapon's system to ensure it had sustained no damage during shipping and setup.

Benning smiled. They would be ready right on schedule. This bird would fly right on schedule. POVO would rise to power right on schedule. And, best of all, George Mackey would die right on schedule.

***

A nasty traffic accident on the highway east of Orney held up Doug's departure for Fishbone's farm. No one was killed in the crash, but two people were injured and damage was done to three vehicles. The accident was a result of an elderly driver cutting a lane change too close and clipping the bumper of a farmer's pickup. The Oldsmobile sedan was spun sideways and struck on the passenger side. The injuries occurred when the third vehicle swerved to avoid the accident and ended up rolling over into the ditch. Two college students would now be spending the weekend in the hospital instead of at the welcome back party planned by their fraternity for the beginning of the new semester. The accident was the kind of thing a small city daily paper covered.

By the time Doug drove his RAV4 into Fishbone's lane, there was only an hour or two of daylight left. He knew he needed to check the fields first as best he could. The farm buildings could be examined after dark.

He knew from the official reports of Fishbone's death that the deputies had found a room in the home that had a chair set facing a window, with a telescope and camera equipment nearby. Curiously, they had found no film in the camera. It suddenly occurred to Doug that this could add some credence to Ben's suspicions. *Surely Fishbone would have kept film in the camera. Why else go to all that trouble? If the camera was empty, then maybe the killer took it.*

Setting that aside for a later conversation, Doug focused on what the room setup revealed. Clearly, Fishbone had spent some time watching something out the south window, so Doug headed south. He climbed over a rail fence and found himself walking through a hayfield. The alfalfa was cut short, having been harvested before the first frost the previous fall, but the snow was several inches deep, so progress was slow and tiring.

As the aches in his legs grew more pronounced, and the cold burrowed deeper into his skin, Doug asked himself over and over why he was wasting his time in an empty farm field.

Eventually, he came across a path in the snow, so walking was somewhat easier. *Probably Fishbone's tracks in and out of here. I should have looked for that to begin with*, he chastised himself. When he reached the back of the field, he could see where the old man had climbed over the fence and kept going south. Doug did likewise.

This area was overgrown with dead or dormant native plants, mostly weeds, and Doug was more grateful than ever to have a path to follow. Soon his feet felt the change from topsoil to gravel beneath the snow. The vegetation cleared, and the view opened up. Doug was standing in what appeared to be a former farmstead. Iowa was filled with these places, where farmhouses had long ago been razed or moved, and only remnants of farm buildings remained.

He could see parts of a stone foundation protruding up out of the snow on his left. It appeared to be all that was left of a large barn. To his right, at the edge of a stand of trees, was the only building still standing—a brick grain silo. Its round walls were intact, but as was true of almost every silo Doug had ever seen, the domed roof was missing.

Far more interesting than the old building were the things he could see near it. Obviously, there had been a lot of activity here recently. He could see multiple tire tracks in the snow, and boxes and wooden packing crates were piled up next to the building.

Walking over to examine the tire tracks, Doug's brow knitted into a tight, continuous line. His dad, Harold Tenney, was an over-the-road truck driver. Doug knew the tracks of an eighteen-wheeler when he saw them.

*Why would a semi be out here? Just using it for parking? Not very convenient for that. Cattle rustling? Maybe. Fishbone always said someone was stealing his cows.*

When Doug looked up, he realized he had moved far enough past the silo to see a pickup truck parked on the side opposite from where he had come. He glanced at the license plate and groaned. "Ah, shit."

He knew the fancy new truck with the four-letter plate. It belonged to Grady Benning, a man well known to frequenters of the Iron Range Tap as someone to avoid when he was drinking. To Doug, Benning appeared to be one of those people who was never happy and wanted everyone around him to share his misery. When he was filled with alcohol, Benning was outright abusive and welcomed a fight with whomever challenged him.

Doug had made it a practice to go elsewhere whenever he encountered Benning in the bar. Life was too short to spend it arguing with assholes.

Knowing that Grady's home was on the northwest side of the county, nowhere near Fishbone's, Doug again found himself baffled, and more than a little nervous. The sun had inched down below the tree line, and the long shadows created an ominous atmosphere.

"Benning?" Doug called out. "Anybody? Anyone here?"

Only a slight rustling of the breeze through the weeds responded.

Emboldened by the fact that he was alone, Doug walked over to the silo, noticing for the first time the extent of work that had been done to the far side of the structure. A vertical opening at least two stories tall had been cut into the bricks and replaced with steel panels. The lowest panel was hinged to swing out, clearly serving as an oversized door. The sheen on the panels indicated they were new, and the door featured a modern electronic keypad.

"What the hell?" Doug tried the handle, but the door wouldn't budge. The keypad appeared to be connected to a deadbolt lock.

Undaunted and determined to see inside, Doug walked a quarter of the way around the silo to where the original series of grain unloading doors also ran vertically up the side. Each door was about three feet square. They were spaced approximately two feet apart all the way to the top. Originally, a metal ladder had overlaid the doors, allowing the farmer to climb up to whichever door he or she needed to open. The ladder had long since disappeared, a victim of rust, vandalism, or an insurance agent's insistence. *Most likely a mix of all three*, Doug thought.

Two of the unloading doors were easily reached, located at the levels of his shins and his head. Unfortunately, they and two others appeared to be sealed shut with similar steel panels and brackets. However, the remaining doors—those twenty feet and more above his head—looked old. Doug wasn't surprised. If people were using the silo, it was easy to understand why they would skip the added work of replacing the doors that were too high for anyone to reach.

He was tempted to see if the keys or the code to the main door were in Benning's truck, but decided he didn't want to give the prick an excuse to give him grief. Instead, he walked around to the north side of the building, grabbed an empty packing crate, and dragged it around to a spot beneath the wooden doors. He made several more similar trips. When he was finished, he had a crude kind of staircase.

He carefully climbed the rickety structure. When he stood on the top, the fifth grain door stared him in the face. It was very old and partially rotted away. Doug tried to peer through a crack in the wood, but it was now dark enough that he couldn't see anything inside.

He took a deep breath, pushed the fingers of one hand through the crack, and grabbed the bricks beside the door with the other. One serious heave and the old door splintered. A couple more pulls and the remnants of the door were lying in pieces on the ground below him.

He reached into his pocket and pulled out his smart phone, activating the flashlight function and pointing it through the opening.

He was mystified by what he saw. It appeared that someone had built a huge smokestack, or vat, or something cylindrical, inside the silo. *Beginnings of a craft brewery? Some kind of moonshine operation? A new way to cook meth?*

His wild speculations came to an abrupt end as his light scanned down the stack and came to a rest on a pair of fins. Scanning up, he could see the cylinder tapered to a point on top.

*A rocket ship? Dear God, Fishbone wasn't crazy. Well, not completely crazy. There's a rocket sh…*

"Oh shit," Doug said aloud, rearing back and nearly dropping his phone. "Oh shit, shit, shit. It's a missile!"

His hands started to shake, and he had trouble getting his phone switched over into camera mode.

"Don't bother," a voice said. It wasn't a suggestion.

Doug looked down. On the ground below him were Grady Benning and another man. Both held very large, very ugly pistols. Both were aiming at Doug's head.

"Pick up your phone and toss it down here. Then climb down nice and slow," Benning said.

Doug nodded and did as he was told. When he reached the ground, he turned to the men, held up his hands, and said, "No need for guns, guys."

"I believe you're right," Benning said, smiling.

In his peripheral vision, Doug saw the second man move, just as his own head exploded in pain and he crumpled to the ground.

***

Darcy spent Friday in a continuous state of anxiety. Tony was in Chicago, probably trying to expose political corruption, end bullying in the schools, and fix all the potholes in the streets before deciding it was okay to come home, and oh by the way, find a damn missile hiding somewhere in Iowa. Rich Davis hadn't returned her texts asking for an update on the search. Even Doug was ignoring her.

Rather than pace and eat more pieces of coffee cake, she spent her time scouring the internet for information about POVO. She knew it was a waste of time—the FBI and CIA undoubtedly had dozens of analysts doing the same. However, she desperately needed to do *something* that might help.

She spent a few minutes debating whether to call the director of the movie she was making. She was due back in London in a few days but hadn't even made flight reservations yet. She suspected she would not be ready to leave when the time came. In the end, she decided the call could wait until she knew for certain if she would be delayed or not.

She made one trip out to a local clothing store to replace her winter coat and to mail Sheriff Ballister's coat back to him. Thinking of him caused her to wonder if Tony had kept his promise to write a full report for him quickly. She filed the thought away as a worry for another day.

However, thinking of Ballister caused her to think of the dead man back in the snowdrift at the POVO camp. Tony had seemed fine after killing the man, but she worried about how it might affect him later. He was so sensitive and so committed to not hurting others. Would a measure of PTSD show up at some point?

She found it interesting that she didn't have the same worries about herself. The man had terrified her, threatened her, kidnapped her, and even burned her—she reached up and touched the spot on her neck—all things that should give a person nightmares. All Darcy felt was a wave of relief that the man was dead. He got what he deserved. End of story. Move on. *Does that make me a brave and pragmatic modern woman, or just a cold-hearted bitch?*

She chuckled to herself just as the doorbell chimed.

Through the window pane at the side of the door, she could see it was Sheriff Mackey. She pulled open the door.

"Hi, welcome, come in," she said.

"Thank you. Sorry to show up at your door unannounced."

Mackey was wearing a Quincy County Sheriff's Department uniform, but otherwise still looked like he'd been living under a bridge. His face was covered in hair. It was obvious he hadn't shaved since Darcy had seen him at Tony's on New Year's Eve.

"Don't be silly. You're always welcome here. Let me take your coat."

"Thanks, but I can't stay. I happened to be driving past, and I decided at the last second to stop and pick your brain."

"I've been wondering all day if you were having any luck. I take it you haven't found anything."

"Right," the sheriff said grimly. "I've got all my people plus a dozen volunteers scouring the county, but so far, nothing. I thought maybe you learned something this week that could help."

"I can't imagine what."

"I don't know either. I'm probably wasting your time and mine. I just thought that maybe something you saw or heard could give us a lead. My briefing on what Agent Tabors and the CIA have pieced together was pretty thorough, but I'm sure they didn't take the time to tell me everything."

"Makes sense," Darcy said, "but if I have to do some thinking, then I insist we do it in the kitchen over beverages and coffee cake. I just made a fresh pot of coffee."

Mackey nodded, pulled off his coat, and followed her down the hall to the kitchen.

After placing the coffee, soft drinks, and a plate of goodies on the table, Darcy sat and said, "Let me begin by ticking through some things quickly to make sure you know the obvious." She held up her index finger. "The missile was probably sent here in a semi."

Mackey nodded.

Darcy held up a second finger. "If it was like the others, it was a newer Kenworth."

A nod.

A third finger. "The truck's probably painted in one or more of the flag colors."

A nod.

A fourth. "The missile's painted white with the POVO logo on it."

A nod.

"Okay, let me think." She took a sip of coffee, set down the mug, and said, "It looked to us, I mean to Tony and me, like the camp had housed about fifty people right up until the day they disappeared. If you assume they had that many people for a reason, then probably each missile was accompanied by a crew." She looked out the window to the back yard, turned back and said, "I wonder if they expected to have more than five missiles? The FBI's mole wrote that all twelve Russian missiles were delivered to the camp in Missouri. POVO might have expected to salvage eight or nine working weapons from that."

"And?" the sheriff prompted.

She smiled ruefully. "And in the end, it probably doesn't matter. My actual point is that it's safe to assume each missile has a crew of at least four people traveling with it to assist with transporting, assembling, and operating the thing. Maybe as many as six or eight. Have you checked the motels and other lodging options? What about people who are away for the winter? Any houses that are supposed to be empty that suddenly aren't?"

Mackey shook his head and pulled out his phone. To Darcy, he said, "That, my dear, is why I'm here. I'm so wrapped up in searching for a weapon, I haven't thought much about searching for its nursemaids." He typed a long text message, pressed send, and set the phone down on the table.

"What else?"

Darcy took a deep breath. "Well…I suppose you know this guy named Grady Benning is a suspect in Deputy Jebron's death, and is a leader in POVO?"

Mackey nodded. "Do I ever."

"Were you surprised to learn he was mixed up in an extremist group?"

"Not even a little bit. Considering his history, I would have been surprised if he *wasn't* plotting to overthrow America."

"Do you think that's why one of the missiles was sent here? Because Benning's here?"

The sheriff stared at Darcy for a long beat, then slumped back in his chair. Darcy was shocked to see tears form in the sheriff's eyes and begin working their way down his cheeks and into his beard.

"Can I be honest with you?"

"Of course," she said, getting up and grabbing a box of tissues from the counter. She sat back down and pushed the box across the table toward the sheriff. He ignored it.

"Benning is living here, that fucking missile is hiding here, and Tim Jebron is dead, all because of me."

Darcy felt like she'd been tased. She couldn't move or breathe. She couldn't fathom what Mackey meant, but she could tell he was dead serious. She also had no idea how to respond. She held her tongue and the sheriff continued, "Grady Benning's little sister was killed by an ATF agent in Montana years ago. Benning was fourteen at the time and saw it happen. Obviously, it fueled a deep rage in him."

Darcy managed enough breath to say, "Tony told me about that."

"What Tony didn't tell you is the worst part of it. The ATF agent who killed that beautiful little girl was me."

Darcy couldn't help herself. A gasp of shock escaped her mouth as her hand flew up to stop it. She still didn't know what to say and found a hundred questions spinning in her mind, but all was pushed aside as she saw the tears now streaming down the grizzled face of Sheriff George Mackey.

She reached out, place her hand gently on his forearm, and said, "Tell me about it. If you want to, of course."

"Believe me, I don't want to tell anybody," Mackey said. "But the fact is, Benning brought these horrors to my county because of what I did."

Darcy remained silent, and the sheriff eventually sighed and resumed speaking.

"I was an ATF agent. I went up there—we all went up there—to protect those children. When things escalated and the guns came out, we all found ourselves in the middle of a horrible situation. The details don't matter, but the fact is, I was scared. When someone took a shot at me, I unloaded my weapon in that direction. Foolish, indiscriminate shooting toward a house filled with people. When I heard the screams of anguish from the mother, I knew what I'd done. I was horrified, tempted to end it all right there."

"I'm glad you didn't," Darcy said.

"What I did," Mackey said, finally wiping his face with a tissue, "is drop my gun, turn, and walk down the mountain to our field operations center. I turned myself in and sat out the rest of the conflict. The ATF and the Justice Department conducted their investigations and found me guilty of no wrongdoing. Someone in the house had shot at me, so I had the right to return fire. It was bullshit of course. Another case of the feds looking after their own. Don't get me wrong. I was glad to be cleared. I didn't want to sit in a prison cell for twenty years. But the day after the ruling, I turned in my badge and moved back home to Orney. I worked in the bottling plant on the highway for five years before I had the courage to apply for an opening in the Sheriff's Department.

"You did the right thing. You're a good sheriff."

"I've tried to be, but I've always known there was a risk the past would come back to haunt me. When Benning moved here, I knew it had started. I just never imagined it would end with one of my deputies lying in a grave or a damn missile hiding in my county."

It occurred to Darcy to ask, "Since you know this all is tied to Benning, I assume you've gone after him."

"First thing I did," Mackey said. "We took six men to his place. No one was there. We searched every inch of his property and found nothing. I've got a couple of guys watching the place, but I don't think he'll go back there until this is over."

Darcy was shocked again when the sheriff looked at her with every feature on his face drawn tautly into a plea for help. He said, "We can't let this happen. We can't."

"You're right," she said. "With your permission, I'll enlist a few people we can trust, and we'll join the search."

"Short of violating my promise to the FBI and CIA, I'll take any help I can get."

"I assume you mean all this has to be kept under wraps."

"Right. If we go public or tip off POVO that we know where to look, it could push them to unleash this nightmare sooner."

"We'll be careful," Darcy said.

# Chapter 35

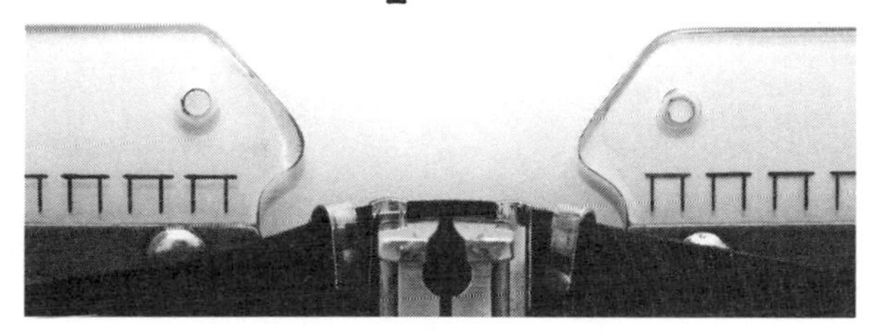

Friday, January 9, Orney, Iowa

Grady Benning was irritated that a newspaper reporter had stumbled across the missile. However, he wasn't overly concerned about it. The old man who had lived in the farmhouse across the field from the silo had been a well-known nutcase. Benning had known about Fishbone's "observatory," and had decided early on that the old man had to be eliminated. Obviously, he had failed to do it before the old codger had called the paper.

*He who hesitates is lost*, Benning thought, pleased that this time, he hadn't hesitated. The overly curious reporter would be dead by now. His body wouldn't be found until long after the operation had concluded. His vehicle would be found near the Iron Range Tap, where Benning had seen the guy drinking and playing pool in the past. People would naturally wonder where he had gone but would have no way to know what had happened to him.

Benning smiled and checked the speedometer for an unnecessary tenth time. He was driving the reporter's SUV into town, followed by another POVO member in a truck. As long as he drove attentively and picked his parking spot carefully, there was almost no chance of being seen. The reporter's phone stood propped in the cup holder in the center console. His friends or the authorities would have no trouble finding the vehicle and phone. They would have a lot of trouble finding the man.

***

Consciousness leaked into Doug's brain despite his best efforts to hold it off. With each passing moment, the splitting pain in his head grew stronger, surpassed only by the dread and fear in his heart.

He was cold, he could barely move, and when he opened his eyes, he could see only vague shapes in the dark. However, his other senses gave away his location. He was in a dirt cellar, lying sideways on hard-packed earth. *Probably the old man's basement,* he thought. *Even if he had a separate tornado shelter, it'd probably be hidden under the snow in the yard.*

He could hear two men talking, their voices growing more distinct as his head cleared. "…just an electrician. I'll do a lot for the cause, but I'm not gonna kill an innocent man in cold blood."

A second voice said, "Benning's an officer. He ordered us to eliminate the threat. You and I both know what he meant."

"I don't care if he's King Tut. I'm not doing it. Look at that poor slob. He's tied up more tightly than a load of pipe on a flatbed. This'll all be over tomorrow. He ain't going nowhere before that."

"If you won't do it…"

"Don't say it. I don't want you doin' it neither. That makes me an accomplice. Just leave him here. You can tell Benning we did him if you want. But we're not killin' him."

"If this comes back to bite me in the ass, I swear I'll kill this bastard first, and then I'm comin' after you."

"Just chill out. This fat turd is no threat to anybody. Now let's get outta here."

Doug ignored the nasty comment and allowed himself a quick sigh of relief as he heard two sets of boots climbing the stairs. A door slammed loudly, followed by the faint sound of a key turning in the lock. It appeared he was safe for the moment, but Benning or another goon could show up at any time to finish what these two men hadn't. Even if no threat of violence returned, Doug knew he was at risk of dying from exposure in the unheated basement if he remained there overnight during January in Iowa. Perhaps most importantly, he knew he had to get free so he could report what he had seen. *It was a missile. Not my imagination, but an honest-to-God missile. Grady Benning has an effing rocket in that old silo.*

Unfortunately, the ropes that bound him were tight, and his fingers were numb from the cold. Even if he could reach the knots, he was doubtful he would be able to untie them.

*First things first.* He was able to move his ankles, so he pushed hard against the ground with his toes, feeling his body move an inch on the dirt. With his head throbbing and his thirst growing, it was going to be a horrible task, but he was determined to reach a wall or a support post or something. He knew that lying in the middle of an empty room was not a solution. Maybe on a wall or in a dark corner, or somewhere, he'd find something that could help him. He wasn't optimistic, but he also wasn't willing to just lie there and die.

*I wonder what Tony would do? That little shit has a way of getting out of everything.* Then it dawned on him that Tony usually escaped peril because he, Doug, came along to save his ass. He grimaced at the thought that Tony wasn't even in Iowa. There would be no reciprocal rescue from him. *If this is all because of something you're doing, Tone-man, I'm gonna haunt you for a thousand years.*

Darkening his mood even more was the thought of Alison. She was expecting him to show up at her apartment for dinner, a movie on Netflix, and with any luck, a good toss in her four-poster bed. When he didn't arrive, she would assume he'd stood her up. He had a reputation for being a bit of a lazy lug, maybe a little unreliable when it came to personal relationships. She'd be pissed, but there was no way she would leap to the conclusion that he was in trouble.

Despite these thoughts, Doug wasn't completely without hope. His boss, of course, knew where he had gone. When Doug didn't show up for work on Saturday, Ben would send out the cavalry. Mid-morning Saturday was a long time from now, assuming it was still Friday night. So to have any chance, he needed to survive the night. He also had to hope he'd been dumped in Fishbone's basement, and not some other building miles from where Ben had sent him. "With my luck, they'll probably save me just in time to amputate a couple limbs due to frostbite," he muttered.

He tried to put all thoughts, good and bad, out of his mind in order to concentrate on his task. Once again, he pushed with his toes, grunted, took a breath, pushed with his toes, grunted, took a breath…

***

Tony's phone began playing "'Til There was You," just as he was driving into Orney. He answered it using the Jeep's hands-free connection.

"Hey," he said. "I'm just about home."

"Thank God," Darcy said. "You can't believe…"

Her tone put Tony on edge immediately. "You okay?"

"As good as can be expected, considering our country's about to be destroyed by lunatics, Sheriff Mackey's been in our kitchen crying, and your best friend is missing."

Tony sat up rigidly in the driver's seat and gripped the steering wheel with both hands. "Doug? What do you mean missing?"

"We can't figure out where he went. A couple of hours ago, I told Sheriff Mackey I'd put together a group of trusted friends to help search for the damn missile. When I called Doug, he didn't answer. So I called Alison. She said he hadn't shown up for dinner and hadn't answered his phone. When she used her 'Find Phone' app, she saw he was near the Iron Range. She was mad as hell, having assumed of course that Doug had blown her off or forgotten their date."

"So was he there?"

"No, and that's the point. When I went to the bar, I found his car parked on a street about a block away. His phone was in the car, but there was no sign of him."

"He's in trouble," Tony said, his conviction growing even as he spoke the words. "He wouldn't have missed a night with Alison. He has it bad for her. Not to mention he's never missed a free meal in his life."

Tony winced at his own quip. It was the wrong time to try to make light of anything, especially Doug.

Darcy said, "He could have gone off with a friend or something, but it's hard to believe he'd leave his phone in the car. Even if he simply forgot it, he almost certainly would've gone back to get it. With you out of town, Ben's probably relying on him for a lot of stuff."

"You're right," Tony said, feeling a sting of guilt at the comment. "Have you talked to Ben?"

"That was going to be my next call."

"I'm pulling into the driveway now. Wait a minute for me and we'll do it together. Then you'll have to tell me about the sheriff's visit."

"Yes, and you won't believe what he told me. Hurry, please. I'm so glad you're home."

## Friday, January 9, Pawnee Lake Recreation Area, Nebraska

One hundred and seventy miles west of Orney, a small convoy of military vehicles pulled into the Pawnee Lake Recreation Area near Lincoln, Nebraska. A Nebraska State Trooper waved them in. Once the convoy passed the front gate and headed down the blacktop lane into the park, the trooper pulled the long steel gate closed, locked it, and drove away. When the convoy reached a point far enough into the park that it could not be seen from the public road, it stopped.

Nine men and women jumped from the vehicles, four Marines, four Airmen, and one Air Force colonel. They worked quickly and quietly. In less than twelve minutes, the PADS anti-missile system was set up and poised to fire. An airman, a young woman who had grown up in Cedar Falls, Iowa, activated the radar system from inside an enclosure at the back of a second vehicle. When Colonel Terrence Jackson looked through the door, she gave him a thumbs-up. He nodded and shut the door. The airman inside the PADS launch vehicle gave a similar thumbs-up. Each of the four heavily armed Marines stationed at the corners of the temporary base repeated the sign. The colonel nodded, looked at his watch, and smiled. He climbed into the cab of the lead truck, pushed "Talk" on the encrypted SATCOM phone, and reported, "Unit One is five-by-five." A single "beep" was the only acknowledgement. No other radio communication would occur unless a bogey was spotted and fired upon.

Colonel Jackson climbed back out of the cab. He opened the doors to both the radar truck and the weapons vehicle so everyone could hear him. "We're live. This is not a drill. Be diligent. Somewhere near here is a surface-to-air missile armed and ready to launch. We don't know exactly where it is. We don't know when it will launch. We can't even be sure of its target. But ladies and gentlemen,

I assure you, the missile is real, and the threat to America is real. If you detect a missile launch, you cannot hesitate. You may have only seconds to respond, to have any chance to catch it and bring it down before it destroys an airliner or some other target. Your orders, therefore, are simple. Do not fuck this up."

In two other locations, similar speeches were being delivered to similar teams—highly trained men and women who were devoted to serving and protecting their country. A scattering of three mobile missile defense systems in a laughably feeble attempt to cover an area of about 400,000 square miles. Near Lincoln, Nebraska, nine devoted men and women looked to the cold January sky and prayed it would be enough.

### Friday, January 9, Mile Marker 44
### Weigh Station, Interstate 80, Iowa

Meanwhile, in Iowa, the fourth PADS unit was moving at a snail's pace; not down the highway, but vertically, as a hydraulic jack slowly raised the left rear corner of the launch vehicle. Major Rodney "Ramrod" Gally was about to come unglued. He and his crew had waited for hours, in the truck weigh station off Interstate 80 in western Iowa, for the delivery of the parts needed to repair the faulty wheel bearing. When the parts had finally arrived, they had been horrified to find the jack provided with the PADS vehicle was undersized. It simply had not been able to lift the exceptionally heavy unit, built of reinforced steel and carrying a full payload of ordnance. They had been forced to call in a commercial tow truck.

It had taken the truck another forty minutes to arrive. By the time it did, the major was pacing back and forth in the weigh station's parking lot, oblivious of the cold. He knew every second of delay could mean the difference between success and failure in the most important mission of his career.

The tow truck was equipped with a hydraulic jack that routinely was used for lifting semis, for tire replacements and other repairs, so it was up to the task. It also was slow. The major stared at the PADS unit's dual rear wheels, willing them to rise up off the cold concrete. When they finally did, he shouted, "Halt!"

As soon as the jack grew still, a crew member rushed up to the outer wheel and began spinning off the lug nuts with an electric drill, placing each lug nut into the pocket of her parka. When finished, she set aside the drill and nodded to another crewman. Together they pulled on the wheel. It didn't move.

"What's wrong?" the major barked. "Get that thing off of there!"

"Sorry sir, it's stuck." The two pulled harder but the wheel remained in place.

"What the…" the major growled, desperately wanting to scream or hit something.

The tow truck driver spoke from behind them. "Not the kids' fault. I see this all the time. The heat and grime from the road create a kind of bond, holding the wheel in place. Some hard tugs from side-to-side usually do the trick."

"You heard the man," the major said. "Pull harder! First left, then right."

The two crew members did as ordered. As the wheel failed to respond, they amped up their efforts. The entire unit began to rock, and no one noticed that at its corner, the hydraulic jack was rocking with it.

Suddenly someone cried, "Look out!" The jack slipped free, toppling over, and the entire unit crashed back and to the left. The two crew members jumped back as the full weight of the vehicle came down hard on its wheels. This time, the outer wheel came free and the inner wheel bore the full force of the unit's weight. A loud metallic bang sounded as the unit came to a rest on the concrete.

"Son of a bitch!" the major shouted. "Everybody okay?"

Confirmations came from everyone. The airman who had shouted the warning dropped to his belly and scooted past the outer wheel, now lying flat on the ground. From under the edge of the vehicle's steel frame, he inspected the damage.

"Well, let's hear it!" the major barked. "What's the report?"

The man wriggled back out, turned and sat up. "I'm sorry sir, but it's bad. The axle's broken."

The major spun on his heels and headed for the cab of the lead vehicle. As much as he dreaded it, he knew he needed to report in quickly. Command needed to know they were now down to three banks of PADS.

***

"Fishbone's?" Tony asked. He was talking to Ben Smalley, who was still at the *Town Crier*, as the Saturday paper went to press.

Ben said, "Yeah, I asked him to go back out there, look around, and see if he could find whatever it was that set off the old man. He left here late this afternoon, so he couldn't have been out there more than a couple of hours before it got dark. If his car was found downtown, it's obvious he came back. I can't imagine where he went from there."

"Did he report back to you from Fishbone's? Did he file a story about it?"

"No," Ben said, "but it was a bullshit assignment. Fishbone has ranted for years about aliens on his farm. I don't know why I thought this time was any different. If Doug had found something, I'm sure I would've heard from him."

"Can't argue with that," Tony said. "But he has to be somewhere."

"You guys keep looking in Orney," the editor said. "I'll buzz up to Viscount before I go home for the night. There's a bar up there he could be hanging in."

"I know the place," Tony said, "but I've never known Doug to go there. Problem is, I can't think of anything better to suggest, so I'm not going to discourage you."

"Let's be sure we touch base again before either of us goes to bed," Ben said. "I'm sure he's fine, but I'll rest easier if one of us finds him."

Tony agreed and ended the call.

Darcy said, "You didn't tell him one of those missiles is here."

Tony nodded. "I've lost track of what I've told whom, and what I'm allowed to tell. I told him about the missiles at the camp, so he knows they exist. If he spots one in Quincy County, I'm pretty sure he'll tell someone."

At 2 a.m., when all the bars in Iowa closed, Doug was still missing. Tony, Darcy, Alison, and Ben agreed there was nothing more they could do until morning. They reluctantly decided to get some sleep and resume the search early.

Tony was exhausted, but still had trouble sleeping. The idea that Doug might be hurt, or lost, or, God forbid, in the clutches of Benning and the other POVO wackos, was more than he could bear. He was trying to imagine who could have attracted Doug away from his car and phone on a side street in Orney when sleep finally overtook him.

# Chapter 36

Saturday, January 10, Orney, Iowa
Three Hours, Forty Minutes to Wheels-Up, Flight 244

"Agent Tabors?" Tony was surprised to hear from her. It was just after 8 a.m. on Saturday. Tony and Darcy were in Tony's Jeep, parked just behind Doug's RAV4 in Orney. They were about to step out for a closer look at the SUV.

"I wouldn't have bothered, but my boss said I should call you." Her voice still had an edge, so Tony refrained from trying to be witty.

"Good news, I hope. Did Jugg give you something helpful?"

"Jugg hasn't given us anything except a demand for a lawyer and a smug smile that scares the hell out of everyone who sees it."

Tony's fingers clenched against his palms at the thought of Jugg sitting quietly, content to let hundreds of people die, perhaps more, to fulfill the aims of some foreign power.

Tabors continued. "The good news is that we've found and secured three of the missiles. Seventeen POVO members are in custody, charged with conspiracy to commit murder, terrorism, possession of illegal weapons, and anything else we could think of in order to keep them under wraps until this is over."

"That's fantastic!" Tony and Darcy turned and shared a high-five. "How did you manage it?"

"That's why my boss insisted I call. The credit for these three raids goes mostly to you. Your photographs of the trucks and their license plates allowed us to find the three missiles that you saw in the camp on Monday night."

Tony felt his heart pounding. It was overwhelming to think he might have played a role in stopping that much death and destruction. He also felt Darcy's hand squeezing his bicep. He reached out, pulled her to him, and kissed her.

"I don't know what to say," he croaked out.

Tabors ignored him. "Some of us wanted to wait to do the raids until we had locations on all five weapons, but the leadership in D.C. ordered us to go early this morning. They said it was too risky to wait. They were probably right."

"But now…" Tony began.

"Now we have to assume the word is out that three of the weapons are compromised. The two remaining sites will be on high alert and more dangerous than ever."

"They'll also push up their schedule."

"Of course they will. They've spent years and millions of dollars developing this plan. They'll be desperate to launch whatever they can as fast as they can."

"Any idea what that means?"

Tabors sighed. "Sadly, yes. All the evidence that the strike teams found says that the missiles we captured were planned to launch at 4 p.m. today."

"Today?" Tony gasped as he heard a similar sound escape from

Darcy. "You're saying the remaining two missiles will launch soon; maybe any minute?"

Tabors was silent for a moment, then said, "Sadly, in this case, the bad news outweighs the good. We appreciate all you've done so far, but now you people in Iowa *must* find that damn missile and put an end to this."

Tony would have agreed, but the agent was already gone. He and Darcy stared at each other.

She said, "So what do we…?"

Tony turned and looked at his friend's SUV. He said, "I love you buddy, but you're gonna have to wait. The needs of the many outweigh the needs of the one." It was a line he'd learned from *Star Trek* as a kid. It made sense back then, as a nice piece of logic. Today, nothing made sense, and abandoning the search for Doug created an all-consuming anguish in his heart.

"Maybe not," Darcy said.

Tony was confused. "Maybe not what?"

"Maybe focusing on finding the missile will also result in finding Doug."

Tony nodded, seeing where she was headed, but he let her continue.

"If our big worry is that POVO took him, then we're saying that he was a threat to them."

"A threat?"

"I don't know, *threat* may or may not be the right word, but you get my point. POVO members aren't going around snatching citizens off the street. They're focused on the biggest operation in their history, maybe in *anyone's* history. They wouldn't have bothered with Doug unless they had a very compelling reason."

"Yeah…like he saw or heard something he shouldn't have." Tony warmed to the idea. "It's the same as Tim Jebron. He overheard something about their operation, so they killed him."

The excitement disappeared along with the air from Tony's lungs. "You don't think…He couldn't be…"

Darcy reached over and touched his face. "Keep your head. Stay focused on the task. If Doug's alive, he may not have much time. Either way, disaster is about to be unleashed. We have to figure this out quickly, and we can't make any mistakes along the way."

Tony nodded and started the Jeep. "We're going to Fishbone's," he said.

Darcy didn't look surprised.

Tony said, "It's the last place Doug went that we know about. If he saw something he shouldn't have, it might've been there."

"Maybe the missile?"

"Think about it. Fishbone calls Ben screaming that he saw an alien ship—even touched it. So maybe he did. After all, the missile is just another version of a rocket ship."

"Makes sense."

"And God help us, that's another death to consider. If we assume Fishbone saw the missile, it's not much of a stretch to think these POVO bastards blew his head off with his own shotgun. Then Doug heads out there, sees something, and…" Tony's jaw set and his knuckles whitened. He said, "Well, shit. There's just no sign of a hopeful note in any of this."

He crushed the SUV's accelerator. They were ten or twelve minutes from Fishbone's farm. Tony thought he could make it in eight.

Darcy took out her phone. Tony glanced at her quizzically.

"I'm calling the sheriff. No excuses this time. When the fate of your best friend, not to mention our country, hangs in the balance, we're not going to take this on ourselves."

"No arguments," Tony said. "I was about to suggest it."

*Well, that's a load of crap*, Darcy thought as she dialed Mackey's direct number.

He answered immediately, and Darcy explained where they were headed, and why.

"Don't know if you're right," the sheriff said, "but we got nothing else, so we'll join you. By the way, tell Tony the State Patrol is coming toward him on the highway. I heard the call on my radio. Some motorist was pissed about being passed on a yellow line, so she called 911 to report him."

"Perhaps you'd like to get in touch with the trooper and suggest he not stop us but turn around and escort us to the farm. No lights or sirens, of course."

"Good idea. But tell Harrington to slow down. He can't help anyone if he's bleeding to death in a ditch."

"I'll try," Darcy said, and ended the call.

# Chapter 37

Saturday, January 10, Pawnee Lake
Recreation Area, Nebraska

Colonel Jackson supposed all soldiers hoped their weapons would never be deployed in actual combat. Well, maybe not all, but most. They trained hard, worked hard, planned and prepared, while simultaneously praying for peace. That was his M.O. anyway, and he wasn't embarrassed to admit it.

In the past three days, he had prayed longer and harder than at any time in his career. So far, his prayers had been answered. No rocket-powered spears of death had appeared in the sky over central Nebraska. Unfortunately, the colonel had no way to know if God had intervened, or if the moment just hadn't arrived yet.

He had traveled with the first PADS team to Pawnee Lake, west of Lincoln and just a few miles north of I-80. The campground in the state-run recreation area was empty this time of year, making it the ideal spot to set up and watch the air lanes between Chicago and

Denver, and Minneapolis and Phoenix, and Omaha and…He stopped trying to make a list. The fact was, a shitpile of commercial airliners flew over the skies of Nebraska every day. He had no idea what location would be best. No matter what this PADS unit did, if a hostile missile was launched, the chance of successfully bringing it down was about equal to the chance the Blair, Nebraska, High School Basketball Team had to win the Superbowl in a couple of weeks.

He took another swallow of coffee and climbed out of the truck. He was concerned about the crew. They were among the best he had, but no matter how talented or well-trained they were, it was impossible to stay diligent every minute of every day for days at a time. He wondered how people like air traffic controllers and early warning radar operators managed it.

He walked up to the PADS truck and pulled open the door to the control room.

"You awake?"

Airman Cynthia Akers spoke crisply, "Yes, sir! Thank you, sir!"

Jackson smiled. "Relax, airman."

"Thank you, sir. Permission to speak freely, sir."

"Of course, airman. Anything."

"That was a bullshit question, sir. I will not let you down on this assignment. I am not only awake, I have commanded my eyes not to blink."

Jackson laughed. "Very good, airman. I apologize, and I'm glad to hear it. I'm just nervous about the effects all these hours of waiting can have."

"Perhaps on others, sir, uh, if you don't mind me saying so."

Jackson chuckled again. "I don't mind at all. I admire you for speaking out. If you turn out to be as good as you say you are, I may send you on a temporary assignment to view the flora and fauna at PACAF."

"Hickam Field, sir? In Hawaii?"

"Just a thought." Jackson smiled. "Don't let thoughts of white sand and surf bums distract you."

"No, sir. Of course not, sir. One other thing, sir."

"Yes?"

"Thank you, sir, for being here. We know the other teams didn't get a full bird to lead them. We're honored to serve with you."

"I worried you would hate it. Back when I was on field assignments, there was no way I wanted a colonel looking over my shoulder."

"Perhaps on routine assignments, sir. Not this. If we get a chance to act, having you at our backs will be a huge help."

"Thank you, airman. I've just increased your orders to two months at Hickam, with no official duties to tie you down. Now let's kill us a bogie soon so we can go home."

"Yes, sir!"

The colonel walked away, thinking he didn't really want to kill a bogie. He wanted this whole mess to be a big hoax. However, he was smart enough to know he had to speak to the team as if the worst was inevitable, in order to keep everyone as alert as possible. *Hope for the best, but expect the worst.*

Sadly, he was about to learn how right he was to expect the worst.

***

Saturday, January 10, Chicago, Illinois
Ten Minutes to Wheels-Up, Flight 244

Joel Fitzgerald was angry and scared, but mostly scared. After five years of careful planning, hard work, and the investment of more money than he could imagine, it felt like the operation was coming apart. Three hot sites were offline. It was unfathomable that local cops or even the FBI had found and shut down all three, but he couldn't imagine what else might have happened.

Equally concerning, the POVO leader, Arvin Jugg, and his camp commander, Jon Slapp, also were unresponsive. On the day of POVO's glory, Jugg and Slapp would not have disappeared of their own accord. Somehow, the authorities must have taken them. Again, Fitzgerald couldn't imagine how.

Regardless of what had gone wrong, Fitzgerald knew the operation now depended on him. It felt like a city bus was parked on his shoulders. He swallowed hard and picked up his phone.

*If only two hot sites are answering, then so be it. We fire from two sites. This operation is not going to fail on my watch. We've worked too hard. The world is going to know POVO's strength. The new society, the America we dreamed of, begins today.*

He dialed a cell phone number from memory.

"Eighteen," a man's voice said.

"Go," Fitzgerald said. "One hour."

"You mean…?"

"Yes, of course. Pick a target and fire."

"Confirmation code?"

"Frank, Tango, Frank, Frank."

"Confirmed. We're go," the voice said shakily.

Fitzgerald ended the call and dialed Grady Benning's number. They had an identical conversation.

It was done.

# Chapter 38

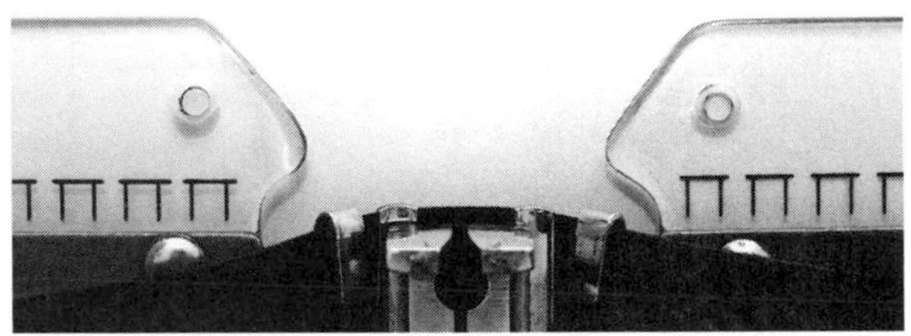

Saturday, January 10, Chicago, Illinois

Randy Lundgren guided the Boeing 737-400 through its final turn on the taxiway, stopping short of the runway. He waited patiently for a United heavy to lumber down the mile and a half of concrete and take to the sky.

While he waited, his eyes flicked over every dial and switch on the instrument panel. It was a well-established habit. Lundgren had been flying for more than three decades. He now enjoyed what he believed to be the perfect job.

As a small carrier, Wingdance Airlines didn't have the prestige or opportunities of the major airlines, but it also didn't have the corporate bureaucracy and other headaches associated with the "big boys."

A second plus in Lundgren's book was the fact that most of Wingdance's flights were relatively short. Chicago to Denver or Kansas City or Minneapolis. It meant he would take off and land several times a day. He couldn't imagine being the pilot of an overseas flight, sitting and doing nothing for six hours or more and having one opportunity to actually fly each day.

Perhaps best of all, Lundgren loved the equipment employed by Wingdance. The Boeing was a safe, reliable plane, big enough to be comfortable, but small enough to land at almost any airport if he ever had a problem. Equally important to Lundgren, the plane had all the avionics necessary to fly anywhere in any weather, but it was not overly computerized. As a pilot, he had the confidence that his movements of the flight controls were manipulating the plane's surfaces and functions, rather than a computer interpreting his moves and flying the plane for him.

The 737-400 was an older plane. Wingdance bought its equipment used from other airlines who were modernizing. If properly maintained, this Tin Mouse would fly forever. Lundgren hoped he would fly it and others just like it all the way into his final retirement.

In short, Randy Lundgren was a pilot. He wanted to *fly* his aircraft.

All of these thoughts were floating around in his subconscious. His attention was focused on the instrument panel, the runway in front of him, and the ground controller's voice in his ears. Also, if he was being honest, a portion of his brain was preoccupied by his co-pilot, a young woman named Theresa Otley, whom he would love to see out of that uniform someday.

Lundgren had a weakness for smart, capable women with dark hair and the right proportions. It had caused him and his family heartache and had led to his divorce. Occasionally, it had led to trouble with the Wingdance HR department. Unfortunately, when he was seated next to a woman like Theresa, who met all his requirements and more, his past difficulties were forgotten and his current desires occupied the pilot's seat, so to speak.

*Wingdance Flight 244, advance to Runway 27 Right and hold,* said the voice in his headphones.

"Advance to 27 Right and hold, Wingdance 244." To his co-pilot, Lundgren said, "Do you want the controls?"

"And deprive you of your second-favorite thing in the world? Not a chance," Theresa Otley said, smiling warmly.

*Wingdance Flight 244, you are cleared for takeoff, Runway 27 Right.*

"Cleared for takeoff, Runway 27 Right, Wingdance 244," Lundgren replied.

As he pushed the throttles forward, he heard the twin jet engines respond with a roar and felt the acceleration. He thought, *A bright, sunny morning, a full flight, a beautiful woman at my side, and the sky waiting with open arms—it's going to be a great day.*

At 11:44 a.m., the wheels came up on the Boeing aircraft, and it climbed steeply toward its cruising altitude of 28,000 feet. None of the nearly two hundred people on board Flight 244 had any reason to suspect it was *not* going to be a great day.

***

Fifty minutes into the flight, as Lundgren and Otley were sipping coffee and chatting, a surprise communication crackled in Captain Lundgren's ears.

*Wingdance 244, contact company on your secure SATCOM.*

Lundgren was baffled, but as an experienced pilot, didn't bother the air traffic controller with his questions. The woman probably didn't know anything more than the instruction she had given him.

He glanced at Otley, who already was retrieving the satellite phone from its storage compartment behind the pilot's seat. Lundgren knew every Wingdance plane had a secure phone, used primarily to talk with dispatch about weather delays or with maintenance about problems with the plane. Neither situation applied today. Wondering to himself how long it had been since he'd used the phone, he dialed Dispatch.

When a woman's voice answered, he said, "Captain Randy Lundgren, Wingdance Flight 244. I was instructed to call."

"Yes. Thank you, Captain. We are contacting all of our assets in the air over the Midwest today to share with you that we've received a disturbing notification from the FBI field office in Chicago."

"The FBI? Hang on."

He turned to Otley, who was wide-eyed at hearing him mention the FBI. To her, he said, "I'm turning the controls over to you for a minute. In three, two, one, now."

She was ready and simply nodded as Lundgren returned to the phone. He said, "I'm ready. What did the FBI report?"

"They say they have received reliable intelligence that a group of domestic terrorists have secured two surface-to-air missiles and intend to fire them on domestic aircraft today."

Lundgren's mind exploded with questions about how terrorists had acquired SAMs, why the FBI believed today was the day, and what was being done on the ground to stop them. He especially wanted to ask how long the authorities had known about this and why in the hell was his aircraft in the air.

He didn't ask any of these things. He surprised even himself as he felt his mind slip instantly into military mode. The only questions that mattered now were the ones that would help him get his plane safely on the ground.

"Do they have locations on the SAMs?" he asked.

"Only in general terms. They believe one to be in central Iowa and one to be in Nebraska, maybe near Lincoln."

"I just flew over Iowa," he responded tersely. "Omaha is out my starboard window. I'll be over Lincoln in ten minutes."

"Understood," the woman said.

Lundgren shook off his anger and said, "Specifics on the SAMs?"

"They're armed with C-4 and able to reach your top altitude."

"Understood, but I want more. Did they give you specifics?"

"Hang on, Captain."

The pause was agonizing. Finally, the woman said, "Believed to be Russian-made older models. Something called a Bear-Cat?"

"The Berkut S-25. I know it," Lundgren said. "Big and dumb and deadly. I'll look for the nearest place to land."

"It's your aircraft and your call, Captain, but just so you know, we're not recommending that."

"What the hell?"

"There are a lot of planes in the air. Leadership here is concerned that if you reduce altitude to land, you risk becoming the missile's first and easiest target. If you stay at altitude, you have a very small chance of being fired upon."

Lundgren covered the mouthpiece on the phone and said to his co-pilot, "Ask air traffic control for permission to reduce altitude to 12,000 feet. Declare a fuel emergency and ask to be diverted to Omaha."

Otley didn't question him, and made the call.

To Dispatch, Lundgren said, "I'm lowering our altitude while I consider our options. If we get struck, I don't want to lose the plane in a catastrophic pressure drop."

"But…"

"I'm guessing a lot of other planes will be doing the same. It won't affect the odds much."

"Understood. As we said, it's your call."

"That's why I love you guys," Lundgren said. "Anything else?"

"Only to wish you godspeed and good luck."

"Thanks," he said, ending the call and adding, "for nothing."

He quickly pushed the alert to signal the lead flight attendant.

She picked up soon after. "Yes, Captain?"

"Announce to the passengers that we've spotted some bad weather up ahead. Get all the food and beverage stuff packed up tightly. Dump the coffee pots first. Then get the passengers to stow their things and button up the tray tables as best you can. Don't make a scene over it."

"Captain?"

"Just do as I ask. When you're done, gather the attendants and come to the flight deck door. Hurry."

He hung up and turned to Otley. "Controls back to my command in three, two, one, now."

He glanced at the altimeter. They were flying level at 28,000 feet. The compass showed they were still flying west.

Otley didn't wait to be asked. She said, "ATC refused our request. They said dozens of planes have asked for diversion to Omaha, and no more can be accommodated there."

"Well, shit," Lundgren muttered. Into his radio, he said, "Minneapolis Center, Wingdance 244, requesting a revised flight path around Lincoln."

*Wingdance 244, Minneapolis Center. Stand by.*

The comm board signaled a call from the lead flight attendant. To Otley, Lundgren said, "Answer that. If she reports the cabin is secure, then open the door and ask her and the others to come in here."

Otley's face darkened. Opening the flight deck door during a flight was strictly forbidden, not only by the airline, but by the FAA. She bit her tongue and did as Lundgren instructed.

*Wingdance 244, Minneapolis Center. Change course, heading 290.*

He turned the autopilot to 290 as he replied, "Turning heading 290, Wingdance 244."

*It's not enough*, he thought. *We're too close. It won't be enough.*

As soon as the flight deck door was open, three flight attendants, two women and one man, crowded into the narrow space behind the crew. Lundgren told them as succinctly as he could what they faced. He reassured them they would probably be fine, but asked them get into their seats, buckle up, and do all they could to keep the passengers seated.

He was proud of his crew. Everyone exited quickly, without questions or complaints.

Without taking his eyes from the open sky ahead of them, Lundgren said, "Watch the radar, and steal a glance out the window from time to time as well."

Both pilots knew the radar was designed to track weather, not missiles or even other aircraft.

As if reading his mind, Otley said, "Roger that. If that thing comes our way, radar probably will get a ping, but I have no idea how early. If we spot it, you may only have a few seconds to react."

Lundgren nodded. He didn't say what he was thinking. *It won't matter if we see it from one mile away or ten. I can't outrun or outmaneuver a Berkut in a Tin Mouse fully loaded with passengers and luggage.*

# Chapter 39

Saturday, January 10, Quincy County, Iowa

By the time Tony and Darcy reached Fishbone's farm, they were part of a convoy. A state patrol car led the way, followed by Tony's Jeep, Sheriff Mackey's SUV, and Rich Davis's state-issued sedan.

"I'll be damned," Tony said. "There he is."

As they neared the farmhouse, they could see Grady Benning and two other men walking across the front yard and up the steps onto the porch. All three turned to watch the vehicles pull to a stop in the farmyard.

They could see Grady was wearing a sidearm in a holster around his waist. The other two men held nasty-looking assault rifles.

"Tony..." Darcy said, gripping his arm as the Jeep and other vehicles slid to a stop in front of the house.

Before Tony could reply, Grady said something to the two men, and they laid their rifles on the frozen planks of the porch floor. Grady then smiled and waved at the convoy, gesturing for them to get out and come join him on the porch.

"What's he doing?" Tony wondered aloud.

"I don't like it," Darcy said. "Why isn't he running or shooting at us or something? He must know that Mackey's here to arrest him."

"Maybe he doesn't care," Tony said. "If so, that can't be good."

Before Darcy could object, he was out of the Jeep and following the other three men toward the house. All three had their guns out, so Tony left his in the back of the Jeep.

Darcy sighed and climbed out of the Jeep to join him.

"Sheriff Mackey, gentlemen, and—oh, look at this—Ms. Gillson," Benning said. "Nice to see you all. Come on in."

Mackey stepped up to the foot of the stairs. "Not so fast. You and your colleagues are under arrest. It's over, Grady. Now come with me and don't make any trouble."

Benning crossed his arms and didn't move, the smile still on his face. "You're right, George. It's over. Sadly for you, you're too late. You might as well come inside where it's warm."

Tony couldn't help himself. He pushed forward, joining Mackey at the foot of the stairs. "What do you mean too late? What have you done?"

"Are you asking about the missile, or your dead friend?

"My dead…?" Tony thought he might faint. He fought to retain his footing. "Tell me what you've done!"

"That missile you've been trying to find is fueled, prepped, programmed, and, I'm happy to say, in countdown mode. You can't stop it. Neither can I, even if I wanted to, which I don't."

"My God, man. Do you realize…?" Mackey began.

"I know exactly what I'm doing," Benning said. "I'm finally getting revenge on the man who destroyed my family."

"And the hundreds of people in that airplane?" Mackey said. "Your target's an airliner, right? Those people never did a thing to you. They're innocents. Christ, man, there's probably children on that plane. How can you just calmly butcher…"

"Hang on, Sheriff. As much as I enjoy seeing the agony on your face, let's be clear. POVO doesn't kill innocents unless we have to, like with Deputy Jebron and that newsman who came poking around where he didn't belong."

"You son of a bitch," Tony hissed, making a move toward the stairs. Darcy and Rich Davis simultaneously reached out and pulled him back.

Davis looked at Benning and said, "I don't understand. You said the missile is about to fire, so why claim no one's going to die?"

"The missile's programmed to explode near the plane, but not close enough to harm it. It'll show the world what POVO can do if things don't change. It will ignite our supporters and terrify our enemies. Our voice will..."

Mackey interrupted what was turning into a political rant. "I want to believe that, but how can you be sure? What if something goes…"

"He's wrong."

All eyes turned toward Darcy, who had spoken forcefully. She strode forward, walked up the stairs onto the porch, and looked up into Benning's eyes.

"You're wrong," she said. "I don't know if you're lying, or if your POVO bosses have fed you a line of BS, but you're wrong."

Benning's smile faded a little as he asked, "What makes you say that? Like I'm gonna believe some actress rather than the men I've trained beside and worked with for five years."

"I read Ted Janssen's journal," she said.

"The traitor?" Benning scoffed. "He was a liar and a thief. I don't care what he said."

"He was an agent, yes. But when he worked in POVO's camp

office, he had access to information at the highest levels, right?"

"Right..." Benning nodded reluctantly.

"He knew the weapons and the money came from the Russians. He found out that, from the beginning, the plan was to destroy commercial airliners in America, to bring the country to its knees. That's why they killed him."

"Bullshit. I don't believe you," Benning said, looking shaken for the first time. "We bought Russian weapons from an arms dealer, yes, but the money came from our supporters. Good people from all over the country."

"That, I can assure you, is not true," Tony said, admiring how Darcy had taken their assumptions and the facts and woven them together to make a compelling case. "Janssen reported all the details about the money in his journal. It came to POVO in one lump sum of $30 million, from a source in Russia."

Re-establishing eye contact, Darcy said, "Mr. Benning, you must believe us. If you've been told this is some kind of demonstration, that people aren't going to die, then you've been duped. Maybe nearly everyone in POVO has been misled. You are helping someone in Russia execute an ingenious and hideous plot to murder hundreds, maybe thousands of people. You must help us stop it."

She reached out and touched his arm, "Please. You must."

Benning looked at the other two men on the porch.

One said, "She's scaring me, sir. I don't wanna be parta no plot to kill women and children. Maybe we should do somethin'."

The second man simply nodded.

Benning's shoulders slumped. To the floor, he said, "Can it all have been for nothing? I can't just let it go. We worked so hard. I *killed* people." He looked at the sheriff, pointed, and said, "And you! You still have to pay."

Mackey immediately turned his pistol around in his hand so he was holding it by the barrel. He held it out to Benning.

"Take it," the sheriff said, dropping to his knees in the snow. "Take my life. Now. Quickly. Kill me, but then help these people stop this horror."

Benning looked lost. He stared at the sheriff's gun, looked frantically out at the crowd, his eyes darting from face to face, and said, "But I told you it's too late. There's no abort code. It can't be stopped."

He then looked up at the bright winter sky and said, almost in a whisper, "Dear God, what have I done?" His hand jerked up, grabbed the sherriff's gun, and before anyone could even cry out, shot himself in the temple.

A chorus of gasps and screams erupted as Benning's body rolled down the steps and stopped in the snow in front of the sheriff.

Mackey didn't even look at it. He quickly stood and looked at the two POVO enforcers on the porch.

"Where is it?"

"It don't matter. Like Grady said, it's too…"

"God dammit!" the sheriff thundered. "Where is it?"

The man on the right pointed south across a barren hayfield. He said, "There. An old silo on the next place south of here. Prolly less than half a mile across that field."

"Give me your rifle."

The man handed Mackey the assault weapon and said, "Won't help. It's a brick silo with a new steel door. By the time you blast through there, it'll be long gone."

"Shit!" The sheriff looked to the others.

Davis said, "The shot gun in the cruiser?"

"Not a chance," Mackey said. "Not if this won't do it."

Darcy said, "Could you crash through the wall with one of our vehicles?"

"Maybe, but that could easily be a suicide mission," Davis said.

"If it'll work, then I'm on it," the sheriff said, heading for his SUV.

"Sheriff Mackey…" Darcy said, a pleading tone in her voice.

As he climbed into the car, he said, "This is all my fault. It's up to me to set things right."

Darcy's instinct was to look to Tony, but she realized he wasn't there. "Where's…"

A loud roar erupted from behind them, and everyone jumped, naturally fearing the worst. Instead, what they saw was a green John Deere tractor driving out of an open machine shed door.

"Tony!" Darcy screamed.

Tony didn't look her way, fearing the sight of her would cause him to reconsider. He shifted the tractor into high gear and pushed the throttle to full. He knew how to do this. It was amazing the things you learned when writing news and feature articles for a rural newspaper.

He cranked the steering wheel to the left and headed south across the hayfield.

# Chapter 40

Saturday, January 10, Pawnee Lake Recreation Area, Nebraska

"Launch detected!" shouted Cynthia Akers from the radar unit of the PADS system near Lincoln, Nebraska.

"PADS volley away!" shouted a voice from the weapons control station.

Colonel Jackson was horrified to hear it was really happening, but thrilled to hear his team react instantly to the threat. He was already was moving, shouting the order, "Fire volley two!"

"Volley two away, sir!"

Jackson yanked open the door to the radar unit.

"Any hope?"

"I doubt it, sir," Akers replied crisply, trying to hide the despair in her voice.

"Distance and time?"

Launch was six kilometers south by southwest. Trajectory is east listing about 12 degrees, so that helps."

"But still not enough."

"No, sir. Target appears to be a commercial liner westbound at 28,000 feet. I've already alerted ATC in Minneapolis, so the pilot should get word in a few seconds."

"How much time does he have?"

"Ninety-two seconds."

"Dear God. Our time to intercept?"

Akers didn't hesitate. The sophisticated computer-assisted targeting system had the answer displayed in front of her, "Two minutes, a little less."

Agony seeped from every pore on the colonel's face. "So close. So damn close!"

"Yes, sir."

Jackson looked back at the screens, willing the missile to falter, explode, disappear, something. After a moment, he said, "He's turning."

Akers studied the screen for a moment. "He's turning northeast, away from the bird, and accelerating, sir."

"Of course. That's what anyone would do," Jackson said.

"Hang on, sir. Copy that, seventy-nine seconds."

The colonel realized Akers was talking to someone else.

"Sir, that was ATC in Minneapolis. The pilot requested the precise time to intercept."

"Any idea what he can do with that intel?"

"Not a fucking clue, sir."

***

## Wingdance Airlines Flight 244

Theresa Otley held her iPhone in her right hand, the stopwatch function open.

"Minneapolis, 244. Confirm time to intercept."

The response came quickly.

*244 Minneapolis. Time to intercept twenty seconds from this mark, now!*

Randy Lundgren looked to his co-pilot, who nodded grimly.

She said, "On the button."

"Theresa, I'm sorry you're here, for your sake. But I couldn't ask for a better second in command."

"It's been a privilege to fly with you."

"We're not done yet. Count 'em off."

Otley nodded. "Nine, eight, seven, six, five, four!"

Per their plan, she dropped the phone, announced through the intercom, "Brace! Brace! Brace!" and simultaneously dropped the landing gear.

At the same instant, Lundgren jerked back the throttles and pushed the yoke forward.

A terrible shriek emitted from the belly of the plane as they were thrown forward against their restraints and plunged downward.

Lundgren hoped it was the sound of the landing gear being damaged, as a result of being lowered at full speed.

*There's a thought I never imagined I'd have*, he mused grimly, knowing it would be preferrable to the sound coming from the fuselage being ripped apart.

An instant later a sharp crack sounded above them and a gleaming white projectile shot into the clouds over their heads.

"You did it!" Otley screamed. "It glanced off our two o'clock!"

*Not yet*, Lundgren thought, noting the missile appeared

undamaged, and would quickly turn in an attempt to re-acquire its target. In addition, he was fighting to regain control of the plane. He knew if it started to spin, he would have no chance to get it level before they drilled a canyon-sized furrow into the Nebraska farmland below.

"Mayday! Mayday! Wingdance 244 damaged and losing altitude."

There was no response. *That explains the crack we heard when the missile went by. It sheared off our antenna.*

Otley understood immediately and fought through the G-forces to retrieve the SATCOM phone. She called in their mayday as Lundgren continued to fight with the controls. Finally, at 8,500 feet, he managed to get the plane level.

"Radar?"

"Bogie at our eight o'clock and turning."

"ETA?"

"Sorry, there's no way to tell on this. Best guess, thirty seconds, maybe less."

"Well, shit," Lundgren said, searching the horizon for another rabbit to pull out of his hat.

Suddenly, the cabin was flooded with light, followed instantly by an enormous boom and shock wave. The plane shuddered but didn't appear to sustain further damage.

"Incoming call on SATCOM," Otley reported.

"You take it."

After a brief exchange, Otley turned to him and said, "According to Minneapolis, the USAF out of Offutt destroyed our bogey from a ground-based anti-missile launcher. We're in the clear. Now all we do is get this beast on the ground."

"Yeah, that's all," Lundgren said, trying to sound serious but unable to keep a smile from forming. He pushed the call button for the flight attendant. It was several seconds before she answered. She didn't have to ask what he wanted.

"Six injured Captain, two with broken bones, the others with more minor cuts and bruises. Despite my pleas, we had one man up in the aisle when we, uh… did whatever we did. The other injuries were from luggage flying around. Some of the overhead bins relieved themselves of their contents. That's why it took me a moment to get to the phone."

"You have a doctor among your passengers?"

"A couple of them. The retired dermatologist isn't too excited about setting bones, but we hit the jackpot with an ER doc on his way to a week of skiing in Aspen."

"Well done. Do what you can quickly. You'll need to get everyone buckled down again soon, injured or not. We almost certainly have a damaged undercarriage. Prepare for emergency evacuation as soon as we're stopped."

"Understood. Any idea where?"

"Hang on." He looked at Otley.

"Minneapolis says if we have control, we should land at Offutt Air Force Base. The runway there is over two miles long, and they're equipped to handle emergencies."

He nodded and said into his comm, "It's Offutt. We'll land in a few minutes."

"We'll manage," the flight attendant said, and was gone.

### Pawnee Lake Recreation Area, Nebraska

Cynthia Akers couldn't stop screaming as sheer joy erupted from her core. "Sir, we did it! We did it!"

Colonel Jackson was more composed, but he couldn't help grinning. Anyone looking closely could see his fists clenched and pumping imperceptibly as he thought, *Yes! Yes!*

The airliner's pilot had somehow maneuvered a miss on the weapon's first pass. By the time the missile had turned to follow, the PADS volleys had arrived and destroyed it.

They were lucky, but Jackson knew it wasn't all luck. The combination of sophisticated defense technology, good training and planning, and some unbelievable flying by a civilian pilot had saved the day.

He allowed himself to take a deep breath. Then, forcing a somber tone, he said, "Stay vigilant. We can't be certain our intel knew it all. God forbid, there could be more of those things."

"Yes, sir!" Akers said as she and the other members of the team refocused on their stations.

The cheers emanating from that remote campground in central Nebraska were exceeded only by the cheers in Langley, Virginia, Chicago, Illinois, and Washington, D.C., as the nation's leaders, from the president on down, watched the action unfold in their various situation rooms.

Four bogies down and one to go. Could they really get them all? Only a few people dared to hope.

# Chapter 41

Saturday, January 10, Quincy County, Iowa

"Tony!" Darcy screamed and began running toward the tractor, which was gaining speed in the snow.

Rich Davis quickly caught up to her. He threw his arm around her waist and picked her up off the ground.

She kicked and clawed at him. "Let me go! Please! Let me... Tony!"

Rich spoke softly into her ear. "You can't stop him. You'll only get yourself killed."

"But Rich, he can't, he just…" She looked across the field to where the tractor was moving at a brisk pace away from them. Through tears, she said, "Please Tony, *please*…"

She turned and threw her arms around the DCI agent, sobbing into his coat. "What will happen? Please tell me. What's going to happen?"

They were only seconds from finding out, but Davis said, "He'll be fine. The warhead is loaded with C-4, which is extremely stable. Detonation requires a specific kind of blasting cap to be activated. If he gets there in time, maybe he'll topple the thing and save the day. If he's too late, the silo should protect him from the missile's exhaust."

It might have worked just like Davis said, except he hadn't accounted for the large amount of fuel stored in the rocket's tanks.

***

Sitting in the cab of the enormous John Deere 4455 four-wheel drive diesel tractor, Tony felt like he was barely moving. *Faster, faster*, he pleaded with the machine.

He estimated he had about one minute before he reached his destination. He pulled out his phone. Keeping the tractor on course with his knee, which was all it required, Tony typed a text to Darcy.

*Find Doug. I love you.* He pressed send and returned the phone to his pocket.

As he reached the clearing in the neighboring farmstead, he knew he was moving at a top speed of perhaps twenty miles per hour. However, he also knew his basic physics. Velocity times mass equals force, and the tractor's mass was something over seven tons. If anything could breach the silo's brick exterior, it would be this behemoth.

Tony knew he couldn't be on the tractor when it hit. Even at this modest speed, the impact of the crash would be devastating. If the bricks stopped the tractor, he would be slammed forward against, or maybe through, the windshield. On the other hand, if the tractor succeeded in penetrating the wall and reaching the weapon, Tony would much prefer to be somewhere else—like Tahiti.

He was nearly there. He stood, double checked the tractor's trajectory, looked for a snowdrift to soften his landing, and jumped. He was in mid-air when he remembered his injured ankle. "Oh, shi-i-t!"

He screamed, as he twisted, landed on his left side, and rolled away.

He was up and moving as fast as he could manage when he heard the crash. A moment later, the world exploded into a mammoth ball of flame, smoke, dirt, and debris. He could feel himself being lifted off of his feet and hurled forward.

When he landed, he heard, then felt, the crack of bone against… something. A second deafening explosion knocked the air from his lungs. Then the world faded away.

***

Davis had barely finished his reassurances when they heard the crash. They all turned in time to see the top of the silo disappear into the trees. Suddenly a gigantic fireball erupted, followed instantly by a second explosion and a shock so loud and powerful, it broke windows in Fishbone's house. Everyone in the yard was knocked to the ground.

Darcy's was not the only scream of horror at the thought of Tony being a half-mile closer to the dual explosions.

Through tears and cries of anguish, Sheriff Mackey could be heard shouting orders. Everyone was headed for the two SUVs, with the obvious intent to race across the field to the blast site. Darcy stopped in her tracks when she felt her phone vibrate.

Tony!

She opened it, read his message, and gasped. *Did he know this would happen? Was he hurt, or worse?*

Every molecule in her body wanted to run to the man she loved, but she couldn't. Five men would help Tony. She would do as he asked and find Doug.

She grabbed the arm of one of the POVO men as he climbed into the sheriff's car.

"Where's our friend? The reporter Benning killed?"

"We didn't kill him, though I can't promise he's still alive."

A flicker of hope awoke in her gut. "Where?" she demanded.

"Basement," the man said, indicating the house. "I gave Grady the key."

Darcy took off at a run as the two vehicles drove away behind her.

***

When she stopped next to Benning's body sprawled in front of the porch steps, she was tempted to spit on it, but she fought the urge and concentrated on her task.

*You can do this, Darcy. You've dealt with gruesome before. Just treat him like a movie prop.*

Slipping off her gloves and pushing them into her pockets, she knelt on one knee and began searching Benning's pockets. She found it in the second breast pocket of his winter camos. She was glad she hadn't needed to dig any deeper into his clothing.

She ran up the steps and into the house. At the far side of the kitchen, she found the basement door, unlocked it, flicked on a light switch on the wall, and headed down the stairs.

"Doug? Are you here? Doug? It's Darcy."

She heard a whimpering sound. Hoping it wasn't a watchdog or a wounded animal trapped in the basement, she kept moving.

What the POVO man had called a basement was better described as a dirt cellar. Her small stature allowed her to stand upright beneath the exposed floor joists, but just barely. To her right, the room was just open space between moss-covered stone walls. She turned left and saw an old workbench, a vertical pipe, probably for the sewer, and, in the corner, a water heater.

The side of the appliance facing Darcy had a water spigot near the floor. From it, a small stream of water spewed, ran across the floor's rough surface, and disappeared into a drain. On the other side, pushed up into the corner behind the heater, was a body.

"Doug!" She ran to the corner and saw Doug Tenney huddled up in the tiny space.

*No, not huddled up. Tied up. Dear God.*

His hands were a frightening shade of purple, and his coat was torn. Skin was scraped from his forehead and dried blood was on his upper lip and chin.

"Doug!"

He looked up at her and managed a weak smile.

"Hey," he said hoarsely. "If I'd known you were coming, I would have showered."

She smiled back, tears forming in her eyes.

"Don't worry," she said. "I'll get you out of this. I'm sure there are knives in the kitchen."

"Thanks."

She stood and turned to go but stopped as Doug tried to speak again.

"The boom?"

She understood immediately and said, "A missile. Long story, but we got it in time. It blew up on the ground."

Doug nodded, as if an exploding missile on an Iowa farm was an everyday event.

Despite Doug's calm, Darcy could see he was in agony from the ropes and the cold. Saying, "Just hang on one sec," she started up the stairs.

"Darce."

She stopped again. Doug rasped through a grin, "Bring back a sandwich."

***

The telephones in the *Town Crier* newsroom began ringing at the same moment Ben Smalley heard sirens. Something big was happening.

With Doug missing, and Tony and Alison out searching, Ben knew he would have to return to his former role as a reporter.

He walked out into the newsroom to the desk with the police scanner. He turned up the volume as he simultaneously answered the nearest phone.

"Ben Smalley," he said, as he heard the dispatcher's voice coming out of the scanner's speaker, sending half the county to whatever it was.

"There's been an explosion. A big one. My wife and I saw a fireball as big as our barn. It cracked a couple of windows in our shed."

Even though Ben knew that callers tended to exaggerate, he felt the adrenaline kick in. He got the caller's name and contact info, asked for details about when and where the explosion had occurred, and ended the call.

He quickly pulled out his phone and entered the address into the map app. Suddenly, he felt nauseous.

*Oh, no.*

The address was a farmstead next door to old man Fishbone's. *South of Fishbone's. Exactly where I sent Doug yesterday morning. Why in the hell didn't I go out there to look for him? What has happened?*

He yelled at the *Crier's* photographer, Shawna Jackson, to grab her coat and camera, then pulled on his own parka as he ran out the door to his old Chevy Fleetside pickup.

***

After freeing Doug, Darcy tried to help him up. He couldn't stand. Because of the cold, he wanted to stay next to water heater, explaining that the old, poorly insulated tank had kept him warm enough to survive in the cellar.

It seemed obvious to Darcy that, at some point, Doug had wriggled around to the front of the water heater and with his hands tied behind his back, had opened the spigot to allow the tiny flow of water.

She smiled at Doug and said, “Water to drink too.”

He rasped, “Flow...important. Water never too hot. Kept burner lit.”

It made perfect sense. He had figured out how to get a continuous flow of water, which had never reached its peak temperature. That had ensured the gas burner never shut off.

“Smart,” Darcy said, removing and folding her scarf. She placed it between his head and the wall, to provide a tiny measure of comfort until help arrived.

When she called 911, the operator said an ambulance was already en route to the site of the explosion.

Darcy squeezed her eyes shut and took a deep breath. Her voice shaking, she said, “We need a second one. Next door to the explosion site. I don’t know the address, but it’s Mr. Fishbone’s farmhouse, just north of the explosion. Please hurry.”

“You okay?” Doug croaked. “That thing kill somebody? Even I felt the ground shake, and I can’t feel a fuckin’ thing.”

“I’m fine,” Darcy said, forcing a smile. “It’s nothing. I’m just glad you’re safe.”

# Chapter 42

Saturday, January 10, Quincy County, Iowa

Black smoke filled the sky southeast of Orney. Ben and Shawna could see it from the edge of town and followed it all way to the site of the blast.

The gravel road that ran past the farmstead was clogged with every type of official vehicle, so Ben parked his pickup on a short access road to a nearby cornfield. He and Shawna walked the remaining half mile.

As they approached, they could see firefighters battling blazes in two places. A thick grove of trees to the west had been set on fire by the blast. A dozen people utilizing two tanker trucks were struggling to get it under control. Closer to the driveway, in what had probably been the west edge of the gravel expanse connecting the barn to the other buildings, an enormous lump of steel, rubber, and other materials smoldered.

"Holy shi…" Ben caught himself, conscious of the young

employee at his side. “That was a tractor.”

“No way,” Shawna said, raising her camera and snapping pictures.

“Get some video, too, for the website,” Ben said, hurrying off to talk to the sheriff. When he reached him, he said, “Any sign of Doug?”

The sheriff looked completely spent, his face blackened by soot and, Ben suddenly realized, his hands scarred with burns.

Ben said, “What the hell?”

“Darcy’s with Doug. They’re at Fishbone’s. I heard the call go out for an ambulance. He’s alive, but I don’t know any more than that.”

Ben began to exhale a sigh of relief, when Mackey added, “It’s Harrington we’re worried about.”

Ben was stunned. “Tony? What about Tony? Was he here? Not *here*. Dear God.”

Mackey reached up and placed his hand on Ben’s shoulder, wincing as his fingers came to rest on his coat.

“The last we saw Tony, he was driving that.” The sheriff nodded toward the burning rubble.

*“What?!”*

“He drove Fishbone’s tractor right into the silo. He destroyed the missile. Probably saved the lives of everyone on board an airliner flying overhead.”

“What in the hell are you talking about? What missile? What silo?” Ben looked past the firefighters and saw only a huge crater in the ground. “Tony was here? Where is he now?”

“I honestly don’t know. The good news is, we haven’t found any sign of him. The bad news is, we haven’t found any sign of him.”

Ben felt like he was living in an alternate universe. *How could a missile silo be in Orney? Has everyone gone crazy?*

To the sheriff, he said, “Tell me everything. Tell it fast, but tell me what happened here.”

Mackey quickly walked Ben through their confrontation with

Benning, Tony's heroic, albeit insane, use of the tractor, the double explosion caused, presumably, by the rocket fuel and the missile's warhead, and their scramble to find and save Tony immediately after the blast.

"'Cept there wasn't anything to find. He was either vaporized, which seems unlikely, or he got away somehow, which seems even more far-fetched. I'm as confused as you."

"No one is as confused as me right now," Ben said, his anger and frustration growing by the minute. *I didn't even know he was out here.* He pushed his anger aside and said, "Walk me through it."

"I just told…"

"No, I mean literally. Show me the tractor's path. What Tony did."

Mackey walked him to the north edge of the farmstead, pointing out where the John Deere had crashed through the barbed-wire fence. Retracing their steps, he then turned right and pointed at the ground.

"Look at the tracks. You can see he made a hard turn to the west here and headed straight for the silo."

"There was a missile silo here?"

"Well, sorta. There was an old grain silo, a brick one. POVO used it to hide and prepare the missile for firing."

Ben thought, *So Tony's in the cab of a huge old John Deere. He's pushed the throttle to full and a brick building is straight ahead. He would jump before it hit.*

Aloud, he said, "Was there snow here?"

"Probably," Mackey said. "You can see that the heat and the shock wave wiped out the snow for quite a radius around ground zero."

"But before the blast, there could have been a sizable drift here."

"Yeah. The wind break from the trees and the buildings would have caused the snow to drift in the farmyard."

"So Tony jumped." Ben was convinced. Tony was foolish and all too eager to put himself in harm's way, but he had strong survival instincts.

"Makes sense," Mackey agreed.

Ben started walking east. "He lands in a snow drift, jumps up and starts running away from the silo." He picked up his pace.

"No way to know how far he got, but a few seconds later, the tractor hits the building. Maybe it takes a few seconds for the silo to topple or collapse, so he has maybe ten seconds before the first blast erupts, which brings him to here."

Ben stopped walking. He was standing in front of the remains of a barn foundation.

"This building was here before the blast?"

"Nah," Mackey said. "Barn's been gone for years.

Ben looked down at what had probably been a shallow crawl space under the original structure. Now it was filled with rubble. He turned to the sheriff.

"Gather everyone you can. He's here."

"What?"

"He jumped or was thrown into the trench behind this foundation wall. Then the blast covered him in rubble. Hurry, dammit! He's here!"

Ben dropped to his knees and started pulling clods of dirt, rocks, shards of brick, and a host of other trash out of the space behind the wall.

Soon, a dozen men and women were at his side doing the same thing.

Ben started shouting. "Tony! Are you there? Tony!"

The shouts became a chorus as everyone else joined in. Every few minutes, the sheriff raised his hand and the group fell silent, listened intently for thirty seconds, then resumed digging and shouting. On the third pause, a firefighter twenty feet to Ben's right cried out,

"Here! He's here!"

In less than two minutes, the rubble covering Tony had been cleared away. They could see that he was pale and bruised. His right pantleg was soaked in blood. Ben held his breath, afraid to voice the question, alive or dead? Tony answered it for him when he coughed, then cried out in pain.

He opened his eyes. "I hope you're all here to help me, 'cause my leg hurts like a son of a bitch."

Ben's face turned red, and he felt tears coming. As the EMTs moved in to take over the extraction of Tony from the foundation, Ben looked down at him and said, "I'm so glad you're alive because once you're healed, I'm going to kill you."

***

A second group of EMTs was loading Doug into the back of an ambulance when Darcy's phone chirped. It was Shawna, the *Crier's* photographer. Darcy punched "Answer" and was greeted by a shout, "He's alive!"

Darcy shrieked and clutched her chest with her free hand. "Really? He's okay? How could he…?"

"Slow down. I didn't say he was okay. He's hurt. Looks pretty beat up, but he's awake and talking."

"Oh, thank God. Oh, thank God. Oh, thank... I'll be right there."

"Don't come over here. They're lifting him into the ambulance now. Meet us at the hospital."

"I will. Of course, I will. Oh my…Thank you. Oh my…"

She ran to Tony's Jeep, climbed in, and started the engine. It took several seconds as her hand was shaking uncontrollably. Before putting the vehicle in gear, she waited for the ambulance carrying Doug to drive past her and out onto the road. She watched the flashing emergency lights disappear, then slumped against the Jeep's steering wheel and sobbed.

**Town Crier**

**EXCLUSIVE**

# Terrorist Plot Thwarted

Foreign government allegedly funded domestic terrorists
*Crier* reporter uncovered plot, saved hundreds of lives
Local man accused of involvement in plot committed suicide

**Ben Smalley**, Editor and Publisher

***Editor's note:*** *The following account was assembled with input from Tony Harrington and Doug Tenney, staff writers at the Town Crier and KKAR Radio. Harrington was on assignment for the news organizations when he uncovered the terrorist plot and played a key role in preventing a devastating attack on innocent people. Tenney was assigned to investigate unusual sightings near the farm owned by Darrell Fishbone, who was found dead in his home on January 5. Both reporters are currently hospitalized with injuries sustained in the performance of their assignments.*

ORNEY, Iowa—Last Saturday was only seconds away from being remembered as another day that would "live in infamy," when an armed missile, fueled and aimed at a domestic airliner flying over Orney, was destroyed before it could launch, according to Quincy County Sheriff George Mackey. The missile had been hidden in a farm silo southeast of Orney and prepared for launch by a domestic terrorism group known as "Patriots of Victory One," or POVO, Mackey said.

Tony Harrington, 30, of Orney and a reporter for the *Orney Town Crier* and KKAR Radio, destroyed the missile when he drove a John Deere field tractor from a neighboring farm into the brick silo, destroying the structure, toppling the missile, and causing it to explode on the ground, Mackey said.

Harrington was injured in the explosion. He was taken to the Quincy

County Medical Center by ambulance, where he is listed in good condition, a hospital spokesperson said.

"Mr. Harrington saved 198 men, women, and children on that one commercial jet," the sheriff said. "However, his investigation over the two weeks leading up to the incident uncovered a plot that involved a total of five missiles, four of which were hidden in other Midwestern states."

Doug Tenney, 32, of Orney, is listed in fair condition at Quincy County Medical Center with damage to his limbs as a result of being kidnapped by members of POVO on Friday. Tenney said he discovered the missile in the farm silo near Orney shortly before he was captured. He was tied with ropes and left overnight in an unheated cellar. At the time of his capture, he was following up on a news tip made to the *Town Crier* a few days earlier, describing suspicious activities in the area.

**Threat eliminated—all missiles accounted for**

When asked the status of the other four missiles, FBI Special Agent Anna Tabors reported that earlier Saturday, three of the missiles were located and secured by the US military, working with the FBI and the CIA. She said the remaining missile, assembled and hidden west of Lincoln, Neb., was launched by the terrorists.

"Luckily, the pilot of the plane targeted by the fifth missile was a former Navy pilot with combat experience. His quick actions saved his plane from destruction," Tabors said. She noted the plane was damaged in the attack but managed an emergency landing at Offutt Air Force Base, near Omaha. Several people were injured, but there were no fatalities, Tabors said.

The agent said the anti-terrorism task force that found and secured the missiles also arrested a total of 28 people. She said the POVO website has been shut down, and efforts are underway to find and arrest other members of the group involved in planning and/or executing the plot.

When asked, Tabors acknowledged that authorities were investigating evidence that a foreign government was involved in funding POVO's purchase of the missiles and other activities leading up to Saturday. She refused to comment further, citing national security interests.

Tabors also said Harrington's investigation into the activities of POVO was instrumental in helping authorities understand the gravity of the threat and in locating three of the missiles and securing them before they could be launched.

**At least four deaths tied to terrorists**

One death on Saturday directly

related to the POVO plot was the suicide of Grady Benning, 42, of rural Viscount. Benning shot himself in the head with a handgun in front of multiple witnesses after being informed that the plot to fire missiles at airliners was likely funded by a foreign government and was intended to destroy the planes, Sheriff Mackey said.

"Benning told us he believed the missiles were programmed to explode a harmless distance from the planes as a show of POVO's capabilities. When he learned he had been fooled by his POVO leaders, he took his life before anyone could stop him," Mackey added.

In addition to Benning, at least three other deaths are believed to be directly tied to POVO, Tabors said.

"Sadly, one of those deaths was that of Quincy County Deputy Sheriff Tim Jebron," Tabors said. "We now know that Deputy Jebron overheard information about POVO's plans while in Chicago on Dec. 27. He was killed to prevent him from reporting what he learned. We were told this by Grady Benning. Before taking his own life, Benning admitting killing Deputy Jebron."

The third local casualty was Darrell Fishbone, a local farmer who was found dead in his home on January 5, Tabors reported. "The death initially was believed to be accidental. However, members of POVO arrested on Saturday have told us Fishbone discovered the missile on the farmstead abutting his own. He was killed to prevent anyone else from learning about it.

She said the fourth death known for certain is POVO Camp Commander Jon Slapp, killed at the camp in Missouri last Thursday, when struck by a truck as he attempted to shoot Tony Harrington, who was at the camp seeking evidence about the terrorists' plans.

Two additional deaths are suspected but not certain. One is an FBI agent who had been working undercover at the POVO camp. The other is a POVO security guard at the camp. Both are missing and presumed dead. She declined to release either name.

The events of Saturday were the culmination of a complex scheme spanning more than five years. It is believed to have begun in Russia with the purchase or theft of several surface-to-air missiles from a military installation there. An international arms dealer then sold the missiles…

# Chapter 43

Wednesday, January 14, Orney, Iowa

Making love was difficult when sporting a cracked bone, a sprained ankle, and a head wound. However, on Wednesday night Tony was relieved and happy to find his pleasure exceeded his pain. He knew he had Darcy's patience and tenderness to thank for it. He only wished he could have done more for her.

In fact, she had surprised him when she had initiated it. Sex had been off the table since his release from the hospital two days previously. Perhaps she had finally believed him that his injuries weren't nearly as serious as she'd feared.

It was true he'd suffered a concussion and several cuts in the explosion, but doctors assured him there was no permanent damage. Even his hearing was returning to normal. His left fibula was cracked, but no actual treatment was required. The lower portion of the leg was wrapped in a lightweight vinyl brace, hidden during the day by his trousers. He could walk almost normally. He actually was experiencing more pain from the sprain, which was improving but not yet fully healed.

Officials speculated that Tony was saved when the first explosion threw him into the trench behind the stone foundation that once had supported a barn. When the C-4 ignited, Tony was, in effect, at the bottom of a foxhole. The fire inspectors were calling it "incredible dumb luck," but Tony was choosing instead to say a prayer of thanks every day.

Doug, too, had escaped the worst. His left hand had required minor surgery, and the doctors had reported he would need therapy to regain the full strength in his hands and legs, but they had predicted a full recovery.

Now, as Darcy lay stretched out beside him, he found himself hoping her desire for him was a result of her love and her relief he was okay. Those were probably a part of it, he knew. Sadly, he also knew the bigger issue was her reluctance to have the next inevitable conversation.

As they watched the barren branches of the trees outside dance in silhouette on the window blinds, Tony finally said, "I have to go back to Chicago."

"Do you?" There was no anger, resentment, or even challenge in her voice, just resignation.

"I want to check on our young friend, Elena Church, to see how she's doing, and I'd like to hand-deliver the gift we bought her." Tony and Darcy had pooled their money and purchased a new high-end laptop computer for the girl after talking to Elena's mother to ask what her daughter needed. They had agreed they should do something as a thank you and reward for the girl who had tried to protect them.

Tony continued. "While I'm there, I have a source I need to see—the woman who confirmed POVO's involvement and put us onto Benning. She deserves to know how her willingness to talk saved all those people."

What Tony didn't explain was that Homeland Security had contacted him about his anonymous source. The government wanted to reward the person who had made it possible for authorities to stop the horrific plot against America. Because Tony had refused to give up the name, Homeland Security had deposited a sizeable sum of money in an encrypted account. Tony had the pleasant task of communicating the information to Wedders.

"I understand," Darcy said.

"I'm sorry," Tony added. "Because I promised her anonymity, I have to go alone."

"It's okay. I'm due in London anyway. When I'm done there, I'm going to head back to California for a while."

Tony tensed. This was a turn he hadn't expected but had always feared.

Darcy twisted around to face him. "I'm coming back," she said.

The relief flowed through him like beer through a frat party keg tap. "Me, too," he said, smiling, trying to pretend he'd never thought otherwise.

She said, "I need to check on my house and spend a little time with the Hollywood mucky-mucks. I don't want them to forget about me."

"Couldn't happen," Tony said, "but I get it. You have a career that needs attention from time to time. And I wondered about the house. I assume you have good security."

She rolled onto her back and pulled the sheet up, covering them both to their shoulders. She said, "All the usual stuff, plus a nosy neighbor. And no, it's not someone stalking me with a telephoto lens. Mrs. Parks, Charlotte, is a former receptionist at Warner Brothers and a widow. She keeps a lovely flower garden and likes to bring me cookies. She thinks I shouldn't live alone."

"I agree," Tony said. "I'm glad…"

Darcy interrupted. "I was going to put it on the market, but I'm not sure the time is right."

All the tension returned to Tony's muscles in an instant. He knew Darcy could sense it. His heart fell as she didn't respond. She remained silent, staring at the ceiling.

He reached out and stroked her cheek with his index finger. "You're not talking about the market, are you?" It was a statement, not a question.

She turned her head to look at him. "Tony, I love you, I do. And I'm committed to this relationship."

"But..."

"But I don't know if I can survive another day like Saturday. When you ran from me and drove off in that tractor on a suicide mission, I thought I might die. I've never known such sheer terror, such a crushing sense of being abandoned."

"I didn't want to leave you. I did the only thing I could think to do. What I *had* to do."

"Of course you did," she said, "and I can't fault you for it. You saved that plane and probably a lot more. I'm proud of you. The problem is, it reinforces what I've learned about you. This is who you are. You're the hero. You're always going to choose the path that puts you in harm's way."

"I don't think that's true," he said, pushing back.

She rolled up onto her side and ran her fingers through his hair. "My love, don't be a dick. Think about it. I've known you for less than a year, and you've been hospitalized four times. Except for dumb luck, three of those incidents would've killed you."

Tony wanted to point out that he'd only been admitted to hospitals three times. In the fourth, he was treated and released. He was smart enough to change the subject.

He said quietly, "We're a team, you know. You were as important in finding and eliminating those missiles as I was—probably more so."

"I want to believe that," she said, a tremor finding its way into her voice. "I'm just not sure I want to live in a constant state of anxiety."

"I'll do whatever it takes to keep you," he said. "If it means changing jobs, I'll do it."

She shook her head, but before she could speak, he said, "I mean it. I love you. Completely. Deeply. Everlastingly. And despite my uncertainties and missteps that led to our spat in Chicago, I know beyond any doubt that we are a team. You are as essential to me as air or water. You make me a better person."

He stroked her face and added, "I don't have all the answers tonight, but I swear this relationship—you—are the most important thing in my life. No matter what happens, whatever we decide to do, we stay together. Deal?"

Darcy leaned over and kissed him warmly. "Well said, newsboy. You should be a writer or something."

His lips curled into a grin but quickly morphed into a look of astonishment as he felt her hand gripping him beneath the covers. As soon as he was ready, she rose up, straddled him, and rode him hard until they reached a shared climax. Then she bent down, kissed him lightly on the lips, and said, "Deal."

Later, despite knowing it could be foolish to continue the conversation about the future, Tony said, "Maybe we're both making too much of my job. This may have been the last time I have to deal with anything dangerous. I work for a tiny newspaper in a small city in a state that's usually boring. The past couple of years have been unlike any in the *Crier's* history. Let's be optimistic and assume we're headed into a new era of a front page dominated by school board meetings, crop yield reports, and Little League tournaments."

"You'd go stir crazy in about two weeks, and you'd soon have us pulling up stakes and moving to Chicago or New York. Besides, it won't happen. There will always be murder, and human trafficking, and domestic terrorism, and a host of other horrendous crimes. Sadly, there seems to be more of it every day. Things may settle down for a short time, but eventually, evil will revisit Orney, and you'll bc in the thick of it."

Unfortunately, Darcy was as smart as everyone claimed.

# Chapter 44

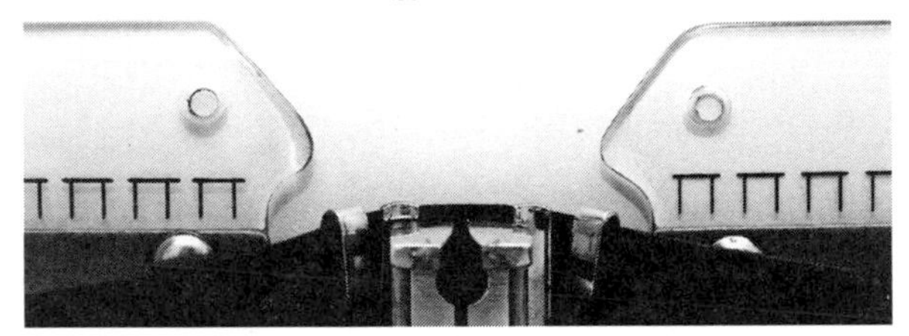

Wednesday, January 14, Port of Rotterdam, Netherlands

The Port of Rotterdam, on the coast of The Netherlands, was everything the websites claimed and more. Andros Turgenev would have been in awe of its enormous size, modern facilities, and incredibly efficient operations, if he hadn't been distracted by his two constant companions: anxiety and greed.

He had been summoned to the port by a simple message, received as a text from an unknown number. *More of the same at a better price. Max*

It was followed by a date, time, and berth number here, at one of the largest commercial shipping ports in the world.

Turgenev knew more than one Max, but he had no doubt from which one the message had originated. So he had come. His previous transaction involving the Russian woman had netted him enough money to last three lifetimes. Rather than satisfy him, it only fueled his desire to do it again, to profit even more.

And out of the blue, from the woman who had said he would never hear from her again, had come another opportunity. Of course he had come. She had proven herself in the past, and he had no reason to doubt her now.

He was not surprised to be meeting her in southwest Holland. Things in Russia had deteriorated in the past two years. Travel there was difficult and exceedingly dangerous. While he never felt safe during a weapons transaction, he was a hell of a lot more at ease here than he would have been in Sochi. He also hoped the meeting place indicated that the missiles, assuming they were discussing another purchase of missiles, were already loaded on a container ship and ready for departure to America.

As an arms dealer, Turgenev was familiar with all the norms and nuances of shipping. Success in his business required him to be an expert, and he routinely visited seaports all over the world. Still, the scale of this place was mind-boggling. The port was nearly forty kilometers long and docked more than 100,000 ships every year. It was the largest in the world outside of eastern Asia.

He drove into the port on a highway system that would evoke envy from many large cities. It was essential to ensure the safe passage of thousands of cars and trucks through the maze of nearly 19,000 acres of shipping containers, warehouses, oil refining and storage facilities, railroad tracks, service and support facilities, and a thousand other obstacles.

Following the signs, and with the help of the navigation system in his rented Lexus, he had little trouble finding the specific port area and finally, the precise berth. Docked there was another awe-inspiring sight—a container ship the width of a football field, and nearly four times as long.

He parked in the designated lot and walked to the security

entrance. His British diplomatic passport, impeccably created for him with a false name, allowed him to enter with few questions and no search of his briefcase. He strode across the open dock and crossed a gangway to an entrance in the side of the ship.

He was greeted by two armed men. They welcomed him inside, but, once out of sight of the dockworkers, searched him carefully. Turgenev's anxiety increased a notch. He didn't recall being searched when he and Max had met in Sochi.

The guards also examined his passport but only sneered when they saw the name. It was obvious they knew who he was. Handing the document back to Turgenev, one of the men indicated he should follow him. The other stayed behind at the door.

The walk into the bowels of the ship was almost as confusing, and took almost as long, as the drive through the port. It occurred to Turgenev that if this meeting wasn't what was promised, no one would hear him scream or find his body.

Finally, the guard pulled open a door and nodded at Turgenev to enter. When he walked through, he found himself in a modestly-sized commercial kitchen. Seated on a stool, on the left side of a long stainless-steel table, was the woman called Max. Turgenev felt relief flow though him like a long pull of vodka.

She was looking away from him toward an empty seat across the table. With a nod, she indicated he should sit, then said, "Andros, it is good of you to come. I hope your trip was pleasant."

"A short trek across the channel," Turgenev said, walking around toward the empty seat. "No trouble at all. Thank you for making this convenient."

The woman nodded again.

Turgenev continued. "I should thank you, too, for contacting me at all. I had the impression I would not be seeing you again."

Max smiled. "Some, uh…arrangements…are too good to forego."

"My sentiments exactly," Turgenev said. He reached the empty stool, lifted his briefcase onto the table, and looked up. For the first time, he could see a full view of Max's face. He couldn't help himself; he cringed. The left side of her face was horribly scarred. Her eye was permanently closed by poorly grafted skin tissue, and her left ear was missing completely.

"Unpleasant, yes?"

"I'm sorry," Turgenev said shakily, averting his eyes. "I didn't know."

"Of course not," Max said. Her smile widened, which only made her appearance more grotesque. "Your CIA friend didn't make it out of Sochi alive, so she never had a chance to tell anyone what she did."

"My CIA friend? What does that mean? I have no friends in the CIA."

"Friend or foe, no matter," Max said. "You led her to the warehouse in Sochi, and she did this to me."

"I did not," Turgenev nearly squeaked, his anxiety morphing into primal fear. "I couldn't have. I flew to Sochi in a private plane. You saw it. No one knew where I was. If someone else was there, it wasn't because of me."

"Andros, you are wasting your breath." Her smile returned as she said, "Not a commodity you can afford to waste, as it turns out. Within seconds of your departure from the warehouse, the woman entered. Whether she was smarter than you, or just lucky, makes no difference. She is already dead, killed by one of my men. I cannot seek my revenge against her, so I choose to do so against you."

Turgenev realized the two of them were not alone. Four men carrying assault rifles emerged from an adjoining storeroom. He said, "Max, please. I was careful. I kept our deal. I paid well. I even brought you a gift. I am not your enemy."

"You are no longer anyone's enemy. Your carelessness has

ruined my face. It is time for justice to be served."

As the four men approached, Turgenev frantically looked in every direction for something he could use as a weapon. He reached for his briefcase, but the men were on him instantly. As he pleaded, and then screamed, the men forced him onto the table and onto his back. In seconds, his hands and feet were handcuffed to the four corners.

He began to cry as he continued begging for his life.

Max was no longer smiling. In a voice as cold as ice, she said, "Very soon, Andros, you will be begging for your death. Can you smell that? This ship's crew has learned to like things prepared in what the Americans call a deep fat fryer."

"Oh, God, please…" Turgenev could feel the dampness in his trousers as he wet himself.

"They can't use the fryer while on the open sea. It's too dangerous. If the hot grease spills on you, it creates horrible, excruciating burns. Rather like an exploding CIA telephone held too close to one's face." She leaned in, apparently wanting Turgenev to see her disfigured features up close. "Here in port, the fryer is fired up and ready to cook…what? Maybe potatoes, maybe poultry. Anything, really." Turgenev yanked against his restraints, crying, "No! Please no! Anything. Take my money. You can have it all. It's more than…"

She reached out and placed her finger on his lips. "Shhh… I don't want your money. I only want to hear you scream."

One of the men went to the fryer, where the grease was boiling in a deep vessel. He drew out a ladleful and carefully walked it to the table.

Max carried Turgenev's briefcase to a second countertop. As she examined the contents, the arms dealer accommodated her wish. His screams could have peeled the paint from an older ship's walls.

She let it continue until Max passed out. As soon as he did, she nodded at a second man, who slipped a military knife from his belt and drove it into Turgenev's heart.

She said, "Wait until you're in deep water, then toss him overboard."

The men quietly went about the business of wrapping the body in plastic and cleaning up the mess. Max closed the briefcase, picked it up, and exited the room. As she departed the ship, she didn't look back, only thinking to herself, *It was nice of him to bring me another gift.*

# Chapter 45

Thursday, January 15, Chicago, Illinois

Lethal, angry, and desperate combine to make a terrifying enemy. Joel Fitzgerald was all of those things and more. His closest friend and mentor, Jon Slapp, was dead. Dozens of other friends and colleagues were in jail, and their leader, Arvin Jugg, was missing. The organization they had all devoted their lives to building for the past five years was in shambles, maybe even obliterated for good. And Fitzgerald himself was forced into hiding, suddenly at the top of the FBI's Most Wanted list.

Equally infuriating was the utter failure of the operation they had planned so carefully. Millions of dollars and untold hours of hard work wasted. They had come so close. Hours, perhaps minutes, from a glorious strike against greedy, corrupt bastards who called themselves the leaders of America, and then…nothing. Not a single missile had found its target.

It was inconceivable they had failed, and even more so that it was all due to a handful of people from rural Iowa. A deputy sheriff, a newspaper reporter, and an actress had destroyed him and his dreams.

The deputy was already dead. Nothing he could do about that. But Tony Harrington and Darcy Gillson were very much alive.

*Well, not for long*, Fitzgerald vowed. *Not for long*. He woke up his phone and dialed.

***

Joel Fitzgerald's anger didn't leave him, but it was pushed to the side by his excitement as well as his smug self-satisfaction. That Iowa newsman was every bit as clueless and naïve as he had hoped To lure the reporter back to Chicago, Fitzgerald had claimed to be a CIA agent with information to sell about Arvin Jugg's ties to the Russians. Harrington hadn't just swallowed it hook, line, and sinker, as Fitzgerald's papa used to say. *Hell, he swallowed the whole fishing pole, reel, and tackle box.*

The icing on the cake was the fact that Harrington was coming to Chicago the day after tomorrow. He wouldn't have to wait long to take care of this bit of business. He just needed to stay out of sight for a couple more days, then he could kill the bastard and head west to take care of the girlfriend.

While staying out of sight was crucial, Fitzgerald didn't perceive it as problematic. He was in a place where he wouldn't be found.

As a former wrestler, he felt at home in a gym. His go-to spot was the opposite of a modern health club. Plunky's Escape was located in the back of a depression-era brick commercial building in an old working-class neighborhood on the near northwest side of Chicago. No treadmills or stair-steppers could be found at Plunky's. It was home to punching bags, medicine balls, and free weights. If a wrestler or boxer wanted to work out with anything made after 1950, he or she would have to look elsewhere.

The gym was named for the owner, Petros "Plunky" Smith. The second half of the name—the word "Escape"—came from Smith's legendary career on the wrestling mat, where he won more than a hundred matches by points, many of which were earned by escaping holds from his opponents.

The reference to an escape had a second meaning. Plunky's was the place where many old or washed-up fighters came to work out or, more often, sit and drink beer and tell stories of past glories, some of which were true. Many of the patrons had questionable histories, from either pre- or post-fighting days, and no one asked any questions.

Cold, angry, and frustrated, Fitzgerald had found his way there after dark, just minutes before the gym closed at 9 p.m. He had slipped the old woman at the desk a C-note in exchange for permission to stay in a back room for a few days and to use the showers.

Once he was alone in the building, he was drawn to the mirror in the locker room. He needed the reassurance that his disguise was perfect. His clothes consisted of green cargo pants, a flannel shirt, hooded sweatshirt, and waist-length winter coat. All were intentionally old, tattered, and over-sized. He admired how effectively they created the image of a hapless drifter.

He hadn't shaved since the day POVO had moved out of the camp in Missouri. He had completed the look by bleaching white his scraggly beard and hair. When combined, these things explained why the intensive manhunt underway had failed to find him, even though he hadn't yet been more than thirty minutes away from the FBI field office.

He opened his knapsack and removed a Ruger Mark IV .22 handgun. Many called this weapon the "Hitman .22," because it was designed for stealth, including a threaded barrel.

Fitzgerald spun the noise suppressor in place, checked the magazine, and slid the weapon into the right-hand pocket of his pants. He drew it out again, checking to be sure the pocket held no loose threads that would interfere with its quick removal on Saturday. Satisfied, he returned the weapon to his pack and removed his clothes. He was looking forward to a hot shower.

***

His go-pack held no pajamas, so he selected sweat pants and a sweater for sleeping attire. As he pulled the sweater on over his head, he heard a noise. He paused for a moment to listen, then completed the move, his head popping up through the crew neck.

"Hello, Fitz."

Fitzgerald froze. A young man with curly blond hair stood just eight feet away. He was holding a large-caliber automatic.

In a panic, Fitzgerald realized his go-pack was next to the stranger. The noise he had heard had been his pack being moved out of his reach. He was effectively unarmed. *This kid is unbelievably quick*, Fitzgerald thought, his anxiety increasing.

"Just relax," the stranger said.

"Who are you? Want to you want?" Even in his agitated state, Fitzgerald could process the fact that this was not a cop. He didn't look or act like a cop, and he displayed no badge.

"I'm going to tell you who I am," the stranger said, "because it's important for you to understand I mean what I say."

"What does…?"

"It means, when I make threats, they're backed by people with the will and the means to carry them out."

"Threats? Why threaten me? What the fuck are you talkin' about?"

The stranger's smile never wavered. "Mr. Fitzgerald, I am an operative. What many in the business call an embedded asset. I live here in America, I study at a school here in Chicago, I 'hang' with my friends, I go to all the Marvel movies and eat cheeseburgers and speak impeccable English, all to ensure my true identity is never known. As you may have guessed, I work for the same people as you."

"You're *Russian?*" Fitzgerald was astonished. Very quickly, his surprise morphed into anger. "Then put that thing away. If you know who I am, then you know we're on the same side. I'm gonna need your help."

"Unfortunately, Fitz, you're going to get it, but not in the form you hoped."

"What does that mean?"

"It means," the man said, "you have been a big part of a colossal screw-up. It means the people at home are desperate to cover their asses. Surely you're not surprised that they're moving fast to eliminate any trace that this rogue scheme with the missiles ever existed."

"Rogue scheme?" Fitzgerald nearly spit out the words. "You little shit. We worked and planned and sweated for five years to accomplish the greatest victory for Russia in its history. We risked everything for you and your Kremlin buddies."

"That is exactly right," the man said, nodding. With his free hand, he reached into his pocket and drew out a small pill bottle. He tossed it, and Fitzgerald snatched it out of the air.

Looking at the bottle, Fitzgerald could see it had no label. "What's this?"

"You've probably guessed. As you said, you risked everything. You lost. Now you die. That's cyanide."

"What! No. Hell, no!" Fitzgerald's muscles tensed, but the stranger reacted just as quickly. The gun came up and pointed at his chest.

"Now you understand why I had to share with you who I am. You are going to commit suicide. Right here. Right now."

"No, I won't. I can't."

"You will because if you don't, we are going to kill every member of your family. We'll begin with your mother in the retirement village in Arkansas, then your ex-wife in Kansas City, and finally, of course, those two adorable children. What were their names? Bec…"

"No! Stop! Please, no." Fitzgerald was suddenly trembling and trying to hold back tears.

"Take the pill, Fitz. It will all be over quickly, and those children will have a chance to grow up to be spoiled American teenagers."

Fitzgerald sank to his knees on the cold, dirty concrete floor and accepted the fact that he had no choice. Surprisingly, he also realized he didn't really care. His life was over anyway. With every cop in the country looking for him, he would have to flee and live out the time he had left as a fugitive with diminishing resources and no meaningful opportunities to earn a decent living. In all likelihood, he would end up in a federal prison or, God forbid, at a hell-hole like Gitmo. In any case, he would never see his children again. The thought of that was unbearable. His trembling subsided, and he blinked away any remaining tears.

He looked up at the smiling blond, wishing only that he could get in one good punch before dying. "Tell everyone in Russia to go fuck themselves," he said, and swallowed the capsule.

The young operative's smile widened. This was the first time Moscow had pulled him out of deep cover to take care of a problem, and it had gone perfectly. The target was lying on the floor in the throes of death without a shot being fired or even a scuffle. When the body was found, it would be 'obvious' to the authorities that Joel Fitzgerald had killed himself out of desperation, fear, remorse, or some combination of the three.

He returned the pistol to an inside pocket of his parka and glanced at his watch. He would have plenty of time to get home, freshen up, and get to his girlfriend's brownstone for dinner. With luck, they would forego dessert for a couple of hours entwined in her small but comfortable bed.

He was lucky in many ways. He was dating a beautiful and talented woman, he was getting a first-rate American education, and he was living in an exciting, beautiful city. Now, he would enjoy the gratitude and favor of some of the most powerful men in the world.

He realized he should hurry. Thoughts of his girlfriend, Rita Harrington, were getting him aroused. Yes, Ryan Stenford was a lucky man indeed.

# Acknowledgements

During the pandemic, as I sat at the computer working on my novel *Performing Murder*, my son Luke opened my office door and said, "You should write a novel about domestic terrorists." I responded, "Good idea," and Luke disappeared again, to resume whatever college students did to stay busy during the lockdown. More than a year later, when considering a topic for my sixth novel, I remembered Luke's suggestion. As you now know, that simple seed of an idea grew to become this story.

I mention it here in order to properly thank Luke for thinking about a possible future book, and for taking the time to share his idea with me. Likewise, I want to thank everyone who routinely provides support such as this to me and other writers. We rely on your ideas, feedback, and encouragement to complete manuscripts that have any chance of accomplishing our goals, and of meeting or exceeding your expectations. I am blessed to be surrounded by family members, friends, beta readers, and others who are engaged with me and my work. My appreciation of them knows no bounds.

Related to this, I want to thank my lifelong friend and fellow writer and musician, Don Myers. He read an early draft of this novel and suggested a couple of sentences, which I happily added. No, you don't get to know which ones. I don't want you to look them up and start wishing Don had written the entire book.

A heartfelt thank you also goes to the extraordinarily-gifted James Rollins, the #1 New York Times bestselling author of the Sigma Force series and many other novels. In the middle of a tour, introducing his astonishing thriller *Tides of Fire*, James took the time to read this book and send me a lovely email relating how much he enjoyed it. I am extremely grateful for his interest and support.

Likewise, I owe a debt of gratitude to Max Allan Collins, one of the best and most prolific writers of mystery and suspense fiction working today. His creative genius can be found in novels, graphic novels, short stories, comics, TV shows, movies, and musical compositions. I mention these things in order to emphasize how generous it was of him to take the time to review and comment on my work.

This may seem odd, but I want to take a moment to thank the people who create and maintain online databases and search engines. Some parts of this novel, such as the scenes in Russia, would not have been possible without Google and Google Earth. I try to physically visit all actual locations that appear in my stories (as I write this, I'm just back from a trip to Ireland, to do research for my seventh novel). Of course, a trip to Russia during the time in which this was written was not feasible. The electronic tools allowed me to see in detail the places where travel was impossible. In addition, official government websites and other online resources provided the education I needed about airplanes, weapons, the military, and other key factors in the story. In short, the electronic resources enabled me to write this book. As an aside, I must admit I worried a bit about some of the research I did online. I told my family not to be surprised if

Homeland Security knocked on our door. I was only half joking.

A friend and former colleague, Chelsea Van Vark, provided me with some background information and thoughts regarding Chicago, where she now lives and works as a healthcare leader. Her input helped me choose the South Loop as the setting for the murder with which the book begins and, hopefully, allowed me to create a realistic picture of the Windy City. Chelsea was extremely helpful and generous with her time. Be assured, any errors are my fault alone.

As always, thanks to my editor, Jason Brandt Schaefer, and to the people at Bookpress Publishing. I couldn't ask for better partners in getting my books from manuscripts to finished form and into international distribution.

Lastly, thanks to you, dear reader. Your love of books, and especially of fictional mysteries and thrillers, makes it possible for me to continue to enjoy a fun, exciting and fulfilling career. Keep reading, and keep supporting your local bookstores and libraries. I hope we'll have the chance to chat about books sometime. In the meantime, please sign up for my mailing list at josephlevalley.com, and feel free to reach out to me at joe@josephlevalley.com. It's not always possible, but I try to respond personally to emails sent from individual readers.

BURYING
THE LEDE
JOSEPH LEVALLEY

CRY FROM AN UNKNOWN GRAVE
BY JOSEPH LEVALLEY
A TONY HARRINGTON NOVEL

THE THIRD SIDE OF
MURDER
JOSEPH LEVALLEY

PERFORMING
MURDER
JOSEPH LEVALLEY
A TONY HARRINGTON NOVEL

THE
SOPHOCLES
RULE
JOSEPH
LEVALLEY
A TONY HARRINGTON NOVEL